NEW YORK TIMES & USA TODAY BESTSELLING AUTHOR

MARIE FORCE

THE Gansett Island COMPENDIUM

VOLUME ONE
BOOKS 1-14

Gansett Island Compendium, Volume 1, Books 1-14
By: Marie Force

Published by HTJB, Inc.
Copyright 2026. HTJB, Inc.
Books Copyright 2011-2015. HTJB, Inc.
Cover & Interior Design by Qamber Design & Media
ISBN: 978-1966871507

HTJB, Inc.
PO Box 370
Portsmouth, RI 02871 USA

marie@marieforce.com

A Note from Marie...

I'll never forget where I was the weekend before I published MAID FOR LOVE on April 28, 2011. I'd attended the annual conference for the New England Chapter of the Romance Writers of America and was out to lunch with several of my writing friends after it ended on Sunday. I think the conference was in Salem, Massachusetts, that year, but don't quote me on that. Anyway, I told my friends I was going to publish the first book in my Gansett Island Series, the one that had been shopped around to all the romance publishers and rejected by every one of them.

At this point, I'd already had five books traditionally published, including LINE OF SCRIMMAGE, LOVE AT FIRST FLIGHT, FATAL AFFAIR, FATAL JUSTICE and EVERYONE LOVES A HERO, and had self-published TRUE NORTH, THE FALL and THE WRECK. Despite having eight books on sale, my career had been off to a slow start. I was really excited about the McCarthys of Gansett Island Series and my fictional island, inspired by Block Island, Rhode Island, where I'd spent so much time throughout my life. We're told to "write what we know," and after growing up on yet another island—albeit one connected to the mainland by three bridges—I understood the assignment.

I planned to publish MAID FOR LOVE, FOOL FOR LOVE and READY FOR LOVE three months in a row in April, May and June of 2011. That was something no traditional publisher ever would've done at that time, and I was hoping it would jumpstart things. And that's exactly what happened. The series took off, and by the end of 2011, I resigned from my sixteen-year day job to write full-time. As the series expanded beyond the original McCarthy family, I tweaked the name to the Gansett Island Series, which is now a registered trademark with the U.S. Patent & Trademark Office.

Twenty-eight books later—plus a couple of novellas—multiple *New York Times, USA Today* and *Wall Street Journal* bestsellers and numerous foreign translations—Gansett Island is my bestselling series. I've enjoyed every minute I've spent on our favorite not-so-fictional island over the last fifteen years, and I'm still amazed by everything that's come from the first book about Mac and Maddie and how much fun I've had continuing to write their story. I believe much of the series' success is due to keeping Mac, Maddie, Joe, Janey and the entire cast front and center as the series unfolded, rather than sending them off to live their happily ever after "off stage." I've always thought that "I love you" is just the start of a couple's story, and I wanted to show how life unfolded for these beloved characters. As a result, Book 1 stars, Mac and Maddie, remain front and center throughout the series, and along with Mac's parents, Big Mac and Linda, provide the heart and soul of the Gansett Island community.

I ended the initial series with DELIVERY AFTER DARK in 2025, and I'm hoping to write another series about the Gansett Island kids—and there are a lot of them! I can't promise I'll write stories for all of them, but I'm hoping for updates about their shenanigans as well as those of their parents. You know Mac will never really grow up, and I don't know about you, but I can't wait to see him dealing with three teenage daughters at the same time!

Wrangling the details of the Gansett Island Series for this two-volume compendium was a BEAST of a task! So many people, so much happens! Fun facts: When laid out in its entirety in paperback format, Gansett Island is 8,836 pages, and the series is 2,375,865 words from start to finish! Yes, as in 2.3 MILLION words! I'll have some more stats for you in Volume 2!

We did our best to accurately capture it all, and I owe a huge thank you to my reader friend Jennifer Anderson who stepped in to help summarize the books when I realized I couldn't possibly handle this entirely on my own—and write new books, too! Thank you to Janell Parque for proofreading and to my Gansett Island beta readers: Kara Conrad, Tracey Suppo, Juliane Sullivan, Andi Lawrence, Jaime Reynolds, Judy Evans, Gwen Neff and Amy Altieri for your input! The gorgeous design of the covers of both volumes and the interior pages in the paperbacks were done by Qamber Design & Media.

Oh, and that conference I attended right before I pressed publish on MAID FOR LOVE? I was invited back as the keynote speaker a few years later, thanks mostly to the success of Gansett Island. This series has been a dream come true in every possible way. Thank you for coming on this journey thus far and watch for more to come from the next generation of McCarthys and their friends!

Much love and gratitude,

Marie

MARIE FORCE

Maid *for* Love

Book 1: Maid for Love
Published April 28, 2011

She's a single mom with no patience for a playboy until he proves he's playing for keeps.

Maddie Chester is determined to leave her hometown of Gansett Island, a place that has brought her only bad memories and ugly rumors. Then she's knocked off her bike on the way to her housekeeping job at McCarthy's Gansett Inn by Gansett's "favorite son," Mac McCarthy.

He's back in town to help his father with preparations to sell the family marina and has no intention of sticking around. When Mac accidentally sends Maddie flying over the handlebars, badly injuring her, he moves in to nurse her back to health and help care for her young son. He soon realizes his plans for a hit-and-run visit to the island are in serious jeopardy, and he just may be "maid" for love.

Main Characters:

Madeline "Maddie" Chester, housekeeper at McCarthy's Gansett Inn, mother of Thomas, daughter of Francine Chester and deadbeat dad Bobby Chester.

Thomas Chester, nine months, son of Madeline "Maddie" Chester and Tom Wilkinson.

Malcolm John "Mac" McCarthy, Jr., co-owner of a Miami construction company, eldest child of Malcolm John "Big Mac" McCarthy, Sr., and Linda McCarthy, brother of Grant, Adam, Evan and Janey McCarthy.

Indicates recurring throughout the series

Supporting Characters:

Tiffany Chester Sturgil, daycare and dance studio owner, mother of Ashleigh, 10 months, wife of Jim Sturgil, younger sister of Maddie Chester.

***Captain Joseph "Joe" Cantrell,** co-owner of the Gansett Island Ferry Company with his mother, and Coast Guard-certified ferry captain, son of Carolina Cantrell and the late Peter Cantrell, best friend of Mac McCarthy.

Roseanne, Mac's assistant and ex-girlfriend in Miami.

***Janey McCarthy,** vet tech at the Island Veterinary Clinic, youngest child and only daughter of Big Mac and Linda McCarthy, sister to Mac, Grant, Adam and Evan McCarthy, engaged to Dr. David Lawrence.

***Dr. David Lawrence,** Boston-based medical intern, fiancé of Janey McCarthy.

Nicki Peterson, Mac's first kiss in eighth grade.

***Libby,** manager of The Beachcomber Hotel, part-time volunteer paramedic, friend of Mac's.

***Ethel,** head of housekeeping at McCarthy's Gansett Inn.

***Jim Sturgil,** attorney, husband of Tiffany Chester Sturgil, father of Ashleigh Sturgil.

***Ned Saunders,** island cabdriver, land-owner and giver of wisdom, best friend of Big Mac McCarthy.

***Aunt Joan,** Linda's sister.

Janet, daughter of Joan, cousin of McCarthys.

***Royal Atkinson,** member, Gansett Town Council.

***Linda McCarthy,** co-owner of the McCarthy's Gansett Island Marina and the McCarthy's Gansett Inn, wife of Big Mac McCarthy, mother of Mac, Grant, Adam, Evan and Janey McCarthy.

***Malcolm John "Big Mac" McCarthy, Sr.,** co-owner of the McCarthy's Gansett Island Marina and the McCarthy's Gansett Inn, husband of Linda McCarthy, father of Mac, Grant, Adam, Evan and Janey McCarthy.

***Luke Harris,** second in command to Big Mac at McCarthy's Gansett Island Marina, classmate of Mac McCarthy and Joe Cantrell.

***Evan McCarthy,** musician in Nashville, son of Big Mac and Linda McCarthy, brother of Mac, Grant, Adam and Janey McCarthy, classmate of Maddie Chester.

Teensy, town gossip.

Josh, McCarthy cousin, married to Ellen, expecting second child.

***Grant McCarthy,** screenwriter in Los Angeles, son of Big Mac and Linda McCarthy, brother of Mac, Adam, Evan and Janey McCarthy.

Darren Tuttle, owns a body shop on Sunflower Road, former high school football player, friend of Evan McCarthy.

***Betty, Sylvia, Patty, Sarah and Maude,** housekeepers at McCarthy's Gansett Inn, Maddie's coworkers.

***Daisy,** housekeeper at McCarthy's Gansett Inn, Maddie's friend.

***Doro Chase,** realtor.

Carol Ann, bartender at McCarthy's Marina Tiki Bar.

Tom Wilkinson, bestselling author, Thomas's biological father.

Doc Robach, veterinarian, Island Vet Clinic (name changes to Doc Potter in Book 2—whoops).

***Mrs. Gold,** co-owner of Gold's pharmacy.

Sam Pressley, retired Gansett police chief.

Cliff Sutter, Big Mac's friend.

Mrs. Jergenson, works at the post office.

Connor and Tony, Mac's business partners in Miami.

📍 Places

- **McCarthy's Gansett Inn,** North Harbor.
- **Gansett Island Ferry Company,** co-owned by Carolina Cantrell and her son, Captain Joe Cantrell, founded by Carolina's late parents.
- **The Ferry Landing,** South Harbor, where all the ferries serving the island arrive and depart.
- **Island Veterinary Clinic,** South Harbor.
- **The Beachcomber,** iconic hotel in South Harbor.
- **Victorian Portside Inn,** South Harbor.

- **Mario's Pizzeria and Ice Cream Parlor,** South Harbor.
- **McCarthy's Gansett Island Marina,** North Harbor.
- **The White House,** Big Mac and Linda's home overlooking North Harbor.
- **Gansett Boat Works,** marina in North Harbor.
- **North Harbor Yacht Club,** marina in North Harbor.
- **Coast Guard Station Gansett Island,** North Harbor.
- **The Tiki Bar,** McCarthy's Gansett Island Marina, North Harbor.
- **Galilee, Rhode Island,** ferry landing for boats coming from Gansett Island.
- **Abby's Attic,** toy and gift shop in South Harbor, owned by Abby Callahan.
- **Dominic's,** Italian restaurant, south side of the island.
- *Gansett Gazette,* island newspaper.
- **Gold's,** island pharmacy, South Harbor.
- **South Harbor Diner,** South Harbor.
- **McCarthy Construction,** Mac's company.
- **Hydrangea House,** Bed & Breakfast, North Harbor.
- **Sweet Meadow Farm Road,** location of Mac and Maddie's home.

66 Headlines from MAID FOR LOVE:

- Joe is in love with Janey McCarthy, who's engaged to David Lawrence!
- Mac steps off a curve and crashes into Maddie on her bike!
- Mac moves in to help take care of Maddie and Thomas!
- Tiffany's marriage to Jim Sturgil is in trouble!
- Mac goes to work at his family's hotel to cover for Maddie!
- Mac will help his dad fix up the marina and hang out for a while on the island!
- Linda doesn't approve of Mac spending time with Maddie!
- Maddie's mother is in prison!
- Mac punches Darren Tuttle!
- Thomas's biological father shows up unannounced!

- The men who once started rumors about Maddie publish apologies in the *Gansett Gazette*!
- Maddie breaks up with Mac!
- Tom agrees to surrender paternal rights to Thomas!
- Linda apologizes to Maddie and offers her a promotion!
- Maddie sees Mac hugging another woman and thinks he's moved on!
- Mac makes things right with Maddie, and they get engaged!
- Mac shows Maddie the house he bought for them!
- Mac wants to adopt Thomas!

The Gansett Island series begins as Maddie Chester gets her nine-month-old son, Thomas, ready for another day at her sister Tiffany's daycare. Maddie rides her bike to her housekeeping job at McCarthy's Gansett Inn. Mac McCarthy is on the ferry to Gansett Island, visiting with his childhood best friend, Captain Joe Cantrell, as Joe steers the ferry to South Harbor. The old friends catch up about Mac's father's surprising plan to sell the family's marina, Mac's booming construction business in Miami and Joe's ongoing crush on Mac's younger sister, Janey, who's engaged to Dr. David Lawrence.

Mac no sooner lands on the island when he steps off a curb right into the path of Maddie and her bike, a crash that launches their epic romance. Not that they know it yet, but they'll look back at the moment of impact as one of the best things to ever happen to them. But in the meantime, Maddie is left badly injured and worried about how she'll take care of Thomas and do her job at the hotel. Much to her dismay, Mac says he'll take care of her and Thomas and will fill in for her at work since he feels responsible for the accident that injured her.

The last thing Maddie wants is everyone whispering about Mac McCarthy staying with her, when they already think she slept around in high school because of a rumor started by Darren Tuttle and spread by his friends, including Mac's brother Evan. Her sister, Tiffany, immediately disapproves of Mac helping her, but before Maddie knows what's happening, he's taking Maddie's place helping out at Tiffany's daycare while she teaches dance, feeding Thomas his dinner and giving him a bath.

Mac and Maddie spend the night talking, sharing confidences and building a friendship that soon has Mac wondering if he belongs on the island he once ran away from the minute he was old enough to leave. He agrees to help his dad fix up the marina and to see how he feels about being there for a few weeks. Big Mac says if his son wants to run the marina, he'd never sell it. His mother, Linda, on the other hand, is deeply distressed by Mac's growing affection for Maddie, due to the pervasive rumors about her. That Maddie won't tell anyone who fathered her child only adds to the controversy. Maddie's mother, Francine, is in prison for three months for repeatedly writing bad checks to businesses on the island. Linda is outraged that Mac is working as a maid at the hotel his family owns, and he's furious that Maddie always gets the filthiest rooms. He and his mother argue.

As Maddie starts to soften toward Mac and considers giving him a chance to be more than a temporary roommate, Linda's obvious disapproval becomes a bigger problem for them. Determined to set the record straight about the past, Mac confronts Darren about the rumors he spread and tells him he's going to fix it. He talks to his brother Evan and tells him the same thing. Maddie notices his bruised knuckles and asks who he punched. He doesn't want to tell her about the fight he got into with Darren, so he evades the question and leaves to pick up the vehicle he bought to get them around the island.

Maddie realizes he's serious about making a life together and begins to trust him, to fall in love. He takes her on a romantic dinner date, and they make love for the first time. She appreciates that he sees her, understands her insecurities and seems to genuinely care for her and Thomas, who adores Mac.

They take a trip to the mainland together, and on the ferry back to the island, they run into Tom Wilkinson, the man who fathered Thomas. When Mac realizes who the man is, he thinks fast, introducing himself as Maddie's husband and referring to Thomas as their son. Maddie is weak with relief that Mac managed to diffuse her biggest fear, that Thomas's father would show up one day and want to take him from her. Later, when Mac and Thomas are at the diner, Tom approaches Mac to say he knows they're not married and that Thomas is most likely his son. Mac tells him they want nothing from him, and Tom agrees to surrender his paternal rights. Mac keeps that information to himself until it's a done deal, so Maddie won't be frantic about it.

Mac begins to look for a place for them to live together. His father's friend Ned, who, it turns out, has been buying real estate while driving a cab, shows him a house that would be perfect for their little family, with plenty of room for more kids. Mac is excited to tell her about it, but when he returns to the marina, his dad tells him Maddie was there and she's upset about the letters to the editor that ran in the local paper from the men who started the rumors about her. Big Mac is annoyed that Mac didn't tell him that his son Evan was involved in. Maddie is devastated to once again be the center of attention in their small island town. She packs up Mac's things and leaves them on her porch, where he finds them when he goes after her.

He begs her to understand that his intentions were good, and he intended to tell her what he'd done, but she's not having it. While Thomas cries inside, Mac's heart breaks outside her door, wondering how he'll go on without them. He loves them both desperately and only wanted to fix things for her. Janey comes to get Mac, urges him to give Maddie some space and takes him to her house for the night.

Devastated to lose her and Thomas and the future they'd planned, Mac throws himself into work at the marina, hoping she might change her mind. He's not sure he can stay on the island if his life there doesn't include them. Maddie's friends urge her to consider that Mac's heart was in the right place and to remember how he stepped up for her and Thomas when she was injured. Since the letters ran, others in the community have treated Maddie respectfully, and she has to admit he succeeded in changing their opinions of her. Linda apologizes to Maddie for believing the gossip, offers her the housekeeping director position at the hotel and tells her Mac is miserable without her.

Maddie decides to give him another chance and is on her way to the marina when she sees a dark-haired woman throw herself into his arms and kiss him. Maddie turns back to the hotel, heartbroken to think she waited too long and he's moved on. In fact, Mac has no desire to see his ex-girlfriend, Roseanne, from Miami, and tells her he's met someone else. Roseanne asks Ned to take her to the ferry so she can get out of there.

At dinner that night, Linda asks Mac if he saw Maddie, and when he says no, they realize she would've been arriving at the marina right as Roseanne was hugging and kissing him. Mac runs out of his parents' house and drives straight to Maddie to tell her what she saw was nothing, and the only woman he wants is her. He proposes to her, and she accepts. Then he takes her and Thomas to see the house he bought for them, which she thinks is a mansion. While they're there, he shows her the paperwork Thomas's father sent, surrendering his paternal rights. Maddie is outraged that Mac didn't tell her he'd arranged that, but he didn't want her worrying herself sick over it until he had the paperwork in hand. She realizes he's right. She would've suffered, and she's thankful she didn't know about it.

Mac says Thomas's father will always love and care for Thomas and his mother, and she'll never again have to worry about his biological father resurfacing. They're on their way to happily ever after.

Some of Marie's favorite scenes in the series...

Will we ever forget Janey's condom run?

Mac realized Janey was his only other option. His father would do it for him, but he couldn't ask him. Even at almost thirty-five, he just couldn't. Swallowing hard, Mac called Janey.

"Hey, brat, what're you doing?"

"Heading into work. Why?"

"I need another favor."

"You want to go out *again* tonight?"

"Not exactly."

"Then what?"

"I need you to, um, well… If you could go to Gold's," Mac said, referring to the island drugstore, "and just, you know…"

"*What*, Mac? Spit it out, will ya?"

"I need you to buy condoms for me. A lot of them."

Dead silence.

"Janey?"

"You gotta be kidding me."

"I can't do it! It'll be all over the island in ten minutes, and Maddie can't deal with that."

"Get Joe to do it."

"He's off-island until tomorrow."

"So, *abstain* for one night!"

"Janey, *please*. I'm desperate here."

"You can't ask me to do this. It's too embarrassing."

"How do you think I feel about asking my baby sister to do this for me?" He let out what he knew was a pathetic wail. "*Janey… I need you.*"

"Don't do that. Don't you dare play the need card."

"*Pretty please.*"

She let out a swear that shocked him to his core. "Fine," she said through gritted teeth. "But you'll owe me forever, do you hear me? There's no statute of limitations on what you'll owe me."

"I understand."

"I don't think you do. For the rest of your natural life, anytime I say, 'Jump,' you say, 'How high, Janey? How high can I jump for you?' Anytime I snap my fingers, you come running. Any. Time. Am I clear?"

"Crystal."

"I'll need at least a hundred dollars."

"What the hell for?"

"Buffer items, you buffoon. I can't just go in there and buy a gross of condoms and walk out."

"So, you're going to soak me for a year's supply of nail polish and tampons?"

"That's the very *least* of what you'll owe me."

"Fine. I'll bring it to the vet clinic."

"Pay me later. I can't look at you right now. Meet me at noon behind the Beachcomber, and do not look at me. Just take the bag, give me the money, and walk away."

"I love you, Janey. Have I mentioned that lately?"

"Screw you."

Holding back a laugh, he said, "Get the extra-large ones, okay?"

"I hate you."

Janey was waiting for him when he arrived at the back steps to the Beachcomber.

As Mac approached, her eyes narrowed. *Uh-oh.*

She swung the bag and smacked him right upside the head.

"Hey! That hurt!"

"Mrs. Gold herself was working the register. You know what she said to me?" Without taking a breath, Janey launched into Mrs. Gold's nasally New York accent. "My oh my, *Janey*, Doctor David must be coming for a *good* long visit this weekend."

Mac knew it wasn't a good idea, but he laughed anyway.

She pelted him again with the bag. "It's not funny! I have to live in this town!"

He attempted to wipe the smile off his face and withdrew a wad of twenties from his pocket.

Janey snatched the money and thrust the bag at him. "It's going to take *years* of therapy to recover from this."

"You're the best, Janey." Mac gave her a noisy smooch on the cheek.

She pushed him away. "I hate you more than anything."

He poked her ribs. "Do not."

"I'm off to get a brain scrub to erase this unsavory incident from my memory."

"Come by Maddie's this weekend. Let's hang out."

"No way I'm coming near the two of you until the supply is exhausted."

Mac grinned. "We'll be giving thanks to Janey McCarthy *every time*."

Hands over ears, she shrieked and stalked off.

Mac laughed all the way home.

 An interview with Mac and Maddie...

Here we are, fifteen years later, with Mac and Maddie McCarthy. We've just revisited your love story. What do you remember most about this time in your lives?

Mac: I remember every detail of that first day with Maddie, especially how she wanted me to get lost and never come back.

Maddie: (laughing) I can't deny that's true because I thought you were too good to be true. But I'm so glad you made me fall in love with you.

Mac: As if it were a choice.

At the time, you had nine-month-old Thomas, and now he's about to be sixteen! What's he up to these days?

Mac: He's counting the days until he can get his driver's license.

Maddie: While I want to rewind the clock. I'm so not ready for him to be driving.

Mac: He's obsessed with baseball, like I was at his age, but he's better at it than I ever was. He also plays basketball and lacrosse. But baseball is his first love.

Maddie: He's an excellent student and a wonderful big brother to his brother and sisters. We're very proud of him.

Does he know what he wants to do after high school?

Maddie: He's pursuing an appointment to the Naval Academy.

Wow, that's impressive. What sparked his interest in the military?

Mac: It's something that's always interested him. We don't remember a time when he wasn't talking about joining the military.

You have two other teenagers now, right?

Maddie: We do. Hailey is fourteen, and Mac is thirteen. The twins are nine already. The time is going by so fast.

Mac: We also celebrate Connor's birthday every year. We never stop thinking of the baby we lost.

Mac, we always wondered what you'd be like with daughters who were interested in boys. How's that going for you?

Mac: It's hell.

Maddie: (laughing) He's handling it better than expected. Hailey has a lot of friends, some of whom are boys, but isn't interested in having a boyfriend just yet.

Mac: Thank God for that.

Maddie: Mac doesn't want to hear that we're on borrowed time when it comes to boyfriends and such things.

Mac: You're right. Mac doesn't want to hear about that.

How are your parents doing?

Maddie: Mom and Ned are great. They're traveling a lot. Last year they went to Paris, and this year they're planning an Alaskan cruise.

Mac: My parents are doing well, too. My dad had knee replacement surgery last year, and he's getting around a lot better since then. My mom has taken up pickleball, and no one can beat her. They're looking forward to an African safari next week with their travel crew.

Maddie: We're very thankful for their continued good health. They're surrounded by grandchildren when they're home, and they wouldn't have it any other way.

When you look back over the last fifteen years, what's the thing you're proudest of?

Maddie: Definitely our family. The kids are close and enjoy being together. We never miss a chance to remind them their closest friends are right here in our home. They're also very close to their cousins.

Mac: That philosophy comes right from my dad. He used to say that to us, and my siblings and cousins are still my closest friends.

Maddie: We're also proud of all the things we've been through together and how our relationship has grown and evolved over the years.

Mac: She's still madly in love with me.

Maddie: (rolling her eyes) I can't deny that, even if he is still insufferable.

Mac: Her love is the greatest gift of my life.

Maddie: See how he messes up and then fixes it? Nothing has changed.

Mac: One thing has changed. I love you a thousand times more than I did fifteen years ago.

Maddie: Likewise, my love.

MARIE FORCE

Fool *for* Love

Book 2: Fool for Love
Published: May 26, 2011

He's always been like her fifth brother, but her feelings for him are far from platonic.

Joe Cantrell, owner of the Gansett Island Ferry Company, has been in love with Janey McCarthy for as long as he can remember. At the same time, Janey has been dating or engaged to doctor-in-training David Lawrence. When things go horribly wrong between David and Janey, she calls her "fifth brother" Joe, one of the few people in her close circle who lives on the mainland.

Janey decides a few days with Joe is just what she needs before she goes home to the island to face her parents and family with the news of her broken engagement. It was bad enough for Joe to love Janey from afar but having her in his house is absolute torture. Will he take advantage of this opportunity to show her what they could have together? And what will Joe's best friend and Janey's protective older brother, Mac, have to say about it?

Main Characters:

Joe Cantrell, co-owner of the Gansett Island Ferry Company and a Coast Guard-certified ferry captain.

Janey McCarthy, vet tech at the Island Veterinary Clinic, engaged to Dr. David Lawrence.

Indicates recurring throughout the series

Supporting Characters:

Mac McCarthy, Jr., partner in McCarthy's Gansett Island Marina and owner of McCarthy Construction in MAID FOR LOVE, engaged to Maddie Chester in MAID FOR LOVE, father of Thomas Chester McCarthy in MAID FOR LOVE.

***Maddie Chester,** mother of Thomas, engaged to Mac McCarthy in MAID FOR LOVE.

***Dr. David Lawrence,** ex-fiancé of Janey McCarthy

Leroy, ferry boat captain, Gansett Island Ferry Company.

***Doc Potter,** veterinarian, Gansett Island Vet Clinic, Janey's boss.

***Chelsea,** bartender at the Beachcomber.

***Blaine Taylor,** chief, Gansett Island Police, classmate of Mac's and Joe's.

***Big Mac McCarthy,** grandfather of Thomas Chester McCarthy in MAID FOR LOVE.

***Linda McCarthy,** grandmother of Thomas Chester McCarthy in MAID FOR LOVE.

***Luke Harris,** partner, McCarthy's Gansett Island Marina, ex-boyfriend of Sydney Donovan.

Trio, Janey's three-legged cat.

Sam, Janey's blind dog.

Dexter, Janey's cocker spaniel, who was found with his ears missing.

Muttley, Janey's dog who was malnourished when he was found.

Riley, Janey's German Shepherd, has no back legs.

Pixie, Janey's Jack Russell, has a persistent skin infection.

***Kay Lawrence,** David's mother.

***Ned Saunders,** island cabdriver, land-owner and giver of wisdom, best friend of Big Mac McCarthy.

Rob, mate on the ferry.

***Francine Chester,** mother of Maddie and Tiffany, grandmother of Ashleigh Sturgil and Thomas McCarthy.

***Tiffany Chester Sturgil,** daycare and dance studio owner, mother of Ashleigh, wife of Jim Sturgil.

***Sydney Donovan,** Luke Harris's ex-girlfriend and Maddie's friend, recently lost her husband and children in a drunk-driving accident that left her badly injured.

***Grant McCarthy,** screenwriter in Los Angeles.

***Evan McCarthy,** musician in Nashville.

***Adam McCarthy,** owns a computer company in New York City.

66 Headlines in FOOL FOR LOVE:

- Janey catches David in bed with another woman—they're done!

- Janey's car breaks down and Joe comes to her rescue!

- Back at Joe's house, Janey asks him to make her feel something other than devastated!

- She has the best sex of her life with Joe!

- Joe encourages Janey to consider all her options, including vet school!

- Joe tells Janey he loves her and has for as long as he can remember!

- Janey tells Maddie she slept with Joe!

- Afraid of how he'll react, Maddie keeps Janey's secret from Mac!

- Joe punches David and gets arrested!

- Hello, Blaine Taylor, Gansett Island Police Chief!

- David's mother has coffee with Linda, hoping to Janey and David back together!

- Francine is released from prison and doesn't approve of Maddie's plan to marry Mac!

- Mac and Maddie hit a speed bump right before their wedding!

- David has cancer!

- Janey is going to vet school *this* fall!

- Luke Harris's ex-girlfriend and recent widow, Sydney Donovan, is back on Gansett!

- Grant, Adam and Evan McCarthy come home for Mac's wedding!

- Luke rows his boat across a pond to check on Sydney, who's crying on the porch!

- Mac and Maddie get married!

- Joe and Janey get engaged! He's going with her to Ohio for vet school!

FOOL FOR LOVE has one of Marie's favorite opening lines: *The phone call Joe Cantrell had waited half his life to receive came in around nine on an otherwise average Tuesday evening.* And doesn't that phone call change everything? Hearing Janey needs him, Joe is in his truck and on his way to her location south of Boston before he takes one second to question the wisdom of this mission.

Something has happened between her and her fiancé, Dr. David Lawrence, and whatever it is must be bad if Janey is crying by the side of the road and calling Joe for help after her car breaks down. As far as he knew, she was on her way to surprise David, who is finishing his medical training in Boston, on their thirteenth anniversary. "Lucky thirteen," she'd said when he'd seen her earlier.

So why hadn't she called David when her car broke down? Maybe she called Joe because he's the only other person she knows on the mainland. Or maybe she called him because she knows he'd come running. His burning love for his best friend's little sister is the biggest secret in his life. Only her brother Mac is aware of it, but due to her thirteen-year relationship with David and a wedding planned for next summer, Joe knows there's no point in harboring hopes where she's concerned.

Until she calls him for help.

When he arrives, he learns Janey caught David in bed with another woman. While Joe is secretly glad to hear her relationship with David is probably over, he's focused only on whatever Janey needs. After calling a tow for her car, he loads her into his truck and takes her home with him to hide out while she figures out her next move. Her heartbreak makes him want to punch David Lawrence in the face, but as far as Joe is concerned, David never deserved the magnificence that is Janey McCarthy.

Back at his house, Joe lets Mac know where his sister is and tells him not to come running to get her. Janey needs a minute to catch her breath, and she'll be staying with Joe for a couple of days. Mac expresses concern for Joe in this situation, which Joe appreciates, but it doesn't change his mind about giving her a sanctuary for as long as she needs it—and as long as she needs him. Joe and Mac are angry with David for treating Janey this way.

With her asleep in his bed, Joe settles on the sofa, wondering if now that things have blown up between her and David, there might be a chance for him. But this isn't the time, no matter how much hope he feels. He wakes later to hear her sobbing and goes to her, holding her while she cries and losing his heart and mind to her as he holds her in his bed. He immediately realizes his mistake when she clings to him, and then she asks him to make her feel something other than devastated….

"You have no idea what you're asking of me. No idea."

"I'm asking someone who loves me and who I love to hold me and love me and make this awful, unbearable pain go away."

He shakes his head. "I can't, Janey. I just can't."

"Joe." Her lips find his, her hand sinking into his thick hair, her fingers caressing his scalp, as he trembles. "I need you. Don't say no. Please, don't say no."

His hands frame her face as he draws back from her. "You can't ask me for this, Janey. I'll get you anything else you need, but not this."

"No one else could give me this." She caresses his chest and belly, his rippling muscles responding to her touch even as he continues to resist. Emboldened, she rises so she's on top of him. The press of his erection against her belly tells her his body is with her even if the rest of him isn't.

His hands travel over her back, stopping at the waistband of her shorts. He studies her as if he's making some sort of decision.

"We can't, honey," he says softly. "It's not going to make anything better. It'll only make everything worse."

"No. It won't."

"You're using me to get back at him. Evening the score won't make you feel any less devastated."

She shakes her head and slides her lips back and forth over his. "I'm not thinking about him right now. I'm thinking about you, and I already feel better." Straddling him, she sits up and reaches for the hem of her shirt.

He stops her. "You'll hate yourself in the morning. And worse yet, you'll hate me."

"I could never, ever hate you."

"You don't think so now…"

"I know so."

Oh, Joe… Now he's in big trouble! He knows it's wrong to act on his overwhelming desire for her, but with her pleading with him to hold her and love her, how can he resist? Making love to Janey is the most amazing experience of his life, and Janey realizes what she's been missing with David. Both their lives are changed forever after that first night together. For Joe, it's confirmation of what he's always known—he and Janey belong together. Janey is beginning to understand she may have spent thirteen years with the wrong man.

The next morning, Joe calls out of work for that day and the next so he can be with Janey, and they face the morning after in a charged state of disbelief. They decide to spend the next two days together at his home, in a "bubble," away from everything and everyone, while she contemplates her next move. While Joe is at the store, she removes the two-carat ring David gave her and realizes he didn't even call her for their thirteenth anniversary. He was too busy sleeping with another woman.

When Mac calls, she tells him what happened with David and asks him not to say anything to anyone on the island, especially their parents. Mac is stunned to hear Joe took two days off during Fourth of July week when the ferries are running at full capacity. When Joe returns from the store, Janey tells him she has no idea what to do now, and he encourages her to consider all her options, including veterinary school.

Everyone in Janey's life was outraged when David talked her out of going, so they wouldn't have to take on debt from two medical school educations. She thinks it's too late to apply to vet school, since she graduated from college six years ago. Joe says it's never too late. He notices she took off her ring and recalls that she doesn't eat meat because she's such an animal lover.

Joe finds it difficult to hide his feelings from her, and at the end of the day, the truth spills out of him.

"Janey," he sighs, dropping his head to his hands.

She doesn't know what to say or do. Keeping her hand on his back, she gives him a minute. "Joe—"

He stands up straight, frames her face with his hands, and captures her mouth in a deep, searing kiss. "I love you. I love you so much, and I have for as long as I can remember." Before she can say anything, he kisses her again. "I hated watching you care for a guy who didn't deserve you. I hated how he would go weeks, sometimes months, without visiting you. I hated watching you waste your time with him, *knowing* he would never love you like I do."

She'd suspected there was something…. But she'd never imagined he'd spent *years* silently in love with her. Flabbergasted, she stares up at him. "I, um… I…."

"I shouldn't be saying these things to you, especially right now. But I needed you to know the truth."

Janey struggles free of him. "I shouldn't be here. I shouldn't have called you yesterday." Her hands begin to shake as images from their erotic night together run through her mind like a movie. "Oh, God, Joe. I didn't know. I didn't know it was like *that*." Sure, she'd suspected he had a little thing for her, but madly in love? For *years*? No, she hadn't known that. She hadn't had the first inkling.

"There's no way you could've known. I worked very, very hard to keep it hidden. Only one person has ever figured it out."

"Who?"

He smiles and tilts his head.

"Mac."

Nodding, Joe draws her back in close to him. "I don't want you to go."

"What happened between us…"

"Was the best thing to ever happen to me. Someday, when you're ready, maybe you'll see it was the best thing to ever happen to you, too."

After two blissful, erotically charged days together, it's time for Janey to return home to the island, and neither she nor Joe is ready to face reality. They're on the ferry when Mac calls to tell Joe that David is looking for Janey. Mac plans to meet the boat and will take Janey back to his and Maddie's house for the night. Joe, who is heartbroken to be separated from her after what they've shared, asks him to take good care of her. Mac reminds Joe of the Fourth of July party they're having at their house, and he's relieved to know he'll see Janey again soon.

Mindless of the prying eyes that surround them, Janey drops her head to Joe's chest and rests her hands on his hips. "I never would've survived this without you."

Joe aches. How can he tell her he'd never survive the rest of his life without *her*? He can't. It would be so unfair to add to her burden.

He holds her close. "You know where I am. You know how I feel. You know what I want."

She nods.

"No time limit, no statute of limitations, no pressure."

She looks up at him again, slaying him with the array of emotions that dance across her expressive face. "Thank you."

Gratitude was the least of what he wanted from her, but being the needy fool he was, he took what he could get. He kissed her forehead, and even though it cost him more than he could bear, he let her go.

Janey and Joe go their separate ways, trying to cope with everything that's happened. Janey confesses to Maddie that she slept with Joe, and her emotions are all over the place after learning Joe has been in love with her for years. Maddie struggles with keeping the news that Joe and Janey slept together from Mac. Janey listens to voicemails from David, who's wondering where she is, while Joe gets drunk at the Beachcomber bar. He wakes up horribly hungover the next day and is heading to work when he runs into David. Joe punches him in the face, breaking David's nose. Joe gets arrested, and while sitting in jail waiting for Mac to bail him out, he begins to wonder whether Janey will appreciate him punching David.

Along with Gansett Island Police Chief Blaine Taylor, classmate to Joe and Mac, Big Mac comes to have a talk with Joe. Joe is upset to have disappointed the man who's been a father figure to him since he lost his own father as a child. Big Mac bails him out. Janey hears about the incident and is shocked that Joe actually broke David's nose. Maddie takes Janey to the clinic to see David. She tells him what she saw that day in his apartment, says they're over and gives him back the ring while he tries to explain.

Janey doesn't want to hear it. She needs to tell her parents the engagement is off before they hear it from someone else. Maddie takes her to the McCarthy's home. They encounter Joe and his swollen hand there.

Joe and Janey have a moment together outside. She asks him to come to her house later that night.

When he's leaving the Beachcomber to go to Janey's, knowing it's probably a bad idea to go back for more, he runs into Luke Harris, who razzes him about punching David. They discuss Mac's upcoming bachelor party. Joe gets to Janey's, intending to talk and only talk, but quickly finds himself in her bed. He learns she has five dogs and three cats in her home, all of them special-needs animals.

Joe is worried about trouble with Mac after Janey says she told Maddie about what really happened between them on the mainland. After another night in bed with Joe, Janey's glad she didn't get married before she knew what it was like to be with him. He asks her to come back to the mainland with him that night to pick up her car and spend the night at his house.

With Joe in her shower, David shows up at Janey's wanting to explain himself. She tells him to leave. He says it's not over between them. Linda has coffee with David's mother, Kay, who's trying to get David and Janey back together. Linda pushes back because David cheated. Kay says David is having some challenges that he needs to tell Janey about. Linda doesn't think that'll matter to her daughter. Joe isn't happy to hear that Kay and Linda might be trying to get Janey and David back together. Mac notices Joe is using Janey's favorite cow mug and is suspicious of how he came to have it.

Ned shocks Joe when he tells him to give Janey some time, that she'll come around. How does he always know what's going on? Janey talks to Maddie about the strange transition from friend to lover with Joe and how to know if she *loves him*-loves him as more than a friend. Mac asks Janey about the coffee mug, and Maddie advises Janey to tell him the truth before their wedding. If Mac finds out that Maddie knew about Joe and Janey and didn't tell him, there might not be a wedding.

When she's preparing to catch the ferry with Joe, Janey runs into David again. He wants to know where she's going. Meanwhile, Joe is afraid he might have to leave without her if she doesn't get to the ferry landing soon. They make the crossing in deep fog with Joe at the helm, and at his house, they make love in front of the fireplace on a chilly night. Joe shows her his paintings, and Janey is shocked to realize there's so much about him she doesn't know.

Maddie takes the first boat off the island to pick up her mother, who's being released from prison after serving three months for writing bad checks. She is nervous about telling her mother that she's marrying Mac McCarthy, since Linda was one of the merchants who reported Francine to the police. Maddie tells her she's getting married to Mac in a week. Francine says she'll marry a McCarthy over her dead body.

Maddie and Janey meet up on the ferry ride back to the island. Janey encourages Maddie not to allow anyone, even her mother, to steal her happiness with Mac. Janey wonders how it's possible she could be falling in love with Joe when she was engaged to David a week ago. Finding him in bed with another woman helped to move things along, Maddie says. Mac and Thomas meet the boat, and Francine is rude to Mac.

Janey looks into vet school at Ohio State and takes a call from Kay, pleading with her to give David another chance, that there are things she doesn't know. David shows up at Mac's party and insists on talking to Janey. She makes a comment about him thinking he's the only one allowed to have cheap, meaningless sex that Joe overhears.

Stunned and hurt, Joe walks away.

Before Janey can go after him, David tells her he has cancer.

Mac goes after Joe, asks if it's true, and Joe says it is and he did *not* take advantage of Janey. Joe accidentally lets on that Maddie knows about them. Mac is incredulous.

David has stage-two Non-Hodgkin's lymphoma and has started chemo. Janey can't believe he never told her. She's sorry for what he's going through, but they're done. This incident has shown her that marrying him would have been a mistake. He apologizes to her, and they agree to part as friends.

Mac and Maddie argue about her keeping the news about Janey and Joe from him. Later, they make up, and she asks him to understand that she wants to be good friends with Janey and needed to follow her lead on who to tell and when. She mentions her friend Sydney Donovan, Luke Harris's ex-girlfriend, who recently lost her husband and children in a drunk driving accident that left Sydney badly injured. Sydney is back on the island.

After Janey drops David off at his mother's and convinces Kay that they're really over, she goes to the Beachcomber to see Joe. She apologizes for what he overheard and tells Joe that David has cancer. He wants to know if they're back together. They're over, Janey says. Joe wonders if she'll ever *love him*-love him, and she says yes, she's very close to that, and suggests they date like normal people in the meantime. They agree to wait to have sex again until she's sure of her feelings. He sends her flowers to the vet clinic. Janey tells Doc Potter that she's considering vet school, and he's supportive.

Mac comes to see her at work, notices the flowers, asks if they're from Joe, and wonders why she didn't tell him. "I'm a grown woman, Mac. I can sleep with anyone I want to, and believe it or not, it's none of your business."

"You're right." He's happy for her and Joe and promises not to let their relationship come between him and Joe.

Janey tries to convince Francine to come to Maddie's shower at Linda's house. Grant, Adam and Evan McCarthy come home to Gansett for Mac's bachelor party and wedding. Mac and Joe make up, and Mac gives his approval of Joe being with Janey, not that either of them needs his approval. And then Joe has to deal with Big Mac, who's heard about Joe and his "Princess." Joe tells Big Mac he loves Janey and is encouraging her to go to vet school.

They find out Sydney Donovan was on the ferry with the McCarthy brothers, news that shocks Luke Harris. Drunken Mac blurts out he's glad Joe is sleeping with Janey, who's with Maddie during the bachelor party. The news is out. Joe gives Janey a ride to town, and they have sex in his truck. The next day, Janey and Linda host Maddie's shower.

During the shower, Doc Potter calls with big news that he pulled strings as an alumnus and got her into Ohio State Veterinary School for that fall. She decides she has to end things with Joe because she can't do another long-distance relationship. His whole life and business are rooted in Gansett. Right when she's sure she *loves him*-loves him, her long-time dream comes true out of state. Maddie is thrilled when her mother comes to the shower.

Later, Janey cancels plans with Joe. He's immediately on alert for trouble and goes to her house, where she tells him she made a mistake and they're done. He calls Mac and tells him something is wrong with Janey.

Luke Harris rows his old boat across a pond to check on Sydney Donovan, the only woman he's ever loved. She suffered devastating injuries in the same crash that claimed the lives of her husband and kids. He sits in silence, watching over her, wishing he could do something to help, and vows to keep coming back to watch over her.

Mac checks on Janey, and she tells him about vet school. He tells her how Joe gave up his dream of art school to run the ferry company after his grandfather died. Mac says it's not fair for her to make decisions for him and says he'll fix it for her. Janey waits for days to hear something from Joe but doesn't see him again until Mac and Maddie's wedding. After they dance together as best man and maid of honor, Joe picks her up over his shoulder and carries her away.

"I missed you so much, and it was only *four days*. Oh, Joe, how will we ever be apart for *four years*?" The idea alone was enough to reduce her to tears.

"Who said anything about being apart?"

"But you live here. Your business, your whole *life* is here."

Staring down at her, he shakes his head, his eyes filled with what looks an awful lot like regret. "I guess I haven't done a good enough job."

"Of what?" she asks, confused.

"I thought you'd know by now that everything I want, everything I *need*, is right here in my arms. The rest is just details, Janey."

He'll get someone to run the business so he can go to Ohio with her. She *loves him*-loves him. He tells her not to cancel the wedding she has planned for next summer and says Dr. Janey Cantrell has a nice ring to it as he gives her an engagement ring.

Janey holds him close. "Thanks for waiting for me, Joe."

"You were well worth the wait, my love. Very well worth it."

 **An interview with Joe and Janey...**

Here we are, fifteen years later, with Joe and Janey Cantrell. We've just revisited your love story. What do you remember most about this time in your lives?

Janey: What a week that was… I left the island, planning to marry David, and came back a few days later, halfway in love with Joe.

Joe: Only halfway?

Janey: Haha, it took me a minute to catch up to you.

Joe: That was the happiest week of my life, even if it was tough for you. Janey had a bit of whiplash.

Janey: That's a good word for it. My entire life changed in the course of one afternoon and evening, but it changed for the better.

Joe and your parents encouraged you to finally go to veterinary school. What did their support mean to you?

Janey: It meant everything. When Joe told me he'd hired Seamus to run the ferry company so he could come with me to Ohio… I still can't believe everything he did to make it possible for us to be together while I was in school.

Joe: You can't? Really? I finally had the chance to be with my dream girl. There was nothing I wouldn't have done to make it work.

Janey: Sigh.

How is it going being Dr. Janey Cantrell, DMV, and running the Gansett Island Vet Clinic?

Janey: It's a dream come true. Every day is a different challenge, and I get to work with my favorite 'people.'"

Joe: She means the animals.

Janey: Haha, yes, they're the best. They make it so much fun. And the actual people aren't bad, either.

Joe, when you hired Seamus to run the ferry company, you never could've imagined how he'd become part of your family.

Joe: (laughing) Ain't that the truth? And now he's my stepdaddy.

LOL! Do you call him that?

Joe: Every chance I get. He's made my mother very happy, and he's one of my best friends. We're very lucky it worked out the way it did.

Your children, PJ and Vi, are growing up quickly. How old are they now?

Janey: PJ is fourteen and a freshman in high school, which we cannot believe. Vi is eleven and in sixth grade. They're active in the island children's theater, and both play soccer. They keep us busy.

Joe, are you still captaining the ferries?

Joe: I fill in as needed, which allows me to drive the kids around and wrangle the special-needs pets my wife continues to bring home regularly.

Janey: What can I say? It's what I do.

Joe: And we're all thankful for what you do. (With a wink for his wife...) Some of us more than others.

MARIE FORCE

Ready *for* Love

Book 3: Ready for Love
Published: June 28, 2011

After unspeakable tragedy, will her heart take a new journey… or walk a well-worn path?

For four of the best summers of his young life, Luke Harris was in love with Sydney Donovan, a wealthy seasonal visitor to Gansett Island. Then Sydney went off to college and never came back. She married another man and had two children while Luke remained on the island, working at McCarthy's Gansett Marina and wondering what had gone wrong between him and the only woman he ever loved.

Fifteen months after Sydney suffers the tragic loss of her husband and children, she has returned to Gansett to figure out what's next, and that may very well be a rekindled love affair with the one man from her past she's never forgotten. But is she ready for a second chance at love?

Main Characters:

*Luke Harris, partner, McCarthy's Gansett Island Marina.

*Sydney Donovan, widow of Seth, mother of the late Max and Malena, Luke Harris's ex-girlfriend.

*Indicates recurring throughout the series

Supporting Characters:

*Buddy, Sydney's golden retriever.

Max, Sydney's late son.

Seth, Sydney's late husband.

Malena, Sydney's late daughter.

*Maddie McCarthy, mother of Thomas, married to Mac McCarthy in FOOL FOR LOVE.

*Tiffany Chester Sturgil, mother of Ashleigh, wife of Jim Sturgil.

***Janey McCarthy,** engaged to Joe Cantrell in FOOL FOR LOVE.

***Abby Callahan,** owner of Abby's Attic, engaged to Dr. Cal Maitland, ex-girlfriend of Grant McCarthy.

***Dr. David Lawrence,** ex-fiancé of Janey McCarthy.

***Joe Cantrell,** engaged to Janey McCarthy in FOOL FOR LOVE.

***Mac McCarthy, Jr.,** married to Maddie Chester in FOOL FOR LOVE, father of Thomas McCarthy in MAID FOR LOVE.

***Big Mac McCarthy,** grandfather of Thomas McCarthy in MAID FOR LOVE.

***Owen Lawry,** musician, best friend of Evan McCarthy.

***Ned Saunders,** island cabdriver, land-owner and giver of wisdom.

***Grant McCarthy,** screenwriter in Los Angeles.

***Dr. Cal Maitland,** physician, Gansett Island Medical Clinic, engaged to Abby Callahan.

Mary Alice Donovan, Sydney's mother.

Allan Donovan, Sydney's father.

Wendell Sturgil, Jim's father, an old friend of Ned's.

***Francine Chester,** grandmother of Ashleigh Sturgil and Thomas McCarthy, wife of Bobby Chester, only love of Ned Saunders.

***Bobby Chester,** deadbeat father of Maddie and Tiffany, husband of Francine.

***Chelsea,** bartender at the Beachcomber.

***Stephanie,** restaurant manager at McCarthy's Gansett Island Marina.

***Blaine Taylor,** chief, Gansett Island Police.

***Slim,** pilot.

***Thomas McCarthy,** son of Maddie and Mac McCarthy.

***Linda McCarthy,** grandmother of Thomas McCarthy in MAID FOR LOVE.

***Adam McCarthy,** owns a computer company in New York City.

***Evan McCarthy,** musician in Nashville.

◉ Places

- **Harris Boat Works,** Luke's restoration business.
- **Gansett Island Clinic**

▭ Gansett Island Soundtrack:

- "Summer Breeze"
- "Sister Golden Hair"
- "God Only Knows"
- "Peaceful Easy Feeling"
- "Southern Cross"

❝ Headlines from READY FOR LOVE:

- Luke and Sydney talk for the first time in 20 years!
- Sydney is giving herself a month on Gansett to make some decisions!
- Sydney reconnects with Maddie!
- Maddie is pregnant!
- Luke still loves Sydney but gives her space to decide what she wants!
- Sydney is tortured about whether she should be with Luke again!
- Luke and Sydney spend time together and kiss!
- Sydney's dog Buddy is sad to meet Thomas, he misses her son Max!
- Big Mac wants Luke to be careful not to get hurt again!
- Sydney dreads the sentencing of the drunk driver who killed her family!
- Luke and Sydney are nearly hit head-on in his truck, she is traumatized!
- Buddy needs emergency surgery and only Janey can save him!
- Ned and Francine were a couple years ago—who knew?
- Hello Owen Lawry!
- Grant is back on Gansett Island and can't believe Abby has moved on!
- Big Mac, Mac and Luke are injured in an accident at the marina!
- Tiffany meets Blaine!

- Maddie's on bed rest!

- Joe and Janey get married!

One year after FOOL FOR LOVE...

"Are you ever going to say anything?" Sydney's question at the beginning of READY FOR LOVE shocks Luke. He thought she didn't know he was lurking next to her parents' front porch, like he has many times before, since she tragically lost her husband and children to a drunk driver. Sydney knew he was there but wasn't ready to talk the summer before.

Now it's a year later, and she'd like to see the man who was her first love. She tells him she'd know the sound of his rowboat scratching on the shore anywhere, as it was a sound she used to listen for when they were together. She invites him to the porch and mentions her parents are away for a few weeks for a family reunion. Sydney apologizes for the way she left him without a word seventeen years earlier. She says the summers they spent together were magical, and she was an idiot to treat him the way she did.

"I had this idea, you know, of how my life should be. Who my husband should be. What he would do for a living. Where we would live—I was a snobbish fool."

"I suppose the boy you'd left behind on the island, who worked at a marina and never made it to college, didn't quite fit the bill." Luke tries to keep the bitterness out of his tone, but after so many years of suspecting what had driven her away, hearing confirmation of what he'd most feared is hardly a balm on the still-open wound.

"I know there's nothing I can say to change what happened all those years ago, but I want you to know I regretted the way I treated you. I *always* regretted it."

She fears the accident was payback for how she treated Luke, but he says no, that's not possible. He accepts her apology, says they've got a clean slate to be friends again, and promises to come back and see her.

She's never forgotten him. She thought of him, missed him, and regretted their parting. *God, what does that mean?*

She's no longer married. Her husband and children had been gone for more than a year. Luke could tell just by looking at her that she was doing much better at accepting the awful hand life had dealt her than she was last summer, when the pain of her loss was still so fresh and new.

"Ugh," he says out loud as he rows away from her. "Don't go there, man. It was over and done with years ago. Leave the past where it belongs."

But even as he tells himself there's no point, a pesky burst of hope refuses to be ignored.

Sydney has come back to Gansett Island, her favorite place in the world, to make some decisions about her future. She can no longer bear to work as an elementary school teacher in a school full of kids the same ages as her late children. She resigned from her teaching job and is now trying to figure out what's next. Sydney has given herself a month on Gansett Island to make plans for her future. She regrets how she treated Luke once upon a time, when she was influenced by her parents, hoping she'd marry someone other than a marina worker on a remote island.

Sydney is delighted to see her old friend Maddie Chester, who's now Maddie McCarthy after marrying Mac McCarthy. She's expecting her first child with Mac. Later, after dinner, Sydney tells herself she's not waiting for Luke to come back, but she's thrilled to hear the distinctive scrape of his boat on the beach. All day, he'd told himself to stay away. He had the closure he needed, so why go back for more? Big Mac McCarthy had noticed his disquiet and asked if he was okay.

Luke is worried about getting attached to her again, only to watch her leave the way she did before. He realizes he still loves her, even after all these years, and having to stand by while she married someone else. He tells her he can't be just friends with her when he wants so much more, but he doesn't want to be her rebound or transition guy.

Sydney shares that a year ago, the thought of moving on or starting a new relationship would've been unimaginable, but she's in a better place now.

Luke can't resist the urge to brush a soft kiss over those perfect lips that have dominated his fantasies for such a long, lonely time.

The moment their lips connect, her eyes fly open with awareness.

"Think long and hard, Syd. Be sure it's what you really want. Be sure you're ready."

"Luke—"

He rests a finger over her lips. "If it's tomorrow or next week or next summer or two summers from now, it doesn't matter. I'll be here, and you'll always be welcome. If you never feel ready, that's okay, too."

"That's crazy," she says. "You can't wait forever for me."

"I already have. I've never met anyone I like better than you. After a while, I stopped looking." He kisses her forehead because he didn't dare kiss her lips again. If he does, he might not be able to stop kissing her. "You know where to find me."

Before he can let the possibility of never seeing her again set in, he gets out of there. Without looking back, he goes down the stairs, across the yard and into the reeds. Only when he's rowing his boat across the pond does he breathe again. What the hell has he done?

Sydney spends a long week thinking about Luke's offer, tormented by the push-pull of past and present. She's invited to a girl's night out with Maddie and her friends. Mac, Joe and Luke crash the party, and Luke asks Syd to dance. They admit to being miserable over the last week, and when they go outside together, Luke kisses her. He invites her to his house for dinner the next night, even as she confesses to being scared to start things up again with him when she doesn't know what's next for her. He's willing to risk it.

The entire next day, she debates whether to go and decides she really wants to. Over dinner, they discuss whether he's happy and if he'd ever consider living somewhere else. He says he's content and living elsewhere would depend on who's asking him to relocate. After dinner, they walk on the beach, where they used to escape to have sex. They talk about his mom, who died too young, and how he never regretted staying on the island to care for her and about whether she'd want more kids. She's not sure she could handle the worry of losing them, too. They take his rowboat out to go stargazing like they used to as kids. They make out in the boat and go back to his house. He's the only man who's ever made her weak in the knees. She's not ready for more. "We have the rest of the summer," he says.

Sydney goes to Maddie's with Buddy, who's sad when he meets Thomas because he reminds him of Max. They talk about how much she loved Seth, but Luke has always been different, the one who got away.

"I used to think my feelings for Luke took on such mythic proportions because everything about our relationship was new and exciting and a bit forbidden."

"And now?"

"I'm not so sure it was any of those things. Seeing him again, I've begun to realize it was *us*. That what we had was that special thing they write about, but I was too young and stupid to know it at the time."

Maddie reaches across the counter to squeeze Sydney's hand. "Oh, Syd."

"I walked away from him like he meant nothing to me. How could I have done that to him, Maddie? It ruined him. *I* ruined him."

"If he wasn't capable of getting past that, I doubt he would've been looking at you the other night like he wanted to take you home and keep you in bed for the next year."

"Sometimes I wonder if it's the comfort. Am I attracted to him—again—because it's comfortable? Because I know he won't crush me? Or is it more than that?"

"You thought about him for seventeen years. That has to count for something."

"True."

"Don't overanalyze it. Just enjoy it. After all you've been through, you deserve some joy. If being with Luke brings you joy, there's nothing wrong with that."

Being with Luke had always brought her joy.

She tells Maddie she has to be home in Massachusetts on September 5 for the sentencing hearing for the drunk driver who killed her family. At the marina, Luke cleans his truck, and Big Mac asks if he's being careful with Sydney, recalling how devastated Luke was the last time she left and didn't come back.

"I don't want to see that happen again."

"It won't," Luke says with more confidence than he feels. He'll do whatever he can to make sure it doesn't.

"She's been through an awful thing. People come out the other side of something like that changed."

"I can't see how it wouldn't change a person."

"See to it she doesn't use you to put the pieces back together and then move on like she did last time."

"Now wait just a second—"

Big Mac held up a huge hand. "I'm sorry. I don't mean to overstep."

"You didn't. You can't overstep with me. You know that." Luke drops the rag and rests his hands on his hips, fighting a range of emotions, including anger, fear and a bit of despair. "I hear what you're saying, and I appreciate why you're saying it." Luke pauses, takes a moment to get himself together, and then looks up at the man who means the world to him. "Am I a chump for giving her another chance?"

"Nah," Big Mac scoffs. "You're only a chump if you ignore the handwriting on the wall telling you history is about to repeat itself."

When Luke picks Sydney up for dinner, they're immediately drawn to each other again and have to remind themselves they're going to dinner.

"Syd…"

"Yes?"

He had to know. He *needed* to know. "Do you feel it, too?"

Her breath seemed to catch in her throat as she looked at him. "Feel what?"

"*Everything.*" How else to put it?

She ran her fingers over his jaw. "Yes."

Overcome with relief that he wasn't in this alone, Luke gazes into her eyes. "I'm worried we're moving too fast."

"We probably are."

"So, we should—"

"Enjoy it." She kisses him. "We should enjoy it."

"For how long?" He hates that he needs to ask.

"I don't know the answer to that. I wish I did, but all I can give you is right now. I'd understand if that wasn't enough—"

Luke kisses the words off her lips. "Do you promise you'll talk to me about your plans? That you won't leave me out of it?"

"The way I did before."

"I'd rather not go through that again."

"I promise I'll talk to you."

He twirls a lock of strawberry-blonde hair around his finger. "Then it's enough. For now."

"Most guys never would've given me a second chance."

"I'm not most guys."

"Believe me, I know that. Why did you give me another chance?"

Continuing to play with the strand of hair, he shrugs. "I've never felt everything with anyone else."

They're driving to the restaurant when they nearly have a head-on collision with a car coming the other way. Sydney is immediately transported back to the worst moment of her life and is so traumatized that Luke is scared. He calls Mac to come and help him get her home to his house. Mac then goes to retrieve Buddy from her house and brings him to Luke's. He and Mac have become good friends since Big Mac made them partners in the marina.

After she sleeps for a while, Sydney tells Luke about the accident that took her family and introduces him to the loved ones she lost. She wants to make love, but he wants to wait until it's about them. Tonight is about the family she lost. He convinces her to stay with him and let him take care of her.

Her parents call, freaking out because they couldn't reach her, and Syd says she understands why they hover after the accident, but it's tough to deal with sometimes. After a trip to the beach with Buddy, they go back to Luke's house and make love all afternoon. Maddie calls to invite them to the Tiki Bar to see Owen Lawry perform. Before they go, she tells Luke she can't have more kids naturally because she had her tubes tied after Malena was born.

They have a great time out at the Tiki Bar. Sydney is taken back to Seth when Owen Lawry plays his favorite song, "Southern Cross." Ned warns Luke to be careful with Syd, and Luke encourages Ned to take another chance with his former love. Grant McCarthy shows up, home for Janey's wedding. He's upset that his ex, Abby, is engaged to Cal Maitland, the island's doctor. Sydney is going to decorate the nursery for Maddie's baby, and Luke says she can redecorate his place, too, which is all part of his plan to get her to stay forever. They come home to find Buddy in distress and rush him to the vet clinic.

Janey is minding the clinic this week while Doc Potter is off-island at his niece's wedding. Buddy needs emergency surgery to remove a blockage from his intestines, and Janey is the only one who can do it. She asks Dr. Cal Maitland to assist. Sydney is cold and remote to Luke while Buddy is in surgery, and that hurts him. She doesn't want him to see her undone again after the incident the night before. He figures that out and goes back to comfort her.

"Syd. Let me in. I know you're upset. You don't need to be alone."

Riveted by his voice, she can't bring herself to move.

"Come on, baby. Let me in."

Tears cascade down her face.

"Sydney." His voice is so soft, so tender. "I'm not leaving you alone. I figured out about two seconds after you walked away that you were on the verge of a meltdown and didn't want me to see you that way again. But I'm not going anywhere. You can melt down every day if you need to. I'll be right here with you."

Sobs hiccup through her, one right after the other. Suddenly, she's on her feet, opening the door. Braced in the doorway, arms over his head, his tall frame takes up most of the space. He scoops her up with one arm and carries her into the house.

"Hold on," he whispers. "Hold on to me."

Sydney wraps her arms and legs around him and buries her face in his neck, comforted by his familiar scent.

He lowers them into a big easy chair, settling her on his lap. "It's okay, baby. Get it all out. I know how scared you must've been all night long. I was scared, too. Buddy is such a good boy, and he's been right by your side when you needed him most."

All the fear and dread and worry about Buddy melds with the ongoing grief she lives with every minute of every day, making her feel weak and defeated. She's tried so hard to put her life together again, but two frightening episodes have set her back. Luke and Sydney fall asleep at her house while Buddy recovers at the clinic.

Grant is trying to figure out how to approach Abby after their bi-coastal, ten-year relationship fizzled. He's devastated that she's engaged to someone else. While he's at her store trying to get her to talk to him, Cal comes in. She introduces Grant as her old friend. He's the love of her life, and he's determined to make her see that. He tells her he's back home for as long as it takes to fix this.

Sydney and Luke are asleep when her parents come home. Her mom sees them in bed together. After saying hello to her parents, who are less than thrilled to see her with Luke, he leaves. She stands up to her parents and their disapproval of Luke, packs a bag and leaves to check on Buddy before going back to Luke's.

Ned thinks about Francine, mother to Maddie and Tiffany, and how they were in love twenty-five years ago before Bobby Chester showed up and stole her away. Seeing Luke back with Sydney inspires Ned to go to Francine's apartment and ask her out to dinner. Francine would be honored to have dinner with the nicest boy she's ever known.

Sydney finds Luke working in the barn on his property, where he restores old boats. His work is beautiful. She asks why he didn't go to college after his mother died. Luke wonders if her parents put that question in her head. He had a choice: pay off his mother's medical debt and keep their house or go to school. He chose the house, and he's never been sorry. He's not the same guy he was before. A lot has changed. She sees that.

Distraught over Abby, Grant gets drunk at the Beachcomber. Big Mac comes to get him and take him home. They see Ned and Francine together, giggling like kids. Ned took Francine to Dominic's and had a great time. She invites him in for coffee. He says he wishes he'd come by sooner and is alarmed to find out that Tiffany has been looking for Bobby Chester because she has no memory of him. Ned promises to come back and see Francine again.

Luke goes back to work expecting to be the center of attention because of his romance with Sydney, but he finds out that Ned is the one setting everyone abuzz with his rekindled romance with Francine. Stephanie, the restaurant manager, brings doughnuts to the guys. A drunk boater pulls Big Mac right off the dock. Mac jumps in after his father, while Luke jumps onto the boat.

"Kill the power, *now!*" Luke lands on the boat's deck, his left ankle at an unnatural angle. "We've got two guys in the water!"

With Mac screaming for help for his father, Luke is relieved to know at least one of them is okay.

Mac realizes Big Mac is badly hurt and not breathing. He performs rescue breathing and is relieved when Big Mac starts breathing on his own again. Paramedics tend to Big Mac, Mac and Luke, while Stephanie goes to find Linda. Police Chief Blaine Taylor arrests the boat captain. Big Mac has a head injury, a broken arm, and is hypothermic. Mac is hypothermic, and Luke has a badly sprained ankle.

Sydney is at Maddie's, looking at catalogs for the baby nursery, and talking about Sydney maybe staying for the winter on the island. Janey calls to tell them there's been an accident at the marina, and Big Mac, Mac and Luke have all been taken to the clinic. Janey only knew that one of them was hurt badly. They're terrified of what they'll find at the clinic. Maddie and Sydney are relieved to see that Mac and Luke are mostly all right. Everyone is worried about Big Mac.

Janey can't bear to see her dad unconscious and badly hurt. Joe, who'd been on the mainland, was flown back over by Slim, the island's top pilot. Janey is so glad to see Joe. They agree they can't get married without Big Mac.

Grant wakes up hungover and demoralized and finds out about his father's accident. He goes to the clinic and learns his father's life rests in the hands of the man Abby is engaged to. She comes to the clinic to be with the McCarthys. Big Mac has a concussion and should be okay in time. Grant is outside getting himself together when Stephanie appears to tell him Big Mac will be okay. He has to be. She loved his movie *Song of Solomon* that won him an Oscar. She advises him to act like he doesn't care that Abby is engaged to Cal. Back inside, Grant asks the others what's going on with Ned and Maddie's mom. Everyone is shocked to hear that anything is going on. They find out that Ned and Francine were together before Francine met Bobby.

Maddie starts having weird pains, and Mac wants her checked. Sydney wants to get Luke home. He asks Grant to help out at the marina. Sydney calls her parents to help her get Luke home. Her parents offer to care for Buddy so she can take care of Luke. Sydney worries about whether Luke can afford to be out of work. She asks her parents to give Luke a chance. She's sick with guilt when, during an argument with her parents, she says she was happy with Seth but never loved him the way she loves Luke. She says Luke has brought joy and optimism back to her life. Her parents invite them to dinner.

Grant and Abby talk about how she got tired of waiting for something that was never going to happen with him, and she loves Cal differently than she loved him. Grant asks for another chance. She loved him so much, but it's over now. She's going to marry Cal in October. Stephanie is waiting for Grant with a hangover remedy and points out that he didn't exactly act like he didn't care about Abby and Cal.

Maddie might be in pre-term labor and is on bed rest for the remainder of her pregnancy. Mac needs Grant to help out at the marina. Stephanie offers to show him the ropes. She tells Grant he's lucky to have a big family around when times are tough. She doesn't have that. Big Mac wakes up, confused and disoriented.

Sydney tells Luke that she knew, as she was marrying Seth, that she didn't love him the way she'd loved Luke. He says it was all meant to be, and you can't have regrets. Maybe they weren't meant to get their shot until later in life. Mac is driving Maddie crazy, wanting to take her to the mainland because of her pre-labor. She refuses, and she's about had it with him. Maddie tells Sydney that Big Mac made Luke a partner in the marina. Sydney wonders why Luke didn't tell her that. Syd agrees to help Maddie with Janey's bridal shower. Sydney takes Thomas to see Buddy and for dinner at Luke's. Mac and Maddie make up, and he agrees to try to chill out about her being pregnant on a remote island.

Sydney's mom offers to help with Thomas while Maddie is on bedrest. Ned tells Big Mac how scared he was about his accident, while Big Mac needles him some more about Francine. Big Mac says it's turning into a recycle summer between Ned and Luke taking up with old loves. Janey breaks down with Joe about the close call with her dad. Grant stops by Luke's to catch up, and says he's not happy in LA, his career has gone to shit and he's lost Abby, too. Luke says Abby's not married yet, and a lot can happen before October.

Tiffany visits Maddie at the clinic and tells her that Jim is accusing her of cheating on him, in the latest saga in Tiffany's marital woes. Tiffany is fed up with the entire situation and wants to separate from Jim. Police Chief Blaine Taylor comes into the room, looking for Mac to tell him the boat driver is being charged. Maddie introduces him to Tiffany, who thinks he's hot, and she'd like to have an affair with him. Maddie encourages her sister to deal with her husband. Francine comes in, and her daughters tease her about having a boyfriend. Maddie tells her mother that Ned owns half the island, and Francine is incredulous. When she confronts him about his real estate business, Ned tells her all the money in the world can't make him as happy as being with her again.

The next day, Luke asks Sydney why she's shut down on him. She wants to know if he was ever going to tell her he's now a part-owner of McCarthy's Marina. Luke wants her to stay for him, not for what he has. She realizes he's never really forgiven her for what she did in the past. Money is important to her. She looks at his home and sees that nothing has changed and thinks it's because he doesn't have the money. They end up going to her parents' house for dinner with nothing resolved. Luke tells her parents that Syd is annoyed with him because he didn't tell her about the partnership. Syd realizes he didn't tell her because he wanted her to stay for the right reasons, and she loves him. That's all that matters. Syd's aunt has had a heart attack, and her parents need to go to the mainland. Luke calls Slim to fly them over, and they appreciate it.

Luke asks her to redecorate his house and see how she feels about island life. He'll go with her to the sentencing and help her pack up her house in Wellesley.

Big Mac rallies to walk Janey down the aisle, and Janey and Joe exchange vows with everyone they love there to witness the big day.

 An interview with Luke and Sydney...

I love your second-chance story so much!

Sydney: Thank you! We do, too. Sometimes we can't believe the way it all happened. I give Luke most of the credit. He never gave up on me. The way he rowed his boat over to check on me after I lost Seth and the kids... He's the sweetest.

Luke: I couldn't stay away.

Does it seem like it's been fourteen years already?

Sydney: We can't believe that! It's so strange that I've been married to Luke twice as long as I was to Seth. I've always appreciated the way Luke keeps Seth, Max and Malena close to us as we make a life together.

Luke: They're part of our family. We celebrate their birthdays every year, and our kids know they had an older brother and sister.

That's so sweet! I'm afraid to ask about Buddy...

Luke: We lost him about six years ago, and we miss him every day. In his honor, we got two puppies who look a lot like him. We like to think he picked them out for us.

It's not fair that dogs don't live forever.

Sydney: I couldn't agree more. I like to think that Buddy is with Max and Malena in heaven, taking care of them.

I'm sure he is. Tell us about your kids! What are they up to?

Luke: Lily is twelve and in seventh grade. She's big into dance and theater and has a beautiful singing voice. Elias is nine and in fourth grade. He's big into video games like Minecraft and loves comic books.

Sydney: In a total surprise, we had another son, Jonah, three years after Elias. Jonah is in first grade and is the family comedian. We would've said our family was complete until he showed up to prove otherwise. He's been such a blessing to all of us. To say our lives are busy is putting it mildly!

Congratulations on your second son! How exciting. Syd, are you still doing interior design?

Sydney: I am! I just did a big project for Joe and Janey Cantrell, who needed a space for their kids to hang out with friends. We did a basement rec room that they love. It helps to be friends with most of the island's residents.

Luke, how are things at the marina?

Luke: Busier than ever. Big Mac still gets one of his "big ideas" at least once a year. The latest is a bocce court that the guests are enjoying.

Do you still restore boats?

Luke: I try to do one per year, and most years I sneak in a second one where I can. Elias has taken an interest and helps me a lot. It's even more fun to do with him as my sidekick.

Sydney, your journey from tragedy to a second chance with Luke really touched our hearts. How did you find the courage to start over?

Sydney: I think a lot of it had to do with Luke, who's been my rock through it all. His love and encouragement gave me the courage to continue dreaming, loving and hoping. I also appreciate the way he helps to keep Seth, Max and Malena present in our lives.

Luke: (reaches for her hand) She's the strongest person I know. It's an honor to walk through life with her by my side. And she's a wonderful mother. Our kids are lucky to have her—and so am I.

Syd, how are your parents doing?

Sydney: Quite well, thank you. My dad has joined Big Mac's morning meeting at the marina, and he enjoys that very much. He also goes fishing with the guys while my mom is big into pickleball. She and Linda play together a lot. They also travel together. And of course, they love being grandparents and hosting weekend sleepovers.

Glad to hear they're doing well. The get-togethers with family and friends must be quite something these days...

Luke: It's a madhouse, and we love every crazy minute of it.

Sydney: We're so blessed that our children are best friends with our best friends' kids. What could be better than that?

Nothing at all!

NEW YORK TIMES AND USA TODAY BESTSELLING AUTHOR
MARIE FORCE
Falling for Love

Book 4: Falling for Love
Published: January 15, 2012

The wrong woman rocked his world. Is fate rewriting his future?
Since he won the Academy Award for best original screenplay a few years ago, Grant McCarthy's personal and professional lives have fallen apart. Abby, the woman he was supposed to marry, is engaged to someone else, and Grant is back at home on Gansett Island helping to run the family marina while his father recovers from a serious injury.

While all of Grant's focus should be on winning back the love of his life, pesky Stephanie, who runs the marina restaurant, is working her way under his skin and into his bed. As Tropical Storm Hailey cuts off Gansett Island from the mainland, Grant suspects Stephanie is hiding something big from her past. When he finds out what it is, what will be more important to him? Winning Abby back or helping Stephanie to right a terrible wrong?

Main Characters:

***Grant McCarthy,** screenwriter in Los Angeles.

***Stephanie Logan,** restaurant manager, McCarthy's Gansett Island Marina.
***Indicates recurring throughout the series**

Supporting Characters:

***Ned Saunders,** dating Francine Chester in READY FOR LOVE.

***Captain Seamus O'Grady,** general manager, Gansett Island Ferry Company.

***Joe Cantrell,** married to Janey McCarthy Cantrell in READY FOR LOVE.

***Janey McCarthy Cantrell,** married to Joe Cantrell in READY FOR LOVE.

***Mac McCarthy, Jr.,** married to Maddie Chester in FOOL FOR LOVE, father of Thomas Chester McCarthy in MAID FOR LOVE.

***Maddie McCarthy,** mother of Thomas, married to Mac McCarthy in FOOL FOR LOVE.

***Laura McCarthy,** daughter of Judge Frank McCarthy and the late JoAnn McCarthy, sister of Shane McCarthy, first cousin of Mac, Grant, Adam, Evan and Janey McCarthy, came to Gansett for Janey's wedding in READY FOR LOVE.

***Owen Lawry,** musician.

***Francine Chester,** grandmother of Ashleigh and Thomas, wife of Bobby Chester, dating Ned Saunders in READY FOR LOVE.

***Luke Harris,** dating Sydney Donovan in READY FOR LOVE.

***Sydney Donovan,** interior designer, dating Luke Harris in READY FOR LOVE.

***Linda McCarthy,** grandmother of Thomas McCarthy in MAID FOR LOVE.

***Big Mac McCarthy,** grandfather of Thomas Chester McCarthy in MAID FOR LOVE.

***Adam McCarthy,** owns a computer company in New York City.

***Evan McCarthy,** musician in Nashville.

***Hailey McCarthy,** infant daughter of Mac and Maddie, born during Tropical Storm Hailey in FALLING FOR LOVE.

***Judge Frank McCarthy,** brother of Big Mac, father of Laura and Shane, Superior Court Judge in Providence.

***Shane McCarthy,** brother of Laura, son of Frank and the late JoAnn McCarthy.

***Justin,** Laura's ex-husband.

***Dan Torrington,** celebrity defense lawyer, close friend of Grant McCarthy.

Jim, Grant's agent.

Tony Zuckerman, a big-time producer, wants Grant to write a movie.

⦿ Places

- **Sand & Surf Hotel,** owned by Russ and Adele Kinkaid, grandparents to Owen Lawry.

📼 Gansett Island Soundtrack:

- "You've Got a Friend"

❝ FALLING FOR LOVE Headlines:

- Tropical St orm Hailey hits Gansett Island!

- Grant slept with Stephanie!

- Newlyweds Joe and Janey can't get off the island for their honeymoon!

- Mac is worried about Maddie's high-risk pregnancy when the power goes out!

- Grant cuts his hand and fights with Stephanie all the way to the clinic for stitches!

- Laura and Owen meet and he gives her a tour of the Sand & Surf Hotel!

- Cal's mother has a stroke in Texas—there's no doctor on the island while he's gone!

- Francine breaks up with Ned over a big secret she's keeping from him!

- Stephanie's stepfather Charlie is in prison for a crime he didn't commit!

- Laura's new marriage is over because her husband never stopped dating!

- Maddie is in labor early (see above—no doctor)!

- Hailey McCarthy arrives during Tropical Storm Hailey!

- Dr. David Lawrence's redemption arc begins when he saves Hailey!

- Laura is worried about her brother Shane, whose wife is in rehab!

- Francine needs to speak to Bobby Chester because she wants a divorce!

- Owen's grandparents hire Laura to manage the Sand & Surf Hotel!

- Grant calls in his uncle Frank, a judge, and his friend, defense attorney Dan Torrington, to help Stephanie and Charlie!

- Owen finds Laura getting sick and finds out she's pregnant with her ex-husband's baby!

- Bobby Chester returns to Gansett and wants to see his daughters before he'll give Francine a divorce!

- Grant is returning to LA to write a new screenplay!

- Stephanie drops him at the airport!

- Grant realizes his mistake and goes after Stephanie—the only story he wants to write is theirs—and hers and Charlie's!

- Stephanie loves him, too!

- Hello Seamus O'Grady, Laura McCarthy, Dan Torrington, Judge Frank McCarthy, Dan and Charlie Grandchamp!

Grant McCarthy awakens on the morning after his sister Janey's wedding, in bed with the wrong woman! All he wants is a second chance with his long-time love, Abby Callahan, who's now engaged to that overgrown cowboy, Dr. Cal Maitland. So, what in the hell is Grant doing naked in bed with Stephanie, who manages the restaurant at his parents' marina? And why can't he remember what happened the night before? FALLING FOR LOVE begins with a bang, literally. Too bad Grant can't remember it.

He's housesitting and pet-sitting for Janey while she's on her honeymoon, so he can't exactly leave his one-night stand sleeping in his sister's bed while he tries to fix things with his ex-girlfriend. What a mess of his own making, and so much for trying to make Abby jealous by dancing with Stephanie. Look at what that had gotten him. He watches Stephanie get out of bed and get dressed, desperately trying to remember how they'd ended up in bed together and what had transpired between them. After she leaves, he finds a condom wrapper in the bed and can't deny that more than sleeping took place. Shit!

Stephanie knows he used her to make Abby jealous, and she went along with it because he's the first guy she's been attracted to in years. He rocked her world in bed and probably doesn't even remember it. She's walking back to the marina in the rain when Ned pulls up in his cab and offers her a ride. Ned says the storm is a "doozy of a Nor'easter." He doesn't think the newlyweds will make it off the island that day.

Ned talks to Stephanie about Grant, how he was the smartest kid Ned had ever met, but he's confused and has lost his way a bit. He tells her to watch out for herself in the midst of Grant's mess. How does he know everything?

On the morning after his wedding, Joe gets a call from Seamus O'Grady, whom he hired to run the Gansett Island Ferry Company while Joe is in

Ohio with Janey. Seamus is thinking he should suspend service for the rest of the day due to the weather but doesn't want to mess up Joe and Janey getting off the island for their trip. Joe looks outside and reluctantly tells Seamus to make the call. Janey is disappointed that their trip to Aruba has been delayed, but they're both glad to spend the day in bed.

The storm is stressing Mac out since Maddie's pregnancy was determined to be high-risk. Knowing they can't get off the island if they need to sends him into a panic. Maddie is feeling huge and hideous, and Mac is trying to reassure her when the electricity goes out.

Memories of Grant's erotic night with Stephanie start to come back in bits and pieces that remind him of some of the best sex he's ever had. He immediately feels guilty because he still loves Abby, who gave him an ultimatum after Mac's wedding last year: If he went back to LA, they were done. "You can write anywhere in the whole wide world, Grant. Why can't you write in the one place where I want to be?" He'd wanted one more shot at fixing his career in LA and had expected her to wait for him. She hadn't, and now she was engaged to Cal Maitland, who was all wrong for her.

While Grant gets dressed to work at the marina during the storm, Janey's pets seem to be judging him for the way he treated Stephanie. He arrives at the marina to find Stephanie struggling with a generator, and more memories from their night together come back to him as they snap at each other. He doesn't even like her. Why does she turn him on? While he's busy thinking about Stephanie and what to do about her, his hand gets slammed in the door of the shed. Mac and Stephanie determine Grant needs stitches, and Stephanie says she'll take him to the clinic. Mac invites them to a tropical storm party at his house, where Joe and Janey will open their wedding gifts.

Grant and Stephanie do nothing but fight on the way to the clinic.

Stephanie presses harder on the accelerator.

"Easy does it. I think you're going thirty now."

"Shut up."

"You shut up."

She shakes her head, seeming regretful. "I told you it was a bad idea to sleep together."

"*When* did you tell me that?" Of course, he has no recollection of that but has had plenty of other vivid memories torturing him all morning.

"Before we slept together. We got along just fine before."

"We did not. We've never gotten along."

"We got along pretty well in your sister's bed last night, but you probably don't remember that."

"I remember it," he snaps.

"You don't need to bite my head off just because you're pissed with yourself."

Stepping over a downed tree, they end up falling into each other's arms.

Cousin Laura McCarthy is in town for Janey's wedding and is staring up at the Sand & Surf Hotel, wishing she had thirteen million dollars to buy it, when Owen Lawry finds her there. He knows the owners and offers to give her a tour.

Ned takes the day off from cab-driving to spend some time with his lady, Francine, who's worried about marital trouble between her daughter Tiffany and Jim Sturgil. Francine is upset about something else, but she won't tell Ned what it is. She says maybe they shouldn't see each other anymore. Ned leaves heartbroken. Francine, who may still be married to Bobby, asks Tiffany if she found her father. No, but she found his sister, Marion. Tiffany says Jim is moving out of their house. Francine asks for Marion's number.

Stephanie is puzzled by Grant and knows she shouldn't get involved, especially since she has to get back to Providence after the summer to deal with the most important thing in her life. She suggests Grant hasn't yet met the love of his life if he didn't marry Abby during all the years they were together. She offers to help him get Abby back if that's what he wants and gives him advice.

Abby is at the clinic—Cal has gotten a call that his mother in Texas has had a stroke, and he's leaving. The nurse practitioner, Victoria, can take care of Grant's wound.

Ned goes to visit Big Mac and asks Linda for advice about Francine. She advises him to be patient. Adam and Evan are wrestling, and Ned is happy to see Big Mac engaged with his family as he recovers from his head injury.

Laura is in love with the Sand & Surf Hotel. Owen admits the owners are his grandparents, and he spent summers with them there. His father is an Air Force general, and his family moved around a lot. His grandparents live in Florida and are trying to sell the hotel. He doesn't want it because it would require him to stay in one place. He calls her "Princess" because there's something regal about her, and says he's staying to play at the Tiki Bar until October. It'd be more fun if she were there, too.

On the way to Mac's party, Grant stops at the marina to check on Stephanie, who lives in one of the back rooms there. He doesn't like thinking of her alone in the dark with no power. He finds her at a table with a battery-powered light, poring over stacks of papers. She's startled by his sudden appearance. He wants to know what she's doing, and they bicker about minding their own business.

He pushes her to tell him what's wrong.

"Fine!" The word seems torn from her very soul as she spins around, her eyes wild with rage, fear and pain unlike anything he's ever seen. "If you want to know so bad—here it is. Charles Grandchamp is my stepfather—the one person in my whole, entire, miserable life who was ever good to me, who ever loved me or gave a shit about me. And guess where he is?" Before Grant can begin to form a coherent statement, she answers her own question. "In prison, serving a life sentence with no chance of parole, for kidnapping and assault of a minor." Her chest heaves, and tears fall freely down her face.

Riveted by her outburst, Grant can't seem to move as he absorbs what she said. "Who did he kidnap and assault?"

"Me," she says so softly he almost doesn't hear her over the howling of the storm.

He finds out that she's been trying to get Charlie out of prison and goes to visit him on Fridays. They share an embrace, and he offers to help her. He talks her into coming to Mac's with him so she can help make Abby jealous. She turns him on and makes him mad, often in the same second.

Stephanie is mad at herself for telling Grant about Charlie. They arrive at Mac's, and Grant tells Maddie that Cal left the island that day, and now there's no doctor. She pleads with him not to tell Mac that. Grant talks to Abby, finds out Cal made it to the mainland, and is on his way to Texas. Abby tells him again they're over, and he ought to give Stephanie a chance if he likes her. Grant is upset. Luke is going to the mainland for an MRI because his ankle isn't healing. He's cranky with Sydney and then feels bad.

Watching Janey and her husband open wedding gifts is torture for Laura. She goes outside for air, and Owen finds her there. She tells him her new marriage is already over because her husband never stopped dating. Owen's grandmother wonders if Laura might be interested in running the Sand & Surf. Evan asks him to play. Owen asks Laura if she has any requests. Something by James Taylor. He plays "You've Got a Friend."

Francine tells Ned she has some things she has to take care of and that she's sorry for being distant. She knows where to find him when she's taken care of her stuff.

Maddie can't deny she's having contractions, and she's in a panic knowing there's no doctor on the island. She's in labor two months early. She should've listened to Mac and gone to the mainland. She asks Stephanie to help find Victoria, the nurse practitioner at the clinic. When he realizes what's happening, Mac fights through the panic to help her to bed.

Grant takes Stephanie home to Janey's house, so she doesn't have to stay at the marina alone in the dark.

Janey tells Joe that her ex-fiancé, Dr. David Lawrence, called her the day before the wedding to wish her well. Joe is miffed that she didn't tell him. David is home on the island visiting his mother. She wants to call David to help with Maddie. Do it, Joe says. David says he'll be right there.

Stephanie helps Grant care for Janey's pets. They sit by the fire, and he gets her to admit she's not sorry he and Abby are done. He gets testy with her and is alarmed by her reaction to his anger. He assures her she has nothing to worry about with him—ever. Then he shows her how being in the same room with her makes him hard. They have sex again, and this time he's totally sober and realizes he's begun to have feelings for her.

They talk about whether they want kids and his career woes since he won his industry's top award. He says her story about her stepfather gave him the first buzz he's had to write in a long time. She says he can't write about her. He promises he won't.

Mac is out of his mind with worry about Maddie. Big Mac offers comfort. Maddie gives birth to a girl, whom they name Hailey, in honor of Tropical Storm Hailey. The baby is perfect, and David suspects Maddie was further along than the doctors thought. Mac says they're never having sex again. Maddie just laughs.

Janey realizes David saved Hailey's life because she wasn't breathing at birth. He tells her he's still in remission after being treated for lymphoma a year ago. Joe sees David kiss Janey on the forehead, and she quickly gets her husband out of Mac's house and back to their honeymoon.

Ned gives Francine a ride home after her granddaughter's birth. She promises to call him soon.

Grant wakes up thinking he's with Abby and realizes he slept with Stephanie again, and just that quickly, he wants her. They have hot sex and are interrupted by a knock on the door. Big Mac has come to tell Grant that Hailey McCarthy was born, and everyone is doing well. He warns Grant that if he hurts Stephanie, he'll answer to him. After overhearing the conversation with his dad, Stephanie tells him all she wants is sex, not a relationship. Grant is oddly wounded by her withdrawal.

Laura tells Big Mac about what happened with her husband. He's outraged. She says she's worried about her brother Shane because his wife had been hiding a pain medication addiction that landed her in rehab. Her dad, Frank, couldn't make it to Janey's wedding because he had a big trial starting and couldn't risk getting stuck on the island with the storm coming. She tells Big Mac about the job offer at the hotel. He suggests asking Shane to come over to help her renovate the hotel. Laura decides to take the job.

Mac takes care of Maddie the next morning. While she's in the bath, she thinks about how happy Tiffany looked talking to Blaine Taylor the night before. They introduce Thomas to his baby sister.

Francine calls Bobby's sister, Marion, to ask for his number because Francine needs a divorce.

Laura tells Owen she'll take the job. He calls his grandparents so she can talk to them. Grant talks Stephanie into continuing to stay with him at Janey's. She's worried about coming up with $1,000 to pay her new lawyer by the end of the month. With the storm expected to last another day, the island is beginning to run out of food, beer and other essentials. When Grant sees that Stephanie is really worried about running out of food, he asks if that was a problem in the past. She says her mom did her best, but she was an addict. Her mother would forget about her, once for a week when she was six or seven.

Stephanie has spent close to half a million dollars on lawyers for Charlie over the last fourteen years—every dime she's ever made, except a small amount to live on. His uncle is a judge, Frank McCarthy. Let us help you, Grant says. If he can write about her story, they might be able to get even more help. In all the years she's been fighting this battle, he's the first one to offer to help. She matters to him.

She tells him the whole story of what happened to Charlie—and her. Charlie saved her from her mother beating her and paid for that with imprisonment. Her mother overdosed six weeks later without ever telling the truth that she was the one who'd beaten Stephanie, not Charlie. He mentions his friend, Dan Torrington, a lawyer who specializes in getting innocent people out of prison. She can't believe Grant knows him. Grant offers to call him the next day.

"I'm afraid to hope."

"Don't be afraid. Whatever happens, you're not alone in this anymore."

"It's not just Charlie and the case. It's you, too." She reaches up to comb her fingers through his hair. "You make me want things I've never wanted before."

"Don't be afraid of that either."

Her brows knit with aggravation. "What about Abby?"

"Who?" he asks, kissing her again.

"Grant…"

"I'm not thinking of anyone but you, Stephanie. Only you."

As they have sex again, Stephanie realizes she's fallen in love with Grant.

Owen and Laura spend the day together, playing Monopoly and passing the time while the storm rages on. They talk and flirt and he makes her feel better about what happened with her husband. Adam and Evan show up with beer, looking for fun. They tell Laura and Owen about Grant being shacked up with Stephanie. Evan, Adam and Owen swear they'll never let a woman get her hooks into them while Laura laughs.

A phone call from his mother wakes Grant the next day. The storm is over, the sun is out, and everyone is going to the ferry landing to see off Joe and Janey. Stephanie needs to get to the marina to open the restaurant. Grant doesn't want her to go yet. After she leaves for work, Grant's agent calls with a big new offer. They want him back in LA in a week. He asks for some time to think about it.

When Grant goes to say goodbye to Janey, he asks if it was different with Joe than with David. No comparison, she says. "When it's the right person, it's *earth-shattering*." Grant is shocked to realize that's how it is with Stephanie, and maybe he was with the wrong person for all the years he spent with Abby.

Grant has one more week before he'll have to return to reality in LA. He has a nice moment with Abby and gains closure there. She reminds him that he can write anywhere. Cal's mom is not doing well and may not survive the stroke. Dr. David Lawrence is staying for a few weeks to cover at the clinic while Cal is away. Ned offers Grant a ride to the marina, tells him he knows what Stephanie is dealing with, and says she can come to him if she needs money. Ned advises him not to let Stephanie get away.

Grant hears Stephanie arguing with someone on the phone, realizes it's her lawyer, and tells her to fire him. She has stomach pains after firing her new lawyer. Grant will have someone better for her before the end of the day. She tells him she's on the pill, and they have sex without a condom in her room at the marina. After she goes back to work, he leaves a message for Dan Torrington.

When he emerges from the marina, Big Mac and the other guys tease him about what he's been doing. Dan calls back, and Grant tells him Stephanie's situation. He offers to come to Gansett to help. Grant runs back to the marina restaurant, scoops up Stephanie in front of everyone, and shares the news. She can't believe Dan is coming there. There's nothing Grant won't do for her.

Owen finds Laura getting sick. He picks her up off the floor, and she tells him she was married just long enough to get pregnant.

Ned goes into Gold's, where Francine works, and buys a truckload of condoms to mess with her. He meets up with Luke and Sydney at the ferry landing, who are leaving for the mainland to get an MRI on Luke's ankle. A man asks for Francine, and Ned realizes Bobby Chester has come back to Gansett. When he goes back to Gold's to ask Francine why Bobby is there, she faints.

Grant wants to read Charlie's case files. Because Stephanie expects nothing of him, he wants to give her everything. Linda tunes into Stephanie's feelings for Grant, reminding her of Big Mac at the same age. She appreciates the way Stephanie challenges Grant. She invites them to dinner. Stephanie will never love anyone the way she loves Grant. She's storing memories for when it ends.

Ned takes Francine home, Bobby shows up, Francine confronts him and says she wants to marry Ned but needs a divorce. Bobby wants to see his daughters before he'll give her a divorce. Francine is outraged. Tiffany shows up, sees Bobby, and is upset. Ned loves Francine—always has, always will.

When Grant's uncle Frank returns his call, he tells her about Charlie's case and Stephanie's efforts to free her stepfather. Frank looks up the case and sees that the assigned judge had Alzheimer's and that there were irregularities in some of his cases. Grant plans to meet his uncle next Friday, the day Stephanie visits Charlie at the state prison. Grant is torn between the LA offer and staying with Stephanie. He's in love with her.

Grant tells Stephanie that Luke needs surgery on his ankle, and that his Uncle Frank called. They're meeting with him on Friday. They go to dinner at Grant's parents' home. Linda tells them Laura is staying to manage the Sand & Surf, and her new marriage is already over. Linda suggests that Stephanie talk to Laura about the restaurant at the Surf. Grant encourages Stephanie to tell his parents about Charlie. They want to help. Cal has resigned from the clinic to stay home in Texas with his mother, and David Lawrence is taking the job. Grant asks about how Cal's decision affects Abby, which upsets Stephanie. He tells her he wants only her.

Laura is leaving for the mainland to take care of some things before she moves permanently to Gansett. Owen walks her to the ferry and tells her he'll miss her while she's gone.

Ned and Francine sleep together, and he goes with her to tell Maddie that her deadbeat father has resurfaced. She hates dropping this news on her daughter just days after the baby was born. He's here on the island and wants to see Maddie before he'll give her mother a divorce. Mac says no way. Maddie says, "Take me to him right now so we can get this over with, and I can dance at your wedding." Maddie confronts Bobby and says, "Now you've seen me. Give my mother a divorce." When she gets home, she collapses in tears in Mac's arms.

When they pack to go to the mainland on Friday, Stephanie asks why he's taking so much for one night. He says it's because he's going to LA for a couple of days. She's upset he didn't tell her about his big new offer. He's not sure what he's going to do and didn't want to upset her. They talk about whether their relationship would work outside the bubble they've been in on the island.

After Charlie is chilly to Grant and they have dinner with Frank, Grant takes her to a nice hotel for the night. They get Charlie to agree to let Dan represent him. Stephanie says it feels like it's their last night together. Grant says it is not. "Everything is different now. When I said I'll be back, I meant it. I'll be back for you. I promise."

Minutes after Stephanie drops Grant at the airport and leaves to head back to the island, he realizes he's made a huge mistake letting her go. He grabs a cab to the ferry landing. Stephanie is crying on the ferry when Grant takes the seat across from her. Before he tells her what he's doing there, he says his uncle Frank called, and a new hearing will be held in Charlie's case on Halloween.

Grant wants to write her story—her story and Charlie's—and she'll be getting a call from his agent with an offer in the next couple of days. He's taking a chance on her and her story. She thinks he's making the offer, so she'll be okay without him. "I really buried the lead here. I love you. I'm in love with you." This kind of thing doesn't happen to her, but she loves him, too.

 An interview with Grant and Stephanie...

Here we are, fourteen years after Tropical Storm Hailey changed everything. How are you guys?

Grant: We're great. Couldn't be better.

Stephanie: Fourteen years. That's how long Charlie was in prison. Meeting Grant changed my life—and Charlie's—in every possible way. As soon as he heard our story, he wanted to help. I was already halfway in love with him before that, but when he stepped up for us the way he did, that was it for me.

Grant: How could I not step up for you?

Stephanie: I couldn't believe you knew Dan Torrington, and now he's one of my best friends. Life is funny.

It is indeed. How's it going with Stephanie's Bistro?

Stephanie: Fantastic. We're open from May to October, and then we shut down for a long winter's nap.

Do you still go to LA in the winter?

Grant: Sadly, no. We now have children we're required to educate, and they've ruined everything.

Stephanie: Hahahaha, he doesn't mean that.

Grant: (laughing): Of course I don't, but I miss warm winters in Southern California. Stephanie tells me we can go back to that when we're empty nesters in two hundred years.

Stephanie: It'll be here before we know it.

Grant: I don't even want to think about them growing up and leaving us.

Tell us about them. Last we knew, you had a son named Oren Charles.

Stephanie: He goes by Charlie because his favorite person in the whole world is his Grandpa Charlie.

Aw, that's so sweet!

Stephanie: One of the great joys of my life is seeing my beloved Charlie as a doting, indulgent grandfather.

Grant: I'm not sure who spoils them more—her dad or mine.

Stephanie: It's a close competition. Our Charlie is about to be nine, and our daughter, Avery, is six. They're best friends with all their cousins. Avery's favorite thing is sleepovers with her cousins Emma and Evie.

I love to hear that the kids are so close.

Grant: How could they not be when their parents are best friends?

True! How's the writing going?

Grant: It's been great. I added another Oscar to the shelf for best original screenplay with *Indefatigable*, Stephanie and Charlie's story. That was such a thrill.

I'm sure it was. How do you juggle life on Gansett with a career in LA?

Grant: As a writer and producer, I help put all the pieces together and then step back to let the experts see it through to completion. I get out there a couple of times a year for in-person meetings, but most of it can be done by Zoom these days.

Stephanie: Thank goodness for Zoom, because we need Daddy with us.

Grant: There's nowhere in the world he wants to be more than with you and our kids.

Tell me you still bicker the way you did at the beginning.

Stephanie: That's all we do! It's our love language.

Grant: What she said. Bickering with her is my favorite hobby.

NEW YORK TIMES AND USA TODAY BESTSELLING AUTHOR

MARIE FORCE

Hoping for Love

Book 5: Hoping for Love
Published: March 4, 2012

He gave her a hand when she needed it. Can he give her forever?

Heavy all her life, Grace Ryan was taunted, teased and ignored by her peers, while trying every diet ever invented to no avail. Desperate to change her life as her twenties slipped away, she had lap-band surgery. More than a year later, she's lost 130 pounds and is venturing into the dating world for the first time. During a boat trip to Gansett Island with the new guy in her life, Grace refuses to have sex with him and finds herself abandoned without a dollar to her name at McCarthy's Gansett Island Marina.

At home for the summer, awaiting the launch of his debut album, music star-in-the-making Evan McCarthy is performing at the Tiki Bar when he notices Grace looking lost in a sea of happy people. Evan comes to her aid and quickly finds himself smitten. But the last thing Grace needs after all she's been through is a guy who "doesn't do relationships." Will Evan change his ways to win Grace's heart?

Main Characters:

*Evan McCarthy,** musician in Nashville.

*Grace Ryan,** pharmacist from Connecticut.

*Indicates recurring throughout the series**

Supporting Characters:

Trey Parsons, Grace's crush since fourth grade.

Tom Quigley, Trey's best friend.

*Owen Lawry,** grandson of the owners of the Sand & Surf Hotel.

*Linda McCarthy,** grandmother of Thomas Chester McCarthy in MAID FOR LOVE and Hailey McCarthy in FALLING FOR LOVE.

***Big Mac McCarthy,** grandfather of Thomas Chester McCarthy in MAID FOR LOVE and Hailey McCarthy in FALLING FOR LOVE.

Mrs. Gold, owner of Gold's Pharmacy.

***Ned Saunders,** Engaged to Francine in FALLING FOR LOVE.

***Francine Chester,** grandmother of Ashleigh Sturgil, Thomas McCarthy and Hailey McCarthy, engaged to Ned Saunders in FALLING FOR LOVE.

***Grant McCarthy,** screenwriter, involved with Stephanie Logan in FALLING FOR LOVE.

***Stephanie Logan,** restaurant manager, McCarthy's Gansett Island Marina, involved with Grant McCarthy in FALLING FOR LOVE.

***Luke Harris,** involved with Sydney Donovan in READY FOR LOVE.

***Sydney Donovan,** involved with Luke Harris in READY FOR LOVE.

***Laura McCarthy,** manager of the Sand & Surf Hotel in FALLING FOR LOVE.

Mr. Gold, co-owner of Gold's Pharmacy.

***Mac McCarthy, Jr.,** married to Maddie Chester in FOOL FOR LOVE, father of Thomas Chester McCarthy in MAID FOR LOVE, father of Hailey McCarthy in FALLING FOR LOVE.

***Tiffany Sturgil,** separated from Jim Sturgil in FALLING FOR LOVE.

***Abby Callahan,** engaged to Dr. Cal Maitland.

***Blaine Taylor,** chief, Gansett Island Police.

***Justin Newsome,** Laura's ex-husband, father of her unborn child.

***Maddie McCarthy,** mother of Thomas, married to Mac McCarthy in FOOL FOR LOVE, mother of Hailey McCarthy in FALLING FOR LOVE.

***Jim Sturgil,** separated from Tiffany Sturgil in FALLING FOR LOVE.

***Buddy Longstreet and Taylor Jones,** superstar singers, touring with Evan.

***Seamus O'Grady,** general manager, Gansett Island Ferry Company.

***Jack Beaumont,** Evan's manager.

***Bobby Chester,** father of Maddie and Tiffany, husband of Francine.

66 HOPING FOR LOVE Headlines:

- Grace and Evan meet at the marina after her date ditches her!

- Evan takes Grace home to Linda's house for the night and pays for her ferry ride home!

- Jim Sturgil moves out and takes all of Tiffany's furniture!

- Abby is moving to Texas to be with Cal!

- Luke has surgery on his injured ankle!

- Grace returns to reimburse Evan and is buying Gold's Pharmacy!

- Tiffany is opening a store in the former home of Abby's Attic!

- Laura's ex-husband plans to fight the divorce!

- Grant and Stephanie host a going-away party for Abby!

- Evan's record company files for bankruptcy!

- Owen cancels his fall gig to stay on the island with Laura!

- Dan gets an emergency hearing in Charlie's case!

- Tiffany handcuffs herself to Jim and then has an explosive encounter with Blaine!

- Charlie is freed from prison and comes to Gansett!

- Grace and Evan are in love!

Gansett Island Soundtrack:

- "Brown-Eyed Girl"

- "Turn the Page"

- "Bad Moon Rising"

- "Take it Easy"

- "Love the One You're With"

- "Sister Golden Hair"

- "Please Come to Boston"

📍 Places:

- **The Lobster House Restaurant,** South Harbor

Grace Ryan is on a boat at McCarthy's Gansett Island Marina, about to have sex for the first time with her long-time crush, Trey Parsons. Until, that is, she sees a text from his best friend reminding him there's $500 on the line if he "nails the whale," referring to the horrible name kids called her before she lost 130 pounds. She leaves Trey's boat and walks up the dock to look for somewhere else to stay. An older man, who turns out to be Ned, tells her she's missed the last ferry, and the island's hotels are sold out on for the weekend. She'll have to sleep on the small sofa in the boat's salon because she's not sleeping with Trey.

In no rush to get back to the boat, she watches two men perform at the marina's Tiki Bar. Then she returns to the boat to find it's gone, along with her clothes, purse and money. What was supposed to have been the greatest night of her life has turned into another disaster.

Evan McCarthy is having the time of his life playing at the marina his parents own with his best friend, Owen Lawry, as he counts down to the release of his long-awaited first album in December. While he plays, he's flirting with a table of young women, hoping for a weekend fling. Owen nudges him and gestures to a dark-haired woman crying at one of the tables. When they take a break, Evan is compelled to check on her because that's what his father would want him to do. He goes over to sit at Grace's table. "Now tell me this—what in the world could've ruined such a great night for such a pretty lady?"

Grace tells him that her date for the evening has left her stranded on the island without so much as a toothbrush or any money. Evan is gorgeous, sweet and talented. Before she lost the weight, a man like him never would've spoken to her. Now, he wants to help her. He offers her a room at his parents' home up the hill and the money to take the ferry home the next day.

When Evan returns to the stage, Owen encourages him to play the first single off his new album, "Here for You."

Owen teases Evan that if he takes Grace home, his mother will have them married with four kids by morning, which is true. With no other options on a sold-out weekend, Evan takes one for the team.

Grace tells Evan she can't believe what an asshole Trey is, and that swearing is one of her character flaws, along with inappropriate laughter. Evan says his are an overload of ambition as well as beer, women and a commitment-free life. Linda makes Grace feel welcome and cooks breakfast for them in the morning. Big Mac is cranky and out of sorts as he recovers from a head injury. Grace doesn't eat much but can't tell Evan it's because lap-band surgery reduced her stomach size.

Grace, a pharmacist, is intrigued by Gold's, the island pharmacy, and asks to check it out as she and Evan walk to the ferry landing. Mrs. Gold asks if Grace might be interested in buying the pharmacy. She gives Grace a flyer, and she's excited about the idea. Evan gives her $100 to get home. She vows to pay him back, but he says it's not necessary. He enjoyed meeting her. They share an awkward hug before she gets on the ferry. She plans to come back to the island to reimburse Evan.

Evan is sorry to see her go, even if she's a forever kind of girl and he's a temporary kind of guy. Ned gives Evan a ride, and they discuss being worried about Big Mac. Evan teases Ned about getting married and asks to be dropped off at Mac's. Evan says he might wait until he's Ned's age to settle down. "Don't be a fool," Ned tells him. "I missed everything, never got to have kids, had to share yer dad's family." Evan tells Mac that their parents are arguing a lot, and he's worried about Big Mac.

Linda talks to her husband, and they make up. His thoughts are still scrambled weeks after the accident, and he's sick of the cast on his arm. She talks him into an appointment with Dr. David Lawrence, even though he's not keen on seeing the man who cheated on their daughter. Linda reminds him that David also saved their granddaughter Hailey's life.

Tiffany brings Ashleigh to see Thomas and cries on Maddie's shoulder after a rough few weeks since Jim moved out around the same time their deadbeat dad showed up for the first time in decades. She tells Maddie that Jim took everything in the house except beds for her and Ashleigh. She's sad about the demise of her marriage and fears she hasn't done everything she could to save it. Tiffany is curious about the father she doesn't remember.

Tiffany tells Maddie that Abby is closing her store and moving to Texas to be with her fiancé, Cal. Tiffany talks about taking over Abby's retail space to open a store. Maddie asks her about Blaine Taylor, and her sister admits to sparks with Blaine. Celebrated defense attorney Dan Torrington is coming to Gansett and might be able to help Tiffany with her divorce—which would freak out Jim, Maddie suggests.

Stephanie and Grant are going write a screenplay about her story of getting Charlie out of prison.

Grace is on the ferry to Gansett to reimburse Evan and present a proposal to Mr. and Mrs. Gold to buy the pharmacy when she meets Luke, Sydney and Laura. The man who killed Sydney's family in a drunk driving accident was sentenced to twenty years in prison. Luke had surgery on his ankle to fix a torn tendon. Luke has asked Sydney to marry him, but she's not ready yet. Laura's brother Shane is coming over for the winter to help her renovate the Sand & Surf. Listening to Laura and Sydney, Grace wants to be friends with the gutsy women.

She makes an offer to buy the pharmacy, and Mr. Gold shows her the apartment over the store. Mr. Gold promises to talk over her offer with Mrs. Gold and get back to her. Next, she goes to the McCarthy home looking to reimburse Evan, but no one is there, so she walks down the hill to the marina, where she finds him. He doesn't seem happy to see her.. Stephanie offers her chowder and a seat at their table. When it seems like Evan doesn't want her there, Grace puts the money on the table and gets up to leave.

Evan chases after her. He gives her back the money and says he thought about her after she left. He'd been thinking of her when she walked into the marina restaurant. He was surprised by how happy he was to see her. He wants to hang out while she's in town.

After ten days on the mainland, Laura is happy to see Owen, but she has no business being interested in any man, as she's three months pregnant and still married to her ex.

"Are you okay?" Owen asks her.

"Not yet," she says. "But I will be."

Evan is more interested in Grace than he's ever been in anyone, which Grant and Owen pick up on during an afternoon at the beach with Grace, Stephanie and Laura. Owen says he and Laura are just friends. Evan knows that Grace isn't a one-night-stand kind of woman. He's not good enough for her. He invites Grace to take a walk with him. He's out of sorts because he likes her so much. They share a passionate kiss. He asks her to go out with him that night. Grace needs help from the girls to get ready for her date. She tells them she's lost 130 pounds and has no experience with men.

While they're at Gold's, Mrs. Gold tells Grace they accept her offer to buy the pharmacy. Stephanie buys condoms for Grace, just in case.

Mac is getting ready to leave the marina when he finds Big Mac standing at the same spot on the main dock where his accident occurred earlier in the summer. He can't remember what happened. Mac buys him a beer and tells him the upsetting story. They talk about him arguing with Linda, and Mac suggests a romantic date to get back on track.

Tiffany is taking over the lease and helping Abby shut down her store so Abby can join Cal in Texas. The wedding they'd planned for October has been canceled because of his mom's stroke. Blaine comes in, and sparks fly between him and Tiffany.

Evan is strangely nervous about his date with Grace. Stephanie and Laura are leaving the Beachcomber after helping her get ready and warn Evan to be good to Grace. He takes one look at Grace and realizes this won't be just another date. Grace is thrilled by his reaction to her. It's the first time she's ever felt truly beautiful. They share a kiss that makes her realize that her feelings for Trey were nothing compared to what she already feels for Evan. Their kiss gets out of control. Evan reminds her he's not looking for anything serious. He wants to take her out and show her a good time. She wants to sleep with him but needs more time to get to know him and prepare herself for her first time.

Laura returns to the Sand & Surf and finds Owen playing his guitar as the sun sets behind him. She gets a call from her ex-husband, Justin, who's outraged that she filed for divorce. He wants to meet at their apartment, but she's moved them out of there. His stuff will be delivered to his mother's that week. He's furious that his mother will know they've split and that she told her father they're over. Justin will never sign the divorce papers. Owen offers comfort. Laura suspects that Justin, an up-and-coming lawyer, was more interested in being Judge Frank McCarthy's son-in-law than he was in being Laura's husband. Owen invites her out for pizza.

Tiffany sits in one of the only remaining chairs in her empty house with a glass of wine, picking over the slow-rolling disaster that led to her split with Jim. If only she knew what had gone so wrong. Mac stops by to ask Tiffany to help him plan a girls' night out for Maddie, who's been stuck at home since having Hailey. Tiffany shows Mac her empty house, and he's outraged. Mac tells her he'll be there for her and Ashleigh, and Tiffany apologizes for being hard on him when he and Maddie were first together.

Mac decides to confront Jim, jacks him up and threatens to ruin his practice if he doesn't treat Tiffany and Ashleigh with the respect they deserve. Maddie is waiting for him at home and checks his hands to make sure he kept his promise not to punch Jim. He can't bear to be close to her when they have more than three weeks to go until they can have sex again. She takes the edge off for him. Neither of them can wait to get back to normal.

Walking through town holding hands with Evan is one of the most exciting things that's ever happened to Grace. Their dinner at The Lobster House is full of (inappropriate) laughter, romance and sharing of stories about their lives. After dinner, they walk on the beach. After more hot kisses, Grace wants to go back to the hotel with him.

Since she might only have this one night with him, she wants to try everything she's read about in romance novels. She's glad she waited to experience her first time with Evan, who's tender and sweet. After, he says he wished he'd known it was her first time. He would've been more careful. You were perfect, she says. As it's happening, she fears their one perfect night will haunt the rest of her life.

Owen makes Laura laugh as they share a meat-lover's pizza. Then he takes her to an arcade to shoot things to deal with her stress. Laura feelings for him are overwhelming in light of her current situation. When she takes off toward the hotel, he chases after her and kisses her. She can't set herself up for another disappointment. He's leaving soon, and they want different things. Owen watches her go upstairs, wishing he could go with her to tuck her into bed. He doesn't need to be in the middle of a potentially ugly divorce with a child involved that the father doesn't even know about yet. Despite that, the thought of leaving for the winter and not seeing Laura again for months has him deeply unsettled.

Big Mac is picking up Linda at six and taking her out. She is delighted about the date and tells him Grant and Stephanie are having a going-away party for Abby, which he finds funny since Abby is Grant's ex-girlfriend. Evan never came home last night, and Linda heard he was seen in town with Grace. Linda likes her for Evan. Big Mac tells her not to get ahead of herself. Owen and Laura were also seen walking arm in arm in town. Big Mac and Linda share a sexy kiss, and then she tells him Abby's party will be at their house. "That's okay," he says. "We won't be home."

The morning after his incredible night with Grace, Evan tries to make sense of what took place in that hotel room. Freaked out by their intense connection, he's determined to stay the hell away from her, so she doesn't derail his entire life when all his dreams are about to come true with a new album and a tour with superstars Buddy Longstreet and Taylor Jones. Grace is leaving the next day. He has no intention of ever seeing her again.

Grace is disappointed to wake up alone, but has no regrets about her wonderful night with Evan. She wonders if he'll call to make plans for the day and decides she needs to see her new friends Stephanie and Laura to help make sense of it all.

Owen is thinking about Laura and how the ten days she spent on the mainland were among the longest of his life. He's been unreasonably happy to have her back on the island. He goes upstairs to check on her, to make sure they're still friends after he kissed her, and finds her retching from the morning sickness that plagues her. Standing outside her door, he makes a big decision to cancel his annual fall gig in Boston to stay on Gansett with her. What the hell did he just do?

Laura is weak with sickness when Owen appears to pick her up off the bathroom floor and carry her to bed. She shouldn't rely on him this way, but she can't help it when he's so sweet and caring. Owen asks her to go to Abby's party with him and then leaves her to nap. If you'd told him a month ago that he'd be rearranging his life to accommodate a woman who was still married to another guy and pregnant with his kid, Owen would've laughed his ass off. Now he can't conceive of a day that doesn't include her.

Grace goes to visit Laura, who's on the phone with Stephanie, asking how she got roped into co-hosting a party for Grant's ex-girlfriend. Grace tells them they were right that she'd be unable to resist Evan, and they shriek with excitement. She's disappointed that he was gone when she woke up. Stephanie says he's not going to call because he's running away. She and Grant had a huge fight about the screenplay they're writing together. The girls think Evan's behavior is lame and inform Grace that she's coming to Abby's party with them. Grace and Stephanie tell Laura that if her marriage to Justin is truly over, which she says it is, there's no reason she can't date Owen.

Grace talks to Seamus O'Grady about moving her belongings to the island on the ferry. They partake in a flirtatious conversation that bolsters Grace's spirits. Evan isn't the only guy in town.

Evan goes surfing, trying to clear his mind of his confusing thoughts about Grace. He's haunted by the memories of being with her, even though he doesn't want to think about her. He mistimes a wave and is thrown to the bottom, his face smashing into rocks and shells. Owen sees his wipeout and swims out to rescue him. He tells Owen that the date with Grace was the best one he's ever had, and Owen calls him out on his plan to steer clear of her, offering some of the first insight into Owen's family that Evan has ever heard. His father, the general, is a dick. As the oldest, Owen bore the brunt of his father's abusive behavior. Owen says Evan can walk away from Grace as long as he didn't sleep with her. Evan says nothing. Oh shit, Owen says. That changes everything.

Big Mac arrives to pick up Linda on Mac's motorcycle to take her on an adventure. They end up at a camp on the beach where he's planned a romantic dinner for them with Mac's help. They talk things out and reconcile their differences.

Stephanie is upset about the way she and Grant have been fighting about the screenplay. Grant assures her that nothing could ever come between them. Evan arrives with his torn-up face. Grace comes in as Stephanie is cleaning his wounds. She turns the job over to Grace. Evan had no idea she'd be there and is undone by her presence. She's only there because Stephanie invited her, not because of him. He watches her have a flirtatious moment with that Irish charmer, Seamus O'Grady. How do they even know each other? Evan returns a call from his manager, Jack Beaumont, who has bad news. Evan's record company, Starlite Records, has filed for bankruptcy. All its assets, including Evan's album, are caught up in the proceedings. Buddy Longstreet's company wants to buy Evan's album from Starlite and release it on his label, Long Road, which would be a much better situation, but it'll take a while to work that out.

Grant gives a toast, wishing Abby well in her new life with Cal in Texas. A man comes to the door asking for Francine and her daughters. Mac wants to know who he is and what he wants with them. It's Bobby Chester, and they nearly come to blows as Mac tries to get rid of Maddie's deadbeat father. Maddie comes out and asks her father what he wants. There'll be no divorce until Maddie and Tiffany spend some time with him. When Francine hears what Bobby is asking of her daughters, she says there'll be no divorce. She and Ned still get to spend the rest of their lives together. They don't need to be married. Tiffany wants to see her father. She has nothing of him, not a single memory. If Tiffany sees him, then only Maddie would be standing in the way of her mother marrying Ned.

Grace has a great night talking to Seamus, and then with Blaine about people breaking into pharmacies trying to get drugs. Blaine has heard about her buying Gold's and congratulates her. Laura tells Grace that Evan is seething with jealousy as she flirts with Seamus and talks to Blaine. Stephanie encourages Grace to give Evan a second chance. After what she went through to lose weight and get fit, she wants a real man, not a boy pretending to be one. Seamus drives Grace back to town.

Evan shows up at her door, fearing Seamus is in the room with her. He's a little drunk and a mess from his injuries. She lets him in but says nothing will happen. He accuses her of casting a spell on him and asks if it can be undone. No, she says, I don't think it can be. He tells her about his record company bankruptcy and how he gets stage fright. He wakes up with a horrible hangover and hears her talking about state licenses and other business. She tells him she's buying Gold's and how it was in the works before they slept together. He wants to be with her. While they're having sex, he tells her he doesn't want her to do this with anyone else.

"Is that going to be a problem?"

She makes him wait a long, breathless moment before she says, "No."

With that single word, she seals her fate—and his.

Owen takes the stairs to the third floor and hears Laura getting sick again. He scoops her up off the floor, tucks her into bed and makes her tea.

Owen can't deny he's falling hard for her. When she asks what she'll do when he leaves, he tells her he's not going.

"What do you mean you're not going? Of course you are! It's the great gig in Boston that you do every year—"

Owen places a finger over her lips. "I'm not going."

"Why?"

His face twists into a wry smile. "You know why, Princess."

None of this is his problem. He knows, but that doesn't seem to matter.

"You're really staying?"

"I'm really staying."

"Because of me?"

"No, because of Evan. He needs constant supervision." Owen cuffs her chin. "Yes, because of you, silly. Someone has to pick you up off the floor every morning. It may as well be me."

"Oh."

"Is that okay?"

"You really don't have to…."

Burying his fingers in her soft blonde hair, he presses his lips to her forehead. "I want to, Laura. I really want to."

She's worried that he'll regret staying. He proposes they spend the winter together until the baby arrives and then see where they are. The idea of being domesticated no longer horrifies him, he says. They seal the deal with a kiss.

Grace gives up her spot on the ferry so Stephanie and Grant can get a car on the boat. Dan Torrington has succeeded in getting an emergency hearing for Stephanie's stepfather, Charlie. That gives Grace another night with Evan. He introduces her to shower sex, and she tells him about the lap-band surgery, how she's lost more than one hundred pounds and the whale nickname. He shares what he and the other boys did to Maddie once upon a time and how ashamed he is to have been part of that. He swears he's not that guy anymore.

She's worried they're going in different directions, with her putting down roots on the island while he's chasing a career that'll keep him far from home. He wants to take a chance on love, something he's never said to a woman before.

After Sydney tells a story she read about a woman who cuffed herself naked to her husband to get him to talk to her, Tiffany decides to give it a try with Jim. The mission is a disaster, leading Jim to call the police. Blaine arrives, and Jim demands that charges be filed. Tiffany is mortified that Blaine is seeing her naked and desperate. Jim wants her arrested. Blaine takes her to the station until they work things out.

Blaine can't believe a woman like her has to resort to cuffing herself to a man. He talks Jim out of filing felony charges, but she has to make restitution for the four flat tires on Jim's car. Jim is also demanding a restraining order to keep her away from him. Blaine asks what a nice girl like her is doing with a tool like Jim. Blaine is on fire with desire for her. He offers to give her a ride home. She invites him in to see the condition of her empty home. They share a hot kiss that spirals out of control. He gives her the best orgasm of her life. Before she can return the favor, he gets called back to work.

He studies her for another long moment. "If you'd cuffed yourself to me and wrapped those beautiful lips around *my* dick, I would've been calling for mercy, not the cops. You can bet on that." Pressing a soft kiss to her cheek, Blaine revels in the tremble that ripples through her. "Take care of yourself." He won't soon forget the image of her delectable mouth hanging open in surprise.

Evan is panicked about losing Grace. He wants her, he wants them, he wants it all with her. She suggests they take the next two weeks while she's back home in Mystic packing to move to make sure this is what they really want. While the drama over his record unfolds in Nashville, Evan gets through the first week after Grace leaves. Stephanie's stepfather, Charlie, is released from prison after fourteen years. They bring him home to the island. Ned finds Charlie a rental while Mac offers him a job helping to renovate the Sand & Surf.

Sensing that Evan is suffering without Grace, Linda tells him she understands how it feels to want someone so badly and to see only obstacles standing in the way. She and Big Mac dealt with some of that when they were first together. Later, when he calls Grace, they have phone sex. They can't wait to see each other in two more days.

When Grace comes off the ferry, she throws herself into Evan's arms.

"Did you think long and hard while I was gone?"

"So long and *so* hard," he says in a tone rife with double meaning.

She smacks his arm. "I'm being serious."

"So am I." He takes her hand and leads her away from the maelstrom of people, cars and bikes. Behind the ticket office, he presses her against the wall and kisses her senseless again.

"What did you decide?"

"I decided I'm no good without you. I decided I'll do anything I can to keep you in my life." As he'd practiced this declaration over and over during the last few interminable days, he'd expected this last bit to be the hard part. But with her in his arms, looking up at him with her heart in her eyes, he finds it isn't hard at all. "And I decided I love you."

"That works out perfectly," she says with the cheeky grin he so adores. "Because I love you, too."

 An interview with Evan and Grace...

Look at you guys going strong after more than a decade together!

Evan: No one is more surprised than I am that I haven't screwed it up yet.

Grace: He's tried like hell.

Evan: (laughing) True story. Grace is a saint, and I'm as lucky today as I was all those years ago that she loves me for some reason.

Grace: It's the sex.

Evan: I knew it!

(They laugh).

What's life like for you guys these days?

Grace: Our kids keep us busy. Maddox is almost nine, our daughter Luna is six and our younger son, Jack, is four.

Wow, you have three kids! Are you done?

Evan: Grace says we're definitely done. I say let's have three more because we make really cute, funny kids.

Grace: They're amazing, but three is a perfect number.

Are you still touring, Evan?

Evan: We hit the road for a few weeks every summer, and it's become a fun family tradition. The kids love being on the road—for now anyway. I'm not delusional about the teenage years when they'll want to be home with their friends and cousins.

Grace: We all look forward to touring with Daddy in the summer.

Evan: It helps that we tack on a family vacation at the end of the tour.

How are the studio and pharmacy doing?

Evan: The studio is great. We've recorded twelve number-one songs now, so we've grown a nice reputation for being a hit maker. We've got artists waiting months for a chance to record with us. My engineer, Josh, runs the studio, and I help out when I'm here.

Grace: The pharmacy is humming along. It helps to be the only one in town. My manager and friend, Fiona, is a huge help to me there and has been such a godsend.

Evan: Fun fact—Fiona is married to Josh!

Wow, when did that happen?

Evan: About five years ago. We joke that it was inevitable because they were always hanging out at our house at the same time. One thing led to another…. They're really happy together and have two little ones, who our kids adore.

I love that! I'm so glad to hear you guys are happy and doing well.

Grace: We're so happy. I often think about that first night at the marina and everything that came from it. I feel incredibly blessed to have met Evan and the rest of our friends and family here on Gansett.

Evan: What a life.

Indeed.

NEW YORK TIMES AND USA TODAY BESTSELLING AUTHOR
MARIE FORCE
Season for Love

Book 6: Season for Love
Published: June 3, 2012

His idea of permanence is the VW van that takes him from one gig to the next…

Owen Lawry has made a living as a traveling musician and enjoys his footloose-and-fancy-free lifestyle. But after meeting Laura McCarthy and helping her to land the job as manager of his grandparents' hotel on Gansett Island, Owen decides there's something to be said about a roof over his head and a warm, sexy woman in his bed.

Laura, a newlywed who discovered that her husband never quit dating, came to Gansett for her cousin Janey's wedding, but ended up staying after she met Owen and took on the renovations of the dilapidated Sand & Surf Hotel.

As Owen and Laura's attraction simmers during months of close proximity, they form a tight bond that will be tested when her estranged husband refuses to grant her a divorce. As summer turns to autumn and Laura and Owen take baby steps toward love, favorite characters from past Gansett Island stories continue to live their happily ever afters.

🏮 Main Characters:

*Laura McCarthy,** involved with Owen Lawry in HOPING FOR LOVE.

*Owen Lawry,** involved with Laura McCarthy in HOPING FOR LOVE.

*Indicates recurring throughout the series

⛭ Supporting Characters:

*Linda McCarthy,** grandmother of Thomas Chester McCarthy in MAID FOR LOVE and Hailey McCarthy in FALLING FOR LOVE.

*Grace Ryan,** owner of Ryan's Pharmacy in HOPING FOR LOVE, involved with Evan McCarthy in HOPING FOR LOVE.

***Stephanie Logan,** involved with Grant McCarthy in FALLING FOR LOVE.

***Maddie McCarthy,** mother of Thomas, married to Mac McCarthy in FOOL FOR LOVE, mother of Hailey McCarthy in FALLING FOR LOVE.

***Jenny Wilks,** lighthouse keeper.

***Justin Newsome,** Laura's estranged husband.

***Mac McCarthy, Jr.,** married to Maddie Chester in FOOL FOR LOVE, father of Thomas McCarthy in MAID FOR LOVE, father of Hailey McCarthy in FALLING FOR LOVE.

***Luke Harris,** involved with Sydney Donovan in READY FOR LOVE.

***Sydney Donovan,** involved with Luke Harris in READY FOR LOVE.

***Big Mac McCarthy,** grandfather of Thomas McCarthy in MAID FOR LOVE and Hailey McCarthy in FALLING FOR LOVE.

***Kara Ballard,** from Ballard Boat Works in Bar Harbor, Maine, starting launch service in the Salt Pond/North Harbor.

***Judge Frank McCarthy,** Superior Court Judge in Providence, brother of Big Mac, father of Laura and Shane.

***Shane McCarthy,** son of Frank McCarthy and the late JoAnn McCarthy, brother of Laura, estranged husband of Courtney.

***Courtney McCarthy,** estranged wife of Shane.

***Allan Donovan,** father of Sydney.

***Buddy,** Sydney and Luke's dog.

***Grant McCarthy,** involved with Stephanie Logan in FALLING FOR LOVE.

***Charlie Grandchamp,** Stephanie's stepfather, freed from prison in HOPING FOR LOVE.

***Evan McCarthy,** involved with Grace Ryan in HOPING FOR LOVE.

***Joe Cantrell,** married to Janey McCarthy Cantrell in READY FOR LOVE.

***Carolina Cantrell,** co-owner of the Gansett Island Ferry Company, mother of Joe, widow of Pete Cantrell.

*** Seamus O'Grady,** general manager, Gansett Island Ferry Company.

***Dan Torrington,** celebrity defense attorney, writing a book about working to free unjustly incarcerated individuals.

***Ned Saunders,** engaged to Francine Chester in FALLING FOR LOVE.

***Tiffany Sturgil,** planning to open a lingerie and novelties shop in FALLING FOR LOVE, had a sexy interlude with Blaine Taylor in HOPING FOR LOVE.

***Blaine Taylor,** chief, Gansett Island Police, had a sexy interlude with Tiffany in HOPING FOR LOVE.

***Francine Chester,** grandmother of Ashleigh Sturgil, Thomas McCarthy and Hailey McCarthy, engaged to Ned Saunders in FALLING FOR LOVE.

***Janey McCarthy Cantrell,** married to Joe Cantrell in READY FOR LOVE.

***Slim Jackson,** island pilot.

***Sarah Lawry,** Owen's mother, estranged wife of Air Force General Mark Lawry, mother of Julia, Katie, Josh, Cindy, John and Jeff, daughter of Russ and Adele Kinkaid, longtime owners of the Sand & Surf Hotel.

***Dr. David Lawrence,** medical director, Gansett Island Medical Clinic in HOPING FOR LOVE.

***Mark Lawry,** Air Force general, estranged husband of Sarah, father of Owen, Julia, Katie, Josh, Cindy, John and Jeff, arrested for abusing Sarah.

***Julia Lawry,** sister of Owen, twin to Katie, an office manager in Texas.

***Katie Lawry,** sister of Owen, twin to Julia, a nurse in Texas.

***Josh Lawry,** brother of Owen, engineer in Virginia.

***Cindy Lawry,** sister of Owen, hair stylist in Texas.

***John Lawry,** brother of Owen, police officer in Tennessee. ***Jeff Lawry,** youngest sibling of Owen, attempted suicide at 14 and was addicted to drugs. In recovery now, lives in Florida near grandparents and is going to college.

***Adele Kinkaid,** mother of Sarah, grandmother of Owen and his siblings, co-owner of the Sand & Surf Hotel with her husband, Russ.

***Victoria,** nurse practitioner-midwife, Gansett Island Medical Clinic.

***Holden Francis Newsome,** Laura's son with ex-husband Justin Newsome, stepson of Owen Lawry, born in SEASON FOR LOVE.

📼 Gansett Island Soundtrack:

- "Something"

- "Love of a Lifetime (Luke & Sydney's song)"

66 SEASON FOR LOVE Headlines:

- Owen stays on Gansett Island to be with Laura!

- We meet Jenny Wilks, the new lighthouse keeper, Kara Ballard from Bar Harbor, Judge Frank McCarthy, Carolina Cantrell, Slim Jackson and Sarah Lawry!

- Luke and Sydney get engaged!

- Janey is pregnant!

- Grant and Stephanie get engaged!

- Seamus and Carolina did *what*?!?

- Ned suggests that Evan open a recording studio on Gansett!

- Daisy will be the new housekeeping manager at McCarthy's Gansett Inn!

- Jenny loves Sydney's friends and is thrilled to be part of their group!

- Dan and Kara meet!

- Blaine tells Tiffany to call him the second she's divorced!

- Seamus sees a mortified Carolina at a party and angles to drive her home!

- Sarah Lawry arrives on the island in rough shape!

- Owen's father is arrested and charged!

- Shane McCarthy arrives on the island!

- Laura's son, Holden Francis Newsome, is born!

- Justin signs the divorce papers!

- Laura and Owen plan a wedding for next summer!

- Luke and Sydney get married!

It's Labor Day weekend when Owen Lawry stands on the front porch of the Sand & Surf and watches the last ferry of the day leave without him. He's calling himself ten kinds of fool for staying on the island to be with Laura, who's pregnant with another man's child and staring down a difficult divorce. Despite the many obstacles that stand in their way, Owen has never wanted anyone the way he wants Laura, and as long as she seems to like having him around, he's not going anywhere.

Laura loves being with Owen, but she's about to have a child and is tied to the island through her new job managing the Sand & Surf Hotel, which Owen's grandparents own. He makes a living traveling from gig to gig on the mainland. Though their plans are vastly different, she can't deny the sizzling chemistry between them or that she likes him more than any man she's ever met—including the one she married.

Linda McCarthy has called Laura, Stephanie, Grace, Maddie and Sydney to breakfast. Sydney reports that Luke is recovering well from ankle surgery, and they may be getting married soon. Linda reads them a letter from Jenny Wilks, the new lighthouse keeper, which tells the story of losing her fiancé in the 9/11 attack on the World Trade Center. Years later, Jenny is still trying to get her life moving forward again and hopes a stint on Gansett Island might be restorative. Jenny's story deeply moves the women, and they plan to befriend her. Having survived her own tragedy, Sydney offers to reach out to Jenny.

Maddie wants to hold a benefit to raise money for the seasonal employees whose income drops after the summer ends. She's heading to her six-week post-partum checkup with Dr. Lawrence. Hearing Jenny's story, Laura realizes her problems are trivial in comparison to what Jenny went through. When she voices her concerns about Owen changing his way of life to stay on the island with her, Maddie says Mac is perfectly content to be "trapped on the island" and jokes about how to keep him that way. Laura still wonders if Owen will be happy on the island long term.

After hearing the baby's heartbeat for the first time during an ultrasound at the clinic, Laura returns to the hotel and tells Owen how glad she is that he stayed. They share a passionate kiss. They both want more from their relationship. Before they move forward, Owen wants her to resolve things with her estranged husband, Justin. She vows to take care of it as soon as possible, and they agree that kissing is allowed in the meantime.

While Mac waits to hear from Maddie that they have the green light to resume having sex, he works with Luke and Big Mac to repair the marina roof. Luke has been asked to teach at the International Yacht Restoration School in Newport for a month over the winter, which affects the off-season projects Mac has lined up for the construction company since Luke is going to work with him there, too.

Kara Ballard, from Ballard Boat Works in Bar Harbor, Maine, is hoping to run a launch service in the Great Salt Pond and asks Big Mac and Mac if they'd like to work together to make it happen. They learn that Kara is the sixth of eleven children, and they strike a deal with her to offer the launch service from their marina starting the next summer. Mac gets a text from Maddie and has to go home right away.

Laura reaches out to her father, Judge Frank McCarthy, and they catch up on her new life on Gansett, her work at the Surf and her friendship with Owen. Frank is worried about Laura's brother Shane. His wife, Courtney, has asked for a divorce. Courtney has been battling an addiction to pain medicine. Shane waited for her to get through rehab, hoping they'd put their marriage back together. The divorce request has devastated him. Laura promises to take good care of Shane when he comes to the island to help with the hotel renovations. She tells her father she's planning to inform Justin that she's pregnant. Laura believes Justin, an attorney, was more interested in being Judge Frank's son-in-law than her husband.

Maddie is ready for Mac when he comes home, having taken Thomas and Hailey to her mom and Ned's until dinnertime. They enjoy a passionate reunion.

Kara's arrival and the extra work needed at the marina to account for increased foot traffic has Luke putting off the offer from IRYS for now. He has a ring for Sydney, has her parents' blessing and all he needs is for her to finally say yes to one of his many proposals. Luke is concerned about Sydney being the one to reach out to Jenny, fearing a setback for her. Sydney appreciates his concern and assures him she can handle it. She might be ready to answer that "question" he asked her a while ago. He retrieves the ring, and they get engaged.

Laura texts Justin, asking to meet at his favorite restaurant in Providence. Owen makes dinner for Laura, and they discuss how he cooked for his younger siblings when he was as young as 12. She tells him about the meeting with Justin, and Owen wants to go with her. They share another hot kiss that's interrupted when Stephanie stops by to see Laura. They pick up where they left off after Stephanie leaves.

"Until today, you never told me you wanted me like this," Laura says.

"Yes, I did."

"When?" she asks.

"When the last ferry left on Monday without me on it. Didn't that say it all?"

"I suppose that did make a statement."

While things between them heat up, they're determined to hold off on anything more until she sees Justin.

Grant is intimidated about meeting with Stephanie's stepfather, Charlie Grandchamp, to ask his blessing to propose to Stephanie. He wants Steph to know they're for keeps, even when they argue. He assures Charlie that he'd go anywhere she wants to be, even if that means leaving the island, and he'd support her dream to open a restaurant, which Grant is surprised to hear about from her dad. Charlie is willing to give his blessing as long as Grant promises he'll always be good to her, put her needs before his own and be faithful to her. Those are easy promises for Grant to make. Charlie thanks Grant for everything he did to help him and Stephanie. He owes his freedom to the phone calls Grant made on his behalf. Grant thinks about how he'll propose and hopes that once there's a ring on her finger, they can stop worrying about whether what they have will last.

Owen carries Laura upstairs to bed, and she asks him to stay. She's worried about him not having enough work on the island, but he's saved most of what he's made over the years and could easily take a couple of years off if need be. She's concerned he'll later regret changing his entire way of life for her.

"When I wake up in the morning, usually quite early even after a late gig, I lie in bed and look up at the ceiling, wishing I were up here with you.

I picture your gorgeous face, all your hundreds of expressions and how much I like watching you sleep when you conk out on me. Sometimes, when I'm really lucky, I can smell your scent clinging to me because you hugged me the night before. I lie there wondering how long I have to wait until you come downstairs, all fresh-faced and pretty, full of excitement over whatever job you've got planned for the day. I want to hear how you slept, how you feel and if the baby is moving. I want to make sure you eat enough for both of you. I think about what we should do for dinner and if we might have time for a walk on the beach, or if it's too chilly for you."

Laura barely took a breath as she listened to him.

"At night, after we've spent the entire day together, I go to bed and burn for you. I want to hold you and kiss you and make love to you and sleep with you in my arms. I want to feel your soft skin next to mine and have your hair tickling my face when I'm trying to sleep. I want to know the second you wake up, and I want my face to be the first thing you see every day."

Tears roll down her cheeks. "Owen." She's never in her life been more touched—or seduced.

"Now tell me, how in the world will I get all that if I'm not here with you?"

"I don't know," she says, wiping her face.

"No one knows anything for sure, Princess. All I know is I'm exactly where I want to be right now. I can no longer imagine a day without you in it. That's got to count for something, right?"

Things between Owen and Laura continue to heat up as they count down to her meeting with Justin, which they hope will begin the divorce and custody process.

Evan is on pins and needles waiting to hear what will become of his album and the upcoming tour with Buddy Longstreet and Taylor Jones since his record company has declared bankruptcy. Buddy's company, Long Road Records, may acquire the album. Grace can help support them in the meantime, but Evan doesn't want that. She assures him they can get through anything together.

In Ohio, Joe is worried about how exhausted Janey has been lately. When he calls his mother, Carolina, to ask her how her first date in years went, they talk about Janey's exhaustion. Carolina asks if it's possible that

Janey might be pregnant. Joe is rocked by that possibility. Carolina tells him she's decided to spend the winter on Gansett Island. He asks her to check in with Seamus to make sure he's doing a good job running their ferry business while Joe is away. They agree they need to keep Seamus running the company even when Joe returns to Gansett. Joe is enjoying teaching painting at Ohio State while Janey is in vet school.

As things get more intense between Owen and Laura, he begins to fear he might somehow screw things up with her.

Sydney and Luke plan a Christmas wedding. She goes to the lighthouse to see Jenny. On the way, she spots Stephanie walking by the side of the road, visibly upset. Sydney stops to pick up her friend. She and Grant have had another big fight about the screenplay they're writing about her story and Charlie's, and she's going to stay with Charlie for a while. Sydney promises not to say anything to anyone about the trouble between Stephanie and Grant.

Sydney's dog, Buddy, helps to break the ice with Jenny. Sydney tells her they have lots of fun on the island and would love to include her. Jenny asks if Syd has read her letter and knows her story. Sydney has read it. When Jenny notices her ring, Sydney is hesitant to celebrate her happiness. Don't do that, Jenny says. Of course, you're happy. Jenny is ready to get unstuck and agrees to come to Sydney's house to meet her friends.

Owen and Laura take a rough ferry ride to the mainland for their meeting with Justin. Laura is seasick on the boat.

Carolina's plans to travel to the island are thwarted when the boats are canceled for the rest of the day. Seamus invites her to Joe's house to spend the night. She's incredibly charmed by him. Too bad she's almost old enough to be his mother. Seamus has found her incredibly sexy since the first time he met her. Acting on that attraction could cost him a job he loves. Their night together turns romantic, which takes both of them by surprise.

Joe waits until Janey is done with midterm exams before he suggests she take a pregnancy test. She says there's no way she could be pregnant. He disagrees. The test is positive, and Janey wonders how she'll manage vet school and pregnancy. Joe assures her that they can handle it.

Grant is waiting for Stephanie to come back to their home, but Dan tells him she's not coming back. He needs to go after her. Dan advises Grant to take a step back from the screenplay and focus on the relationship. Grant goes to Charlie's and asks to see Stephanie. After making Grant work for it, Charlie tells him where to find her.

Stephanie explains to him that after growing up the way she did, she can't live with constant strife and arguing. They agree to changes, including no longer working together. She needs to take the money he paid for her story and open the restaurant she's dreamed about. She can't believe he asked Charlie for approval, since Grant is scared of Charlie.

"Stephanie, you're the love story of my lifetime, the one I can't live without. I know it's been rocky at times, and it's apt to be again once in a while, but I promise I'll do everything in my power to make you happy, to give you the family you've always wanted, the life you've always wanted and the security you've never had. You'll never have to wonder where I am or who I'm with, because I'll always want to be with you more than I want to be with anyone else. There's nothing in this world I wouldn't do for you, but I need you to do one thing for me first."

"What?" she asks, breathless.

"Marry me." He releases her hands to retrieve the ring box from his pocket and opens it to reveal a simple square-cut diamond. He knows anything flashier would've been wrong for her.

She gasps, and her hand covers her mouth.

He *loves* that he's taken her completely by surprise.

Her eyes dart from the ring to his face—possibly to gauge his sincerity—and back to the ring.

"Stephanie Logan, I'll love you every day for the rest of my life. Will you marry me?" Grant wonders if his eyes are deceiving him when he sees her nod. "Is that a yes?"

The word "yes" gets caught on a sob, but he hears it. Loud and clear. He slides the ring onto her finger and reaches for her.

Owen drives Laura Frank's home in Providence. Her dad is happy to finally meet Owen. Laura is in rough shape after the ferry ride. Frank is concerned about Justin getting physical with Laura, but she says he'd never do that in public. Owen goes to the restaurant with her and keeps an eye from a distance as she joins Justin at the table. Justin knows all about her new life on Gansett and her "friendship" with Owen. He knows about the baby because he had a private investigator follow her. She smacks him in the face and tells him to sign the divorce papers, or she and her father will make his life a living hell.

After the awful confrontation, Laura asks for some time to herself, which upsets Owen. He calls Frank to tell him that Justin did something to seriously upset Laura. Frank says her withdrawal is similar to how she coped after her mother died. Frank says it's time he had a talk with her "husband" and asks Owen if he loves Laura. Owen says he does. He can't deny it. Frank encourages him to get her back to the island, where she's always been happiest, and to give her time to process what's happened.

Carolina and Seamus sleep together, and afterward she can't believe she is in bed with a man sixteen years her junior and having the best sex of her life.

Evan wakes to someone banging on the door to his and Grace's apartment. It's Ned with a business idea for Evan. Ned will put up the money for Evan to start a recording studio on the island. Ned believes Evan and Owen could make a go of it. He wants to see Evan back on track with a purpose again. Evan is grateful to Ned and eager to talk to Grace and Owen about the idea.

Laura wakes in Owen's arms and apologizes for punching out on him the night before. She tells him how Justin implied that she can't be without a man. And as a result of that, Owen says, you've decided to take a step back from me. Something like that, she says. You're a dope, he replies. Laura is still too upset to focus on the next steps with Owen.

Carolina is mortified to be naked in bed with Seamus when Joe calls to tell his mother that Janey is pregnant. Seamus says, "Congratulations, Grandma," and she chokes on her coffee. By the time he finally lets her out of bed to take a shower an hour later, Carolina is royally screwed—in every possible way.

Maddie has the women over to discuss a Thanksgiving dinner for the community. When Tiffany arrives, she asks if Maddie has heard any more from their father. Maddie hates being the only thing standing between their mom and Ned getting married. Maddie is worried about Tiffany, who tells her sister about a sexy interlude with Blaine after she snuck into Jim's place and disastrously tried to seduce him. Tiffany is rattled to realize she might've missed out on the kind of incendiary passion she experienced with Blaine if she'd stayed with Jim. Maddie has decided to decline Linda's offer to be the housekeeping director at McCarthy's Gansett Inn to stay home with her kids. She suggests Linda offer the job to Daisy.

Laura thanks Owen for being with her during the difficult trip to Providence and tells him things are apt to be messy for a while, but she wants to be with him. He wants that, too, and he can't wait to meet the baby who will change both their lives. When they return to the island, they finally make love. She jokes about how he got "more than his share." They admit they love each other.

Seamus accompanies Carolina to the ferry landing for the ride to Gansett. She can barely bring herself to look at him, which is disappointing to him. He's not going to beg her, but says he had a grand time, best sex of his life, and she knows where to find him if she changes her mind about wanting to pursue a relationship with him.

Linda comes to the marina to tell Big Mac that Janey is pregnant. Then Linda goes to celebrate with Carolina, who has just arrived on the island. Linda notices that Carolina has a rash on her face. Carolina admits she had sex but won't say with whom. It was great sex and she likes him very much, but he's sixteen years younger than her. Linda invites Carolina to Sydney and Luke's party that evening.

When they wake much later in the day, Laura wonders how Owen will feel about the baby. He'll love the baby because he or she is part of Laura. Owen wants to attend her doctor's appointments and be her labor coach.

Jenny arrives early at Sydney's party so she can get situated before the influx of friends. Sydney believes Jenny will fit right in with their group. Kara also attends the party to meet everyone.

Linda wants to kill Grant because he got engaged and didn't tell her. Mac gets Janey on the phone to tell them her news. Luke and Sydney are engaged, too. Maddie tells Tiffany that Blaine is looking at her. She encourages Tiffany to talk to him. Maddie hates that Jim made her fearless sister hesitant and unwilling to go after what she wants. Tiffany admits Maddie is right—she's afraid of her own shadow. If it's meant to be, it'll happen, Maddie tells her.

When she finds out Seamus is at the party, Carolina regrets not bringing her own car. Seamus wants to drive her home. Absolutely not, she says. Seamus corners her in the bathroom, and they engage in a heated make-out session before Carolina storms off, maddened by her unmistakable attraction to the charming Irishman. Seamus offers her a ride home in front of everyone, so she can't very well turn him down without people wondering why. He's infuriating!

Owen and Laura show up late to the party, which has everyone talking about where they've been all day. Evan wants to talk to him about Ned's idea. Owen is excited for Evan to pursue the opportunity, but he's found his calling working at the hotel with Laura. He likes the idea of keeping the hotel in the family.

Frank has talked to Justin, who agreed to give Laura a divorce and primary custody if she ends things with Owen. Frank isn't done working his network to deal with Justin. He and Owen agree to keep this latest salvo from Laura until Frank has time to see what he can do. Owen isn't comfortable keeping it from her.

Laura asks Stephanie to open her new restaurant in the Sand & Surf. Dan Torrington is intrigued by Kara, who isn't his type. When he asks Grant to introduce him, Grant says Dan is far too old for Kara. Big Mac introduces her to Grant, who introduces her to Dan. She's not impressed to hear he's a lawyer. Dan asks her to dinner the next night, and she declines.

Tiffany ventures onto the back deck to get some air and encounters Blaine. They confess to having thought of each other often since their earlier encounter. He asks if she's still married, and she says not for long. "Good," he says. "The minute you're free of him, the very same *second* it's final, you're going to call me."

"Oh, I—"

He brings his face so close to hers that the hint of his whiskers against her cheek and the mild, masculine scent of his cologne make her tremble madly. "You're going to call me, and we're going to pick up where we left off. Are we clear on how this is going to go?"

Tiffany doesn't know whether to be relieved to know there'll be more with him or outraged over his dominant tone. No one tells her what to do!

When she doesn't answer him, he gives the waistband of her jeans a firmer tug that throws off her balance, causing her breasts to mash against his chest.

She gasps when her sensitized nipples rub against hard muscle.

"I *said*, are we clear?"

While she wants to protest his high-handedness, she's so aroused that all she can manage is the briefest of nods. It's a shock to realize high-handedness turns her on.

"I didn't hear you," he growls in her ear.

"Yes," she whispers. "We're clear."

"Good." He releases her so suddenly she nearly stumbles. Only his hands on her shoulders keep her from falling. And then his palm is on her face in a tender caress that steals the breath from her lungs.

When he walks away from her, she goes to find Dan to get her divorce from Jim finalized.

Carolina is infuriated on the ride home. Seamus wants to understand why she won't let herself have something she wants. She doesn't want him to sacrifice the chance to have a real life and children with someone his own age. What would your mother say about this, she asks. He laughs at the question and says his mother would like her. He wants to make a go of this thing with her, but she has to get out of her own way. She agrees to think about it.

Pilot Slim Jackson arrives at the party to tell Owen he just flew his mother to the island, and she's in rough shape. Owen knows right away how she ended up that way and wants to run away and hide the way he did as a kid when his father would beat up his mother or him. Evan, the only one who knows about Owen's family history, offers to drive him and Laura home to the hotel, where his mother is waiting for him. On the way, Owen tells Laura there're things he should tell her, things she should know… Laura insists they focus on his mother. Owen doesn't want his two closest friends in the middle of this latest nightmare, but they won't leave him alone with it.

Owen finds his mother, Sarah Lawry, on the steps to the hotel. The hide-a-key is missing, so she couldn't get inside. He sends Evan to find Dr. David Lawrence. When Owen and Laura get Sarah inside, he introduces the two women. Sarah has traveled from Virginia to Gansett Island, fueled by the determination to get to her son. If David suspects a crime has been committed, he's required to report it. Sarah has severely bruised ribs from her husband punching and kicking her. David calls Blaine, who will work with the authorities in Virginia to arrest her husband. Owen says she may change her mind about reporting the incident in the morning. That's the pattern.

Owen wants to explain his family situation to Laura. He's nothing like his father.

"Owen! My God, do you honestly think you have to tell me that?"

"I wanted you to know because of the baby."

"Owen, *please….*"

The brush of her lips against his neck registers at the same moment he feels new dampness on his face. He hates that he made her cry.

"You could never hurt me or the baby," she says softly. "Never."

"I'm sorry to drag you into this. I didn't want you to know."

She turns his face, forcing him to meet her gaze. "I love you. I love everything about you. *Everything.*" Her sweet, gentle kiss is nearly his undoing. "Close your eyes. It's okay. I'm here, and I love you. Always."

Owen releases a deep breath and closes his eyes. Wrapped in her love, he's able to quiet his mind and sleep.

Evan is undone by what Owen is going through, and Grace offers comfort. Owen only recently told him about his childhood with an abusive father, who was also a decorated Air Force general.

In the middle of the night, Owen fills in some of the details for Laura. He was five the first time his father hit him across the face, and he had to stay home from school for a week because his face was bruised. That's his first memory. His mother, who had three children by then, couldn't defend him out of fear of what her husband would do to her. It took Owen a long time to realize that pretending it wasn't happening was how she coped. He tells her of the nightmare that unfolded throughout his childhood and how he put himself between his father and younger siblings and didn't go to college so he could stay close to them. The only respite they got from the hell of their upbringing was when their father was deployed and during summers with their grandparents on Gansett Island.

"Now you've got the whole ugly story. I can only imagine what you must be thinking."

Laura rests her chin on his chest and meets his gaze. "I'm thinking that you are, without a doubt, the most amazingly heroic man I've ever had the pleasure to meet."

"Oh, *please*, Laura," he says with a groan. "Don't pin me with that. I missed so many opportunities to put a stop to it."

With a hand on his face, she forces him to look at her. "If I want to think you're heroic, I'm allowed to. You were very brave, and you stood up for your younger siblings, protecting them from the worst of it. You sacrificed your own chance to escape to be there for them. If that's not heroic, I don't know what is." She kisses the protest off his lips. "I hate to think about what you went through for so long. I wish I could've been there for you."

"I wouldn't have wanted you anywhere near it."

"If your mom hadn't come here, would you have ever told me?"

"I suppose I would've had to explain at some point why I have nothing to do with my parents other than an occasional call to my mother to make sure she's still alive."

"Where are your brothers and sisters now?"

"Julia and Katie still live in Texas. Julia is an office manager, and Katie is a nurse. I'm really proud of both of them. They lived through the worst of it with me and came out on the other side happy and productive." He has another sister, Cindy, and three brothers, John, Josh and Jeff.

"Are they married?"

He shakes his head. "None of us is. I'll let you shrink the deeper meaning of that."

After they talk more about his family and upbringing, he tells Laura about Justin's conditions for the divorce. She'll live in sin with Owen for the rest of her life if that's what it takes and will fight Justin for custody of a baby he doesn't even want.

The next day, Sarah is checked at the clinic. Her ribs are badly bruised but not broken. Blaine comes to the hotel to take her statement. After Sarah decides to press charges against her husband, Owen is overwhelmed and takes off on his own. Laura aches for him but bonds with Sarah as she tends her. Sarah isn't going back this time, no matter what. Owen later tells Laura the fight was about undercooked chicken this time. He warns her that things are apt to get ugly with his father, and he'd understand if it was too much for her. She's going to pretend he didn't say that. He tries to push her away, but she's not going anywhere. They're in this together—forever.

In the Epilogue, a few months have passed, and Laura gives birth to a son. Her brother Shane joined them on the island after Christmas and has been a big help in renovating the hotel. Sarah has healed, and her husband has been ordered to have no contact with her while the case makes its way through the courts. She's become Laura's right hand at the hotel.

Laura calls Justin to tell him the baby has arrived, and they name the child Holden Francis Newsome. Justin informs her that Frank has the signed divorce papers to give her. They have a long talk, clear the air and agree to work together to parent their son, with Laura having primary custody. The divorce will be final in six months, so Owen and Laura plan an August wedding on the new deck of the Sand & Surf.

Sydney and Luke are married in A Gansett Island Wedding short story. They're thrilled to have forever to spend together.

 An interview with Owen and Laura

When I think about the Gansett Island Series, one of the moments that stands out to me is Owen on the porch of the Sand & Surf watching that last ferry leave on Labor Day.

Owen: I think about that day a lot, and how I wondered then if I was doing the right thing.

Laura: What's the verdict?

Owen: I'm still trying to decide.

(They laugh.)

Owen: Seriously, though, it was the best decision I've ever made. Life is a series of options, you know? We all get to decide what path we take. I thought I'd found my avenue until I met my Princess, and all my plans changed.

Laura: I'll never forget the way you cared for me when I was pregnant with another man's child, who you've raised as your own.

Owen: Holden is my best friend. We have so much fun together.

Laura: Owen has taught Holden to play the guitar, and they sing together, sometimes even in public when Holden gets over his shyness.

Owen: And he's made me into a fisherman.

Laura: They spend hours casting off the jetty. I love watching them from the hotel.

Did you guys ever move out of the hotel?

Laura: We had good intentions but never got around to it. We love being right there, and the kids like living in town. Last year, we took one more room from the hotel to make some space for teenagers. Holden is fourteen, and the twins are twelve. Joanna is our rockstar student. She gets straight A's, while her brothers are a little *less* studious.

Owen: Like I was. But both boys have lots of practical skills, thanks to me and their uncle Shane. We've had them swinging hammers since they were old enough to walk. JoJo loves working at the front desk, especially during check-in, so she can meet all the guests.

Laura: It takes a lot to keep this old building maintained and the hotel running smoothly. The kids love being part of it.

I want to ask about Adele and Russ...

Owen: Believe it or not, they're as active as ever in their nineties. They tell us they're going to live forever, which is fine with us. We can't imagine life without them. The kids are very close to them and spend a lot of time with them. Jon loves to listen to Russ's stories, and he's started recording videos of them, so we'll always have them.

Laura: They're delighted to have a third generation of their family actively involved with the hotel.

And how are your parents?

Laura: My dad and Betsy are world travelers. They've been everywhere in recent years, which is so great for them. We get to live vicariously through their travels. One year, they went on a two-month cruise through the Mediterranean with Big Mac, Linda, Ned and Francine. They have a great time together.

I can picture them causing international incidents and Frank getting them out of trouble.

Laura: You're not far off! My dad and Uncle Mac love to tease Uncle Kevin about raising a second family while they're off having fun, but Kev loves his little ones—and his grandkids.

Owen: My mom and Charlie are homebodies. They've done some traveling, but they prefer to be right here on Gansett, close to their families and their grandkids. My father was released from prison about four years ago. We have no idea where he is, and we like it that way. As long as he stays far, far away from us, all is well.

Congratulations on the beautiful life you've created for yourselves.

Owen: Thank you!

These two... still entertaining us six books in...

"I'll take a shower so fast I'll be back before I'm gone." Mac stole a quick kiss and headed for the stairs, stopping halfway up. "Where are my children?"

"With my mother and Ned until dinnertime."

"God, I love you so much."

Maddie laughed as he bolted up the remaining stairs and disappeared. She thought about going upstairs to meet him after his shower but decided it would be far more fun to make him come after her. Sure enough, he came flying down the stairs less than five minutes later, with a towel wrapped around his waist, his dripping-wet hair standing on end and a small spot of blood on his chin from where he'd nicked himself shaving.

"You're a mess," she said, laughing as she held out her arms to him.

Smelling of soap and sexy man, he came down on top of her and sighed with relief when she hugged him. "I know. I can't help it. Waiting for this day has made me nuts."

She combed her fingers through his hair, attempting to bring some order. "Good thing I love you even when you're a messy nut case."

That drew a smile from him. "So, what did David have to say?"

"Everything looks good."

As she'd expected, he scowled darkly. "You're damned right it looks good. I hate the idea of that guy having his face... *there*."

Once again, she held back a laugh at his ridiculousness. "He's a *doctor*. Seen one, seen them all."

"That's crap. Yours is way better than most. I should know. I did a lot of shopping before I bought."

"Mac!" She sputtered with laughter as she smacked his shoulder. "*Oh, my God!* I can't believe you said that! You're *outrageous*. Don't forget 'that guy' saved your daughter's life."

"I'll never forget that, but it doesn't mean I want his face in my wife's hoo-ha."

She squished his lips together before releasing them. "You really need to stop talking now."

"Why? Is there something else you'd rather be doing?"

"Definitely." She kissed him fully, deeply, letting him know exactly what she'd rather be doing.

MARIE FORCE

Longing *for* Love

Book 7: Longing for Love
Published: September 18, 2012

All his training never prepared him for this kind of shock and ahhhhh…
Series favorite Tiffany Sturgil steals the spotlight in *Longing for Love* as her new boutique Naughty & Nice opens in downtown Gansett, right in time for the annual spring Race Week festivities. Finally divorced and ready for a new beginning, Tiffany wonders if sexy Police Chief Blaine Taylor thinks of her as often as she thinks of him since their explosive encounter last fall. Back then, he directed her to call him the second she was officially divorced, but the opening of her store and her unconventional advertising "campaign" have put the island's lingerie queen at odds with the town's top cop. Despite their clashes, when these two finally get together after months of steamy buildup, readers will need to keep a fire extinguisher close at hand!

Blaine has been burned in the past by love affairs gone wrong, and he's wary about risking too much too soon. But he quickly discovers that Tiffany's sarcastic rejoinders and bitter outer shell hide a badly wounded heart of gold. He also discovers she's a "sex-toy fraud" and convinces her she can't possibly sell the merchandise without trying it out first… While he finds himself thinking of her all the time, the mayor is after him to curb her sexy advertising and his mother worries that Blaine has taken on another "project" who will break his heart.

As Blaine and Tiffany fight for their happily ever after, readers' favorite characters from past books are back for more island adventures. Joe and Janey return to Gansett for the summer and discover the big secret his mother has been keeping. Evan learns that Grace hasn't told her parents about him. Stephanie's restaurant is ready to open in the renovated Sand & Surf. Dan keeps showing up to "visit" Kara at work, Mac is worried about Maddie's upcoming meeting with her deadbeat dad and a Race Week catastrophe reminds everyone what's really important.

Gansett Island takes a decidedly erotic turn in this seventh book! If hot, sexy men in uniform cavorting with hot, sexy women who sell sex toys for a living aren't your thing, this book might not be for you!

Main Characters:

Tiffany Chester Sturgil, owner of Naughty & Nice boutique, mother of Ashleigh Strugil, ex-wife of Jim Sturgil.

Blaine Taylor, chief, Gansett Island Police.

*Indicates recurring throughout the series

Supporting Characters:

Patty, clerk, Naughty & Nice.

Wyatt Abrams, patrolman trainee, Gansett Island Police.

Josh Harrelson, sound engineer in Nashville.

Mr. & Mrs. Ryan, Grace's parents.

Evelyn, secretary, Gansett Island Police Department.

Mona, executive assistant to Mayor Chet Upton.

Chet Upton, mayor, Gansett Island.

Verna Upton, wife of Chet.

Jim Sturgil, ex-husband of Tiffany Sturgil, father of Ashleigh Sturgil.

Kara Ballard, manages a launch service in the Great Salt Pond from McCarthy's Marina.

Dan Torrington, celebrity defense attorney, writing a book about working to free unjustly incarcerated individuals.

Captain Seamus O'Grady, involved with Carolina Cantrell in SEASON FOR LOVE.

Mac McCarthy, Jr., married to Maddie Chester in FOOL FOR LOVE, father of Thomas McCarthy in MAID FOR LOVE, father of Hailey McCarthy in FALLING FOR LOVE.

***Maddie McCarthy,** mother of Thomas, married to Mac McCarthy in FOOL FOR LOVE, mother of Hailey McCarthy in FALLING FOR LOVE.

***Daisy Babson,** housekeeper, McCarthy's Gansett Inn, friend of Maddie's.

***Truck Henry,** Daisy's abusive boyfriend.

***Libby,** volunteer paramedic, manager of the Beachcomber Hotel.

***Dr. David Lawrence,** medical director, Gansett Island Clinic.

***Victoria,** nurse practitioner/midwife, Gansett Island Clinic.

***Rebecca,** owns the diner in South Harbor.

***Linda McCarthy,** grandmother of Thomas McCarthy in MAID FOR LOVE and Hailey McCarthy in FALLING FOR LOVE.

***Billy Weyland,** owner, Island Gym.

***Carolina Cantrell,** involved with Seamus O'Grady in SEASON FOR LOVE.

***Janey McCarthy Cantrell,** married to Joe Cantrell in READY FOR LOVE.

***Joe Cantrell,** married to Janey McCarthy Cantrell in READY FOR LOVE.

***Big Mac McCarthy,** grandfather of Thomas McCarthy in MAID FOR LOVE and Hailey McCarthy in FALLING FOR LOVE.

***Steve Jacobson,** captain of sailboat *Shadow Dancer.*

***Laura McCarthy,** manager of the Sand & Surf Hotel, engaged to Owen Lawry and mother of Holden Newsome in SEASON FOR LOVE.

***Mason Johns,** chief, Gansett Island Fire Department.

***Owen Lawry,** engaged to Laura McCarthy and stepfather of Holden Newsome in SEASON FOR LOVE.

***Holden Francis Newsome,** Laura's son with ex-husband Justin Newsome, stepson of Owen Lawry, born in SEASON FOR LOVE.

***Sarah Lawry,** Owen's mother.

***Charlie Grandchamp,** Stephanie's stepfather, freed from prison in HOPING FOR LOVE, working at the Sand & Surf Hotel in SEASON FOR LOVE.

***Francine Chester,** grandmother of Ashleigh Sturgil, Thomas McCarthy and Hailey McCarthy in FALLING FOR LOVE, engaged to Ned Saunders in FALLING FOR LOVE.

***Ned Saunders,** engaged to Francine in FALLING FOR LOVE.

Mrs. Taylor, Blaine's mother.

***Stephanie Logan,** engaged to Grant McCarthy in SEASON FOR LOVE.

***Grace Ryan,** involved with Evan McCarthy in HOPING FOR LOVE.

***Sydney Donovan,** married to Luke Harris in SEASON FOR LOVE.

***Jenny Wilks,** lighthouse keeper.

***Grant McCarthy,** engaged to Stephanie Logan in SEASON FOR LOVE.

Dylan Torrington, Dan's late brother, Army ranger killed in Afghanistan.

***Evan McCarthy,** owner of Island Breeze Records in SEASON FOR LOVE, involved with Grace Ryan in HOPING FOR LOVE.

***Shane McCarthy,** estranged husband of Courtney McCarthy.

***Luke Harris,** married to Sydney Donovan in SEASON FOR LOVE.

***Linc Mercier,** commander, Coast Guard Station, Gansett Island.

***Royal Atkinson,** Gansett Island Town Councilor.

***Chloe Dennis,** owner of Curl Up & Dye Hair Salon, South Harbor.

Places:

- **Naughty & Nice,** owned by Tiffany Sturgil in South Harbor
- **Island Breeze Records,** studio opened by Evan McCarthy on Gansett Island
- **Island Gym,** South Harbor
- **Stephanie's Bistro,** owned by Stephanie Logan in the Sand & Surf Hotel
- **Sand & Surf Hotel,** reopens in LONGING FOR LOVE
- **Curl Up & Dye Hair Salon,** owned by Chloe Dennis in South Harbor

Gansett Island Soundtrack:

- "Hotel California/Hotel Sand & Surf"

66 LONGING FOR LOVE Headlines:

- Grace hasn't told her parents about Evan!
- Jim threatens to ruin Tiffany and her new store!
- Blaine saves Daisy from a domestic assault!
- Seamus resigns from the ferry company because he can't be with Carolina!
- Kara agrees to go with Dan to Stephanie's grand opening!
- Seamus is in love with Carolina! She agrees to consider talking to Joe about what she wants!
- Blaine buys furniture for Tiffany!
- Big Mac will be with Maddie when she sees her father!
- An outbreak of stomach flu hits the island!
- Steve Jacobson needs a replacement crew for Race Week!
- Meet Fire Chief Mason Johns, Coast Guard Commander Linc Mercier and Chloe Dennis, owner of the Curl Up & Dye Salon!
- Charlie asks Sarah out!
- Stephanie's Bistro opens in the Sand & Surf Hotel!
- Tiffany is being evicted from her store!
- Blaine cares for Tiffany when she has the stomach flu!
- Laura has the flu, too!
- Blaine's mother doesn't approve of his new girlfriend!
- Dan and Kara sleep together!
- Carolina tells Joe she's in love with Seamus!
- Joe and Seamus work things out!
- Maddie sees Bobby and asks him to give Francine a divorce!
- The boat Steve, Dan, Mac, Evan and Grant are on is hit by a freighter in the fog!
- Steve has been killed, Mac, Evan, Dan and Grant are later rescued!
- Kara will take care of Dan while he recovers!
- Blaine defends Tiffany and her store at the town council meeting!

Eight months after SEASON FOR LOVE...

Tiffany Sturgil is excited to open her new shop, Naughty & Nice, on Ocean Road, but is afraid people won't accept a lingerie-and-novelty store on stuffy Gansett Island. She's also concerned about what her ex-husband, Jim, will have to say about it. She unveils the stunning new sign for her store and takes the paper off the windows to reveal her beautiful new business, a badly needed fresh start after a painful divorce. She's thinking about several explosive encounters with sexy Police Chief Blaine Taylor, as she contemplates jump-starting her social life once she gets the store open. She also needs to get some furniture to replace what Jim took when he moved out.

When she returns to the shop the next day, she discovers that someone shot paintballs at her white storefront, brand-new sign and the window displaying her inventory. She changes out of her opening day outfit into a French maid's costume to paint over the damage.

Watching from across the street, Blaine wants to repair the damage before she saw it, but that's the old Blaine. The new Blaine isn't taking on any "projects." But he wants to see what she does about the damage to her store. When she appears in the skimpy French maid costume with a roller and a can of paint, Blaine nearly swallows his tongue. Then she gets to work, and he's reminded of the night he saw her naked after she handcuffed herself to her deadbeat ex-husband.

Blaine is about to go have a word with her when two cars crash in front of the store. He tries to get her to go inside, but she shakes him off, determined to cover the paint splotches and get on with her grand opening. He reminds her of the town's decency laws, and she tells him to write her a ticket. She has work to do. He says she caused an accident, and she argues that the drivers who weren't watching where they were going caused it. When she lets it slip that she's also selling sex toys in the store, Blaine's head is about to explode. Tiffany realizes her sexy outfit is getting more attention for the store than anything else she could've done. Maybe she should do some "creative marketing."

No one can believe what Tiffany is selling in her store, even her own sister and mother, but she's undeterred. After three hours with no customers, she realizes she's being snubbed. She changes into a naughty nurse outfit and goes outside to drum up business. Blaine, who's watching from across the street, sees her come out in the racy outfit and decides she's going to be the living death of him. He's seething with jealousy at the reaction she's getting from cars driving by. He doesn't want anyone seeing the woman he already thinks of as his. He hears his mother's voice warning him of another "project," after being taken advantage of by women in the past. He's heartbroken for Tiffany when she goes inside hours later, defeated at not having attracted a single customer. He's going to do something really stupid.

Grace's judgmental parents show up at her apartment and encounter shirtless Evan, the boyfriend they don't know she has. Grace is surprised that they walked into town from the McCarthys' hotel. "There are other ways to lose weight besides going under the knife," her mother says. Evan invites them to dinner, and after they leave, he wants to know why Grace never told them about him. Grace explains that they ruin everything for her, and she didn't want them to ruin Evan for her, too. Evan says that no one could ever do that, and he gets why she keeps them at arm's length.

Tiffany is shocked and terrified that no one came to her store. Everything she has is invested in her new business. Failure isn't an option. She gets home to news that Dan Torrington has finalized her divorce and custody arrangement for Ashleigh. All she wants is to snuggle her daughter, but it's Ashleigh's weekend with Jim. While she's sad about the failure of her marriage, she knows she did everything she could to make it work. She thinks about Blaine and how she was supposed to call him the minute she was divorced, but she's too dispirited to do anything but take a bath.

When the doorbell rings, she finds Blaine at her door and wonders if he's come to gloat. He's worried she'd be upset about the reception to the store. She tells him she's fine and things will pick up. She realizes he wants her desperately. He asks if she's divorced yet, and she tells him she is as of that day.

"We had a deal," he says.

"I wasn't sure you'd still want to hear from me."

"I think about you *way* more than I should," he confesses.

If he comes in, they'll end up in bed. She invites him in.

He doesn't like the skimpy outfits she wears outside the store and doesn't want anyone else to see how sexy she is. They have the hottest sex of their lives. Blaine never spends the night with a woman, but he can't bring himself to leave her. The next day, Tiffany goes to work with more energy than she should have after a nearly sleepless night with Blaine. Since they have no customers, she gives her assistant, Patty, a makeover. Patty hopes the makeover will help her get a boyfriend because she's never had one. She's thrilled with the results.

When Blaine comes to visit, Tiffany tells Patty to take a long break. He wants to be her first customer, if he's not too late. Unfortunately, he's not too late. He pretends to be shopping sexy things for a newish woman in his life. He goes to see what's behind the beads in the second, smaller room and emerges scandalized. She has to explain each item and answer all his questions. She's about to die from mortification—and desire.

He wants to know if she's played with the items, and she says, of course she has. How could she sell them otherwise? He doesn't believe her and wants her to pick out things for them to play with together so she can tell her customers about them. Hearing that her daughter won't be home until the next day, he tells her he'll be done with work at eleven-thirty and gives her instructions on what to wear and what position to be in on the bed when he arrives, legs apart, ceiling fan set to high. They need a safe word in case she wants to stop whatever they're doing. Before he leaves, they have another sexy encounter in the back room of the store. Blaine discovers that the town's lingerie queen wears white cotton underwear. He suggests she take a little nap when she gets home because they're going to be up late—again.

When Blaine gets to work, he learns the mayor wants to see him. Mayor Chet Upton wants Blaine to do something about the distraction Tiffany is causing outside her store. Blaine defends Tiffany, saying there's nothing he can do and that she's within her rights, so the mayor puts the matter on the town council agenda to possibly reconsider her business license. He tells Blaine to keep control of the situation outside the store or else. Blaine tells the mayor not to threaten him, or he'll quit—the mayor needs Blaine more than Blaine needs the mayor. As he leaves, the mayor tells him to get a haircut.

The mayor's wife, Verna, comes into Tiffany's store and becomes her first real customer. The spark has gone out of Verna's marriage, and she needs some help. Tiffany realizes the mayor's wife might be her most important customer ever and tells her she's come to the right place.

As Tiffany is leaving the store, Jim confronts her, asking what she thinks she's doing, peddling filth and acting like a common tramp. Listening to him spew his vitriol, she's thrilled to discover she doesn't love him anymore. She lets him know she's now got something to compare him to in the bedroom and knows what she's been missing out on. He vows to do everything he can to ruin her. Despite her bravado with Jim, she's scared he might succeed in shutting down her business. When she gets home, she falls asleep in the one chair in her living room, exhausted by the constant battles in her life.

Blaine finds her there instead of where he told her to be, and understands something is wrong. He needs to stick to the sex and not get overly involved, but she touches him. He wants to know what upset her. She tells him about Jim and his threats. Blaine doesn't like her creative marketing any more than Jim does, and he might have to "punish" her if she keeps it up. She's not at all threatened by him. He tells her to go upstairs and assume the pose he asked for earlier. Things between them are even hotter the second night they spend together.

She decides *naughty* will be her safe word, and they play with the things he bought at the store. He tells her the mayor is putting the issue of her store on the agenda for Monday's town council meeting. Blaine refused the mayor's order to cite her for indecency. She's worried about him endangering his job for her, but she's also ridiculously pleased that he stood up for her. He suggests she cut out the creative marketing until after the meeting.

"How will people know what I'm selling in the store?"

"Trust me, honey," he says, laughing, "they'll know."

In the morning, Mac asks Evan to help him at the marina for a few hours. Evan is worried that Grace hasn't told her parents about him and isn't sure what it means that she hasn't. It's Race Week on Gansett Island, and everything is super busy, including the marina. Evan is glad that his friend Josh from Nashville has decided to accept the sound engineer job at the new studio. He talks to Mac about Grace not telling her parents about him. He's worried that she's ashamed to be shacked up with a loser who doesn't have a real job. Mac says he's not a loser. He had a tough thing happen with his record company going bankrupt, and he needs to cut himself a break. Mac also encourages Evan to talk to Grace about why she didn't tell her parents about him. Evan thinks Mac and Maddie make it look easy, but it's not. She wants to see her deadbeat father, so he'll give her mother a divorce, but Mac doesn't want her subjected to him after the way he hurt her by leaving when she was five. They've been fighting about it.

Stephanie is still running the marina restaurant while she works on getting her own restaurant up and running at the Sand & Surf Hotel. Mac tells her they can hire someone else to run the marina restaurant, but she's got it covered. They're all looking forward to the opening of Stephanie's restaurant.

Kara Ballard's launch service is now operational in the Salt Pond, but she's annoyed that Dan Torrington keeps showing up at the marina. Why won't he take the hint and go away? He pays her to take him on a boat ride and nearly falls overboard when his silly loafers slide across the deck. She knows his type—cocky and entitled—and doesn't want to be interested in him, but she can't help being intrigued. She's never been to LA, where he lives, and he says she should visit sometime.

Seamus comes by the apartment to speak to Grace about how he's fallen in love with a woman who doesn't want to be with him. She can't believe that any woman wouldn't want him. He tells her she's sixteen years older and he works for her son. Joe's mother? Grace is shocked. He hasn't seen Carolina since Luke and Sydney's wedding, and it's killing him. Grace puts a comforting arm around Seamus, and that's what Evan walks into when he comes home. She invites Seamus to stay for dinner, but he has to go. Evan wants to know what was going on, but Grace is annoyed by his attitude. He wants to understand why she didn't tell her parents about him. She has a very difficult relationship with them, which is why she wanted to keep her relationship with Evan private. They ruin everything for her.

Seamus's heartache over Carolina is so intense that he's thinking about resigning from his job and leaving Gansett. He returns to the ferry landing to find Carolina waiting for Joe and Janey's boat to arrive. He tells her he's missed her just as Joe brings the boat into port, and his mother can't take her eyes off her beloved Joe. She's chosen her son over a relationship with Seamus. At least he has his answer, and he knows what he has to do.

Blaine attends a cookout at Mac's, hoping to run into Tiffany. He's called to a domestic disturbance at Daisy Babson's house and breaks in just in time to keep her drug-addict boyfriend, Truck, from killing her. She's transported to the clinic, where David and Victoria tend to her, and Maddie comes to be with her. David is relieved that Janey plans to have her first child in Ohio, so he won't be involved in delivering his ex-fiancée's baby. Daisy tells David that Truck tried to rape her, and she only wants him to treat her. David and Victoria perform a rape kit.

The next morning, Maddie, exhausted after being up all night with Daisy, runs into Tiffany and takes her to breakfast at Rebecca's diner. Tiffany has received her final divorce papers, and Maddie is planning to see their father to clear the way for their mom and Ned to get married. Tiffany blurts out that she slept with Blaine. Maddie is thrilled and wants details.

Blaine is waiting for Tiffany when she gets to the shop. He's sorry their plans for the night before were canceled. He wants to see her later. She has Ashleigh, so he says they'll do it another time. Tiffany wonders if he doesn't want to be around her daughter. After he leaves, Verna Upton returns to say that the advice Tiffany gave her worked to spice up her marriage. She asks Verna to encourage her husband to take the matter about the store off the town council's docket. Verna will take care of it.

Seamus tells Joe he's resigning. Joe is crushed. Seamus has been such a huge asset since he joined the company two years ago. A personal matter has made it impossible for Seamus to stay on the island, and he's clearly devastated, but doesn't want to talk about it. Joe has counted on Seamus to run the business while he is in Ohio with Janey. What will he do without him?

Dan is waiting for Kara when she returns to the dock. He's brought lunch and a Diet Mountain Dew for her. She tells him she's not interested in him. No kidding, he says, laughing. He asks her to go to Stephanie's restaurant opening with him, and she declines. She feels like he's playing some sort of game with her, and she doesn't know the rules. She tells him her ex dumped her for her sister, and now they're married and expecting a baby. He caught his fiancée in bed with his best man two days before the wedding. After sharing confidences with him, she agrees to go to Stephanie's party with him.

Linda McCarthy visits Tiffany's store and buys a robe and a vibrator. Tiffany is very good at what she does, and Linda predicts she'll be a smashing success. Linda will tell her friends. Tiffany appreciates the support of her sister's mother-in-law. Her assistant Patty arrives, having given her appearance significant effort. Still no boyfriend, Patty reports. Kara comes into the shop looking for something to wear to Stephanie's party. She confesses she's going to the party with Dan Torrington, and Tiffany says she so admires his career. Kara doesn't know what she means. Tiffany shows her search results featuring Dan's illustrious career freeing unjustly incarcerated people. Kara wonders why he never told her that when he was trying so hard to impress her.

Blaine hears from Billy, the gym owner, that Truck has hired Jim Sturgil to represent him. Of course, Jim would take the case of a man who attacked his girlfriend. While on routine patrol, Blaine notices a sign for an estate sale at the former home of Mrs. Ridgeway. He buys new furniture for Tiffany, even as he worries he's taken on another project. But she's different. She's not looking to him to solve all her problems, which makes him want to help her.

While Maddie and Thomas are at Tiffany's, Blaine's delivery arrives. Tiffany is stunned by Blaine's gift and his sweet note that says he finds himself thinking about her all the time. After Ashleigh is in bed, Blaine shows up with a pizza that he calls a peace offering. He figures she might be mad that he changed the rules of their sex-only relationship. The furniture is the nicest thing anyone has ever done for her. It made him happy to do it. Tiffany realizes this is already a relationship, whether she's ready for it or not.

Blaine asks to see Ashleigh sleeping. She's as pretty as her mother. He'd like to get to know her, if that's okay with Tiffany. Assured that Ashleigh is asleep for the night, they take some time for themselves. Blaine brings a blindfold and cuffs to her bedroom and makes her crazy with his creativity. Later, he tells her that everything is different with her because she's not out to get anything and everything she can from him the way women in the past have been.

David stops to check on Daisy on his way home from the clinic. She's embarrassed that she "let" the man she loves hurt her this way. David reminds her that none of it was her fault. He checks her ribs, and she offers him some of the food her friends have brought. She asks why, even when he smiles, his eyes are sad. He tells her he's made some big mistakes and has regrets about them. She thinks it matters that he tries to be a good person, despite his mistakes.

Carolina is making Joe's favorite dinner for him and Janey. She's thrilled they're staying with her for a few more days before moving back to Janey's house. Grant and Stephanie have bought a house and will be vacating Jancy's house. They talk about Carolina coming to Ohio when the baby is born. Joe doesn't seem as enthusiastic about his favorite meal as usual. He tells them Seamus leaving because of a personal matter that's made it impossible for him to stay on the island. Carolina has to know if it's because of her. The minute Joe and Janey are in bed, she'll go find out.

Sometimes, Blaine hates being the police chief, especially when he's wrapped up with Tiffany and has to deal with his phone. He never ignores a call. It's his mother trying to find out who he's buying furniture for and hoping he's not getting himself into another situation with a woman that'll end badly for him. She tells him to come by the next day. Blaine wants Tiffany he to meet his mother. He doesn't want to talk about the women who did him wrong. It's ancient history and doesn't matter because he's so over them. He asks if she's over Jim, and she says, "Definitely." She tells him about her father leaving when she was three and how she recently saw him for the first time since then. They both admit to being happy when they're together. Then Ashleigh wakes up sick.

Tiffany sees Ashleigh through two rounds of vomiting and a fever. Blaine waits for her to come back to bed and says he should go so Ashleigh doesn't find him there. It could cause her trouble with Jim. Tiffany doesn't care about Jim, but Blaine doesn't want him hassling her.

Carolina waits until she's sure Joe and Janey are asleep to drive into town to confront Seamus at the Beachcomber, where the company keeps a room for him. She asks him why he quit, and he says, "You know why."

"You can't do this! You love that job. Isn't that what you said?"

"'Tis indeed what I said. I do love it."

"Then *why?*"

"Caro…." He runs his fingers through his auburn hair, over and over until it stands on end. "Do I really have to spell it out for ya?"

Her stomach begins to hurt as she takes in his tortured expression. "I guess you do."

"I'm *in love* with you. If I can't have you, I can't be here. 'Tis that simple."

She shakes her head and holds up her hands, as if to protect herself from the surge of longing his words inspire in her. "You… We… We spent *one* night together. How in the world did you turn that into *love?*"

"Damned if I know. Some things just *are.* There's no explaining them."

"Seamus, please. You can't do this to Joe when the baby is due so soon."

His amiable expression hardens. "'Tis all about poor Joe, isn't it? *Poor Joe* will find someone else. No one is irreplaceable. Especially me."

Carolina has said the worst possible thing by pleading Joe's case. After all, Joe is the primary reason she's kept her distance from Seamus.

"I'm sorry," she says. "I know you can't run your life based on what's best for Joe—or me."

"Are you *serious*? I'd rearrange my entire existence for the chance to be with you. I'd do it gladly for you, Caro. Not for Joe, but for *you*."

"I don't want you to go."

"Let me ask you something."

"What?" she asks hesitantly.

"If there was no Joe, would you give me a chance?"

"That's a foolish question. He's my *son*, my heart and soul. No matter what I might want for myself, he'll always come first. Always."

"And what do you want for yourself, love?"

"That doesn't matter. The day his father died, I made a promise to him that I'd always be there for him, no matter what."

"And you have been. You've made him the center of your life for thirty-seven years. Now he has a life of his own, a good life that satisfies him greatly. Do you think he'd want any less for you?"

She shakes her head. "He'd never understand this. He'd never understand *us*."

If there's no changing her mind, then she should just go, he says. Before she leaves, she says she'll talk to Joe and tell him what she wants.

"Don't do it so I won't quit the business," he says.

"This has nothing to do with the business," she assures him.

Seamus is elated that they might have a shot after all.

The baby kicking wakes Janey. She suggests she take a year off from school to be with the baby and give Joe time to figure out a new plan for after Seamus leaves. The closer she gets to having the baby, the more concerned she is about balancing motherhood with veterinary school. After Joe goes back to sleep, she gets up and catches Carolina sneaking back into the house. Janey is alarmed to realize her mother-in-law has been crying. Carolina tells her about Seamus. Janey is shocked. The reason Carolina couldn't say anything is that Joe won't approve of his mother being with a man two years older than him. Janey promises to be there when Caro talks to Joe about it.

Big Mac is worried about Mac. Thomas has the stomach flu, and Maddie is insisting on seeing Bobby, her deadbeat father, so her mother can marry Ned. Mac doesn't want her anywhere near the man who hurt her so badly. Mac and Maddie have been fighting about it. She won't let Mac go with her because she doesn't trust him to behave. Big Mac offers to go with her.

Steve Jacobson is in town for Race Week. His crew is down with the stomach bug. He asks Mac and Big Mac to help him round up a fill-in crew.

Blaine stops by Tiffany's store with Wyatt to find out how Ashleigh is feeling. He finds out from Patty that Tiffany is home sick with the same bug Ashleigh has. Wyatt is wowed by Patty. Blaine calls to check on Tiffany and offers to stop by later to check on her. He tells her Wyatt asked Patty out. We meet Gansett Island Fire Chief Mason Johns when Blaine checks in with Laura at the Sand & Surf to make sure they're ready for the hotel's reopening. The Sand & Surf is cleared to reopen. Laura isn't feeling well, and Blaine tells her that a stomach bug is going around. Blaine asks Sarah Lawry if she might be willing to visit Daisy, to talk to her about breaking the cycle of abuse and offer her support. While he's there, he notices something may be brewing between Sarah and Stephanie's stepfather, Charlie Grandchamp, who works at the hotel.

Sarah has a world-class crush on the gruff ex-con. They've been paying attention to each other during the months of working together at the hotel. Charlie asks Sarah if she'd like to go to the restaurant opening with him. Owen overhears Charlie ask her out. Sarah wants to know if her son approves.

"Jeez, you certainly don't need my permission to go out with a guy."

"I don't?"

"Mom, come on…"

"You know he was in prison, right?"

"Everyone knows that."

"And it doesn't matter?"

Owen thinks about what he wants to say. When he finally brings his gaze back to meet hers, Sarah aches at the pain she sees in his eyes. "For so long, you were married to a man the whole world thought was a hero, when he's the one who should've been in prison. It doesn't matter to me what baggage Charlie might be dragging around behind him. We've all got our share. All that matters to me is that he treats you with the respect you deserve."

"Owen…"

He puts his arms around her.

Sarah rests her face against his chest and holds on tight. "I don't know how you did it, growing up the way you did, but you're a man any mother would be proud to claim as her son."

"You had an awful lot to do with that."

Owen can't wait until she's divorced from his father, and the trial where she has to testify against him is over.

Tiffany wonders if she's dying from the stomach flu when someone pounds at her door. She signs for a letter from Jim's law firm letting her know she's being evicted from her store because her rent check bounced. Patty deposited the store's money into the wrong account. Tiffany asks her mom to come and get Ashleigh. Then she calls Dan to ask for help dealing with this latest mess. Ned goes with Ashleigh to supervise her packing for a sleepover. Blaine walks in and stops short when he sees Tiffany's mother there.

"Something you want to tell me?" Francine asks.

Blaine says he'll be with Tiffany while she's sick, which makes Francine feel better about leaving her alone. Ashleigh comes downstairs and says hello to Blaine, who asks if it's okay for him to keep an eye on her mommy while she is sick. Ashleigh is fine with that, and Tiffany exhales.

Blaine is on call, which means he needs to be near his home phone, a rule he set for his island-based officers. Can he take Tiffany to his place? A girl could fall madly in love with a guy like him. Dan calls and says he'll be happy to deal with Jim for her—and no charge because the guy annoys him. Blaine is furious to hear about Jim's latest stunt and wonders what the hell is wrong with him. She is the mother of Jim's child. Tiffany so appreciates Blaine's outrage on her behalf.

Kara is thrilled with the sexy red dress she bought at Tiffany's store and the return of some of the self-confidence she lost when her sister stole her boyfriend in the "big betrayal" two years earlier. Dan appears at her door, looking gorgeous. He's brought flowers for her. She's rendered him speechless, which doesn't happen very often. He likes making her laugh.

Three of Stephanie's servers are down with the stomach flu, so she recruits Grace, Jenny and Sydney to fill in for the grand opening of her restaurant. Sydney tells them she saw a doctor on the mainland about having her tubal ligation reversed. She's a good candidate. She and Luke are talking about it, but she's worried about bringing another child into the world when she lost her first two in an accident. Would she be in a panic the whole time?

Grant brings Stephanie's dress and engagement ring to her at the restaurant. It's been months since he proposed, but they haven't planned a wedding. He's so proud of what she's done at the restaurant. She appreciates that he bought the rights to her story, which gave her the money to chase her dream.

"Thank you," she says. "My whole life changed the day I met you. I had no idea it was possible to be this happy."

Her happiness makes him happy. Mac has asked him to sail the next day to fill in for Steve's ailing crew, which is fine with Stephanie because she needs to get some sleep before the restaurant's public opening in two days.

Sarah is excited and nervous about spending time with Charlie and having feelings for him after what she's been through with her soon-to-be ex-husband.

Blaine settles Tiffany in his bed while he does some work and watches the Red Sox game. When she wakes up, water and crackers sound good to her. She's worried about what she must look like. He says she's always beautiful, even when she's sick. He likes being with her—even when there's no chance of sex.

Owen wakes Laura to feed Holden after she's been asleep for hours. She's bummed to be missing Stephanie's grand opening party. Shane, Charlie and Sarah are showing off some of the hotel's new rooms to party-goers. He tells her his mom is on a date with Charlie. Owen is worried about Sarah getting hurt again. They suspect it'll be more than one date with those two.

Dan tries to play it cool with Kara. She compliments his Porsche, which he realizes might've been a mistake as it makes him look like the pretentious fool she already thinks he is. He decides to tell her the truth. It belonged to his brother Dylan, an army ranger who was killed in Afghanistan. Having the car makes Dan feel closer to his only brother. Kara is so sorry for his loss. She asks why he didn't tell her the true story about his work. He didn't want to seem arrogant. Far too late for that, she says, making him laugh.

Blaine falls asleep with Tiffany and wakes to someone at his door. His mother has come to throw cold water on his new romance. She's furious that he bought furniture for Tiffany and that one of her friends is calling Tiffany's store the House of Dildos. She reminds him how he lost his last job because of a woman. Blaine tells her he's a grown man, and Tiffany is good for him. After she leaves, Tiffany appears and would like to go home. She overheard the conversation with his mother. He doesn't care what anyone else thinks. Being with her feels good. He's unnerved when she says nothing. That's not like her.

Stephanie's grand opening winds down to her closest friends on the deck for a nightcap. She thanks everyone who helped her, especially Charlie. She's so glad to get to work with him and be with him every day. She thanks Big Mac and Linda for keeping her on at the marina restaurant while she got her own place ready to open, and thanks Grant for everything. Mac, Grant, Evan and Dan are going to crew for Steve the next day.

Stephanie is intrigued when Charlie follows Sarah inside and doesn't come back. Everyone is worried about Laura's brother Shane and how quiet he is. They love how Kara takes no crap from Dan. Grant assures Stephanie that he never misses LA and is right where he wants to be. He's thrilled to see her dreams coming true.

Charlie and Sarah walk out to the South Harbor breakwater. He opens up a little about Stephanie's mother and what they went through when she was using. Her accusations put Charlie in prison for fourteen years, when it was Stephanie's mother who abused her, not him. He tells Sarah to never to be afraid of him. She's not sure she can do that, and she's not ready to tell him about her past. That's okay with him. She never has to tell him if she doesn't want to.

Tiffany is reeling from the things she learned about Blaine from his mother. He lost a job because of a woman. Every man leaves her. Why would he be different? She's mad at herself for falling in love with him. He finds her crying in the bathroom and draws her a bath. They have sex, and she wants to tell him she loves him, but not until she's sure he won't leave. He asks why she was crying. She's afraid that people who don't approve of her will talk him out of wanting to be with her. That's not going to happen, he assures her. He nearly went crazy waiting for her to be free of Jim. He's not going anywhere.

Dan's not ready to go home yet. Kara suggests a boat ride on the Salt Pond. She irritates him by telling him a guy named Robert, in town for Race Week, asked her out. She wanted to see how tonight went with Dan before she gave Robert an answer. Kara and Dan have sex in the dark on the floor of the boat after he makes her promise she won't hate him in the morning. She won't. After, she invites him back to her place to get more comfortable.

Joe wakes up to Janey telling him his mother needs to tell him something, and he needs to listen and not overreact. He's nervous about whatever it is, but as long as she's not sick, he promises to be reasonable. Carolina is the personal reason for Seamus giving his notice. He's shocked to hear that she and Seamus have feelings for each other, and she didn't pursue them because of him. He's got to go. Where? Anywhere. Janey and Carolina go after him.

Since Carolina's visit the night before, Seamus is trying not to get his hopes up. After bringing the ferry into port at Gansett, he finds Joe sitting behind the desk in the office.

"Love is love, Joe. I love your mom. I want to be with her. I want to make her happy and take care of her. How is that any different from what you feel for Janey?"

"She's a lot older than you, for one thing."

"Is she?" Seamus asks, feigning shock. "I had no idea!"

"Stop trying to be funny. This isn't funny."

"Stop acting like a little boy who's miffed because his mum got a boyfriend behind his back."

Joe is furious. "I'm not doing that!"

"Don't you want your mum to be happy?"

"Of course I do! But what happens a few years down the road when you decide being with an older woman isn't working for you anymore? Or you want kids of your own? What happens then?"

"What happens a few years down the road when you decide being with Janey isn't as great as you thought it would be?"

"That'll never happen! I love her with everything I am. What does that have to do with what we're talking about?"

Seamus smiles as the realization settles into Joe's expression and demeanor.

"You love her that much?" Joe asks in a whisper.

"I love her that much."

Janey and Carolina arrive, relieved that Joe didn't hit Seamus.

Carolina focuses on her son. "Are you going to be able to live with this?"

"You haven't given me much choice."

"Actually," Seamus says, "that's not true. You know as well as I do that if you disapprove or express your disappointment or in any way seem put out by it, she'll throw me over like yesterday's news. So, it does matter. If you're going to do any of those things, I, for one, would appreciate you doing them now before this goes any further."

"I'm not going to do any of those things."

"Are you sure?" Seamus asks. "You don't get to change your mind in a week or a month or a year."

"Neither do you," Joe says pointedly.

Seamus, who understands what Joe is saying, nods in agreement. "Neither do I."

"It might take me a while to get my head around it, but I won't stand in the way." To his mother, he says, "I'd never want to be the cause of your unhappiness. I hate that you thought I would."

Tears fill Carolina's eyes as she hugs him. "Thank you."

"Caro?"

She pulls back from her son and turns to Seamus.

"Come here."

Joe nods and squeezes her shoulder.

Carolina takes a couple of halting steps toward Seamus.

He holds out his arms to her. "Come to me."

She seems hesitant to get close to him with her son and daughter-in-law watching, but Seamus knows it's vital that she take this first, most important step in front of them.

"It's okay, love," he whispers. "Everything's going to be okay now."

They told Joe, and nothing bad happened. Now they have all the time in the world to spend together.

Dan, in bed with Kara, wants to weep when the alarm goes off at six a.m. She says thanks for a great night, but she's not interested in anything more. He's stunned and hurt by her coldness when she promised she wouldn't hate him in the morning. He wishes he hadn't agreed to go sailing so he could stay and work things out with her, but he has to leave.

Carolina wakes up to realize Seamus never went back to work the day before. He called in one of their other captains to cover for him so he could stay with her. He asks if she's prepared to deal with people who won't understand what she's doing with a much younger man. After getting her to admit she loves him, he wants to marry her and have everything with her. She needs to think about it.

Tiffany is relieved that Dan worked things out with her landlord to provide a new check and assured the landlord it won't happen again. The landlord told Dan it was Jim's idea to begin eviction proceedings. Of course it was. Dan tells Jim he's considering relocating to Gansett and opening his own practice. As the island's only lawyer, Jim doesn't take that news well. He orders Jim to leave Tiffany alone, or they'll sue him for defamation.

Maddie and Big Mac wait on her deck for Bobby Chester to arrive. She's a nervous wreck, but Big Mac reminds her that she's strong and resilient, no thanks to her deadbeat father. Bobby wants to say he's sorry. Maddie asks why he left. He says he wasn't cut out for family life, but he loved them.

"You've seen me. Give my mother the divorce and let her be happy."

"Is that the only reason you saw me?"

"Yes."

Blaine connects Sarah and Daisy, who bond over their shared experience with abusive partners. He talks to Sarah about his mother not approving of Tiffany. While he's with Sarah and Daisy, Blaine gets a call from Linc Mercier, commander of Coast Guard Station, Gansett Island, telling him that one of the Race Week sailboats collided with a freighter in the fog with one confirmed fatality. Islanders were on the boat, and he needs Blaine's help figuring out who they might be.

Blaine goes first to McCarthy's Marina to ask Big Mac who might have been on the boat. When he tells him why, Big Mac lets out an agonized howl. Three of his boys are on that boat—Mac, Grant and Evan—along with Dan Torrington and the captain, Steve Jacobson. Luke and Blaine stop Big Mac from going out in the fog to look for them. It's too dangerous.

Someone needs to tell Linda, Maddie and Grace. Stephanie is working at the marina restaurant and breaks down upon hearing the news. Kara hears the shocking news when she comes to work at the marina. She was just with Dan.

Laura buys a gift for Sarah's birthday at Tiffany's store. As they talk about Blaine, she realizes he may be reticent with words, but he more than makes up for it with actions. Francine finally comes in to see the store and is very complimentary of what Tiffany has created. She tells her she heard Royal Atkinson, town councilman, is determined to address the issue of the store at the next meeting. Tiffany is disappointed to hear that Verna didn't get that taken care of for her. Bobby comes into the store, wanting to see Tiffany. Francine tells him to get lost and smacks him across the face. Ned comes in and says someone should've smacked him a long time ago. He tells him to get lost.

"Who are you to tell me what I'm gonna do?" Bobby asks.

"I'm the man who loves Francine and her girls as if they's my own, and I've had just about enough of yer happy horseshit."

Listening to Ned tell off her father, Tiffany realizes two very important things: She loves the man who loves her mother, and she loves Blaine—with her whole heart. As soon as she gets the chance, she'll tell him so. Her mother is right—if she lets fear drive her away from Blaine, Jim wins. She can't let that happen. After Bobby leaves, Tiffany tells Ned they love him, too. Tiffany and Patty don sexy sailor outfits in honor of Race Week and go outside to drum up business.

Blaine has the dreadful job of notifying Grace, Linda and Maddie about the accident. He finds Linda at the Curl Up & Dye Salon, where owner Chloe Dennis is doing Linda's hair. Linda pulls the foils out of her hair and leaves to be with her husband. Chloe will drive her. Blaine walks the two blocks to Tiffany's store and finds her parading around outside in the sailor suits with Patty. Infuriated, Blaine cites her for public indecency. Tiffany tears up the citation right in front of him. Mac and his brothers are missing. That's what he came to tell her. She lets him drive her to Maddie's as long as he's not going to tell her how to run her business. They'll talk about that later.

Everyone gathers at the marina awaiting word of the missing men during an endless day. Big Mac and Linda call Adam in New York to tell him his three brothers are missing. While they wait for news, Blaine takes advantage of the opportunity to ask Royal why he's hassling Tiffany when they have so many bigger problems to contend with on the island. He tempts Royal with talk of the store being a tax-generating gold mine. They can't take the matter off the agenda because it's already been advertised to the public. Blaine was afraid of that.

Ashleigh asks Blaine if he likes her mommy, and he says he does. He's smitten with both of them, but he has to do something about Tiffany strutting around town half-naked.

Mac calls Maddie to tell her he's okay, and so is Evan. The captain, Steve, was killed on impact, and they're still looking for Grant and Dan. All Kara can think about is what an awful bitch she was to Dan that morning. He freaks her out with his intense interest in her. Blaine offers to drive Tiffany and Ashleigh home, and they run into Jim, who's not happy to see Blaine carrying Ashleigh. Tiffany taunts him and makes sure Jim knows they're together. He says Blaine can't leave with *his* family.

"They're not your family anymore," Blaine reminds him. "You saw to that."

Grant and Dan are found, hypothermic and injured but alive. Blaine shares the news with the euphoric family waiting at the marina and rounds up EMS support to meet the injured men when they're brought in. As he drops off Tiffany at home, he tells her he needs a minute to think about things. She's devastated that he might be changing his mind about them. He tells her she has to stop prancing around in skimpy outfits in public if she wants Royal's support at the meeting. She thinks Blaine is the one who wants her to stop. Blaine gets a call from the fire chief, Mason Johns. He has to go.

Blaine works all night dealing with the aftermath of the accident. David asks if he knows Kara Ballard. Dan Torrington is asking for her. Blaine goes to the barn near the marina, where Kara lives, and offers to drive her to the clinic to see Dan. Kara can't believe he's really asking for her. After he drops her at the clinic, Blaine heads home to get some sleep and figure out what he's going to do about Tiffany.

At the clinic, Kara hugs Stephanie, who's tending to Grant. Dan is pale and bruised, but alive. Dan is in a lot of pain from broken ribs and Grant saved his life about fifty times when they were in the water. She apologizes for treating him badly the previous morning. He knows it was because she was freaking out about having sex for the first time since her epic breakup. Thinking about her and their night together got him through the rough day. She'll be there to care for him while he recovers.

Days pass without a word from Blaine while Tiffany helps out with Maddie's kids and helps with Mac, who's a horrible patient. Tiffany talks to Mac about Blaine. She's surprised to hear he drove Mac crazy, asking when her divorce would be final. Mac tells her about the women he was involved with, one of whom was dealing drugs while he was on night duty as a police officer. By the time he could prove he wasn't involved, his reputation was ruined, and he lost his job. The Gansett council knew about that and made him serve a probationary period before they gave him a long-term contract. That's why he can't have another girlfriend ruin things for him, she realizes.

When he comes into Mac's house looking tired and stressed, Tiffany realizes she'll never love anyone the way she loves him. She talks to Maddie about how she can't be a supporting character in another relationship. She won't let him tell her what to do. They need to compromise, Maddie advises. Maddie and all their friends will fight the council's interference in Tiffany's business.

Mac helps Blaine see that he's in love with Tiffany. He knows what he has to do.

Tiffany arrives at the council meeting wearing her most demure dress. She's stunned and overwhelmed when Maddie, Mac and all their friends show up to support her. Dan is out of bed and limps in to be there to help her if she needs it. Jim glares at her, as if he can't wait to defeat her. When the council questions her, she defends her store and has decided to change her advertising strategies. People speak for and against her. while Blaine bides his time in the back. Linda McCarthy speaks in favor of the store.

"I wanted to raise my daughter here because of the values this town has always had," Jim says. "Lately, however, I have to question whether this is the best place for her to live." He glowers at Tiffany. "She's just doing this to spite me for leaving her—"

That's it, Blaine decides. *I've heard more than enough.* He plucks the microphone from its stand.

"What do you think you're doing?" Jim asks indignantly. "It's my turn."

Into the microphone, Blaine says, "It was your turn. Now it's mine. You want to talk about values, Sturgil? What kind of man lets his wife work two jobs to put him through law school and then leaves her when the money starts rolling in?"

Jim's eyes bug out of his head, and for a moment, Blaine wonders if Jim might be stupid enough to hit him. He really, *really* wishes he would.

"What kind of man asks his very nice wife for a divorce, moves out of the house and takes all the furniture, leaving the wife who put him through law school *and* his young child in an empty house?"

Jim's fist rolls into a ball, and Blaine gives him a challenging look that dares him to go for it. Assaulting a police officer could get him disbarred, which Jim well knows.

"Sit down, Sturgil," the mayor orders.

"You heard the mayor," Blaine says. "We've *all* heard enough out of you."

Everyone sitting behind Tiffany whoops and claps. Blaine doesn't dare look at her, or he might lose his nerve. To the council, he says, "This whole thing is ridiculous. For better or worse, the town approved Ms. Sturgil's application, and now you've got to live with it. She has the same right to make a living here that all of you do. She's an accomplished businesswoman who has run two successful businesses on this island for years. She pays her taxes just like everyone else. This is a witch hunt because you're all afraid of something different. To you, this is about sex toys and sexy nighties. To her, it's about food on the table and a roof over her child's head."

"She's caused at least one accident on Ocean Road," one of the councilmen reminds him.

"How was that her fault? Was she driving the car? Did she take her eyes off the road and run into another car? We cited the driver who caused the accident, not her."

"She caused a distraction."

"And she's said she won't do that anymore."

"I'm ready for a vote," the mayor says.

Blaine glances toward the back of the room, pleased to see that everyone is in place. "Before the council votes, I'd like to remind you that you represent the citizens of this town. It might be helpful to gauge where the citizens stand on this matter. With the election coming up in November, I'd think you'd want to be sure you're following their wishes."

After some whispered discussion among the council members, the mayor says, "I'll allow that. With a show of hands, how many are opposed to the Naughty & Nice shop remaining open?"

Quite a few hands are raised, including Jim's and Blaine's mother's in the back of the room.

"And how many are in favor of the shop remaining open?"

All the hands on the side of the room where Tiffany is sitting go up, along with the hands of every police officer, firefighter, first responder, paramedic, ambulance driver and the guys Blaine works out with at the gym. He even got Linc and some of the officers from the coast guard station to come into town for the meeting.

Blaine finally allows himself to look over at Tiffany and catches the exact moment when she realizes what he's done. Her eyes widen when she sees the men and women in uniform lining the back wall, casting their votes for her.

With their help, she has more than enough votes to sway the council.

"Motion to table the matter of the Naughty & Nice store indefinitely," Royal says.

"Second," one of the others says.

"All those in favor?" the mayor asked.

All seven members vote "aye."

After they celebrate the big win, Blaine and Tiffany share a nice moment with Blaine's mother, who invites Tiffany and Ashleigh to dinner. Tiffany tells Blaine to leave his door unlocked, and she sneaks in late at night to handcuff him to the bed, the way she tried to do with Jim. This time, she's sure of how she'll be received.

"Thank you," she whispers. "Thank you so much for risking your job and your career and your reputation and your mother's wrath to stand up for me. No one has ever done anything like that for me before."

"No one has ever loved you as much as I do."

She didn't see that coming and stares at him, almost waiting for him to take it back. "You do?"

Nodding, he says, "For a very long time now, I suspect."

"I love you, too. For probably just as long."

"Now that you have me," he says, smiling suggestively and tugging on the cuffs, "whatever will you do with me?"

She makes him promise he'll never leave her and never use his badge to bully her, and he agrees. He wants everything with her, and she wants the same thing.

 An interview with Blaine and Tiffany

You two nearly set Gansett Island on fire with your incendiary romance back in the day.

Blaine: We were hot from the start. Still are.

Tiffany: Hush. No one wants to hear about that.

Um, yes, we do. Let me ask you this... How's the ceiling fan?

(Blaine laughs while Tiffany hides behind her hand.)

Blaine: We're on our third one.

Tiffany: You didn't have to tell them that.

Yes, he did. We love you two! What's your favorite memory from those early days together?

Blaine: For me, it was finding out she was officially divorced, and we were free to be together. By then, I felt like I'd waited forever for her.

Tiffany: My favorite moment was when Blaine sent the furniture he bought at the estate sale. We had that for years, and I cried when we replaced it with new pieces. That was the moment I knew he was for real, and I was well on my way to falling in love.

Blaine: I think I fell in love that first night, after you ended up in my jail and I took you home.

Oh yeah... The kitchen counter encounter...

Tiffany: You know far too much about what went on between us.

LOL, that's my job! Tell us about the kids!

Tiffany: Ashleigh is sixteen and full of beans.

Blaine: To my horror, she looks exactly like her mother, and the boys are flocking around like bees to honey.

Tiffany: My girl doesn't suffer fools. She holds them all at arm's length while she studies dance, plays the piano and hangs out with her girlfriends.

She's still best friends forever with her cousin Thomas. They're so cute together.

Do you ever tease them about Naked Boy, Naked Girl?

Blaine: (laughing) Not if we want them to speak to us. They prefer to forget that ever happened.

Whereas we'll never forget.

Tiffany: No, we won't. Our Addie is twelve and such a delight. She's also big into dance and is so good with her little brother. Adrian is nine and loves to be with his cousins. They're the best of friends, and the wrestling matches are epic.

I can't even imagine… Are you teaching dance again?

Tiffany: I am! I keep the store open during the season, and I run the dance studio during the school year. It's been so fun to teach our girls, our nieces and friends' daughters—and a few of the boys, too. The studio is as busy as the store.

How's life as the police chief, Blaine?

Blaine: Insane in the summer as always. Manageable the rest of the year. I still enjoy it for the most part, but I entertain thoughts about retiring more than I used to.

What would you do if you weren't the police chief?

Blaine: Mac wants me to work with him in the construction business. Sometimes I dream of not being responsible for the safety of everyone on the island.

Tiffany: I'd be down with that. It can be a lot at times.

Does Ashleigh know what she wants to do after high school?

Tiffany: She's interested in possibly pursuing the law in some way. She's looking at colleges from North Carolina to Boston. When I think about her living off-island, I get a little twitchy. But she's excited, and I'm trying not to let my anxiousness dampen her enthusiasm.

How's that going?

Blaine: Day by day. We can't picture life without her here, bossing us all around and taking care of her siblings and cousins.

The last time we saw Ashleigh, she'd just lost her dad. How has she coped with his death?

Tiffany: It's been a process for sure, but she's much better these days. We still talk about him all the time, and she's close to his parents. They're getting on in years, and she's very good about visiting them and spending time together. We're proud of how she navigated such a big loss so early in her life.

Thank you for sharing your life today with us. We wish you many more happy years together!

NEW YORK TIMES AND USA TODAY BESTSELLING AUTHOR

MARIE FORCE

Waiting *for* Love

Book 8: Waiting for Love
Published: January 10, 2013

Sometimes the best offense is a good rebound…

Adam McCarthy has had a really bad week. In addition to nearly losing his three brothers in a tragic boating accident, his now ex-girlfriend double-crossed him out of the successful computer company he founded in New York City. What he needs is a few days at home on Gansett Island to make sure his beloved brothers are safe and to get back in touch with what really matters—his family, his friends and the tiny island that soothes his battered soul. On the ferry ride home, he runs into an old family friend who's had her own share of heartache, and Adam helps her through some rough moments, sparking an unlikely alliance.

Abby Callahan has come home to Gansett, single once again, after her relationship with Dr. Cal Maitland blew up in her face. After two epic failures in the game of love, she's decided this is going to be the summer she busts loose and finally has some fun—and she's shaking things up in a big way! The new Abby swears, drinks, gets a tattoo, sleeps around and generally does anything her kinder, gentler alter ego wouldn't have dreamed of doing.

Before too long, Adam has appointed himself her guardian and is determined that the only sleeping around she's doing is with him. That is… unless his brother Grant is willing to risk his newfound happiness with Stephanie to keep Adam from rebounding with his ex. And what happens when Adam and Abby realize their summer fling has taken a serious turn, especially when he gets the chance to return to New York and fight for the company that's rightfully his? Abby has already followed two men off the island. Does she have it in her to find out if the third time really is the charm?

Another wild summer on Gansett Island is underway, complete with new stories for many of your favorite couples from past books! You'll also see more of Dan and Kara, David and Daisy, and find out whether Carolina has made peace with her relationship with the much younger and very sexy Irishman, Seamus O'Grady. Ready? Set? Let's go back to Gansett Island!

Main Characters:

***Adam McCarthy,** owns computer company in New York City.

***Abby Callahan,** owner of Abby's Attic, ex-girlfriend of Grant McCarthy, ex-fiancée of Cal Maitland.

***Indicates recurring throughout the series**

Supporting Characters:

***Janey McCarthy Cantrell,** married to Joe Cantrell in READY FOR LOVE.

***Grant McCarthy,** engaged to Stephanie Logan in SEASON FOR LOVE.

***Aunt Joan,** Linda's sister.

***Linda McCarthy,** grandmother of Thomas McCarthy in MAID FOR LOVE and Hailey McCarthy in FALLING FOR LOVE.

***Carolina Cantrell,** involved with Seamus O'Grady in LONGING FOR LOVE.

***Captain Seamus O'Grady,** Involved with Carolina Cantrell in LONGING FOR LOVE.

***Ned Saunders,** engaged to Francine Chester in FALLING FOR LOVE.

***Francine Chester,** grandmother of Ashleigh Sturgil, Thomas McCarthy and Hailey McCarthy, engaged to Ned Saunders in FALLING FOR LOVE.

***Rebecca,** owner of diner in South Harbor.

***Luke Harris,** married to Sydney Donovan in SEASON FOR LOVE.

***Mac McCarthy, Jr.,** married to Maddie in FOOL FOR LOVE, father of Thomas Chester McCarthy in MAID FOR LOVE, father of Hailey McCarthy in FALLING FOR LOVE.

***Big Mac McCarthy, Sr.,** grandfather to Thomas McCarthy in MAID FOR LOVE and Hailey McCarthy in FALLING FOR LOVE.

***Laura McCarthy,** engaged to Owen Lawry and mother of Holden Newsome in SEASON FOR LOVE.

***Maddie McCarthy,** mother of Thomas, married to Mac McCarthy in FOOL FOR LOVE, mother of Hailey McCarthy in FALLING FOR LOVE.

***Hailey McCarthy,** daughter of Maddie and Mac, sister of Thomas McCarthy, born in FALLING FOR LOVE.

***Grace Ryan,** involved with Evan McCarthy in HOPING FOR LOVE.

***Evan McCarthy,** involved with Grace Ryan in HOPING FOR LOVE.

***Josh Harrelson,** sound engineer at Island Breeze Records.

***Alex Martinez,** landscaper, co-owner of Martinez Lawn & Garden, brother of Paul.

***Paul Martinez,** landscaper, co-owner of Martinez Lawn & Garden, brother of Alex, member of Gansett Island Town Council.

***Dr. Cal Maitland,** Abby's ex-fiancé.

***Carol Callahan,** Abby's mother.

Sasha, Adam's ex-girlfriend and business partner.

***Victoria,** nurse practitioner/midwife, Gansett Island Clinic.

***Dr. David Lawrence,** medical director, Gansett Island Clinic.

***Dr. Kevin McCarthy,** psychiatrist, brother to Big Mac and Frank.

***Daisy Babson,** housekeeper at McCarthy's Gansett Inn.

***Laura McCarthy,** engaged to Owen Lawry and mother of Holden Newsome in SEASON FOR LOVE.

***Owen Lawry,** engaged to Laura McCarthy and stepfather of Holden Newsome in SEASON FOR LOVE.

***Sarah Lawry,** involved with Charlie Grandchamp in LONGING FOR LOVE.

***Charlie Grandchamp,** involved with Sarah Lawry in LONGING FOR LOVE.

***Chelsea,** bartender at the Beachcomber.

***Tiffany Sturgil,** mother of Ashleigh, involved with Blaine Taylor in LONGING FOR LOVE.

***Blaine Taylor,** chief of Gansett Island Police, involved with Tiffany Sturgil in LONGING FOR LOVE.

***Holden Francis Newsome,** Laura's son with ex-husband Justin Newsome, stepson of Owen Lawry, born in SEASON FOR LOVE.

***Cissy,** bartender at Stephanie's Bistro.

***Duke,** tattoo artist

***Jeff,** tattoo artist

***Joe Cantrell,** married to Janey McCarthy Cantrell in READY FOR LOVE.

***Rebecca,** owner of Rebecca's Diner.

***Doc Potter,** veterinarian.

Rick Levinson, Adam's attorney.

***Marion Martinez,** owner of Martinez Lawn & Garden, mother of Alex and Paul, widow of George Martinez.

***Shane McCarthy,** divorced from Courtney McCarthy.

***Judge Frank McCarthy,** grandfather of Holden Newsome.

***Betsy Jacobson,** mother of Steve, who was killed in the boating accident.

***Dan Torrington,** involved with Kara Ballard in LONGING FOR LOVE.

***Kara Ballard,** involved with Dan Torrington in LONGING FOR LOVE.

📍 Places:

- Shore Point Road, location of Grant and Stephanie's home.

- Southeast Light, lighthouse on the southeast side of the island.

- Island Breeze Records, Evan's studio, near the Southeast Light.

- Martinez Lawn & Garden, owned by the Martinez family.

- Computronic Solutions Incorporated, Adam's company in New York City.

66 WAITING FOR LOVE Headlines:

- Abby and Cal have broken up!

- Adam lost his business in NYC!

- Something is up with Grant after the boating accident!

- Carolina tells Linda she's seeing Seamus!

- Introducing Marion, Alex and Paul Martinez!

- Janey takes a year off from school to stay home to have her baby!

- Surprise! Laura and Owen are expecting twins!

- Evan and Grace get engaged!

- Sydney is having tubal ligation reversal surgery!

- Steve Jacobson's mother, Betsy, has come to visit the McCarthys!

- Grant is tormented that he couldn't save Steve *and* Dan!

- Abby is going to rent Janey's house in town!

- Adam sells his business and comes home to Gansett to be with Abby!

"I'm absolutely, positively, totally and *completely* done with men. Done. Done. *Done.*" With that statement, Abby Callahan makes her last stand on a crowded noon ferry to Gansett Island, where she grew up. She's chased two men, one to Los Angeles and another to Texas, and is no closer to the marriage and children she craves than she was ten years ago.

Adam McCarthy is sitting near her on the boat and recognizes the voice but can't place it. She's slurring her words as if she's been drinking. The seas are rough, and Adam has enough of his own problems. He isn't about to take on someone else's. When the woman behind him gets seasick, he turns to see who she is and is shocked to see his brother Grant's ex-girlfriend, Abby.

He escorts her outside to get some air and asks when she started drinking. She's done being a good girl because what good has that done for her? She's going to drink and party and swear like a sailor and have sex with strangers. Adam thought she lived in Texas with her fiancé, Cal Maitland, now. Not anymore, she replies as he notices she's not wearing an engagement ring.

He's had a hellacious week with a nightmare at work that resulted in him losing the company he founded, followed by the news that his three brothers were missing after a sailboat accident.

Abby walked away from a successful business, Abby's Attic, to follow Cal to Texas after his mother had a stroke, for all the good that did her after she found out Cal still had feelings for his ex-girlfriend. As she rants, Adam encourages her to test out some of her new swear words, but he doesn't think she can have sex with strangers.

"How do you know? You don't know me at all."

"You dated my brother for ten years."

"He didn't know me either. I've never had the real deal. Have you?"

He thought so until recently, when his girlfriend screwed him out of his own business when the board found out they'd been seeing each other outside of work. The best part is he's the only one who knows anything about how to do the actual work. There's no way they can run the place without him. Abby is upset to hear about the accident that nearly cost Grant his life. They've been broken up for a while, but to hear he could've died…

She's so upset that Adam finds himself hugging her and noticing what a sexy, curvy, beautiful woman his brother's ex is. He has to remind himself that this is *Abby*, his brother's first love. Hands off. They agree to keep each other's secrets. She's staying at the Beachcomber, so she doesn't have to hear her mother say she was right about Abby chasing after another man, only to have it not work out. She tells Adam to come by if he wants to talk, since they don't plan to tell anyone else their tales of woe. He'll be at his parents' house if she needs him. When the ferry lands, he helps her get her luggage across the street to the Beachcomber.

In town, he's happy to see the Sand & Surf reopened and notes the sign for Stephanie's Bistro, opened by Grant's fiancée. Adam stops to see Janey, who's hugely pregnant and emotional to see him after they nearly lost their three brothers in the accident. She's glad he's there because she's having trouble registering for fall classes, and maybe it's a sign that she's not meant to go back to school when she's due to have a baby around the same time. She wants to be a mom.

Adam tells her not to make any big decisions while she's pregnant and helps her navigate the website. He saw her good friend Abby on the ferry and thought she might need a friend since things with Cal are finished. Janey is worried about Grant—he's not bouncing back after the accident. Adam will stop to talk to him while she goes to see Abby at the Beachcomber. Adam is surprised to find Grant still sleeping at one in the afternoon. His brother looks like hell. Something is way off with him, and it's weird that Grant doesn't want to talk about it when he loves to talk things to death.

Abby is settled in a room at the Beachcomber, bemoaning the loss of her adorable shop that would've been booming during Race Week. And she's mortified about crying all over Adam McCarthy on the ferry. She questions why she came back to Gansett, where everyone will know she's a two-time loser in love. She's sad about Cal and how happy they'd been on the island, but it had fallen apart when they were in his Texas hometown. She'd rather be alone than overlooked by the man she loves.

When Janey comes by to see her, Abby sobs all over another friend. This was why she came home to Gansett. For every vicious gossip, there are five real friends who'll help her put her life back together. She left without a word to Cal, which surprises Janey. Laura is looking for someone to run the gift shop inside the Surf. Maybe Abby could talk to her about that. The idea sparks some interest in Abby. She plans to focus on herself for a change. This will be her summer of rebellion. Janey is worried about Abby getting hurt, but Abby assures her friend that she'll be fine.

Adam is seriously worried about Grant, who was hailed a hero for saving his friend Dan Torrington's life after the sailboat accident. As he walks through town, his Aunt Joan mistakes him for Mac, which has been happening all his life. He rushes to get home before his aunt can tell his mother he's there, but they're on the phone when he arrives. He has an emotional reunion with his mother and promises to check on his brothers, who've accused her of hovering since the accident. Linda agrees that something isn't right with Grant, and even Stephanie isn't sure what to do. Big Mac is having nightmares about the accident and waking up in a cold sweat. Linda is so happy to have Adam home and tells him to invite everyone to dinner while she meets Carolina for lunch. After the trauma of being screwed out of his business by the woman he thought he loved, Adam is relieved to be home with the people who love and respect him.

Linda and Carolina talk about the accident and how close they came to catastrophe. Linda wants to reach out to Steve's mother but wonders what she'd say since her three sons survived. Carolina thinks Steve's mother would welcome hearing from Linda. Carolina tells Linda that the man she mentioned she was seeing last fall is Seamus. Linda is stunned and impressed. Carolina relays the excruciating conversation with Joe about Seamus and how they can be together now that Joe knows. Janey was instrumental in smoothing things over with Joe, and Carolina appreciates her. Seamus wants to get married, but Carolina isn't sure that's the right move. Linda reminds her that scandals come and go, but love is forever. Seamus shows up, looking for Carolina, and makes a big production of kissing her in front of everyone. Amused and intrigued, Linda invites them to dinner.

Seamus and Carolina go back to her house and have hot sex on the kitchen table. She tells him she's sorry if she made him feel like she's ashamed to be with him. She's adjusting to what people will have to say about her being with a much younger man. But she loves him. She should take all the time she needs to wrap her head around it because he's not going anywhere.

Adam visits the marina and learns that Luke is also concerned about Grant. Stephanie needs Adam to fix the computer system at the marina restaurant. She reports that Grant has had little to say to anyone, even her, since the accident. Adam sees Mac and Big Mac, who are thrilled he's home for a visit. He has lunch with them and is shocked by Big Mac's ravaged appearance. Nearly losing three of his sons has been devastating for him. To give his dad something else to think about, Adam tells them what happened with his company.

Stephanie checks on Grant, who says all the right things but is definitely not himself. At the Sand & Surf, she's surprised to see Abby. She and Cal have broken up, and she's back to live on Gansett. Abby is interested in running the hotel gift shop if Laura is still looking for someone. Stephanie is immediately on edge about Grant's longtime girlfriend being back on the market when things are so weird between them. Laura would be thrilled to have Abby run the gift shop.

Maddie is worried about Mac. He's been quiet, moody and withdrawn since the accident. She hates that he's hurting and won't talk to her about it.

"I can't talk about what it was like not to know where my brothers were for hours or how it felt to be almost certain they were dead. I can't talk about that, because if I do…"

Maddie is determined to be as strong for him as he always is for her. "What, Mac? Tell me."

"I'm afraid if I do… I might… I might break into a million pieces that can't ever be put back together again the way they were before."

She places her hand over his fast-beating heart. "I won't let you break. I won't let you. Hold on to me. Let me help."

The sight of his face streaked with tears breaks her heart, but she doesn't let him see that. Rather, she brushes away his tears and traces the outline of his mouth. "I love you so much," she says. "I had a very long day to think about what my life might be like without you, and I hope I never feel that way again. Ever."

"I don't mean to make it all about me. I know it was awful for you, too."

"My awful was nowhere near as awful as yours. You don't always have to be strong for me and everyone else, you know?"

"I don't?" he asks with a small, teasing smile that's far more in keeping with her Mac than the grim countenance he's sported in the last week.

"No, you don't. Sometimes you can let me carry the burden for you."

"You just did, baby." He kisses her softly and sweetly. "Thank you."

Adam takes his dad's truck and goes to check out Evan's new studio, Island Breeze Records. He meets Josh Harrelson, the sound engineer, and catches up with Evan. Adam tells Evan he needs to cut back the brush leading to the studio. Alex Martinez is coming to do it this week. He's back on Gansett after working at the U.S. Botanic Garden in Washington, D.C., because his brother, Paul, needs help running Martinez Lawn & Garden and caring for their mother, who has dementia. Evan is scrambling to get ready for their first artists to arrive and might not make it to dinner at home, but Grace will be there. Adam senses things are off with Evan, too.

Cal starts calling Abby around five. He didn't see the note she left him, so she tells him where to find it. He can't believe she's left him. Abby thinks he has unresolved feelings for Candy, his ex-girlfriend at home.

"I can*not* believe you didn't talk to me about this," Cal says.

"I did talk to you. You said I shouldn't worry about your feelings for her. I don't agree. What's there to say?" She's sorry things didn't work out between them and hopes his mother continues to recover.

Abby's mother, Carol, comes by to get the scoop on why she's home and not staying with her parents. She wishes Abby had learned from the past and gotten married before she chased after Cal. Carol is sorry this happened to Abby, but she's a strong person, and she'll get through it. Enough dwelling on the past, Abby is going out to have some fun.

The McCarthy family dinner is the usual comedy show, and Adam loves every minute of it. He's determined to keep his problems to himself so he can support the others in the emotional aftermath of the accident. He's thinking about his ex-girlfriend and business partner, Sasha, who sold him out. When did things go so wrong between them that she'd do such a thing to him? He has no idea. He'd planned to bring her home to meet his family, and he hates himself for missing her. Big Mac wants to know what he plans to do about the fact that he got screwed out of his company. He's not going to do anything because he doesn't care enough to fight for the business. They owe him a ton of money and have sixty days to pay him. After that, he'll see what's next. He doesn't want his dad fretting over the situation. A few weeks at home will cure what ails Adam, Big Mac says. Sasha texts that she's sorry, that she loves him, that she made a mistake, and that she wants to talk. He has nothing to say to her.

Adam, Mac, Janey and the others find out about Carolina and Seamus. Carolina is so mortified to be "coming out" to the McCarthy kids, who were like extra children to her growing up, that she breaks out in hives. When they leave the dinner early, she realizes Seamus is angry that she's so upset about being there with him that she broke out in hives. After he takes her home, Seamus leaves until she can make peace with the situation. He tells her to call him when she's truly ready to be a couple.

Grant goes to see David Lawrence, needing a prescription to help him sleep. His mind is racing. David asks what he sees when he closes his eyes, which is the one question Grant can't answer. Nothing really, he says, which isn't true. David gives him seven days of sleep medication, but Grant is worried about what will happen after the seven days are up. He's afraid he might have to tell people what really happened after the sailboat accident. "Do yourself a favor and unload on someone," David advises. "Before it eats you alive."

Stephanie arrives at the McCarthy's home and is surprised that Grant isn't there. She has no idea where he is. The family discusses how Evan is burying himself in work at the studio, but Grant isn't working at all. Mac says it was tough out there. Not only were they fighting to survive, but they had hours to wonder what had become of their brothers and friends. Adam offers to go looking for Grant. He assures his mother that his brothers are fine, but she knows better. They're not fine.

Linda calls Big Mac's brother, Kevin, a psychiatrist, and asks for his help. He specializes in posttraumatic stress. He advises giving them some space to process what happened. If they're not doing better soon, Kevin will come out to the island. Adam thinks his dad needs Kevin, too, since he can't talk about the accident without crying.

After Grant leaves the clinic, David makes a note to follow up with him in a few days. He's known Grant a long time and can tell something isn't right with him. When Daisy comes by to bring him food, again, Victoria teases him about his not-so-secret admirer. David says they're just friends, but he can't deny he's begun to look forward to Daisy's daily visits. He asks her to keep him company while he eats.

Adam goes into town looking for Grant and stops at the Sand & Surf, where he finds his cousin Laura lightheaded from recovering from the stomach flu. Laura suggests that Grant might be with Abby, who is back on the island. Since Laura isn't feeling well, Owen takes her upstairs to bed while Adam watches the front desk until Sarah comes down to relieve him. Charlie arrives, and Adam witnesses the spark between Sarah and Charlie. He thought he had that with Sasha, but it turned out to be a lie. Stephanie comes into the hotel and is upset that no one can find Grant.

When she's not working, Kara's routine has become focused on Dan as he recovers from a broken right arm, broken ribs and other injuries from the sailboat accident. Every night after work, she brings him dinner and helps type his book, which is due soon. He's grumpy and out of sorts, and she's wondering if she'll ever see the Dan from before the accident again. They're both afraid to talk about what's going on between them since the accident. They finally discuss that terrible day and how they thought of each other constantly. Dan says he's wanted her from the first time he ever saw her and asks her to go steady.

Big Mac can't stop thinking about how he nearly lost three of his sons. Luke finds him on the main pier at the marina. He knows Big Mac is pissed with him. About what? Big Mac asks. That Luke wouldn't let him go out in the fog to look for the boys that day. They'd nearly come to blows over it. At the time, Big Mac wasn't pleased, but he can see that Luke was right to stand in his way. "You're one of my kids, Luke Harris. I could never be truly pissed at you."

"Shit… You gotta put it that way, huh?"

Big Mac hugs him. "'Fraid so."

Luke returns the embrace and pats him on the back. "Thank God they're all right."

"Yes. Thank God. And thank you. You did the right thing, but then again, you always do. You're a good man, and I'm proud to call you one of my own."

When Luke steps back from him, Big Mac sees a tear in the younger man's eyes. They'd all done their share of weeping lately.

"You can't possibly know how much that means to me," Luke says.

"Go on home to your wife, son. Everything's okay here." And it was, Big Mac thinks, as he watches Luke walk up the pier to the parking lot. Everything is okay. If he keeps telling himself that, someday soon, he might believe it.

Big Mac goes home to Linda, who's worried about Grant. Something big happened out there. They end up in bed, talking about how lucky and blessed they are.

Still looking for Grant, Adam goes to the Beachcomber. The bartender, Chelsea, tells him she hasn't seen Grant. Some of the Race Week sailors are teaching Abby Callahan how to do tequila shots. Adam finds her in a circle of men, wearing a sexy outfit and bright red lipstick. She looks amazing. In all the years she dated Grant, Adam had thought she was pretty, but now… He realizes she's hot. He pushes through the group of men to retrieve her, making up a story about their six children waiting for them. She's mad at him for ruining her fun. She was planning to sleep with one of those guys. "Go home, Adam. I don't need you to save me from myself."

Adam gets a text from Stephanie that Grant is home safely. Abby realizes he's worried about Grant. They all are, he says. He tells her he heard from Sasha, and he's not planning to reply to her. They end up resting on Abby's bed, facing each other as they talk. When she burps—loudly—they lose it laughing. He tells her there's no need for her to become someone else when she's perfect the way she is. "That's very sweet of you to say," Abby replies, "but there's lots of stuff wrong with me. I can't keep making the same mistakes over and over without trying to learn *something* from them. You know?"

He confesses to having inappropriate thoughts about his brother's ex-girlfriend. She admits to having trouble reaching orgasm because she never feels she has a man's full attention. She got very good at faking it. She falls asleep, and Adam sets up her phone so he can track her location to keep her safe from herself. Despite warning alarms from his conscience, he's decided that if anyone is going to help her go a little crazy—in bed and out—it's going to be him.

Owen, who's dreading his father's upcoming trial, helps take care of baby Holden. Laura is still feeling awful after having the stomach bug. A thought occurs to Owen… Is it possible she might be pregnant again? Laura is shocked. Holden is only three months old! She can't be pregnant again. They haven't exactly been careful, Owen reminds her. She'll see Victoria the next day to find out if it's true.

Stephanie keeps a watchful eye on Grant, who's still withdrawn as he sits at the bar at her restaurant, not talking to anyone, which is wildly out of character for him. When they get home, she confesses that she feared he might be with Abby. He didn't know she was home or that she had broken up with Cal. He's hurt that she'd think he'd cheat on her. He loves her, and she shouldn't ever worry about that. Despite his assurances, she's lonely for him and wishes he'd tell her what's weighing so heavily on him.

Abby is mortified and hungover. She can't believe she told Adam about her orgasm issues and that one of the men she complained about was his brother. She wants to die and then finds Adam asleep on the bed next to her. Even while dating Grant, she'd thought Adam was the handsomest of the McCarthy brothers, which is another of her deep, dark secrets.

"I'd like to volunteer to be your partner in crime," Adam says. "We'll do anything you want—in bed or out. Skinny-dipping, motorcycle rides, tattoos, tequila shots, all-nighters and as many orgasms as you can handle. Whatever you want, whenever you want it."

Abby stares at him, incredulous—and intrigued. "You'd get a tattoo for me?"

Adam laughs. "That's the part you're fixating on? Did you hear anything else I said?"

"I heard it."

"And?"

"What's in it for you?"

"Seriously? You're really asking me that?"

"Yes!"

"I don't know if you've looked in a mirror lately, but you're a very sexy woman who's looking to bust loose and have some fun. What red-blooded guy wouldn't want to be a part of that? Besides, I could go for some lighthearted fun after what I've just been through with Sasha and the company."

"And the fact that I dated your brother doesn't factor into this at all?"

"It does. In fact, it's one of my two conditions."

"This I've got to hear."

"Condition one is that we keep our arrangement between us. No sharing the dirty deets with Janey, Laura or anyone else. I don't want Grant to know we're seeing each other until I'm ready to tell him, but only because it might upset him, and I don't want to do that when there's something else on his mind."

"This is a small island. If we're seen together, it might get back to him."

"It might, and if it does, I'll deal with it when and if it happens. In the meantime, I'd prefer to keep it between us."

"Fair enough. What's the second condition?"

His expression turns serious. "I don't share with anyone. If you're seeing me, you're not seeing—or sleeping with—anyone else."

She agrees to his conditions and wants to get the tattoos first. Adam's next thought is *holy fucking shit*, getting a tattoo hurts. Next, she wants to rent a motorcycle. She's mad at herself for not listening to Adam and putting the tattoo somewhere people can see it. They agree that this is just fun, nothing serious. She's worried about causing a rift between him and Grant with their deal. Adam might talk to his brother about it. Adam and Abby share a kiss at the beach that turns hot, taking them both by surprise.

Ned is getting frustrated that Francine hasn't received the divorce papers from Bobby Chester. It's just paper to Francine. They have everything they need. But Ned wants her to be his wife and her girls to be his family. It matters greatly to him. When they finally receive the divorce papers, they learn that Bobby set up college funds for his three grandchildren. Ned wants to invite the family over to celebrate her divorce. Francine says he's the best father and grandfather they ever could've hoped for.

Carolina is trapped in purgatory, wanting Seamus but wrestling with what people will think about her taking up with a much younger man. This whole thing is her own fault. She never should've let him tempt her. She's known from the beginning that he's too young for her, but that didn't stop her from walking straight into the flame of his love, knowing all the while she would surely get burned. And now that she knows what it's like to be with him, to be loved by him, to be consumed by him, how can she resist the life he's offered? How can her mouth continue to say *no* when her heart and soul say yes, yes, *yes*? She can't keep saying no because living without him now would be impossible.

Carolina drives into town to the office where Seamus is meeting with Joe. She asks her son for a minute with Seamus. She tells him she no longer cares what anyone thinks of them. All she cares about is being with him. She asks him to come home with her to stay.

Joe has coffee with Mac and talks to him about his mom and Seamus. Mac advises him to count his blessings and not sweat the small stuff. That's what Mac has been trying to do since the wake-up call of the accident. Doc Potter calls to ask if Joe has noticed that Janey seems to have lost her sparkle. Joe feels bad that he hasn't noticed, but he'll take her to lunch. Doc gives her the afternoon off. Joe and Janey go home for lunch, and he tells her Doc gave her the afternoon off because he's worried about her.

Janey doesn't want to go back to Ohio and miss everything with the baby while she's in school. Joe suggests she take this year off from school and see how she feels about it next year. He'd like to see her finish, however, because he fears she'll regret it if she doesn't. She agrees. "Thank you—for this love, this life, for understanding what I need. All of it. Thank you."

"God, Janey," he whispers, overwhelmed by her. "It's my pleasure. Every second of it. Thank *you*." He kisses her, and for a long time, he thinks of nothing else but *her* pleasure.

Adam talks to Sarah at the Sand & Surf about the issues they're having with their reservation system that he's going to fix for them. While thinking about the challenge Sarah presented, Adam is hit by a pang of longing for the company he founded and gave his heart to for fourteen years. The loss hits him like a tsunami, overwhelming him with sadness. All at once, he's ready to fight for what's his and calls his lawyer, Rick, who's happy to hear from him. He tells Rick to do whatever it takes to make this right, even if that means discrediting Sasha.

Adam goes to see Grant, who seems better after getting some sleep. He tells Grant he'd like to "hang out" with Abby. Grant says she's not a fling kind of woman and asks if Adam liked her when they were dating. Of course I didn't, Adam says. Grant doesn't want his brother to hurt her. She's had enough hurt. Adam promises to have some fun and do no harm.

Stephanie hears them arguing and wants to know what it was about. Hearing that Adam wants to date Abby, Stephanie feels like she's been punched because Grant was arguing against it. Grant assures Stephanie that he loves *her*, and he doesn't care if Adam dates Abby. He cares if his brother hurts his friend. That's all it is. For the first time since the accident, Grant makes love to her.

Laura and Owen leave the clinic in shock. She's pregnant with twins and is freaking out. How will they have *three babies* while running a hotel? No matter what happens, Owen says, they'll deal with it together. She tells him to have all the sex he can get while she's pregnant because she's never going near him again if he can get her pregnant this easily—and with two babies! She's relieved that Owen, who never wanted a family of his own, is excited about the babies.

Abby is sick of wishing she were different. She's bored with herself and desperately wants to shake up her life. Sleeping with Adam, something she'd never considered before yesterday, will be a good first step. On her way to get another tattoo in a more visible place, she runs into Tiffany and takes a tour of Naughty & Nice, in the same space that used to house Abby's Attic. Tiffany outfits Abby in two weeks' worth of sexy underwear and new dresses. While

Duke gives her a second tattoo, this one on her ankle, she gets to work on plans for the gift shop at the Sand & Surf.

Abby skinny dips for the first time. Adam has been wondering where she is and is feeling jealous and out of sorts as he tries to reach her. Is she out with one of her new guy friends? He runs into Laura, who tells him the news about the twins. Finally, Adam overrules his conscience and checks her location. What the heck is she doing at the beach at night? When he arrives, he sees her floating in a moonbeam, realizes she's naked, and plays a trick on her by taking her clothes. She's furious at his practical joke until they start kissing, and all she wants is more. They head back to her hotel room.

Ned feeds his family to the point of bursting with lobsters. He loves presiding over a family dinner in the home where he lived alone for most of his life. They tell Maddie and Tiffany that they received the divorce papers and that Bobby set up college funds for each of the grandchildren. He enclosed notes with them, and Tiffany cries reading hers. Maddie doesn't want to look at hers. Not now anyway.

Ned clears his throat and works up his courage. "I wanta say somethin' else. None a you kids will ever want for nothin'. I made a lotta money buyin' and sellin' houses over the years and never spent much of it on anythin'. Mac and his siblings are my heirs, but you girls have been added inta my will as well. And yer kids don't hafta wait for me ta kick it to have their college paid fer. If ya don't want the money from yer daddy, send it back to him. Yer kids won't suffer any if ya do. I waited a long, long time to have a family of my own, and there ain't a one a ya that's gonna want for nothin'. That's all. That's what I wanted to say."

Maddie and Tiffany have waited a long time for a dad who takes care of them. They hug him and make him cry. Francine doesn't want to talk about Bobby anymore. She wants to talk about their wedding. Tell me when and where, and I'll be there with bells on, Ned says.

At home, Mac reads Bobby's heartfelt letter to Maddie, who weeps upon hearing that her father always loved her and that he regrets what he did. They give him credit for owning it and not making excuses.

Tiffany reads and rereads her letter, greedy for every word she can get from the father she has no memory of. She asks Blaine when he's going to move in with them. He wants to get married. She just got divorced and isn't ready to talk about getting married again, even though she loves him so much. He'll do this any way she wants, as long as he has as much time with her and Ashleigh as he can get.

While sneaking back into the Beachcomber, with wet hair and clothes, Abby and Adam run into his parents, who haven't heard she was back on the island. Adam tells them she ended her engagement with Cal. Big Mac invites them to have a drink and makes it sound mandatory. Abby runs upstairs to shower while Adam goes into the bar with his parents. Linda wants to know what he's doing with Abby. Big Mac encourages Adam to tell his mother what happened to his business and his relationship. Linda still wants to know what's going on with Abby and what Grant will think of it. Adam has talked to Grant about it. Big Mac doesn't want him to do anything that might lead to a falling out with Grant, especially when things with Grant are so unsettled. "You're playing with fire, son."

"I'm thirty-five years old, Dad. You know I love you both, and I love Grant, too. But this really has nothing at all to do with him—or with you. I'm sorry if that sounds disrespectful, because I don't mean it that way. I'm asking you not to make it into something it isn't. We're hanging out together. That's all it is so far. She's not looking for anything serious, and neither am I."

"If that's the case, you'd be a fool to let it come between you and your brother," Linda says. "I can see risking your relationship with him if it were serious between the two of you, but to just 'hang out,' it doesn't seem worth the risk."

"Let me decide that. I'm asking you to stay out of it and let me figure this out for myself. And please, give me a little credit where Grant is concerned. I'd never do anything to hurt him intentionally, and I'd never let anything come between us. Ever."

Abby comes into the bar wearing a hot red dress, making Adam stare at her with his mouth hanging open. "Just hanging out, my ass," Big Mac says.

The dress does wonders for Abby's self-confidence, even if it is too much for drinks at the Beachcomber with the McCarthys. Adam is blown away by her. He puts a hand on her leg, and she sucks wine into her lungs. At the worst possible time, Cal shows up asking for a minute of her time. He tells her he loves her. Abby is convinced he's in love with his ex-girlfriend Candy. She wants more out of love than what she found with him. She's throwing away a good thing, he says. It wasn't good for me, she replies, hating that her hands are shaking.

Adam is worried about what might be happening with Abby and Cal. Will she decide to give him another chance? And why does it matter so much to Adam if she did? She's beautiful inside and out, and he hates that she feels she has to turn herself into someone new when there's nothing wrong with who she is. When she returns, Adam is dying to know what happened. After his parents leave, she tells him she stuck to her guns and told Cal it's over. Adam is relieved and asks if they can go upstairs. He notices her new tattoo and is proud of her for getting one that people can see.

She looks up at him with those guileless brown eyes. "So your brother knows, your parents know and Cal knows we're really done. Where does that leave us?"

Because he can't live another second without touching her, he puts his arms around her and draws her in closer to him.

Her hands slide up his chest to link behind his neck.

Bending his head, he kisses from her throat to her ear, drawing the lobe between his teeth. "It leaves us alone together in a hotel room with only this astonishing red dress between us."

This night is all about her, about finding out what she likes and needs and wants. "We have all night," he says. "I have nowhere to be and nothing on my mind except you."

Adam already understands what she needs more than anyone else ever has.

David Lawrence finds himself thinking of Daisy frequently. He decides to stop by her house to see if he can take her to dinner. He wants to take her to Stephanie's, but she doesn't have anything to wear there. He's never dated anyone but Janey, so he's off his game, especially when Daisy kisses his cheek. Before this goes any further, he needs to tell her he cheated on Janey.

Grace has given Evan seven days and nights to bury himself in his work before she goes to get him. After she gets him home, he confesses he promised her father he wouldn't propose to her until the studio is making real money. Grace is shocked and speechless.

"*This* is why you've been working like a madman over there?"

"Not the only reason, but the most important one. I'm determined to show him—"

"Stop." Grace blinks back tears as she covers his mouth with her fingers. "Don't say any more. You don't have to show anyone anything, least of all my family or me. You're *everything*. From the first minute you came over to me after that rat bastard Trey abandoned me here without a nickel to my name, you've been my everything. You always will be. I don't care if you're dirt poor and never have another paying job. None of that matters to me, and if you know me at all, you know I long ago stopped letting my parents' opinions matter to me. If I'd continued to listen to them, I'd still be three hundred pounds and as miserable as any person could possibly be."

"Grace…."

"I love you, Evan. I love you exactly the way you are. The studio could be the most successful in the business, and I wouldn't love you any more than I already do."

He proposes to her with a ring he bought months ago. They plan to get married over the winter.

Abby asks Adam if he thinks it's weird that they never thought of each other this way until recently, and now it's all they can think about.

"I think," he says, as he crawls from the foot of the bed to join her, "it's a matter of timing. It's a matter of both of us being in this place and this time and finding something in each other that we need right now."

"That's a nice way to put it."

He doesn't want her to fake anything with him. She comes three times and can't believe it. She realizes she's in big trouble with Adam McCarthy. After she falls asleep, he goes into the shower looking for relief. She joins him and says, "Let me." Abby can't believe what he managed to do when she was with other guys for years, and they never understood her the way he already does. She's going to pester him for nonstop sex, which is fine with him.

Carolina wakes Seamus with kisses. She wants to talk about his mother. He hasn't told her he is seeing someone much older. Carolina wants him to invite his mother to visit them. He has six sisters who've given her sixteen grandchildren, so she's not waiting on him. His two brothers died young, one of cancer and the other from a drug overdose. Carolina realizes he's the last of the O'Grady line. He says he'll invite his mother, but adds, "Don't say I didn't warn you."

Janey calls Abby to invite her to a girls' night out. She gets dressed and goes to find Adam at the Sand & Surf, where she gets to see him looking sexy with his glasses on, working on the hotel's computer system. Laura is sick again, so Adam calls Shane down to cover the desk. He and Abby are going to get breakfast. They're at Stephanie's, holding hands, when Mac and Luke come in. Mac asks for a moment alone with Adam, who says he can't do it right now, so Mac asks him to find him before he leaves the hotel. He wants to know what's going on between Adam and Abby and if Grant knows about it. Adam tells his big brother to butt out. Mac invites Adam to Luke's house for poker while the women are out together.

After Mac walks away, Adam says he's a pain in the ass. "You know he's already on the phone with Grant, telling him we're having breakfast together." Abby worries about causing trouble between brothers who've always been close.

Mac calls Grant, who tells him he already knows about Adam and Abby. "That doesn't bother you?"

"What do you want me to say? I'm engaged to Stephanie. Why would it bother me?" Grant tells Mac not to make a big thing out of it and to leave Adam alone.

"You're ruining all my fun," Mac says.

Mac mentions how they went through the same thing during the sailboat crash, and Grant says that's not true. But he won't tell Mac what's going on with him since the accident, and Mac is frustrated about that. Luke advises him to give Grant some space. He'll talk about it when he's ready. Luke informs Mac he's going to be off-island for a couple of days because Sydney is having tubal ligation reversal surgery. He asks Mac not to say anything about it because they have no idea if it will work.

Laura awakens from a sound sleep to find her dad knocking at the door. Shane told him that Laura is still feeling poorly, and since he had a few days free from court, he's come to see his kids. Laura is frustrated that she's now slept the day away once again while Owen covers for her at the hotel. She tells her dad the news about the twins. She was afraid he wouldn't approve because she and Owen aren't married yet, but Frank is thrilled for them. Owen comes in and shares the news that Adam and Abby are seeing each other. All Laura wants to know is what Grant had to say about it.

Adam finds Abby mapping out her new store at the Sand & Surf. He's impressed by her drawings and how she managed to create a 3-D image of the store. She's looking forward to having the store open. She missed it while she was away and didn't realize how much until today. She'd like to call it Abby's Attic at the Surf, thinking that the customers who patronized the attic might be more likely to check out the gift shop if she gives it a name they recognize. Adam is still working on the hotel's computer system, but he's done for the day and asks if she wants to take a nap before the evening's festivities.

Adam is thinking about Abby far more than he should and asks if she knows how hard it is to write computer code with a gorgeous, sexy woman occupying so much of his attention. He embarrasses her by talking bluntly about how sweet she looked naked. She confesses to another issue she has with sex. She gets so nervous that she has trouble relaxing enough to allow herself to have intercourse. All that means is we need to make sure you're as relaxed as we can possibly get you before we try that, he says. He's so tuned into her that she's afraid she'll fall for him when they said they weren't going to do that. But he's thinking the same thing. They decide to put off having sex until later when they have more time. Abby hopes it'll be easier with Adam than it was with Grant and Cal in the past.

After visiting Laura and her family, Frank spends an hour with Shane and then decides to walk the short distance to his brother Mac's house in North Harbor. He's pleased that Shane is doing better after spending time on the island with his sister, cousins, aunt and uncle. When Frank gets to Big Mac's house, he finds an attractive woman standing outside the gate, looking for Mr. McCarthy. I'm one of them, but this is my brother's home, he says. I'm Frank McCarthy. She's Betsy Jacobson and was hoping to see Mr. or Mrs. McCarthy. Frank invites her in and offers to call them for her. It was her son Steve, who was killed in the sailboat accident. Frank is sorry for her loss.

When Linda arrives a short time later, the two women embrace as if they've always known each other. Betsy appreciates Linda's kindness and the invitation to visit the island where her son lost his life. She's hoping to meet Linda's sons and, if they're willing to share, to hear more about what happened that day. Frank offers to call them. Linda hands him her phone and asks him to send a text. Tell them I'd like them to come to the house as soon as possible, she says. That way, it comes from their mother. Big Mac arrives and tells his brother how hard it's been thinking about what could've happened to his boys. He can't begin to understand what Betsy is going through. He's glad Frank is there.

Abby wakes from her nap in pain from the tattoo on her leg, and Adam admits that his is killing him, too. Before they go their separate ways for the evening, they agree to meet back at her room afterward.

Annoyed by the text from his mother, Grant almost ignores it. He's with Dan, enjoying some time together, when his mother summons her sons home for some unknown reason. Dan asks if he can come along because he's getting tired of looking at his own four walls. Kara isn't coming over until later, so he has time. He tells Grant he might be in love with Kara. Grant shares that Adam is seeing Abby, and it's weird to have his brother dating his ex, but it's been over between them for a long time. Dan and his late brother, Dylan, dated the same girl once, but Dan ended things with Dylan's ex because it was making things weird between them.

Grant says if it makes things weird between him and Adam, it'll also put a strain between Grant and Stephanie because she'll think he's jealous, which he's not. If Grant is being completely honest, he wishes Adam were "hanging out" with somebody else. He has to keep his mouth shut about it or cause trouble he doesn't need with Stephanie. He refuses to be another disappointment to her.

When they arrive at the McCarthys' home, Adam is there and wants to know why he wasn't invited to the summit. Inside the house, Grant finds his parents and uncle Frank talking to a woman he doesn't recognize. When he hears that the woman is Steve's mother, Grant goes into complete denial and turns to run away from the home where he was raised. His brothers chase after him. Mac catches up to him, hugging him so tightly that Grant can barely breathe.

"Let it go," Mac says. "No matter what it is, we love you. We'll always love you."

Grant is sobbing. "No, you won't." He wants so badly to tell them, but he just can't bring himself to do it.

Big Mac shows up and takes over for Mac. "Tell us what has you so upset. Put it out there and get it off your chest."

Surrounded by the unconditional love of his family, Grant can no longer hold back the words that pour forth. The boat, the crash, landing in the water with Dan and Steve both grievously injured, not knowing where Mac or Evan were, and faced with an unimaginable choice: save one of his best friends or save the man he'd only met that morning. He couldn't save them both and save himself, too.

"Oh, my God," Mac says.

"I couldn't save him," Grant says, choking on sobs, "and now his mother is here, and I have to tell her that. I have to tell her I let him go because I couldn't save him and Dan."

Dan has joined them and is stricken as realization sets in.

"I chose you," Grant says. "I chose to save you, and now he's dead, and it's my fault."

The others are sniffling and wiping their eyes.

Dan hugs Grant as best he can with his injuries. "It's not your fault. It's the fault of the ship that hit us, the fog, and the bad luck of being in the wrong place at the wrong time. There was nothing you could've done but survive. You saved my life. It's thanks to you that Steve and I aren't both dead."

Big Mac asks if Grant gives himself any credit for saving Dan.

"I wanted to save them both," Grant says.

"You couldn't," Adam says, "and no one will blame you for reaching for the one who's been your friend for so long, not even Steve's mother."

Grant can't tell her this.

Mac will tell her. "We've got your back. We've always got your back."

Big Mac is proud of Grant. "You saved Dan's life. You saved my life, your mother's and Stephanie's by saving your own. You faced an unimaginable dilemma, and you did the best you could. That's all anyone can ever do." His father's absolution means everything to Grant and brings a measure of peace.

Mac and Evan are astounded that Grant was able to save his own life and Dan's, too, when all they could do was save themselves.

"Let's go in there and face Steve's mom together," Big Mac says. "She wants the truth. She needs the truth. Let's give it to her, and maybe it'll set you free, too."

After hearing the details of the accident, Adam is shaken by how close he came to losing his three brothers. He's heartbroken for what Grant went through. Evan finds him on the porch and tells him that Steve was Betsy's only child. They agree that someone should call Stephanie to tell her what's going on with Grant. They will stay close to Grant and help him through this difficult time. Evan is glad Adam is home, that everyone is home. There was, Adam thought, nowhere else he'd rather be.

Listening to Mac relay the tale of the epic struggle to Steve's mother is the most excruciating thing Grant has ever endured. The poor woman weeps throughout the telling, during which Mac's voice never wavers from the soft, soothing tone he begins with. Everyone in the room is in tears after hearing the story. Grant is so sorry he couldn't save them both. Betsy asks if it's possible that Steve died on impact. Grant doesn't know.

Betsy thanks them for seeing her and for reliving what had to have been a terrible day for all of them as well. Linda asks her to stay for as long as she'd like. "We've got plenty of room, and we'd love to have you." Big Mac adds that the island is a wonderful place to rest and recover. Betsy accepts their kind hospitality. Stephanie arrives at the McCarthy's home and comes in looking teary-eyed.

"Someone called you," Grant says, relieved to see her.

She wraps herself around him and tells him everything he needs to know without saying a word. Grant holds on to her for dear life.

After Grant leaves with Stephanie, Dan asks Mac to take him down to the docks so that he can see Kara. He's reeling after what he learned about the accident and needs to be with her.

Mac encourages him to come to Luke's later to be among friends. "I don't know you very well, but I can guess how I might feel after hearing what you just heard. There isn't much point to beating yourself up over something you had no control over."

Mac reminds Dan of his brother Dylan, always the big brother. Dan misses him, and it's been a long time since he had a big brother. He tells Mac how his brother died in Afghanistan and thanks him for the words of wisdom.

"Anytime you need a big brother," Mac says, "it's one of the few things I've ever been truly good at."

"By whose estimation?" Dan asks.

"My own, of course."

Dan takes the ramp to the launch landing and sits carefully on the bench, waiting for Kara to return, thinking about what he learned from Grant. Kara is shocked to see him there and obviously in pain. He tells her about the emotional discovery of what really happened after the accident.

"I was right up the hill from here, and I wanted to see you. I needed to see you."

She's so sad to hear what really happened and offers comfort. He wants to tell her something right there on the dock where they began: He loves her. She makes a joke about how he hasn't met her sisters yet.

"I don't care if you have a hundred single, fetching sisters, you're the one I want, the only one I want."

"I love you, too, you knucklehead," she says. "I was just testing you."

Abby goes to the Sand & Surf to join the girls' night out with Janey, Maddie, Tiffany, Sydney, Grace and Laura. She meets Jenny Wilks, the lighthouse keeper, who organized the evening. Jenny has something she wants to say to them before she loses her nerve. She updates Abby about how she lost her fiancé in the World Trade Center on 9-11. She doesn't want to chicken out on telling her new friends that she's ready to date again. She's not looking for anything serious, but she's getting tired of her own company, and if they know of anyone who might be fun to go out with, keep her in mind.

Laura whips out a notebook and pen. "We've been waiting a long time for this moment."

Sydney adds, "If you think we won't take this job seriously, you don't know us at all."

They start listing every single guy they know. They put Mason, the fire chief, on the shortlist, as well as Laura's brother, Shane. Laura asks about Adam. Abby wants to tell them he's not available. Laura looks directly at Abby. "I heard Adam might be seeing someone."

Mac told Maddie that Adam is going back to the city to deal with his business. That news hits Abby like a punch. She's determined to keep moving forward with her life regardless of what happens with Adam.

The others talk about how David seems to be seeing Daisy, so he's not available. Grace says she has some news and puts her engagement ring on the table for everyone to see. Laura tells them she doesn't have the stomach bug after all, but rather a case of twins. Then Janey announces that she and Joe have decided to stay on the island this year after the baby is born. She's taking a year off from vet school. They're looking for a bigger home and will be renting out Janey's place in town. Sold, Abby says, thrilled to be renting Janey's adorable house.

Sydney and Luke are going to the mainland so she can have surgery to reverse the tubal ligation she had after her late daughter was born. There's no guarantee she'll be able to conceive again, but the surgery is an important first step. The women drink to good friends, good times and new beginnings.

Two hours later, the guys crash their party. No one could beat Ned at poker, so they were getting bored. They could either join the girls' night out or find trouble somewhere else, Mac says. Abby can't recall an evening she's enjoyed more than this one. Maybe it's the champagne or the excellent company, but suddenly, it doesn't matter that Adam might be leaving or that she's allowed herself to get more involved with him than she planned to. The only thing that matters is right now. Tomorrow will take care of itself.

Grant wakes up after the deepest sleep he's had in weeks. He's sorry that Stephanie missed the night out with the girls to stay with him. He should've told her what really happened before he told everyone else.

"You talked when you were ready to. I'm glad your dad and brothers were there for you."

He's afraid he scared the hell out of them, but Stephanie assures him they were more afraid when he was silent. Everyone considers him a hero for what he did for Dan, but Grant doesn't want that.

"Don't let them say that about me."

Stephanie loves him, and she's so proud of what he did out there. "I'm choosing to focus on what you were able to do, not what you couldn't."

She wishes he would try to do that, too. He agrees to try.

When Adam and Abby return to her room at the Beachcomber, they discuss feelings of envy after being with so many happy couples. Their friends and family have it all figured out and know who they're going to spend forever with. It must be nice to have all the questions answered so definitively.

"I want that," Adam says. "I want the answers to the questions."

Abby does, too.

"Have you considered that this right here might be the answer for both of us?" Adam asks.

She's considered it, but since she only left Cal a few days ago, she's got no business having fantasies about Adam. Before she tells him what she's thinking, he has a confession that might make her never speak to him again. He programmed her phone to share her location with him and felt guilty the minute he did it. He felt worse when he actually used it. He was worried about her and didn't want someone like the guy in the bar taking advantage of her.

"Selfishly, I wanted you all to myself."

She hands him her phone. "Turn off whatever you did and don't use your mad techno skills on me again."

Adam fills her in on what happened earlier with Grant, and she's upset to hear what Grant went through.

Adam wants her to tell him about the fantasy she has that involves him.

"I had this thought about running my new store while you served as the island's resident computer geek."

But he has to go back to his life in New York at some point.

"What if that's not my real life?" he asks. "What if this is? What if you are?"

Abby begs him not to say those things if he doesn't mean them.

"The last few days I've spent with you have been the best I've ever spent with anyone," he says.

He loves that he can be totally himself with her. He wants to make love to her and show her what might be possible. She's afraid of how he makes her feel, of what will happen when he goes, or what will happen if he stays.

"Let's live the fantasy," he says. "For one night, let's pretend it's exactly the way you imagined it."

She looks up at him, so handsome and dear to her, and decides to take a gamble. "Okay."

Adam knows this is much more than a rebound with Abby. He has real feelings for her. He's determined to make this good for her. He sets out to overwhelm her to the point that she's not thinking about anything other than pleasure as he works his way inside her. He says and does exactly what she needs to fully enjoy the moment. She doesn't understand how she's had all kinds of problems with sex, but not with him. She didn't know it could be like that.

"I felt like I was someone else," she says, and wants him to do it again.

Adam's happy to do it as many times as she can handle.

She's got a lot of fake orgasms to make up for.

Abby has found the answers to her most pressing questions. They do it every which way until she's addicted to sex with Adam McCarthy. He's what she's always wanted and had begun to fear she'd never find. But once again, she's ended up with a man whose home and life are elsewhere. She wishes things were different, that he was planning to stay on the island.

He's not sure when he'll have to go back to New York, which is why he didn't say anything about that to Abby. He's decided to fight for his company, which will take months. Until that's worked out, he's right where he wants to be with her. He wakes up more relaxed than he's been in years, with no responsibilities and nothing to think about but her, until his lawyer, Rick, calls with a development in the case.

Sasha resigned the night before. The board has reached out to Adam with a letter of apology and an invitation to return as CEO. They've set a meeting for four o'clock that afternoon in New York, and they'd like him to be there.

"This is moving very quickly, Adam," Rick says. "We've got them right where we want them. This is your chance to return on your own terms." If Adam doesn't wish to return, they still have to buy him out, and they know it, so the ball is in Adam's court. He says he'll be there at four.

He wakes Abby up to tell her he has to go to New York for a meeting about the company and invites her to come with him. She wishes she could, but Laura is counting on her to open the gift shop, and she's got a lot to do. He promises to call, and she asks him not to.

"Let's not make promises we can't keep. It was lovely. I enjoyed every minute we spent together, but let's not make it into something it's not. My life is here on the island, and I can't do another long-distance relationship, not even for you."

He makes her promise not to sleep with strangers. "Don't ever let anyone try to convince you that you aren't perfect exactly the way you are." She encourages him to fight for what's his. "I fully intend to."

After he leaves, Abby breaks down into sobs. She wants to chase after him, to beg him not to go, to tell him she loves him, but she's done all that before and can't do it again, even if she already loves him more than she ever loved Cal or Grant. Everything is different with him, and it's only taken a few days to know that for sure. She's mad at herself for letting this happen after declaring she was done with men. *How did you manage to make everything worse in only three days?* She's determined to survive the aftermath of her time with Adam and to make this new chapter in her life successful if it's the last thing she does.

Over the next few weeks, she throws herself into getting the store open in time for the start of the season. She helps Maddie and Laura plan a baby shower for Janey and Joe and spends time with her parents, who have plenty to say about her new tattoo. Her parents seem to recognize that Abby is going through a difficult time, and they refrain from asking about her plans. They think she's mourning her breakup with Cal, and she doesn't bother to set them straight.

She gets a text from Adam. *You said I couldn't call, but you never said I couldn't text. I want you to know I miss you, and there isn't any other way to tell you. I hope you're behaving and staying out of the bars. Don't you dare write back to me, do you hear? If you do, that might mean we're having some sort of long-distance relationship, and you don't do those anymore, so I'll say good night, sleep tight, and did I mention I miss you?*

His text makes her laugh, cry and smile. She's absolutely dying to write back. She wants to know everything that's happened since the last time she saw him, but she doesn't reply. She set the rules, and she has to stick with them or risk losing more than her heart this time.

After a few weeks, she finally asks Laura if she's heard anything about whether Adam was able to regain control of his company. Laura is surprised to hear they haven't been in touch. Adam got the company back, Laura says, and Abby is thrilled for him even though her heart is breaking at the thought of him staying in New York to run his business.

Adam continues to text her regularly, saying he's thinking about her, dreaming about her and devastated not to be with her, and tells her not to write back unless she means never to stop writing back. Now that she knows he plans to stay in the city, she simply can't get any more involved with him than she already is. He continues to text her, tempting her with his romantic words and detailed descriptions of the time they spent together. Her resolve is weakening.

Her new store opens to much fanfare. Everyone is happy to have Abby's Attic back in business. She helps out at Janey and Joe's baby shower two Saturdays after the store opens and is amused that the guys are annoyed at having to attend. Abby is shocked when Adam strolls into Mac's house through the sliding door from the deck, wearing a sharp navy blue suit. Slim has flown him over for the shower. Abby's entire body feels like it's on fire the second he trains his intense gaze on her. She's missed everything about him, the sound of his voice, the scent of his cologne, the brush of his whiskers against her cheek...

After Janey finishes opening her gifts, Adam asks Abby to go outside with him. She's annoyed with him for driving her crazy with the texts. He made her want things she said she was done with. He made her wish she hadn't already been through the same thing twice before, so she could say to hell with it and do what she really wants to do. He asks what she would've said if she'd written back. She would've said she's happy he got his company back.

Adam saw Sasha. She apologized and said she screwed up royally. He didn't care about seeing her when he was so busy thinking about Abby all the time. She admits she thought about him all the time, too. She's glad it worked out for him.

"It hasn't worked out for me," he says. "Not yet."

He went back to regain control of the company that was rightfully his, but also to take care of the employees who made the company successful. After he was restored as CEO, his first order of business was to recommend to the board that they entertain one of the many offers they had received when the shake-up hit the news. It took a while to find the right buyer because Adam wanted them to retain his staff. He sold the company and signed the papers earlier that day. That's why he's wearing a suit.

She can't believe he sold the company. It's not what he wants anymore. He wants other things now.

"What other things?"

"For one thing, I thought it might be fun to be the island's resident computer geek. Things are a mess around here. They need me." He describes the fantasy she'd built around him. "And then there's this girl I can't seem to stop thinking about. She looks a lot like you, actually. She's sweet and funny and thinks she needs to become someone else entirely before she'll be worthy of the kind of love she deserves, but you see, she's managed to make this guy fall madly in love with her, just by being her perfectly perfect self."

Abby is sure she is dreaming. Is he really saying these things to her? Is he really in love with her? Is his life in New York really over, and is he home to stay?

"Say something, will you?" he says.

"I love you, too."

A roar erupts from Mac and Maddie's deck as they kiss, with everyone cheering them on.

The only reason Adam went back to New York was to get rid of the company so he could come home to her. "I didn't think it would be fair to tell you what was going on until it was a done deal. I was afraid it would drag on for months. Your fantasy was so much better than any reality I've ever known, and when faced with running the company again or being here with you, it was a no-brainer. It's about time you finally got your happy ending, sweetheart."

"It's about time you got yours, too," she says.

"You're my happy ending," Adam says.

With everyone they know watching them, they've officially gone public.

Back at her house in town, she finds out he dropped his stuff there on the way to Mac's house.

"You were taking an awful lot for granted, mister."

"I was hopeful."

He's brought her a black leather jacket with matching pants and gloves. If she wants to learn to ride a motorcycle, she needs protective gear. He also brought her a sleek silver helmet. That he understands her so well, better than anyone ever has, is the greatest gift. He can't wait to see her ass in those pants. They make love, and it's effortless for her, as if she were born to love this man and this man only. She's traveled a long and winding road to get to where she belongs. It turns out the third time is really the charm. With her heart and soul filled to overflowing with Adam's love, she's finally gotten it just right.

 An interview with Adam and Abby...

You two were so special from the start, although I have to admit it was challenging to write about Adam taking up with his brother's longtime ex-girlfriend. I had to work hard to "sell it" to the readers.

Adam: Challenging is a good word for that time in our lives, but to his credit, Grant was always very supportive of us as a couple, and we're close to him and Stephanie.

Abby: The time I spent dating Grant feels like it was someone else's life, not mine. He's my brother-in-law and close friend now. Everyone ended up with the one they were meant for, so it's all good.

And how are your *five* boys?

Adam: They're positively *feral*.

Abby: Like Adam, his brothers and cousins still are.

Adam: We're not as bad as we used to be.

Abby: According to whom?

Haha, I believe Abby. So Liam would be eleven and the quadruplets are nine, right?

Abby: Yes, and they're into all the sports and Pokémon and Minecraft and—

Adam: Making messes. They're extremely good at that.

Abby: Our house is like a locker room half the time. I've given up on keeping it nice for now.

You had two sets of identical twins. Have they ever been successful in switching places with each other or pranking you guys?

Adam: Not us because we can tell them apart, but we've had some issues with teachers who can't tell them apart and are convinced they're messing with them.

That must be pretty funny...

Abby: Oh, yeah, it's *hilarious.*

Is that sarcasm?

Abby: What do you think? I have *five* McCarthy boys. It's a wonder I'm not in the loony bin by now, and I hear it gets worse as they get older.

If Adam and his brothers are any indication…

Abby: Exactly.

Adam: I'm in the room.

LOL, so how's business?

Abby: The Attic has done great at the Surf. I love working close to Laura and Stephanie and being at the hotel. I've got a great helper at the store who makes the rest of my life possible, which is ideal.

Adam: I'm still tending to all the computers on the island while doing freelance programming for a number of former clients from New York who sought me out after I sold the business.

What's your favorite memory of when you were first together?

Adam: Mine would have to be Abby getting her first tattoos and deciding to go a little wild. It was fun to be her partner in crime during that time.

Abby: My favorite memories involve the texts he sent when he was in New York, and I was determined not to get sucked into another long-distance relationship. Those texts were such a lifeline for me, and they made me fall all the way in love with him. I still have copies of all of them saved on my phone. I also want to include Adam's incredible support when I was certain I'd never be able to have children after I was diagnosed with PCOS. He never wavered in his belief that he'd rather be with me and have no kids than be with someone else and have a houseful of kids.

Adam: Lucky me, I got to have both.

Abby: But it wasn't easy, and you were amazing during that time. I still struggle with the effects of PCOS, but I'm so thankful for our boys.

Did you ever hear about what became of Cal?

Abby: He married Candy and had six kids!

Oh, you called that!

Abby: I sure did.

Congratulations on your lovely life together!

MARIE FORCE

Time *for* Love

Book 9: Time for Love
Published: July 23, 2013

Her life has been full of hard knocks. Will he be one more?

Dr. David Lawrence has spent the last two years atoning for his sins and recovering from the devastating breakup with Gansett Island golden girl Janey McCarthy. As the island's only doctor, he's had ample opportunity to show his fellow island residents that there's more to him than the guy who disappointed Janey so profoundly. Now if only he could find a way to forgive himself, he might be able to move on with his life without the woman he'd expected to love forever...

Daisy Babson, probationary director of housekeeping at McCarthy's Gansett Inn, is in bad need of a fresh start after her relationship with Truck Henry took a violent turn, leaving her battered and broken—in more ways than one. As she recovers from her injuries, her days are made brighter by her visits with David Lawrence. The kind and caring doctor who tended to her after the attack has become much more than a friend to her in recent weeks.

Will these two wounded hearts find comfort in one another and move forward together on a new path toward love? Or will ghosts from the past derail them before they get the chance for their own happily ever after? Catch up with many of your favorite characters from earlier books in the Gansett Island Series and get set for another summer of love on Gansett!

Main Characters:

***Dr. David Lawrence,** medical director, Gansett Island Medical Clinic.

***Daisy Babson,** probationary head of housekeeping at McCarthy's Gansett Island Inn.

***Indicates recurring throughout the series**

🛟 Supporting Characters:

***Maddie McCarthy,** mother of Thomas, married to Mac McCarthy in FOOL FOR LOVE, mother of Hailey McCarthy in FALLING FOR LOVE.

***Mac McCarthy, Jr.,** married to Maddie Chester in FOOL FOR LOVE, father of Thomas McCarthy in MAID FOR LOVE and Hailey McCarthy in FALLING FOR LOVE.

***Thomas McCarthy,** son of Maddie and Mac McCarthy, brother of Hailey McCarthy.

***Hailey McCarthy,** daughter of Maddie and Mac McCarthy, sister of Thomas McCarthy

***Ned Saunders,** engaged to Francine in FALLING FOR LOVE.

***Francine Chester,** grandmother of Thomas McCarthy, Ashleigh Sturgil and Hailey McCarthy, engaged to Ned Saunders in FALLING FOR LOVE.

***Linda McCarthy,** grandmother of Thomas Chester McCarthy in MAID FOR LOVE and Hailey McCarthy in FALLING FOR LOVE.

***Big Mac McCarthy, Sr.,** grandfather of Thomas McCarthy in MAID FOR LOVE and Hailey McCarthy in FALLING FOR LOVE.

***Sylvia,** housekeeper at McCarthy's Gansett Inn.

***Betty,** housekeeper at McCarthy's Gansett Inn.

***Sarah,** housekeeper at McCarthy's Gansett Inn.

***Maude,** housekeeper at McCarthy's Gansett Inn.

***Ethel,** head of housekeeping at McCarthy's Gansett Inn.

***Janey McCarthy Cantrell,** married to Joe Cantrell in READY FOR LOVE.

***Joe Cantrell,** married to Janey McCarthy Cantrell in READY FOR LOVE.

***Doc Potter,** veterinarian, Island Veterinary Clinic.

***Victoria Stevens,** nurse practitioner/midwife, Gansett Island Clinic

***Carolina Cantrell,** engaged to Seamus O'Grady in WAITING FOR LOVE.

* **Seamus O'Grady,** engaged to Carolina Cantrell in WAITING FOR LOVE.

***Sarah Lawry,** involved with Charlie Grandchamp in LONGING FOR LOVE.

***Grace Ryan,** engaged to Evan McCarthy in WAITING FOR LOVE.

***Blaine Taylor,** chief of Gansett Island Police, involved with Tiffany Sturgil in LONGING FOR LOVE.

***Charlie Grandchamp,** involved with Sarah Lawry in LONGING FOR LOVE.

***Marion Martinez,** owner of Martinez Lawn & Garden, mother of Alex and Paul, widow of George Martinez.

***Paul Martinez,** co-owner of Martinez Lawn & Garden, member of Gansett Town Council.

***Alex Martinez:** co-owner of Martinez Lawn & Garden.

***Nora O'Grady,** Seamus's mother.

***Shannon O'Grady,** Seamus's cousin.

***Sydney Donovan,** married to Luke Harris in SEASON FOR LOVE.

***Luke Harris,** married to Sydney Donovan in SEASON FOR LOVE.

***Laura McCarthy,** engaged to Owen Lawry and mother of Holden Newsome in SEASON FOR LOVE.

***Owen Lawry,** engaged to Laura McCarthy and stepfather of Holden Newsome in SEASON FOR LOVE.

***Tiffany Sturgil,** mother of Ashleigh Sturgil, involved with Blaine Taylor in LONGING FOR LOVE.

***Jim Sturgil,** father of Ashleigh Sturgil.

***Ashleigh Sturgil,** daughter of Tiffany and Jim Sturgil.

***Dan Torrington,** involved with Kara Ballard in LONGING FOR LOVE.

***Kara Ballard,** involved with Dan Torrington in LONGING FOR LOVE.

***Jared James,** Wall Street billionaire, David's landlord.

***Kay Lawrence,** David's mother.

***Chloe Dennis,** owner of Curl Up and Dye Salon.

***Jenny Wilks,** Gansett Island lighthouse keeper.

***Stephanie Logan,** owner of Stephanie's Bistro in LONGING FOR LOVE, engaged to Grant McCarthy in SEASON FOR LOVE.

***Evan McCarthy,** engaged to Grace Ryan in WAITING FOR LOVE.

***Grant McCarthy,** engaged to Stephanie Logan in SEASON FOR LOVE.

***Officer Wyatt:** involved with Patty.

***Patty,** involved with Wyatt.

***Charlie Grandchamp,** involved with Sarah Lawry in LONGING FOR LOVE.

***Adam McCarthy,** involved with Abby Callahan in WAITING FOR LOVE.

***Abby Callahan,** involved with Adam McCarthy in WAITING FOR LOVE.

***Mason Johns,** fire chief, Gansett Island Fire Department.

***Tobias "Slim" Fitzgerald Jackson, Jr.,** pilot.

***Betsy Jacobson,** mother of Steve (deceased).

***Shane McCarthy,** ex-husband of Courtney.

📍 Places:

- Stephanie's Bistro
- Carpenter's Beach
- Lighthouse
- Curl Up and Dye Salon
- Martinez Lawn & Garden

💬 TIME FOR LOVE Headlines:

- Seamus's mother is coming for a visit!
- Daisy meets Marion Martinez!

- David talks to Daisy about how his relationship with Janey ended!
- Nora O'Grady arrives and is shocked to learn her son's love is significantly older!
- Carolina is furious that Seamus didn't tell his mother about their age difference!
- Seamus's cousin Shannon O'Grady has accompanied Nora to the island!
- Jim threatens to sue for custody of Ashleigh because Blaine is living with Tiffany!
- David checks on Janey and puts her on bed rest for the remainder of her pregnancy!
- Blaine and Tiffany get engaged—and married two days later!
- We meet David's landlord, billionaire Jared James!
- Janey is hemorrhaging, and David has to save her and the baby!
- Peter Joseph "PJ" Cantrell is born!
- David saves Janey's life!
- Truck Henry has been released from jail and trashes Daisy's house!
- David loves Daisy, and she loves him, too!
- Seamus and Carolina get engaged!

Daisy Babson is nervous after inviting Dr. David Lawrence over to hang out with her while she's babysitting for Thomas and Hailey McCarthy. She worries he's only being kind to her, and she's blowing their friendship into something it's not. David reassures her that his feelings are genuine. Daisy is happy to have her first physical contact with a man following her ex-boyfriend's attack without too much fear or embarrassment.

Before things go too far, Mac and Maddie come home from their night out. David drives Daisy home and says he needs to tell her some things about himself before they go any further.

Thomas McCarthy wakes up and catches Mac and Maddie having sex. He worries about Daddy hurting Mommy. Maddie assures him that Daddy would never hurt her or him. Thomas agrees he's a good daddy, and the crisis is averted, but Mac and Maddie are mortified to have been caught.

Ned Saunders drives Daisy to work, where she's now the probationary head of housekeeping at McCarthy's Gansett Inn. Ned is worried about Daisy's new friend, Dr. David. She appreciates his concern and knows there are things he needs to tell her. Maddie visits Daisy at the hotel and tells her that Thomas caught her and Mac in the act. Linda McCarthy comes in while they're laughing and shares that Mac once caught her and Big Mac on the sofa.

After Linda leaves, Maddie tries to warn Daisy about David. Daisy reassures Maddie that she and David will talk about it when he returns from a trip to Boston. Daisy is grateful for everyone's concern but worries about whether she can trust David.

Janey Cantrell checks in for her thirty-two-week visit at the clinic with Victoria and learns the baby is in the breech position. If he or she doesn't move into position soon, she may need a C-section. Janey and Joe plan for her to deliver at Women and Infants Hospital in Providence. Neither of them wants Janey's ex-fiancé, David, involved in the birth.

Sarah Lawry picks up Daisy for their dinner "date." Police Chief Blaine Taylor introduced them, thinking they could support each other following violent relationships. Daisy looks forward to her time with Sarah. They head to Mario's for pizza and a quiet place to talk. Sarah is worried that Charlie Grandchamp, whom she's been dating for a while, is getting fed up with her. She still hasn't told him about the abuse she suffered at the hands of her estranged husband or his upcoming trial for the abuse. Daisy encourages Sarah to tell Charlie. Daisy shares her excitement about David and her worries that his past might be too much to overcome.

"I think it has something to do with his breakup with Janey McCarthy, which has my brain spinning in a number of unsavory directions," Daisy says.

"Don't forget it's possible for people to make really serious mistakes that they regret tremendously and to learn from those mistakes and never make them again," Sarah reminds her, while acknowledging that her estranged husband is a violent, controlling monster incapable of ever changing. "I don't think there's any comparison between his brand of evil and whatever sins David Lawrence may have committed, but you'll have to be the judge of that. Something tells me that a man who's capable of the sort of kindness and compassion he's shown both of us is someone worth spending time with."

Daisy is worried that she can no longer trust her gut when it comes to men. Only she can decide if she can live with whatever David needs to tell her, and there's no shame in walking away if need be, Sarah says. She's absolutely right, but the thought of walking away from David fills Daisy with an aching sadness.

Carolina Cantrell is getting ready for Seamus's mother to arrive. Seamus comes home to find her obsessively cleaning and carries Carolina outside to a campsite he set up to stop what he calls the "madness" that's overtaken her in preparing for his mother's visit. Carolina is furious that he disrupted her work. They'll soon have a house full of guests, and they need the night to themselves, he says

Janey and Joe invite Big Mac and Linda over for lunch so she can tell them she's taking a year off from veterinary school in Ohio and staying on Gansett with the baby. Linda catches Janey up on family gossip. "Grant is almost done with the screenplay, Evan is recording at the studio for the first time this week and Adam is officially moving into your old house with Abby." Joe glances at Janey and nods at her to share their news with her parents. "So, there was a reason I wanted to see you guys today," Janey says tentatively. "I want to talk to you about school."

"What about it?" Big Mac asks, his brows furrowing. He's always touchy on the subject of veterinary school because no one wanted to see her become a vet more than he did.

"I've decided to take this next year off from school."

Her parents are thrilled to hear Janey, Joe and the baby will be staying home this year, even though they hope she'll go back to Ohio to finish school eventually.

Janey isn't sure if she'll go back. Everything has changed since she got pregnant, and now she wants some time to think and enjoy being a mother. Her parents and Joe support her in anything she decides to do.

While waiting for her date with David, Daisy hears a noise on her front porch and looks out to see a woman sitting in one of her rockers. The woman's hair is standing on end as if it hasn't been brushed in days. She's wearing a sweatshirt with flannel pajama pants. Daisy notices the woman's feet are cut and bruised and wonders how far she walked before landing on Daisy's porch. The woman is Marion Martinez, and she's waiting for her husband, George, to pick her up. Daisy goes inside to get Marion a glass of water and decides to call Blaine Taylor. He tells her Marion has dementia, and her sons are going crazy looking for her. When Blaine arrives, he and Daisy convince Marion to go to the clinic to get her feet checked. David has texted to say he's back on the island but was called into work to check on a patient. Daisy will meet him at the clinic.

When they pull up to the emergency entrance, two dark-haired young men run up to Blaine's police SUV. Alex and Paul Martinez have brown eyes and skin so tanned it might've been August rather than June. They have to keep reminding their mother that their father died quite some time ago. Every time they tell her, she's heartbroken all over again. After tending to Marion and sending her home with her sons, David and Daisy get on with their plans for the evening. He shares his biggest shame, that he cheated on Janey, and how she caught him in bed with someone else. David had been diagnosed with lymphoma and never told Janey about it. He went a little crazy during that time and made a lot of mistakes. David wants to give Daisy the chance to end things with him if it's too much to hear what he did to Janey.

Daisy surprises him when she tells him how her father cheated with a friend's mother and how that ended her parents' marriage. Daisy got married at eighteen in defiance of her parents. At nineteen, she got pregnant, lost the baby and then got divorced. Eventually, she made her way to Gansett. Everyone has a past, and it means a lot to her that he didn't let her hear about his from others.

"I'm sure there were plenty of people trying to warn you away from me," he says bitterly, even though he knows he deserves nothing less.

"I wouldn't let them warn me away from you, and I won't let you warn me away either."

Seamus's mother, Nora O'Grady, arrives on the island with his cousin Shannon. After Nora is introduced to Carolina, Joe, who captained the ferry that brought them to the island, comes over to say hello. Nora is shocked that the love of her son's life is significantly older than Seamus and has a son almost the same age as Seamus. Carolina is upset that Seamus didn't tell his mother about their age difference before she arrived.

Sydney is on the mainland for a tubal ligation reversal surgery. Maddie's sister, Tiffany, calls Maddie, upset that her ex-husband, Jim Sturgil, is threatening to sue her for full custody of their daughter, Ashleigh, because Blaine Taylor is moving in with them. Maddie encourages Tiffany to contact her attorney, Dan Torrington.

David takes Daisy to his apartment to change and salvage their date. They decide to stay at his place and order pizza instead of going to Dominic's. They watch baseball and HGTV.

Blindsided by Seamus not telling his mother about their age difference, Carolina takes a walk after Nora goes to bed. Seamus chases after her. After they've argued and made up, Carolina teasingly runs away from him and accidentally falls into a thorn bush, injuring herself.

When David and Daisy finally have their date at Dominic's, they run into Big Mac and Linda McCarthy. Janey passed out, and they're concerned about her and her pregnancy. David offers to check on her. Their dinner is interrupted when he gets a call that Janey needs him. With Daisy's blessing, he goes to check on his ex-fiancée. David puts Janey on bed rest for the remainder of her pregnancy. Janey has forgiven him. It's time for him to forgive himself and be happy.

With Jim hassling her for custody of Ashleigh because of their plans to live together, Blaine and Tiffany get engaged and decide to marry in two days at the lighthouse. Mac and Maddie's cookout will serve as their reception.

David and Daisy encounter David's billionaire landlord, Jared James, who is upset on his back deck. His girlfriend turned down his proposal. He's heartbroken and hiding out on the island. They offer him friendship and consolation. Later, Daisy and David take a walk on the beach, where she mentions that she's been approved for one of the new affordable housing units and will be getting her own home. David has been offered a job in Boston, but he's not taking it because he is happy with her on the island.

David and Daisy visit Marion and Alex Martinez at their home on the grounds of Martinez Lawn & Garden. David talks to Alex about hiring professional help for Marion. Alex agrees that it's time. David offers to help them find someone qualified to work with dementia patients. Alex thanks him and reminds David how grateful he and Paul are to have him nearby to help them navigate their mother's illness. Alex's praise helps to solidify David's decision to stay put on the island, where he's needed by people he's known all his life.

Blaine and Tiffany get married at the lighthouse, with Judge Frank McCarthy officiating, Evan McCarthy providing music, and photography by Jenny, Grace and Stephanie. Mac, Maddie and Thomas stand up for the new family. When it comes time to exchange rings, Blaine includes a ring for Ashleigh and promises to be the best stepdad to her. Blaine and Tiffany ride away in Ned's vintage Rolls-Royce.

David and Daisy arrive at Mac and Maddie's as they're setting up for the party/wedding reception. Janey is upstairs taking a nap and is mostly sticking to the bed rest that David prescribed. They're outside when a shout from inside catches their attention. Janey won't wake up. She's hemorrhaging, and the baby needs to come out right away, even though it's too soon. They rush her to the clinic in Mason's fire department SUV. Joe begs David to save Janey. David suspects placental abruption, which can be fatal to mom and baby.

The island clinic is ill-prepared for an emergency of this magnitude, but he'll work with what he has. David has never performed a cesarean section on his own but has assisted in plenty of them as a resident, so he knows what to do. He's worried about complications that are beyond his skills. The thought of Janey dying on his watch is unfathomable, so he can't let it happen. No matter what, he has to save her life. He asks Mason to call for a Life Flight helicopter with neonatal support.

David has trained for the last decade for situations just like this one. However, being on a remote island when disaster struck wasn't part of his training, all of which occurred in well-equipped, inner-city hospitals. In this case, he'll be relying on instinct as well as training. Janey's life and that of her baby are in his hands, and even in the midst of a crisis, the irony of that isn't lost on him. He owes her one. Hell, he probably owes her more than one. He owes her his very best, and that's what she—and her baby—will get from him.

David stops Joe from running after them into the room where the procedure will take place. "We're going to do a C-section and take the baby. If we don't, we could lose them both. I need you to know… If I can't stop the bleeding, there's a chance I may have to perform a hysterectomy. Do you understand?"

Joe's face is white with shock, and his shirt, arms and hands are stained with blood as he nods to indicate his understanding of the situation.

"I'll tell you what's going on as soon as I know anything." David starts toward the double doors that lead to the exam rooms. "David!" David spins around to face the man who'd once been his rival and is now his ally in wanting to save the woman they both love. "If it's a choice, save Janey." Joe chokes on a sob. "Please, save Janey." David nods and takes off running.

David delivers Janey's son and passes him off to the Life Flight paramedics and doctor. He works frantically to stabilize Janey so she can be transported with her son. After both patients depart on the chopper, David is overwhelmed with emotion. He locks himself in his office and tries to process everything that happened. He realizes he left Daisy at Mac and Maddie's without so much as a thought and goes to find her.

At her house, the door is open and her house has been trashed, but thankfully, she's not there. He rushes to Mac and Maddie's and professes his love to her. Daisy tells him she loves him, too. They find out that Truck Henry has been released from prison. David takes Daisy home with him while the police look for Truck.

Carolina is frustrated that her injuries keep her from traveling to meet her new grandson. Peter Joseph "PJ" Cantrell is named after Joe's late father. Carolina asks Seamus to be the baby's grandfather, or Da, as he wishes to be called. She suggests it would be best if PJ's Granny and Da were married. Since Seamus has proposed and been turned down before, Carolina proposes, and Seamus gratefully accepts.

Daisy and David return to his apartment. After a shower, David comes into the room wearing a towel around his waist, his chest still damp, and his hair pushed back from his face. In all the weeks she's known him, in all the time it's taken to become close to him, she's never seen him look so happy. He sits on the coffee table facing her. "I want to say something to you, and it's going to sound absolutely insane. But I'd really like it if you could listen to the whole thing before you tell me I'm crazy, okay?"

Daisy loves this euphoric version of David even more than the quiet, thoughtful, caring man she's come to know. She nods, willing to give him anything he needs.

"I've been walking around in a daze for two years. It's been like dragging my feet through quicksand, you know? No matter how hard I tried, I couldn't seem to find my way out of it. It wasn't even about Janey anymore. That was over such a long time ago. It was about me and about finding my way. No matter what I did, I couldn't find a way out until I found my way to you."

He reaches for her hands and bends his head to kiss both sets of knuckles. "Today I realized I have a very real purpose. I'm here, on this island where I grew up, to save people who matter to me. I saved Janey's life. I probably saved her baby, too. I was meant to be here so I could do that for her today. I was meant to be here the day Chris Allston cut off his finger while trimming his bushes, and when Mrs. Murtry had an allergic reaction. I was meant to be here to help Paul and Alex through this journey with their mother and to make it possible for them to keep her at home for as long as they can. I was meant to be here the night Sarah Lawry showed up battered and broken, and when Hailey McCarthy came into the world blue and unresponsive."

Deeply moved by his words and the emotion behind them, Daisy says, "You were meant to be here the night I ended up in your clinic after Truck tried to kill me."

"Yes, and I was meant to be with you just about every night since then. When I went to your house today and saw what he'd done, all I could think about was getting to you. The fog had lifted, the daze was gone and what matters to me—who matters to me—became very, very clear."

She blinks back tears. "David…"

"When I said I love you, I hope you know I meant it. I didn't say that because I'd hurt you by leaving you to take care of Janey." He props his head on their joined hands. "I said it because when I realized you could've been hurt or worse… All that mattered was you and being with you and protecting you and making sure no one ever hurts you again."

She moves onto his lap and wraps her arms around him, bringing his wet head to rest against her chest.

"Don't take that house, Daisy. Move in here with me until we can buy our own place together. I want to wake up with you every morning and come home to you every night and… and I need you. I need you. Just you."

She couldn't believe what he was saying.

He looked up at her. "I need you to keep the fog away. I need you to show me the way."

"But that house… It's my security for the future."

"When we buy a house together, we'll put it in your name. If anything happens between us, you'll keep it."

"You can't do that! Most of the money to buy it would be yours."

"I want you to feel safe and secure. I want you to feel completely at home wherever we are. I don't care what I have to do to make that happen. I just want you with me." He looks up at her imploringly. "I love you, and I want to move forward with you by my side. Will you come with me and live with me and be with me?" His sweet words are punctuated by sweeter kisses.

She knows she ought to think before she leaps, but he's offering her all the most important things. How can she say anything other than, "Yes, I'll come with you." Placing her hand on his face, she kisses him to seal their deal.

 **An interview with David and Daisy...**

I always forget how crazy your story was with Janey's emergency taking place in the middle of it...

David: That was a wild day for sure. I'm so glad I was in the right place at the right time. I don't like to think about what might've happened to her and PJ if I hadn't been right there.

Daisy: I think of that day every time we see PJ, who's growing into such a handsome, sweet young man.

Is he aware that you saved him and his mom?

David: He is. Janey made a thing of it years ago, and since then, he's thanked me a couple of times. Once he said, 'It would've been a bummer to croak before I ever got to live.' That made me laugh. He's got his mother's irreverent sense of humor.

I'm sure you've saved some other island residents in the ensuing years.

David: A few.

Daisy: He's being humble. We're very lucky to have him on our island. He's also pushed to vastly expand the clinic's capabilities to better handle true emergencies.

That must be a great feeling of accomplishment for you and a sense of security for island residents.

David: The upgrades have saved some lives, so we're glad we did it.

Your daughter Helen was born almost nine years ago. How is she?

Daisy: She and her younger sister, Josephine, are the lights of our lives. We call her Josie, and she's five. Their favorite thing is dance classes with "auntie" Tiffany and the other kids.

David, you're a girl dad! How is that?

David: I love being a girl dad. They're in charge of me, and I wouldn't have it any other way.

Daisy: He's great with them. They have amazing tea parties, and he lets them paint his nails and do his hair.

Aw, that's so cute! Daisy, are you still working at the hotel?

Daisy: I am! I'm the general manager these days, since Linda has mostly retired.

Wow, that's an awesome promotion. Congratulations.

Daisy: Thanks. I was afraid to take it on at first, but Linda is super flexible, and she always says family comes first. I love the job, so it's worked out well.

David: She's great at it. She started a networking group for herself, Laura and the other hotel and inn managers on the island. It's been a great source of support for all of them.

Daisy: It's nice to spend time with people facing many of the same challenges.

It sounds like you guys have made a nice life for yourselves.

David: We really have, and it's thanks to Daisy, who makes it all happen.

Daisy: We make it happen together.

NEW YORK TIMES AND USA TODAY BESTSELLING AUTHOR
MARIE FORCE
Meant for Love

Book 10: Meant for Love
Published: November 18, 2013

She's waited a long time for her second chance at love...

It's been twelve years since Jenny Wilks lost her fiancé in the 9/11 attacks in New York City. Since then, she's been floundering, trying to find her way. Taking the job as lighthouse keeper on Gansett Island was the best thing she could've done for herself. On the island, she's found amazing friends and a wonderful new life. The only thing missing is romance. She's recently asked her new friends to fix her up with some of the island's more eligible men. While her friends are busy arranging dates for her, Alex Martinez comes to cut the grass at the lighthouse.

He's given up everything to come home to Gansett to care for his ailing mother...

Alex has gone from cultivating orchids at the US Botanic Garden in Washington to cutting grass on Gansett, as he did as a teenager. Running the family business with his brother while managing their mother's dementia requires Alex's undivided attention until a sexy lighthouse keeper shows him there's much more to life than work and endless obligation. During a scorching summer heat wave on Gansett, Jenny and Alex take comfort in each other, and what begins as a hot summer fling quickly becomes something much more lasting. But will it hold up beyond the heat wave when real life intrudes on their sexy interlude?

Main Characters:

*Jenny Wilks, lighthouse keeper.

*Alex Martinez, co-owner of Martinez Lawn & Garden.

Supporting Characters:

Toby Barton, deceased fiancé of Jenny Wilks.

*Mason Johns, chief, Gansett Island Fire Department.

***Commander Linc Mercier,** U.S. Coast Guard.

***Mac McCarthy, Jr.,** married to Maddie Chester in FOOL FOR LOVE, father of Thomas Chester McCarthy in MAID FOR LOVE, father of Hailey McCarthy in FALLING FOR LOVE.

***Maddie McCarthy,** mother of Thomas, married to Mac McCarthy in FOOL FOR LOVE and mother of Hailey McCarthy in FALLING FOR LOVE.

***Tiffany Taylor,** mother of Ashleigh, married to Blaine Taylor in TIME FOR LOVE.

***Blaine Taylor,** married to Tiffany Taylor in TIME FOR LOVE, stepfather to Ashleigh Sturgil.

***Sydney Donovan,** married to Luke Harris in SEASON FOR LOVE.

***Luke Harris,** married to Sydney Donovan in SEASON FOR LOVE.

***Hailey McCarthy,** daughter of Mac and Maddie McCarthy, sister of Thomas McCarthy, born in FALLING FOR LOVE.

***Laura McCarthy,** engaged to Owen Lawry and mother of Holden Newsome in SEASON FOR LOVE.

***Holden Francis Newsome,** Laura's son with ex-husband Justin Newsome, stepson of Owen Lawry, born in SEASON FOR LOVE.

***Owen Lawry,** engaged to Laura McCarthy and stepfather to Holden Newsome in SEASON FOR LOVE.

***Stephanie Logan,** engaged to Grant McCarthy in SEASON FOR LOVE.

***Abby Callahan,** involved with Adam McCarthy in WAITING FOR LOVE.

***Grace Ryan,** engaged to Evan McCarthy in WAITING FOR LOVE.

***Janey McCarthy Cantrell,** married to Joe Cantrell in READY FOR LOVE, mother of Peter Joseph "PJ" Cantrell in TIME FOR LOVE.

***Joe Cantrell,** married to Janey McCarthy Cantrell in READY FOR LOVE, father of Peter Joseph "PJ" Cantrell in TIME FOR LOVE.

***Peter Joseph "PJ" Cantrell,** son of Janey and Joe Cantrell, born in TIME FOR LOVE.

***Ned Saunders,** engaged to Francine in FALLING FOR LOVE.

***Francine Chester,** grandmother of Ashleigh Sturgil, Thomas McCarthy and Hailey McCarthy, engaged to Ned Saunders in FALLING FOR LOVE.

***Ashleigh Sturgil,** daughter of Tiffany Taylor and Jim Sturgil, stepdaughter of Blaine Taylor in TIME FOR LOVE.

***Thomas McCarthy,** son of Mac and Maddie McCarthy, brother of Hailey McCarthy.

***Evan McCarthy,** engaged to Grace Ryan in WAITING FOR LOVE.

Sharon, store manager, Martinez Lawn & Garden.

***Paul Martinez,** co-owner of Martinez Lawn & Garden, member of Gansett Town Council.

***Dr. David Lawrence,** living with Daisy Babson in TIME FOR LOVE.

***Daisy Babson,** living with Dr. David Lawrence in TIME FOR LOVE.

***Josh Harrelson,** sound engineer at Island Breeze Studios.

***Jack Beaumont,** Evan McCarthy's manager.

***Buddy Longstreet,** country music star and owner of Long Road Records.

Michael, nephew of Jenny Wilks.

Lacey, niece of Jenny Wilks.

Brent, nephew of Jenny Wilks.

Tyler, nephew of Jenny Wilks.

Emma, sister of Jenny Wilks.

Leah, sister of Jenny Wilks.

Mackenzie, niece of Jenny Wilks.

***Adam McCarthy,** involved with Abby Callahan in WAITING FOR LOVE.

***Grant McCarthy,** engaged to Stephanie Logan in SEASON FOR LOVE.

***Dan Torrington,** involved with Kara Ballard in LONGING FOR LOVE.

***Kara Ballard,** involved with Dan Torrington in LONGING FOR LOVE.

***Victoria Stevens,** nurse practitioner/midwife, Gansett Island Clinic.

***Shannon O'Grady,** deck hand on the Gansett Island ferries, cousin of Seamus.

***Rebecca,** owner of Rebecca's Diner.

***Kelly Ballard,** estranged sister of Kara Ballard, married to Matt.

***Matt,** ex-boyfriend of Kara Ballard, married to her sister, Kelly.

***Jared James:** Wall Street Billionaire, David Lawrence's landlord, college classmate of Jenny Wilks.

***Hope Russell,** nurse hired to care for Marion Martinez, mother of Ethan Russell.

***Ethan Russell,** son of Hope Russell.

***Erin Barton,** Toby's twin sister, friend of Jenny Wilks.

***Hugh Wilks,** father of Jenny Wilks.

***Karen Wilks,** mother of Jenny Wilks.

📍 Places:

- Chesterfield Estate
- Oar Bar at Gansett Boat Works Marina

🎵 MEANT FOR LOVE Headlines:

- A heat wave scorches Gansett Island!
- Jenny throws tomatoes at Alex!
- Maddie thought she was pregnant and is disappointed that she's not!
- Evan's album is going to be acquired by Long Road Records!
- Evan and Grace plan a destination wedding for January!
- Jenny goes on a date with Linc, but she really wants to be with Alex!
- Evan sings his new song "My Amazing Grace" for the first time!
- Jenny and Alex have sex and agree to be exclusive!
- After Alex fires their store manager, Jenny offers to help out!
- Alex hears Jenny dreaming about Toby!

- Jenny tells Alex about what happened to Toby!

- Seamus takes Carolina to Providence to meet her new grandson!

- Grant and Dan realized Kara's estranged sister and her husband have come to confront Kara!

- Dan races to the marina to find her before they can blindside her!

- Dan and Kara get engaged!

- Hope Russell is hired to care for Marion! She and her son Ethan will move to the island soon!

- Marion embarrasses Alex in front of Jenny and her parents!

- After a ten-day breakup, Alex proposes to Jenny, and they get engaged!

Jenny Wilks is dreaming of the last morning with her late fiancé, Toby Barton. They're talking about a visit with her parents, and Toby gets up to leave when Jenny is rudely awakened by a loud noise coming from outside. In the skimpy clothing she wore to sleep in the scorching heat wave, she runs down the stairs at the lighthouse and outside to find the largest lawn mower she's ever seen. The town has finally sent someone to cut the overgrown lawn. She yells at him, but the guy on the mower can't hear her. She grabs a handful of tomatoes and starts launching them. One hits him square in the back, and he shuts down the mower.

Alex is sweltering in the heat wave and frustrated to be back to his teenage job of cutting lawns on Gansett. He had a dream job working at the U.S. Botanic Gardens and a life in Washington, D.C. that he enjoyed. He came home to Gansett to help his brother, Paul, with the family business and the care of their mother, Marion, who has dementia. The lighthouse keeper complained to the town because the lawn hadn't been cut. That's what he's doing when something hits him in the back. What the hell was that?

He notices the remnants of two tomatoes on the ground next to him. "Are you throwing tomatoes at me? What the hell?"

"I could ask you the same thing! Do you have any idea what time it is?"

"Ah… five something?"

Despite her rage at being rudely awakened out of a precious dream about Toby, she can't help but notice the shirtless man's muscular chest and belly, dark chest hair, tanned skin and khaki shorts that hang from narrow hips. Dark socks peek out from the top of work boots.

"Five forty-five. *In the morning!*"

"Thanks for clarifying. Do you mind leaving me alone? I've got a long day ahead of me, and you're the one who complained to the town that we hadn't been out to cut the grass. Well, we're here to cut the grass."

"Not at five forty-five in the morning, you're not."

"Ah, yeah, I am."

She takes a step closer to him. "No, you're not."

He takes a step in her direction. "Yes, I am."

The fourth tomato in her hand goes sailing toward his head. He ducks at the last second, avoiding a direct hit. "Are you completely insane?"

As he looks her up and down under the cover of sunglasses, Jenny remembers she's wearing next to nothing as she faces off with the angry lawn guy. The lighthouse doesn't have air conditioning, and the heat has been unbearable, thus the short nightgown and tiny panties. She crosses her arms over her unrestrained breasts.

"Look, lady, I'm sorry if I woke you up, but I need to get back to work if I'm going to keep this already screwed-up day on schedule."

"You're not turning that… *thing* back on at six o'clock in the morning! I thought I was being attacked or something."

"Right. Attacked. On Gansett Island, where it's so unsafe."

Jenny knows what it's like to be attacked in a place where she'd always felt safe, a thought that reminds her of the dream and what she'd missed out on thanks to the roar of his lawnmower. Who knew when or if she'd have the dream again? It's been more than a year since the last time Toby "visited" her slumber.

"You never know when a safe place can become unsafe." As she utters the words, her chin quivers and her eyes swim with tears.

"Oh, my God. You're not going to cry!" He tips his head for a closer look at her. "Are you?"

"No, I'm not going to cry." She has no intention of crying but having that particular dream throws her out of sorts for days every time it happens. Being blasted out of a sound sleep on top of that is a recipe for emotional overload.

"Good." He runs his fingers through straight, silky, dark hair, a gesture that makes his muscles tighten and bulge, not that she's looking or anything, and then he lifts his sunglasses to swipe at the sweat on his face, revealing dark brown eyes.

"Listen, I'm sorry I woke you up," he says in a more conciliatory tone. "I wasn't thinking about someone actually living here. I need to get this done while I can. Since you're already awake, would you mind if I got back to it?" The exhaustion that radiates from him has her softening, too. Slightly.

"And you won't show up here again at this hour?"

"I won't show up here again at this hour."

"Fine."

"Fine." He treats himself to another good look at her barely covered body before he stalks back to his Sherman tank of a lawn mower and fires up the beast.

Later, Alex tries to cool down with a cold hose shower. He catches Jenny watching him.

"What are you looking at?" he asks.

"Not a damned thing. What're you looking at?"

He zeroes in on her lips, which are moist and appealing. The entire package is appealing. Well, except for the tomato incident. But he's not thinking about tomatoes. Strawberries come to mind as he stares at her ripe lips and wonders if they'd taste as sweet as they look. "Nothing."

Alex takes another step, putting him right in front of her. Her lips part with surprise as she looks up at him, probably trying to gauge his intentions. And what are his intentions, exactly? Damn if he knows.

"Who are you?" she asks.

"Alex." Since he has absolutely nothing to offer her, he gives only his first name. "Who are you?"

"Jenny."

He'd begun to rethink his plan to steal a taste of those lips when she moistens them again and makes his decision that much easier. "If you don't want this, say no."

"I, um…"

His hands curl around her hips, drawing a gasp from her as he tugs her against him. "That's not no. Last chance…" She doesn't say no. She doesn't say anything as she continues to look up at him with big, startled eyes that have him thinking about melted chocolate. And then her hands land on his bare chest, and he realizes she's bringing him closer, not pushing him away. They end up sharing a series of hot kisses, moving inside the lighthouse for privacy.

"How did we get here?" he asks a long while later.

She breathes in the scents of freshly cut grass and tomatoes that cling to him. "I'm not quite sure."

"One minute I was borrowing your hose, and the next…"

Jenny smiles at his summary of events. "I don't do things like this."

"Like what? Like this?" He tweaks her nipple again, making her gasp and squirm against his tight hold.

"Yes, like that. And this." She drags him into another torrid kiss, this one skipping right past the preliminaries and going straight to open mouths and tangled tongues. "I, um—"

With his hands on her face, he kisses her softly. "Don't."

"I was only going to apologize for the tomatoes."

"Don't do that either. I've never had a woman throw tomatoes at me or made out in a lighthouse. And here I thought this day would totally suck."

She smiles up at him, dazzled by his gorgeous brown eyes, his darkly tanned skin, the scent of freshly cut grass and the ripple of muscles beneath her hands.

"I gotta go."

She lets her hands drop from his shoulders. "I know."

"I'll see you around, Jenny, the lighthouse keeper."

"See you around, Alex, the lawn mower."

Still reeling from the encounter with Alex, Jenny goes to visit friends. Sydney is recovering from surgery, so the group gathers at her house. The women decide it would be fun to have a surprise post-wedding shower for Tiffany, with gifts from her store. They plan it for the following weekend at the lighthouse.

After his twelve-hour workday, Alex and his brother, Paul, receive good news about the nursing candidates who responded to their ad. David meets with Alex and Paul that evening to help screen the candidates. After they get their mother settled for the evening, Alex takes his motorcycle for a ride and ends up waking Jenny for the second time that day. They venture down to the beach for a nighttime swim that turns heated. Their attraction is incendiary.

Maddie thought she was pregnant and is upset that she isn't. She really wanted the baby, and Mac agrees, even though he put a moratorium on pregnancies in their family after PJ's chaotic delivery. Mac can't handle the scary births or seeing Maddie in pain. She decides to buy a test the next day just to be sure.

Evan McCarthy, high off the recording of his new song at Island Breeze Studios, receives a call that his album, which had been locked up in a Nashville legal battle, is likely to be bought by Buddy Longstreet and Long Road Records. Evan and his fiancée, Grace, plan their wedding for January 18 in Turks and Caicos.

Arriving home after another twelve-hour day, Alex finds employees gathered outside the greenhouses, where Paul is arguing with their naked mother. Paul holds her bathrobe and has obviously been trying to get her to put it on for some time already.

Alex takes off at a run to help Paul, who brightens when he sees Alex heading toward them. Marion's back is turned, so she doesn't see Alex approach, but he hears her sobs.

"I want you to get your father right now and bring him to me, do you understand?"

"I can't do that." Paul looks imploringly at Alex.

"I'm not asking you. I'm telling you. You'll do what you're told."

Ignoring the crowd of employees watching their sad drama unfold, Alex wraps his arms around her shoulders. "I'm here, Marion," Alex says gently in a voice not all that different from his father's. "I'm right here, and I've got you."

She reaches up to grasp his hands. "Oh, George. I've been waiting for you to get home. The boys have been unmanageable this afternoon."

Paul approaches them tentatively.

"I'm here now."

Alex takes the robe from Paul and puts it around their mother's shoulders.

"Why are we outside?" she asks Paul, anger now replaced by confusion.

Paul's face is lined with exhaustion and despair, unlike anything Alex has ever seen, except for when their father was dying.

"You wanted to come find Dad after your shower."

"But Daddy died, didn't he?" she asks in a small voice that makes Alex want to sob with the utter injustice of this horrific illness.

"Yeah, he did," Alex says. "Let's go home and have some ice cream, Mom."

"Not before dinner," she says in a scolding tone that reminds Alex of the mother he used to know.

Paul turns to the employees, who've come out of the store and greenhouses to see what's going on. "Show's over," he says. "Get back to work."

Back at the house, Marion wants to take a nap before her outing with her church friends. She's very sad for what she's putting her sons through, but they love her and are right where they want to be. Alex wants to howl with the outrage of it all.

Jenny goes on a date with Linc Mercier at the Lobster House. After dinner, she asks Linc to join her at the Tiki Bar to watch Evan and Owen play. All their friends are there when Paul and Alex Martinez walk in. Alex and Jenny pretend not to know each other when Grace introduces the Martinez brothers to the group by their nicknames, AM and PM. Jenny is sad to lose their first-name-only status.

Alex heads to the bar while Paul joins the table of friends. Maddie asks about their mom, which is how Jenny learns about Marion's illness. While Alex is at the bar, he overhears a woman talking about his mother and her behavior earlier. Shocked to see Sharon, the manager of their store, calling his mother "bat-shit crazy," he confronts and fires her immediately.

Jenny overhears the exchange between Alex and Sharon. She asks Linc to take her home, surprising him when she passes on a second date. She's anxious to check on Alex, and the minute Linc drops her off at the lighthouse, she rushes for the door to find Alex there. He wants to be with her, and they agree to take their wild attraction to the next level, but only if they're exclusive.

Evan sings his new single, "My Amazing Grace," for the first time to the crowd at the Tiki Bar. He has Grace join him on stage, much to her embarrassment. Everyone loves the song, but nobody more than Grace, who asks him to sing it again at their wedding.

Alex and Jenny are awakened in the middle of the night by a call from Paul. He's concerned their mom is having a heart attack. She's being taken to the clinic. Jenny drives Alex there and then waits for him, even though he told her not to. When Alex comes out in the morning, Jenny offers him a ride home and her assistance with the retail store. She has management experience and an MBA. Alex gratefully accepts her help and tells her how much it means to him that she offered.

Jenny goes home to rest for a bit and wakes up with the flu. She rests all day and misses the planning party for Tiffany's shower. Marion is discharged from the clinic and brought home to recover. After getting her into bed for a nap, Alex lies down and falls asleep. Later, Paul informs him that nurse Hope Russell is coming over on the ferry on Saturday to check out the island—and them. Alex heads to Jenny's with soup and spends the night with her. Later, Alex wakes to her talking in her sleep.

"Toby, wait… Don't go. Please, don't go."

"Jenny," Alex whispers, kissing her cheek and then her lips. "Wake up, honey. You're dreaming."

Undone by her tears, Alex brushes them away. "Are you okay?"

She nods, but he can tell she isn't okay, especially when the tears keep coming. He rubs her back, trying to soothe her.

"I'm sorry," she says after a long period of quiet. "The dream… It was upsetting."

"You don't have to apologize for being upset." He continues to rub her back, wishing he could do something to make her feel better. Alex asks if she wants him to go. She doesn't.

Alex asks who Toby is.

He was her fiancé.

Alex guesses the relationship ended badly.

The next day, Jenny asks Sydney's advice on how to share her story of loss and grief with Alex.

"Do you ever worry about something happening to Luke and having to go through the whole nightmare again?" Jenny asks her friend.

"I worried about that every day when we were first together, especially after the accident at the marina when he was hurt. I was a wreck for weeks after that. I obsessed about what could've happened." They have a long talk about their journeys with loss and grief.

"For what it's worth," Syd says, "I think you'll feel better after you tell Alex about Toby. It's weighing you down at a time when you should be feeling happy at having found someone you want to be with. Tell him sooner rather than later, so you can put the past where it belongs and start to enjoy the future."

"That's very good advice."

Armed with courage following her conversation with Sydney and determined to tell Alex her story before someone else does, Jenny buys lunch and meets Alex at the Chesterfield Estate, where he's working for the day. Alex shows Jenny the beautiful grounds and impresses her with his knowledge of plants and flowers. Jenny shares her story of loving and losing Toby.

"I'm glad you told me, but I hate that you had to go through such an awful thing."

They bond over their struggles and become closer.

Carolina finally convinces Seamus that she feels well enough to go to the mainland to meet her grandson. She's relieved to see Janey and Joe, and to hold her precious grandson. She introduces him to Seamus, who will be his "Da."

Grant McCarthy meets with his friend Dan Torrington weekly at Rebecca's to review his new screenplay. In exchange, Grant is reviewing the novel that Dan is writing about his work to free unjustly imprisoned people. Grant overhears a couple arguing behind him and realizes he's listening to Kelly and Matt, the sister and brother-in-law who betrayed Kara. They're planning to surprise Kara with their visit. Grant urges Dan to warn Kara. Dan's only goal is getting to Kara before they can blindside her. He calls in reinforcements to cover her at work and gets her to leave the dock on the launch before Kelly and Matt arrive.

"You're kind of freaking me out," Kara says as she drives the boat into the Salt Pond at his urging.

"Kelly and Matt are here with the baby."

Her entire body goes rigid with shock. "What? How do you know?"

"Grant and I were in the diner for our weekly meeting, and we heard them talking about you and how they'd come to clear the air and introduce you to the baby."

"Are you kidding me?"

"I wish I were. They planned to force you to deal with them by showing up with the baby."

He tells her he called in her coworker to cover for her, and there's no reason they can't spend the day on the water. Kelly and Matt can't force a confrontation if they can't find her.

Clearing the anchorage, Kara slows the boat, shifts into neutral and turns to him, sliding her arms around his neck. "My hero."

"Hardly."

"Did you or did you not come running, with broken ribs that aren't entirely healed, when you heard what my sister planned to do? And did you or did you not have the foresight to call in another driver so I could actually run away for the day?"

"I might've done those things."

"Then you're absolutely my hero."

"I absolutely love you, and I couldn't let them do that to you. When I think about how they might've succeeded if Grant hadn't heard them…"

"Well, they didn't, and it's all thanks to you."

"While my approval ratings are at an all-time high, I've got something I need to ask you."

"What's that?"

"When are you going to marry me?" After a pause, he adds, "Your mouth is hanging open. Not that I mind that, because it gives me all kinds of ideas, but I was sort of hoping you might say something at this juncture."

"What am I supposed to say when you throw that out there like a live grenade?"

"How about yes?"

"You didn't ask me a yes-or-no question."

"Pardon the error."

He falls gracelessly to his knees before her, grimacing at the flash of pain that radiates through ribs that refuse to heal. "Kara Ballard, center of my universe, love of my life, future mother of my children, will you do me the humongous and probably undeserved honor of being my wife?"

Once again, she stares at him with a flabbergasted look on her face that only makes him love her more, if that's possible.

"That was a yes-or-no question, in case you didn't notice."

"I noticed."

"And? Are you planning to make me suffer?"

Apparently, she isn't, because she drops to her knees in front of him, wraps her arms around him and holds him. "Yes. But—"

He has no interest in any "buts," so he kisses the words right off her sweet lips.

When Jenny goes to meet with Paul at the store, she finds him and Adam McCarthy huddled over a computer. Sharon, the manager they fired, has password-protected the system, and they can't get a hold of her. Paul shows Jenny around the store, then they head to the house to keep trying to access the computer.

Alex is thrilled to have her at the house when he comes home and proceeds to announce to everyone, including his mother, that they're together. They spend the evening visiting with Dr. David and Daisy, who come most evenings to visit with Marion. David brings his landlord, Jared James, with them. They discover that Jared went to Wharton with Jenny and Toby. At the end of the evening, Jenny offers to help Marion get ready for bed. Alex is deeply appreciative of her kindness toward his mother.

Later that night, as a member of the Town Council, Paul shows his brother the letter Jenny sent to apply for the lighthouse keeper job. Alex is deeply moved by what Jenny has overcome. He desperately needs to see her and heads to the lighthouse to spend the night with her.

Evan McCarthy is overwhelmed by the sudden change in his circumstances. He asks his father and Ned how to handle the resurrection of his album now that he's engaged to Grace and running the studio. Following their talk, he contacts Buddy Longstreet and explains how things have changed for him since he first recorded the album. He and Buddy agree to a shorter tour away from home, giving Evan much-needed relief.

Jenny agrees to attend the interview for the nurse Alex and Paul hope to hire to help care for Marion. Thankfully, Hope Russell agrees to take the job and hopes to be ready to move within a few weeks. Help is on the way.

Jenny hosts a successful shower for Tiffany and Blaine. Jenny and Alex have a conversation about having kids in the future, which triggers another dream about Toby, causing Jenny to wake up sobbing. Alex comforts her, saying how lucky Toby was to be loved by her.

Jenny's parents come to visit her for the first time. She enjoys showing them her island and the lighthouse. She tells them about Alex, and they're thrilled to see her so happy. Jenny takes her parents to the Lobster House to meet Alex. He brings his mom to dinner because he can't leave her home alone. Being out in public makes Marion agitated, and he is embarrassed and infuriated when she insults Jenny. He leaves dinner early and apologizes for the scene.

"Well," Jenny says to her parents, "that's Alex. And his mom." She explains the effort Alex and Paul have made to keep Marion at home and how they've recently hired someone to help with her care.

"They say the measure of a man is in the way he cares for his mother," her father, Hugh, says. "If that's the case, then it seems like you've found a man truly worthy of your affection."

Jenny couldn't agree more, but she also can't shake the feeling of impending doom that came over her as Alex left the restaurant. Later, Jenny goes to see Alex, only for him to send her away. He can't subject her to his life. By taking away her choice, he breaks her heart. Jenny avoids her friends for days until Sydney forces her out of her self-imposed solitary confinement.

Ten days later, Alex shows up first thing in the morning with the beast lawnmower, waking Jenny up again. She pelts him with tomatoes, which ends with them wrapped up in each other. Later that night, Alex proposes to Jenny.

"I want you to know I think you're probably the best person I've ever known. You have the face of an angel, the heart of a warrior and the backbone needed to put up with me. I would like for you, Jenny Wilks, to come along with me the rest of the way, to build an amazing future together that also pays homage to the past you shared with Toby. I want to bring him with us, too, because he's part of you and thus part of who we are together. I love you, I need you, I believe I've proven I want you, but I'm available to provide additional evidence upon request."

Jenny laughs as she wipes away tears.

"I know I'm asking a lot of you by bringing you into my family at this particular juncture, but I'm hoping you'll be by my side wherever this journey we're on with my mom takes us."

She happily accepts his proposal.

 An interview with Jenny and Alex...

I have a confession to make. Your story is my favorite of the Gansett Island Series.

Alex: No way! Why is ours your favorite?

Because you were both at such a tender time in your lives when you found each other, and to work things out in that environment took a lot of guts from both of you.

Alex: That was a difficult time, for sure. Things with my mom had gotten so bad. I'll never forget how Jenny stepped in to help, no questions asked, doing whatever was needed. It made such a difference to me—and to my family.

Jenny: I have so much admiration for what Paul and Alex did for Marion for so long on their own. She was truly lucky to have such wonderful sons.

Alex: We were lucky to have her—and our dad.

Jenny, Alex was your first relationship after losing Toby. What made him different from other guys you met in the years after Toby died?

Jenny: That's one of those things that's not easily explainable. But I think he was the right guy at the right time, when I'd decided I was ready for a new relationship. Plus, the connection was instantaneous.

Alex: She was hot for me.

Jenny: Do you want me to throw a tomato at your head?

Alex: (laughing) Behave, honey. People are looking.

Have you ever thrown a tomato at him again?

Jenny: Once or twice, but he always deserved it.

Alex: That's true. I drive her crazy.

Jenny: It's a good thing I love him so much.

Alex: I say that every day.

Tell us about your kids.

Jenny: George is twelve already, which we cannot believe. He loves going to work with Dad, Uncle Paul and his cousin Ethan.

Alex: The next generation of Martinez Lawn & Garden is in training. They love it like we do, which is great.

Jenny: Our Henry is eight, and we also have a daughter named Cora, who's six.

That's so exciting. Three kids!

Alex: I know. Cora was a big surprise, but she completed us.

Jenny: Alex is super cute with her. She's got him firmly wrapped around her little finger.

Alex: I'm in big trouble with that young lady.

Congratulations on your family and your happy life!

NEW YORK TIMES AND USA TODAY BESTSELLING AUTHOR
MARIE FORCE
Chance for Love

Book 10.5: Chance for Love, Novella
Published: January 11, 2014

Billionaire Jared James has everything a man could ever want except for the one thing money can't buy…

After forty days holed up in his house on Gansett Island, nursing a broken heart, Jared James decides enough is enough. Determined to snap out of the funk he slipped into after his girlfriend refused his marriage proposal, Jared organizes a party for the friends who've seen him through the worst of his heartache. Now if only he could stop thinking about the love of his life and how he will survive the rest of his days without her…

She was Elisabeth all her life until Jared made her his Lizzie…

Elisabeth "Lizzie" Sutter knows she has no business chasing Jared after she turned down his lovely, heartfelt marriage proposal in a moment of sheer panic. It didn't take long for her to realize how foolish she'd been. Now all she can do is hope it's not too late to set things right with the one man she can't live without…

🗼 Main Characters:

*Jared James, Wall Street billionaire, landlord of David Lawrence, friend and former classmate of Jenny Wilks.

*Elisabeth "Lizzie" Sutter, runs homeless shelter in NYC, ex-girlfriend of Jared James.

*Indicates recurring throughout the series

⛑ Supporting Characters:

*Dr. David Lawrence, living with Daisy Babson in TIME FOR LOVE.

*Daisy Babson, living with Dr. David Lawrence in TIME FOR LOVE.

*Jenny Wilks, engaged to Alex Martinez in MEANT FOR LOVE.

*Alex Martinez, engaged to Jenny Wilks in MEANT FOR LOVE.

*Toby Barton, deceased fiancé of Jenny Wilks.

*Doro Chase, realtor.

Marcy, personal assistant to Jared James.

***Ned Saunders,** engaged to Francine Chester in FALLING FOR LOVE.

***Hope Russell,** nurse hired to care for Marion Martinez in MEANT FOR LOVE, mother of Ethan Russell.

***Marion Martinez,** owner of Martinez Lawn & Garden, mother of Alex and Paul, widow of George Martinez.

***Paul Martinez,** co-owner of Martinez Lawn & Garden, member of Gansett Town Council.

***Victoria Stevens,** involved with Shannon O'Grady in TIME FOR LOVE.

***Shannon O'Grady,** involved with Victoria Stevens in TIME FOR LOVE.

***Sydney Donovan,** married to Luke Harris in SEASON FOR LOVE.

Melanie, sister of Elisabeth Sutter.

***Judge Frank McCarthy,** grandfather of Holden Newsome in SEASON FOR LOVE.

Forty days after Lizzie turned down his proposal, Jared James woke up ready to return to the land of the living. He takes a run on the beach and decides it's time to host a cookout with friends at his oceanfront home. He invites Dr. David Lawrence, his friend and tenant, and David's live-in girlfriend, Daisy Babson. He tells David to invite others, and David asks Jenny Wilks and her fiancé, Alex Martinez.

On his way to the grocery store, Jared stops at an open house at the Chesterfield Estate. As he walks through the grounds, he thinks it would make a great location for Jenny and Alex's wedding. They've been having trouble securing a venue for their wedding. Maybe it's outrageous to spend so much money on friends, but Jared sees it as a good business opportunity.

Elisabeth Sutter feels foolish as she travels by ferry to Gansett. She made a big mistake by seeming to hesitate when Jared proposed. She hates that she hurt him and caused them both pain. It had taken six weeks of daily visits to Jared's office before his personal assistant had finally told her where he was. Elisabeth hadn't known about his house on Gansett. There were many things she didn't know about him after a year together, but the one thing she knew for certain was that she loved him.

After the final disastrous evening they'd spent together, she'd tried to talk herself out of loving him. Not loving him was easier, cleaner, simpler.

Their lifestyles are as diametrically different as two lives could be. She's low-budget, low-key, low-maintenance. He's all cash, dash and flash.

And she loves him.

By now, he probably hates her and has forgotten all the reasons why he once wanted to marry her. She runs a homeless shelter, and he's a Wall Street tycoon. How could they make this work? Her only goal is to make sure he knows she regrets the negative headshake at his proposal. She can't let him think she doesn't love him.

Elisabeth takes a cab from the ferry landing and tells the driver that she's come to see a friend. She hopes the friend will be happy to see her. Then she shares the whole story, and the man says, "Well, now, I can see why ya think he might not be happy ta see ya after all that."

His words deflate the tiny bit of optimism she's carried with her on this fool's errand. But she's determined to at least try to make things right with Jared. The kindly driver, Ned Saunders, gives her his card with a number to call if she needs another ride.

When she arrives at Jared's, she follows the sound of music and voices to the backyard to find Jared in the pool with two beautiful, blonde women in bikinis. He doesn't seem to be as devastated as she is. She leaves before he sees her and calls Ned for a ride back to town.

David and Alex are arriving at Jared's after David checked on Alex's mom, Marion, who's had a tough day with her dementia. They sent Daisy and Jenny ahead to help Jared set up. As they pull up to the house, David notices a woman waiting by the mailbox. As he opens the window, he sees that she's crying. She looks familiar to David, who recognizes her from photos as Jared's Lizzie. David tells her the blonde women are his girlfriend and Alex's fiancée and says Jared would love to see her, that he's been very sad without her. He talks Lizzie into canceling her cab and coming up to the house with them.

"Hey!" Jared says from the pool when he sees them coming. "You made it. Don't you own a bathing suit, Doctor David?"

"In fact, I do, but I found a friend of yours on the way in." Jared's gaze shifts from David to Lizzie, who stands between him and Alex. Along with the shock that registers on Jared's face, David also sees love and longing and knows he's done the right thing by persuading her to come talk to Jared.

"Lizzie…" Jared says when he recovers the ability to speak.

"Hello, Jared."

Surprised to see Lizzie here, Jared stumbles through introductions. He invites Lizzie to stay for dinner with them. They have a fun evening, especially after Victoria, Shannon and Paul join them. As everyone prepares to leave, Jared tells Alex and Jenny that he may have found a place for their wedding. They've considered the Chesterfield Estate, but they've heard it's being sold to a new owner. The new owner is Jared, and it's all theirs for the wedding. They're shocked and overwhelmed by his generosity.

When they're finally alone, Lizzie tells Jared how much she missed him and how she never meant to hurt him or turn down his proposal. She never actually said no.

"You didn't mean to turn me down? Then why'd you say no?"

"I didn't intend to. I shook my head because it was happening too fast, and I couldn't process it. But I never actually said no."

"Lizzie… Yes, you did."

"No, I didn't."

"So, what you're saying is you didn't actually turn down my proposal?"

"I didn't turn down your proposal."

He tilts his head like he's trying to get a read on her, the gesture so familiar and so totally him that she can't stop herself from placing her hands on his face.

His eyes close as he releases another deep breath that shudders through his big body. "Don't do this to me, Lizzie. I can't handle it. You broke me. You have no idea…"

"I think I do. You broke me when you wouldn't take my calls or respond to my texts. I couldn't sleep or eat. I couldn't find you. No one would tell me where you were. I didn't even know you owned a place out here."

"You couldn't eat?" he asks softly, his gaze filled with concern.

He's asking whether she's suffered a setback in her recovery and appreciates that he remembers and cares so much. "Because I was upset, not because of the anorexia. I swear."

"Thank goodness." He curls his hands around her wrists and presses his lips into one of her palms. Elisabeth feels the charge of that small connection throughout her entire body.

"How did you find me?"

"I finally wore down Marcy, but you have to promise not to fire her."

"What do you mean by 'finally'?"

"I've been to your office every day since that night."

Jared convinces Lizzie to spend the night at his house, although he's not ready to go back to being together like they once were. The next morning, Jared tells Lizzie he's not returning to Wall Street and is staying put on Gansett. She's concerned she caused him to make that seismic decision, but he's tired of it all. He wants to slow down and not be about work all the time.

Knowing how independent she is, he decides to show her the Chesterfield Estate and discuss his plans. He wonders if she wants to use her degree in event planning to make The Chesterfield a premier wedding destination. Jared shows her around the island, including the Oar Bar and McCarthy's Marina. Lizzie loves everything she sees.

They spend the rest of the day in Jared's bed making love. Jared proposes again, and this time, he receives a definitive yes to his question. The next morning, Jared receives word that his offer to buy the Chesterfield Estate has been accepted. He tells the agent he needs the purchase completed within two weeks because he doesn't want to wait any longer than that to marry Lizzie.

Jared moves heaven and earth to have his wedding to Lizzie two weeks later at the Chesterfield with his new Gansett Island friends in attendance. He'll never forget the way Lizzie gazes at him with so much love as he carries her up two flights of stairs to the honeymoon suite Sydney put together for them in record time.

"Happy?" she asks him after a long silence.

"I've never been happier in my entire life."

"Neither have I."

"I'm going to make you happy every day, Lizzie. I promise."

"I promise the same thing."

 An interview with Jared and Lizzie...

Ah, I love your sweet love story and how you overcame a major misunderstanding to put your relationship back together.

Lizzie: That was such an upsetting time. I was so relieved to be with Jared again after more than a month of thinking I'd lost him forever.

Jared: Same. I couldn't believe what I was seeing when she arrived with Alex and David.

Speaking of them, Lizzie, do you ever wonder what might've happened if David hadn't recognized you as the woman Jared loved?

Lizzie: Jared and I have talked about that so many times and how there was something bigger than us involved in making sure we didn't miss out on the love of our lifetimes. We're extremely thankful to David for what he did for us that night. We're still close to him, Daisy and their family.

Jared: In some ways, I owe David everything for what he did when he saw Lizzie about to leave without seeing me. It can still make me a little weak in the knees to think of her being there and me never knowing.

Thank goodness it all worked out the way it was meant to. How is your darling Violet doing?

Lizzie: She's about to be ten years old, and we're in absolute shock at how fast the years have flown by. We were delighted to adopt her a little brother, Miles, seven years ago, and they're the absolute lights of our lives.

Do you hear from Violet's biological parents, Jessie and Brooks?

Lizzie: We're in touch with all four of our children's biological parents, and the kids know them and see them at least once a year. They're part of our family.

That's an amazing arrangement.

Jared: It's worked out well, and we've always felt it was important for the kids to know their birth stories. Being parents has been the most fun either of us has ever had, and we're deeply thankful to the people who made it possible. Vi and Mi, as we call them, adore each other and love being together. She's an awesome big sister to him, and he worships the ground she walks on.

Lizzie: People keep telling us to enjoy that while it lasts because eventually they'll be fighting, but we don't think that's going to happen with them. They're best friends.

That's so lovely. We couldn't be happier for you guys! How's business?

Jared: I'm still working a few hours a day, managing my portfolio and that of several clients. I also teach others the secrets to successful investment. Oliver Watson, who was one of my first students, is a partner with me in that endeavor. He's my star student.

We love to hear you're still working with Oliver. How fun! And what about The Chesterfield, Lizzie?

Lizzie: We did thirty weddings last year, as well as several anniversary parties, a couple of bridal showers and two baby showers. We're busy year-round.

Wow, that is busy. I assume you have some help running the place?

Lizzie: Ironically, Dara Watson has become my right hand there. I couldn't do it without her.

I love that you're both working with the Watsons.

Jared: They're among our closest friends. We have a great time together and have even traveled together with our kids.

Who else are you still close to?

Lizzie: We have more friends here than either of us has ever had anywhere else. We're especially close to Jared's brother Quinn and his wife, Mallory, as well as his sister Kendall and her boys when they're home from college. We love having Jared's youngest brother, Cooper, his wife, Gigi, and their family here in the summers, when he runs his successful party boat business.

We spend time with Alex and Jenny Martinez and their kids, as well as Paul and Hope Martinez and their kids. The list could go on all day.

Jared: Life is good on Gansett Island.

Love to hear that!

NEW YORK TIMES AND USA TODAY BESTSELLING AUTHOR

MARIE FORCE

Gansett After Dark

Book 11: Gansett After Dark
Published: May 12, 2014

Their dreams are within reach. But first, they'll have to put the past away.
Owen Lawry is days away from leaving Gansett Island to attend the trial of his father, who is charged with assaulting his mother almost a year ago. He has spent his entire adult life trying to outrun his violent past, but the upcoming showdown with the father he hasn't seen in more than a decade has him spending far more time in the past than in the present. His biggest challenge is convincing his pregnant fiancée, Laura McCarthy, to sit out the trip. The last thing he wants is to expose the woman he loves to the pain of his past.

Laura is determined to stand by Owen's side throughout the trial and into the life they have planned together. The trial and her final divorce papers are the only things standing between them and the wedding they have looked forward to all year. Can she convince Owen to let her in and allow her to help him through this difficult time? And what will become of the man she loves if his father walks free?

Main Characters:

*Owen Lawry,** engaged to Laura McCarthy and stepfather of Holden Newsome in SEASON FOR LOVE.

*Laura McCarthy,** engaged to Owen Lawry and mother of Holden Newsome in SEASON FOR LOVE.

*Indicates recurring throughout the series

Supporting Characters:

*Sarah Lawry,** involved with Charlie Grandchamp in LONGING FOR LOVE.

*Charlie Grandchamp,** involved with Sarah Lawry in LONGING FOR LOVE.

*Holden Francis Newsome,** son of Laura McCarthy and ex-husband Justin Newsome, stepson of Owen Lawry, born in SEASON FOR LOVE.

***Blaine Taylor,** married to Tiffany Taylor in TIME FOR LOVE, stepfather of Ashleigh Sturgil.

***Dr. David Lawrence,** living with Daisy Babson in TIME FOR LOVE.

***Tobias "Slim" Fitzgerald Jackson, Jr.,** pilot.

***Shane McCarthy,** works for McCarthy Construction.

***Seamus O'Grady,** engaged to Carolina Cantrell in WAITING FOR LOVE.

***Carolina Cantrell,** engaged to Seamus O'Grady in WAITING FOR LOVE, grandmother of PJ Cantrell in TIME FOR LOVE.

***Joe Cantrell,** married to Janey McCarthy Cantrell in READY FOR LOVE, father of Peter Joseph "PJ" Cantrell in TIME FOR LOVE.

***Janey McCarthy Cantrell,** married to Joe Cantrell in READY FOR LOVE, mother of Peter Joseph "PJ" Cantrell in TIME FOR LOVE.

***Peter Joseph "PJ" Cantrell,** son of Joe and Janey Cantrell, born in TIME FOR LOVE.

***Judge Frank McCarthy,** grandfather of Holden Newsome in SEASON FOR LOVE.

***Big Mac McCarthy,** grandfather of Thomas Chester McCarthy in MAID FOR LOVE, Hailey McCarthy in FALLING FOR LOVE and Peter Joseph "PJ" Cantrell in TIME FOR LOVE.

***Linda McCarthy,** grandmother of Thomas Chester McCarthy in MAID FOR LOVE, Hailey McCarthy in FALLING FOR LOVE and Peter Joseph "PJ" Cantrell in TIME FOR LOVE.

***Mac McCarthy,** married to Maddie Chester in FOOL FOR LOVE, father of Thomas Chester McCarthy in MAID FOR LOVE and Hailey McCarthy in FALLING FOR LOVE.

***Maddie McCarthy,** mother of Thomas, married to Mac McCarthy in FOOL FOR LOVE, mother of Hailey McCarthy in FALLING FOR LOVE.

***Ned Saunders,** engaged to Francine in FALLING FOR LOVE.

***Francine Chester,** grandmother of Ashleigh Sturgil, Thomas McCarthy and Hailey McCarthy, engaged to Ned Saunders in FALLING FOR LOVE.

***Tiffany Taylor,** mother of Ashleigh, married to Blaine Taylor in TIME FOR LOVE.

***Adam McCarthy,** involved with Abby Callahan in WAITING FOR LOVE.

***Abby Callahan,** involved with Adam McCarthy.

***Evan McCarthy,** engaged to Grace Ryan in WAITING FOR LOVE.

*__Grace Ryan,__ engaged to Evan McCarthy in WAITING FOR LOVE.

*__Grant McCarthy,__ engaged to Stephanie Logan in SEASON FOR LOVE.

*__Stephanie Logan,__ engaged to Grant McCarthy in SEASON FOR LOVE.

*__Sydney Donovan,__ interior designer, married to Luke Harris in SEASON FOR LOVE.

*__Luke Harris,__ married to Sydney Donovan in SEASON FOR LOVE.

*__Betsy Jacobson,__ mother of Steve (deceased).

*__Daisy Babson,__ living with Dr. David Lawrence in TIME FOR LOVE.

*__Alex Martinez,__ engaged to Jenny Wilks in MEANT FOR LOVE.

*__Jenny Wilks,__ engaged to Alex Martinez in MEANT FOR LOVE.

*__Jared James,__ co-owner of The Chesterfield, married to Lizzie James in CHANCE FOR LOVE.

*__Lizzie James,__ co-owner of The Chesterfield, married to Jared James in CHANCE FOR LOVE.

*__Erin Barton,__ twin sister of Toby Barton (deceased), friend of Jenny Wilks.

*__Mallory Vaughn,__ daughter of Big Mac McCarthy and Diana Vaughn (deceased).

*__Dan Torrington,__ engaged to Kara Ballard in MEANT FOR LOVE.

*__Kara Ballard,__ engaged to Dan Torrington in MEANT FOR LOVE.

*__Judith Ballard,__ mother of Kara Ballad and her ten siblings, from Bar Harbor, Maine.

*__Chuck Ballard,__ father of Kara Ballard and her ten siblings, owner of Ballard Boatworks in Bar Harbor, Maine.

*__Victoria Stevens,__ involved with Shannon O'Grady in TIME FOR LOVE.

__Tom Corcoran,__ assistant commonwealth attorney, prosecuting the case against Mark Lawry.

*__General Mark Lawry,__ estranged husband of Sarah Lawry, father of Owen, Julia, Katie, Cindy, Josh, John and Jeff Lawry.

*__Adele Kincaid,__ mother of Sarah Lawry, grandmother of Lawry siblings.

*__Russ Kincaid,__ father of Sarah Lawry, grandfather of Lawry siblings.

__Eva Lewis,__ friend of Sarah Lawry, who testifies against Mark Lawry.

*__Julia Lawry,__ office manager, daughter of Mark and Sarah Lawry, sister of Owen, Katie (twin), Cindy, John, Josh and Jeff.

*__Katie Lawry,__ nurse practitioner, daughter of Mark and Sarah Lawry, sister of Owen, Julia (twin), Cindy, John, Josh and Jeff.

***Cindy Lawry,** hair stylist, daughter of Mark and Sarah Lawry, sister of Owen, Katie, Julia, John, Josh and Jeff.

***John Lawry,** police officer, son of Mark and Sarah Lawry, sister of Owen, Katie, Julia, Josh and Jeff.

Josh Lawry, engineer, son of Mark and Sarah Lawry, brother of Owen, Julia, Katie, Cindy, John and Jeff.

***Jeff Lawry,** student, son of Mark and Sarah Lawry, brother of Owen, Katie, Julia, Cindy, John and Josh.

***Riley McCarthy,** engineer, son of Deb and Kevin McCarthy, brother of Finn McCarthy.

***Finn McCarthy,** engineer, son of Deb and Kevin McCarthy, brother of Riley McCarthy.

***Dr. Kevin McCarthy,** father of Riley and Finn McCarthy.

Deb McCarthy, estranged wife of Kevin, mother of Finn and Riley McCarthy.

❝ GANSETT AFTER DARK Headlines...

- Owen and Sarah are preparing for Mark Lawry's trial in Virginia!

- After finally hearing her story, Charlie insists on going to Virginia to support Sarah!

- Seamus and Carolina surprise everyone with their wedding!

- Grant convinces Stephanie to finally set a wedding date!

- Big Mac has another daughter! Introducing Mallory Vaughn!

- Jim Sturgil gets arrested after he assaults Dan at his and Kara's engagement party!

- Adam and Abby get engaged!

- Sarah rejects the plea deal becase she wants Mark to admit he's guilty! The trial will proceed!

- When a woman from their past comes to testify against him, Mark pleads guilty and will be going to jail!

- Owen, Sarah and their supporters return to Gansett to prepare for Owen and Laura's wedding!

- We meet Owen's siblings: Julia, Katie, Cindy, John and Jeff!

- Shane rescues Katie from drowning on Laura and Owen's wedding day!
- Hello to Uncle Kevin McCarthy and his sons, Riley and Finn McCarthy!
- Kevin and his wife, Deb, have split up!
- Owen and Laura get married!
- Mac and Maddie host Ned and Francine's wedding, a surprise to the happy couple!
- Ned and Francine finally get married!

Owen Lawry is sitting on the deck of the Sand & Surf Hotel, rocking his stepson, Holden, and thinking about the changes he's made in the last year. He gave up his previous no-commitment lifestyle for Laura, Holden and the surprise twins they're now expecting. He's looking forward to his upcoming wedding but dreading his father's trial. Owen is due to leave in a few days for the trial in Virginia, which stands as a gigantic mountain to climb before he can marry the love of his life.

The upcoming trial is due to the years of abuse his father inflicted on Owen, his siblings and his mother, including the most recent incident in which Mark Lawry beat Owen's mother, Sarah. She came to Gansett Island and Owen for help. For a while now, Sarah has been dating Charlie Grandchamp but has yet to tell him about the history of abuse she and her children endured.

While they sit together on the deck, Owen encourages Sarah to tell Charlie before they leave for the trial. Owen doesn't want Laura to come on the trip because of her pregnancy with twins. Laura wants to support Owen, and Charlie will want to be there for Sarah when he finds out why they're going to Virginia. The thought of Charlie knowing about her past makes Sarah shudder with revulsion.

Sarah and Charlie have dinner at his home that evening. After they eat, she asks if she can hug him, which he sees as an important step forward for them since Sarah has shied away from his touch. While Charlie holds her, Sarah says, "He beat me and my children. He beat me so badly last October that I knew if I stayed, he was going to kill me, so I finally left. It took me way too long to leave. My children grew up in a nightmare, and there was nothing I could do to protect them."

The words, once she lets them out, spill forth in a great rush, almost as though she fears that if she doesn't say them right now, she never will. "He was a general in the air force, and everyone was afraid of him—no one more so than his wife and children. He goes on trial next week in Virginia. That's where I'm going. Owen is going, too. We both have to testify."

"What day are we leaving?" Charlie asks.

She raises her head off his chest to find his deep blue eyes staring at her fiercely. "No… You can't…"

"Try and stop me." He looks away from her for a second, seeming to rein in his anger. "That might not be the right way to put it in light of what you've been through. I want to be with you and support you through the trial. I hope you'll let me do that for you."

After dinner on the beach, Laura's brother, Shane, takes Holden up for his bath. Owen has been quiet all evening, so Laura leaves him to his thoughts and goes to put Holden to bed. Later, Owen finally tells Laura that while he never wants her to be exposed to Mark Lawry or to what happened in his past, he's afraid he won't be able to get through the trial or seeing his father again without her with him. Since all she wants to do is support him, he doesn't have to go through this alone and she'll be by his side through it all.

Seamus O'Grady and Carolina Cantrell are hosting an authentic New England clambake that's going to double as a wedding. They ask Janey and Joe to stand up for them, which, of course, they agree to. Everyone is excited and surprised as the clambake turns into a wedding.

Grant tries to get Stephanie to commit to a date for their wedding, going so far as to suggest they elope. This finally prompts her to tell him she's afraid to have a family because no one ever showed her how, but Grant calms her fears, and they talk about how she'll be a great wife and mother. Betsy and Frank decide to pursue a relationship.

Charlie and Evan are both coming to Virginia. Owen is mortified that people will know the ugly story of his family. "You don't understand how hard it is for the people who love you to watch you suffer," Laura says.

He lets her put her arms around him, but he seems to be merely tolerating her, which is unusual. "And you all don't understand how embarrassing and humiliating this entire thing is for me." Laura and Evan, who were raised by great men, can't possibly understand what it was like for him. Laura helps him see that he has no reason to be ashamed. Owen is nothing like his father and would never hurt their children or her.

Big Mac is enjoying the morning meeting at the marina with Ned and Frank, who's now retired and back in Big Mac's daily life. A striking dark-haired woman approaches them and asks to speak to Mac McCarthy. Big Mac and his son both reply, "That's me." She asks for a moment in private with Big Mac. After they walk down the main dock, she introduces herself as Mallory Vaughn. She's the daughter of Diana Vaughn, a woman Big Mac dated before he met Linda. Mallory has recently found out that Big Mac is her father.

Kara Ballard's parents, Judith and Chuck, host an engagement party at the Summer House for Kara and Dan, much to Kara's dismay. Even though she hates being the center of attention, she's beginning to enjoy the party with their friends when a disruption erupts. Jim Sturgil, drunk and disheveled, wielding a butcher knife, threatens Dan and then Blaine when he intervenes. Jim stabs Dan. Blaine arrests Jim. Dan jokes with Kara as the EMTs tend to his wounds that at least he got her out of the party she never wanted to have. She's not amused.

Adam and Abby get engaged and talk about having a baby as soon as possible. She wants a short engagement.

The next day, as their mother requested, the five McCarthy children arrive at their parents' home to discover that Big Mac had fathered a daughter before he met Linda. He was unaware of Mallory's existence until she came to see him the day before. The kids are overwhelmed by the news. When Big Mac announces that Mallory is on her way to meet them, Janey cannot be there and leaves. Although the brothers want to go after Janey, Mac in particular, doesn't want to disappoint their father. They stay put for the uncomfortable meeting. The McCarthy brothers spend some time getting to know the older sister they didn't know they had.

A few days later, Sarah, Charlie, Owen, Laura, Holden, Frank, Dan, Slim, Blaine, David and Evan leave the island for the trial in Virginia. Upon arrival, Sarah, Owen, Dan and Frank head to the Commonwealth's Attorney's office, where they learn Mark Lawry is willing to plead no contest to one felony count of domestic assault and battery in exchange for the other charges being dropped. Under this deal, Mark wouldn't admit guilt or claim innocence, would avoid the trial and serve time in jail. The trial isn't a slam dunk, since Mark's standing as a high-ranking military officer would be considered, and they can't prove he was the one who beat Sarah. It's her word against his.

"I see the benefit of accepting the plea deal," Sarah says, "but I want to hear him say he did it. I want him to admit, in public, that he beat us while the rest of the world was holding him up as a hero. I want him to say the word *guilty*. If he's unwilling to do that, no deal."

They head to court the next day, where Blaine, David and Slim testify in the morning. As they're breaking for lunch, Owen and Sarah come face to face with Mark for the first time and ugly words are exchanged. When the others walk away, Owen hangs back. "Go away and leave us alone," he says to his father. "You're nothing to us, and we like it that way."

"Your mother will come around," Mark says confidently. "She always does."

The statement has Owen laughing out loud. "Keep telling yourself that."

Sarah's parents, Adele and Russ, had surprised Sarah and Owen by coming to court. As they return from lunch, Sarah's longtime friend Eva Lewis is there and would like to testify. The testimony from someone who witnessed and observed the abuse the Lawrys suffered spurs Mark Lawry to plead guilty to all charges.

Elated that Mark is heading to jail, the relieved group returns to Gansett to prepare for Laura and Owen's wedding. Before the wedding, Laura finds the album from her first wedding and makes a discovery that she shares with Owen.

"You're spectacularly beautiful," he says when he sees the photos. "I still can't believe you picked me to spend the rest of your life with."

"That day," Laura says haltingly, "I knew something was wrong. I didn't know what, but I knew it was wrong."

"I can see that in some of the pictures." Owen points to a photo of her with Justin. "You're glowing and radiant, but I still see the sadness in your eyes."

"I was sad, but I didn't know why then. I do now. It was because I was always meant to be with you, and I've known that for almost as long as I've known you. Please don't look at those photos and think that's what I really want. It isn't." She takes his hand and brings it to her lips. "This is. You are. We are."

Owen has never regretted for a second that he stayed with Laura on Gansett to make a life together there.

With time to kill before the wedding, Shane goes to the beach for a swim. He's thrilled for Laura and Owen, but the wedding festivities have made him miss his wife, Courtney. He still can't believe she hid a raging drug addiction from him. He helped her as much as he could, including paying for rehab, only to have her divorce him when she got clean. Losing her and their marriage had nearly broken him. So while he's happy for Laura and Owen, he's all set with love and marriage. He's headed back to shore when a scream and thrashing catches his attention. He swims out to help a panicked woman. She grabs him and pulls him underwater. He fights to get away from her and then dives down to save her. Pulling her to shore, he realizes she's Owen's sister Katie.

Katie is embarrassed and exhausted. After she catches her breath, she and Shane race to the hotel to get ready for the wedding. She asks Shane not to say anything about what happened. They don't want to upset Owen and Laura's happy day. While Shane agrees, Adele witnessed the incident and thanks him for saving her granddaughter.

Sarah is thrilled to have most of her children in one place. Katie, Julia, Cindy, Josh and Jeff are all there to celebrate their brother's wedding. John, unable to get the time off from work, calls Owen before the wedding.

"The mother of the groom wants a moment with her son." Now that their father's trial is behind them, Sarah's children have a lightness about them she's never seen before. They laugh more easily and smile more often. It's like they finally have permission to be themselves now that Mark Lawry is out of their lives forever. She wishes she'd left him years ago, but hindsight is always twenty-twenty, and she chose to look forward rather than backward these days. Sarah pins the boutonniere on for Owen. When the rose is in place, she flattens her hands on his chest. "I love you more than you'll ever know. You and your little family and this magical hotel saved my life last year, and I'll always be grateful."

"We're equally grateful to you, Mom. You showed up just when we needed you most."

Evan pulls double duty as best man and musician. Katie, Julia and Cindy bring Holden down the stairs to the beach and hand him to Owen.

The wedding party, Adam and Abby, Shane and Janey, Jeff and Stephanie, Josh and Maddie and Grace, the maid of honor, come down the stairs. Then, Laura, on the arm of her father, Frank, comes down the stairs.

Owen can't seem to breathe until she smiles, and the knot of nerves in his chest becomes a feeling of pure joy, the likes of which he's never experienced quite so profoundly. His Princess. His love. His life. Her dad officiates the wedding in which Laura and Owen exchange heartfelt vows.

After the ceremony, Laura and Owen greet their guests and return to the hotel for the reception. Her youngest McCarthy cousins, Riley and Finn, thank Owen for taking her off their hands. Laura wonders where her Uncle Kevin's wife, Deb, is. Kevin talks to his brothers, Frank and Big Mac, who ask about Deb. Kevin shares that she left him a few weeks ago. He plans to stay on the island for a while to regroup. They're thrilled to have him.

Here Comes the Groom, Gansett Island Short Story

Mac and Maddie invite Francine and Ned to a fancy dinner at their house, although Ned isn't sure why he has to put on a tie to have dinner. He's in a foul mood due to the outbreak of weddings and engagements around him. He's waited the longest to marry Francine, and they can't find a date to tie the knot with all the other weddings happening. His best friend, Big Mac, calls him out on his bad mood. Hopefully, soon they can find a date and get it done.

Ned is surprised when they pull up to Mac and Maddie's house to find a driveway full of cars. He thought the gathering was for immediate family. He doesn't want to be around all the other happily married couples. Ned and Francine walk up the stairs to the porch and are surprised when rose petals rain down on them.

Mac and Maddie approach them, holding glasses of champagne and wearing broad smiles. Maddie kisses them both. "Welcome to your wedding."

Ned figures he heard her wrong until things began to happen. Frank McCarthy steps forward with a marriage license for him and Francine to sign. Maddie and Tiffany sign as their witnesses. Next come flowers for both of them. Maddie and Mac and Tiffany and Blaine, their kids, will stand up for them. Their grandkids, Ashleigh, Thomas and Hailey, finish out the wedding party Ned would've chosen for himself.

"I don't understand," Ned says when he can finally get a word in edgewise.

"You wanted to get married and couldn't find a date," Big Mac says, "so Mac and Maddie found one for you. All you gotta do, old pal, is stand there and get married."

Ned is going to cry, goddamn it. Right in front of everyone. He's going to actually cry. Here, standing before him, ready to stand up with him and Francine, is the family he's always wanted but never had. He spares a glance for Francine and discovers she's already crying. To hell with it, he decides as he stops trying to fight the tears.

"'Tis a heck of a thing ya've done here," he says to Mac and Maddie. "Thank you."

"So, you're happy about it?" Maddie asks. "I told Mac if you were mad, it was all his idea."

"It *was* all my idea," Mac says.

Maddie pats his face indulgently. "Yes, dear."

"Well, it was."

"I'm very happy 'bout it," Ned says gruffly as he sniffs. "Never been happier 'bout anything."

"I knew you would be," Mac says with a smirk for his wife.

Frank rubs his hands together. "What do you say, Ned? Francine? Shall we do this? It's been a full week since I married Laura and Owen. I'm starting to get twitchy for another wedding."

Mac and Maddie have even thought of rings for them.

This is the moment he's waited so long for, and nothing can ruin it for him or Francine. He takes a series of deep breaths, hoping to calm his racing heart. He gestures to Big Mac. "Come 'ere."

Big Mac walks over to him. "I'm here."

"Stay. Need ya right here with me."

His best friend hugs him. "You got it, buddy."

With all his favorite people by his side, Ned finally makes Francine his wife.

🎙 **Since we've already caught up with Laura and Owen, we'll chat with some of our other favorite couples, beginning with Dan and Kara...**

That engagement party, though...

Dan: (laughing) One of the crazier days we've had, that's for sure. But it got Kara out of the party she never wanted.

Kara: Still not funny.

Dan: Yes, it is. Every so often, she admits that I'm funny, but I have to really work for it.

Seems to us that you had to work for everything where Kara is concerned.

Dan: She led me on a merry chase, but it was well worth the effort.

Kara: I didn't trip over myself falling into his arms the way every other woman he ever met did, so apparently that counts as a merry chase.

Dan: Point of order, it wasn't all of them. Just most of them.

Kara: Shut it, counselor.

So, nothing much has changed with you two, I see.

Dan: We're still having fun driving each other crazy.

Kara: Speak for yourself.

LOL, I love it. How's Dylan doing?

Kara: She's delightful, even if she's just like her father with an argument for everything.

Dan: The apple doesn't fall far from the tree. She's going to be a lawyer like Daddy.

Kara: She's ready to argue cases in court at nine.

What else has happened since we last saw you?

Dan: We had a son named Noah, who we're crazy about, and another daughter named Alicia, who's hilarious like me.

Wow, three kids. How old are Noah and Alicia?

Dan: He's eight, and she's seven.

Kara: Dan was getting up there in years, so we had to act fast so they wouldn't be raised by a senior citizen.

Dan: VERY funny, love. You're hilarious.

Kara: (grinning) I know. Everyone says so.

Are you still running the launch service?

Kara: I am, and I work two shifts a week during the summer to keep my license.

Dan: And it gives me time to be in charge around here for once.

Kara: Which is usually an unmitigated disaster with cereal for dinner and s'mores for dessert.

Dan: I'm the fun dad.

Kara: It's a very good thing I love you so much.

Dan: It's a very good thing indeed. It's made my whole life worth living.

Kara: See how he saves himself when he's venturing into trouble?

Again, not much has changed. Dan, are you still practicing?

Dan: I have a very busy practice here on Gansett that I share with Kendall James. And I still work with the Innocence Project on occasion, mostly as a consultant these days.

Do you spend time in Maine and California?

Kara: We get to both places at least once a year. And they come to us.

Kara, I wanted to ask after your grandmother, Bertha…

Kara: She's ninety-seven and still lobstering as often as she can. She's unstoppable.

Dan: Thank goodness for that, because she's essential to all of us.

Kara: I'm so thankful for her good, long life and for the fact that she continues to enjoy excellent health. She's still my best friend, along with Dan, of course.

Dan: (smirking) Of course.

I hope all the other Ballards and Torringtons are doing well.

Dan: Everyone is great, which is such a blessing. We're very lucky, and we know it.

 An interview with Ned and Francine...

I loved re-reading the story of your surprise wedding.

Ned: Best day o' my life. Bar none.

Francine: Mine, too. It was so sweet of Mac and Maddie to solve that problem for us the way they did. The wedding was perfect, and the best part was that we didn't have to do a thing. The kids thought of everything.

Ned: They sure did.

Ned, you went from being a lifelong bachelor to having two daughters and eight grandchildren. What's that been like?

Ned: Nothin' but pure joy.

Francine: He's a wonderful husband, father and grandfather. We're all blessed to have him in our lives.

Ned: Aw, doll, I'm the one who's blessed.

Are you still driving your cab?

Ned: A coupla days a week in the summer, but I take winters off these days so that we can travel. We finally got to Paris, and we're hopin' for London next year.

Francine: We're having the time of our lives!

 An interview with Sarah and Charlie...

We loved your story so much! If any two people deserve a beautiful second-chance romance, it was you.

Charlie: I couldn't agree more. Sarah and her family have been such a gift to me—and to my Stephanie, who always wanted siblings. Now she has seven of them.

Sarah: My former life feels like a long-ago bad dream now that I've had almost a decade with Charlie.

There must be a lot of grandchildren by now...

Sarah: We lose count!

Charlie: I think it's around seventeen, but don't quote me on that.

Wow, that must make for some fun family get-togethers.

Charlie: It's total chaos, and we wouldn't have it any other way.

I want to ask about Adele and Russ...

Sarah: We lost them six months apart about four years ago. That was a tough time for all of us, but we're comforted to know they're together and that they enjoyed a wonderful life. We have such fond memories of them and all the good times we had, especially in the last few years when they lived with us. We loved that.

Charlie: We miss them, and the kids do, too. They were very special people.

Any big plans for you guys?

Sarah: We're doing an African safari next year with several couples from the island, including Big Mac and Linda McCarthy, Frank and Betsy McCarthy, Ned and Francine Saunders and Allan and Mary Alice Donovan. We're looking forward to that.

Charlie: We have such incredible friends here and have so much fun playing cards, cooking together and traveling. Life is good!

 **An interview with Frank and Betsy...**

How's life treating you guys these days?

Frank: We're having a great time being grandparents, traveling and hanging out with family and friends.

I hear there's an African safari in the works...

Betsy: Thankfully, Big Mac and Ned, the travel agents, planned the whole thing. We're just along for the ride, but we can't wait. It's a dream come true, even if we'll be missing the kids the whole time we're gone.

Frank: We love doing school pickups, going to soccer and baseball games and weekend sleepovers. We hear those come to an end once the teenage years kick in, so we're enjoying them while we can.

Betsy: Holden is about a year away from wanting nothing to do with us for a while. We know they come back around later, but we're holding on to all the time we can get with him while he still likes hanging out with us.

Frank: I think he'll surprise us and keep coming around, even when he's too cool for us.

Betsy: He's already too cool for us.

Frank: Haha, that's true.

Betsy: We also oversee an annual Race Week fundraiser in Steve's honor, with the proceeds going to summer sailing camps throughout New England.

That's a great way to honor him.

Betsy: He'd be proud of it. He loved sailing more than anything and would want to share that love with kids who might not otherwise have access to it.

Frank, are you still presiding over weddings?

Frank: I do at least a dozen every year.

Betsy: He's in hot demand as always.

I love that! Nice to catch up with you guys.

 **An interview with Seamus and Carolina...**

We so enjoyed your fun—and often funny—romance! What are some of your favorite memories from those early days together?

Seamus: Oh, well… She led me on a merry chase, my Caro, but thankfully, she finally let me catch her.

Carolina: As if you gave me any choice in the matter.

Seamus: The choice was all yours, love.

Carolina: When I look back, it almost seems silly to me that I was ever worried about our age difference. It has no bearing on our daily lives.

Seamus: Except for when you complain about keeping up with your young stud of a husband.

Carolina: When have I ever referred to you as a young stud?

Seamus: (laughter)

Carolina: In your dreams, O'Grady.

I see that nothing much has changed with you guys.

Seamus: We're still deliriously happy.

We were so touched by your generosity toward Kyle and Jackson after they lost their mother. How're the boys doing?

Seamus: They've gone and become *men* on us in recent years. Kyle is a freshman at the University of Rhode Island. It was a tough transition for us to move him to the mainland.

Carolina: I cried for weeks!

Seamus: We both did. But he's enjoying school and planning to major in marine biology. We're very proud of him and Jackson, who's a senior in high school and soon to make his own college plans.

Are you ready to be empty nesters?

Seamus: Not at all. We can't imagine not having them at home, but they'll be back in the summers. They're pursuing Coast Guard licenses to work on the ferries while they're in college.

Carolina: We're keeping the business in the family. Joe's son, PJ, is interested in following in his father's footsteps.

Seamus: That boy is a natural like his dad. Vi has taken an interest in Carolina's jewelry making. They spend hours creating masterpieces together.

Carolina: She's my buddy.

Do you get to Ireland at all?

Seamus: We try to get home at least once a year. The boys love it there, and last year we took Joe and Janey and the kids with us. That was the best.

How are all the O'Gradys?

Seamus: As crazy as ever. My Mam and Da still bicker the day away as always, and I'm a great-uncle many times over. Everyone is healthy and happy, which is all that matters.

Seamus, when you first came to Gansett to manage the ferry company while Joe was in Ohio, did you ever imagine the life you have today?

Seamus: Not in my wildest dreams. I'm the luckiest guy who ever lived to have this life, this family and my beautiful wife, who makes it all possible.

Carolina: We're lucky to have you, too.

NEW YORK TIMES AND USA TODAY BESTSELLING AUTHOR

MARIE FORCE

Kisses After Dark

Book 12: Kisses After Dark
Published: October 1, 2014

She's avoided men all her life…

Growing up with an abusive father, Katie Lawry learned a thing or two about men and has made a conscious choice to stay far away from them, until the day of her brother Owen's wedding, when she's rescued from nearly drowning by Shane McCarthy. With everyone who matters to Katie assuring her that Shane is one of the good guys, she feels safe to give in to the attraction that simmers between them. Katie has waited a long time to take a chance on love, but is Shane the right guy for her?

He's ready to move on…

More than two years after a painful divorce, Shane has a life on Gansett Island that makes sense to him. With his father, sister and beloved baby nephew living close by and a job he enjoys, Shane is content, if not entirely happy. One thing he knows for sure is he's tired of living in the past. Spending time with sweet, sensitive, sexy Katie Lawry makes him feel hopeful again, and he might be ready to risk his heart again. Surrounded by the Gansett Island community, Shane and Katie take an important step forward together, but is their new relationship strong enough to withstand an unexpected challenge?

Main Characers:

*Shane McCarthy,** works for McCarthy Construction.

*Katie Lawry,** nurse practitioner.

**Indicates recurring throughout the series*

Supporting Characters:

*Courtney McCarthy,** ex-wife of Shane McCarthy.

*Holden Francis Newsome,** Laura's son with ex-husband Justin Newsome, stepson of Owen Lawry, born in SEASON FOR LOVE.

*Sarah Lawry,** involved with Charlie Grandchamp in KISSES AFTER DARK.

***Charlie Granchamp,** involved with Sarah Lawry in KISSES AFTER DARK.

***Laura McCarthy Lawry,** mother of Holden Newsome in SEASON FOR LOVE, married to Owen Lawry in GANSETT AFTER DARK.

***Owen Lawry,** stepfather of Holden Newsome in SEASON FOR LOVE, married to Laura McCarthy Lawry in GANSETT AFTER DARK.

***Adele Kincaid,** mother of Sarah Lawry.

***Russ Kincaid,** father of Sarah Lawry.

***Julia Lawry,** office manager.

***Cindy Lawry,** hair stylist.

Josh Lawry, engineer.

***Jeff Lawry,** student.

***Judge Frank McCarthy,** grandfather of Holden Newsome in SEASON FOR LOVE, involved with Betsy Jacobson in GANSETT AFTER DARK.

***Betsy Jacobson,** involved with Frank McCarthy in GANSETT AFTER DARK.

***Stephanie Logan,** engaged to Grant McCarthy in SEASON FOR LOVE.

***Mac McCarthy,** married to Maddie Chester in FOOL FOR LOVE, father of Thomas Chester McCarthy in MAID FOR LOVE and Hailey McCarthy in FALLING FOR LOVE.

***Big Mac McCarthy,** grandfather of Thomas Chester McCarthy in MAID FOR LOVE, Hailey McCarthy in FALLING FOR LOVE and Peter Joseph "PJ" Cantrell in TIME FOR LOVE.

Buster: friend of Big Mac McCarthy.

***Adam McCarthy,** engaged to Abby Callahan in GANSETT AFTER DARK.

***Evan McCarthy,** engaged to Grace Ryan in WAITING FOR LOVE.

***Grant McCarthy,** engaged to Stephanie Logan in SEASON FOR LOVE.

***Stephanie Logan,** engaged to Grant McCarthy in SEASON FOR LOVE.

***Dr. Kevin McCarthy,** father of Riley and Finn.

***Riley McCarthy,** son of Kevin and Deb McCarthy, brother of Finn.

***Finn McCarthy,** son of Kevin and Deb McCarthy, brother of Riley.

***Linda McCarthy,** grandmother of Thomas Chester McCarthy in MAID FOR LOVE, Hailey McCarthy in FALLING FOR LOVE and Peter Joseph "PJ" Cantrell in TIME FOR LOVE.

***Maddie McCarthy,** mother of Thomas, married to Mac McCarthy in FOOL FOR LOVE, mother of Hailey McCarthy in FALLING FOR LOVE.

***Thomas McCarthy,** son of Mac and Maddie McCarthy.

***Abby Callahan,** engaged to Adam McCarthy in GANSETT AFTER DARK.

***Grace Ryan,** engaged to Evan McCarthy in WAITING FOR LOVE.

***Janey McCarthy Cantrell,** married to Joe Cantrell in READY FOR LOVE, mother of Peter Joseph "PJ" Cantrell in TIME FOR LOVE.

***Joe Cantrell,** married to Janey McCarthy Cantrell in READY FOR LOVE, father of Peter Joseph "PJ" Cantrell in TIME FOR LOVE.

***Peter Joseph "PJ" Cantrell,** son of Janey and Joe Cantrell, born in TIME FOR LOVE.

***Dan Torrington,** engaged to Kara Ballard in MEANT FOR LOVE.

***Kara Ballard,** engaged to Dan Torrington in MEANT FOR LOVE.

***Ned Saunders,** married to Francine, stepfather of Maddie and Tiffany, and grandfather of Ashleigh Sturgil, Thomas McCarthy and Hailey McCarthy in GANSETT AFTER DARK.

***Francine Saunders,** grandmother of Ashleigh Sturgil, Thomas McCarthy and Hailey McCarthy, married to Ned Saunders in GANSETT AFTER DARK.

***Captain Seamus O'Grady,** married to Carolina Cantrell in GANSETT AFTER DARK.

***Carolina Cantrell,** married to Seamus O'Grady in GANSETT AFTER DARK.

***Alex Martinez,** engaged to Jenny Wilks in MEANT FOR LOVE.

***Jenny Wilks,** engaged to Alex Martinez in MEANT FOR LOVE.

***Paul Martinez,** landscaper, co-owner of Martinez Lawn & Garden, member of Gansett Island Town Council.

***Dr. David Lawrence,** living with Daisy Babson in TIME FOR LOVE.

***Daisy Babson,** living with Dr. David Lawrence in TIME FOR LOVE.

***Jared James,** married to Lizzie James in CHANCE FOR LOVE.

***Lizzie James,** married to Jared James in CHANCE FOR LOVE.

***Blaine Taylor,** married to Tiffany Taylor and stepfather of Ashleigh Sturgil in TIME FOR LOVE.

***Tiffany Taylor,** mother of Ashleigh Sturgil, married to Blaine Taylor in TIME FOR LOVE.

***Sydney Donovan,** married to Luke Harris in SEASON FOR LOVE.

***Luke Harris,** married to Sydney Donovan in SEASON FOR LOVE.

***Lisa Chandler,** neighbor of Seamus and Carolina O'Grady, mother of Kyle and Jackson Chandler.

***Kyle Chandler,** 6, son of Lisa Chandler, brother of Jackson.

***Jackson Chandler,** 5, son of Lisa Chandler, brother of Kyle.

***Victoria Stevens,** involved with Shannon O'Grady in TIME FOR LOVE.

❝ KISSES AFTER DARK Headlines...

- Shane asks Katie out, but she says no!

- Russ and Adele gift the hotel to Laura and Owen!

- Charlie and Sarah are engaged!

- David offers Katie a job at the clinic! Katie later accepts!

- Shane is going to spend the winter working for Mac!

- Shane's ex-wife Courtney comes to find him!

- Stephanie and Grant are getting married on Labor Day!

- We meet Lisa, Kyle and Jackson Chandler!

- Lisa is dying of cancer!

- Seamus wants to step up for Lisa's boys!

- Maddie has a miscarriage! Later, they name the baby Connor!

- Luke and Sydney are expecting!

- Shane and Katie get a house together and want to have kids right away!

Shane McCarthy awakens the morning after his sister's wedding and reaches for his wife, Courtney. Then he remembers she's not his wife anymore, and he's no longer living in the apartment they shared. Once he gets out of bed, he loses the only moments he gives to Courtney anymore, those first thoughts in the morning. She hid a drug addiction to painkillers. He lost almost everything, including himself, sending her to rehab, only for her to serve him with divorce papers the day she was discharged. The worst part is he still doesn't know why she left him. She didn't give him the courtesy of a conversation. He'd planned to spend the rest of his life with her until she left him.

His sister, Laura, saved him by asking him to come help her get the Sand & Surf Hotel ready to reopen, which was much better than disappearing into despair. He needed to get up and shower before his nephew, Holden, woke up. He was taking care of his baby nephew so Laura and her new husband, Owen, could have their wedding night to themselves. As he lay in bed thinking, his mind drifted to what happened on the beach yesterday. He'd rescued Katie Lawry, Owen's sister, from drowning, and she almost took him down with her. She lost her bikini top in the incident, and the memory of her bare breasts is seared into his mind. He needs to forget about that before sees her this morning at the brunch her grandparents are throwing for the newlyweds. Holden is awake, so Shane gets him dressed and ready for the day.

Katie Lawry dreams about drowning. She's still processing the near-disaster from the day before. She fought to survive for Owen, so her tragedy wouldn't overtake his wedding day. She's in awe of Owen and his ability to love and be loved by Laura. Watching them together has led her to wonder if maybe she can give love a try, especially now that her abusive father is in jail.

"No," she says emphatically. "Absolutely not. Just because he's out of the picture doesn't mean his kind aren't still out there looking for their next victim." She says the words out loud, hoping they'll permeate the unreasonable longing her brother's wedding has generated in her. She wants what he and Laura have. Anyone would, especially a thirty-two-year-old woman who's never been kissed.

She thinks of Laura's brother, Shane, her handsome rescuer. He looked at her with heat in his eyes, which made her feel achy and reminded her that she's a healthy, young woman. She needs to tamp those urges and never forget her violent upbringing.

Sarah awakens with thoughts of her fiancé, Charlie. They made love for the first and second time the night before. Thinking about the discoveries she made, not only about him but also about herself, has her blushing from head to toe, her eyes squeezed tightly closed in embarrassment. How will she ever face him in the bright light of day after the way she behaved? The brush of his lips over her forehead lets her know she's no longer alone with her salacious thoughts.

"Good morning."

"Mmm, morning."

She can't bring herself to look at him, so she keeps her eyes tightly closed. "I come bearing gifts."

"Is that coffee I smell?"

"It is indeed, but you have to actually look at me before you can have it."

"I can't look at you. I might never be able to look at you again."

His bark of laughter rings through the room.

"God, you turned me into a madwoman."

"I love that."

"You're out to embarrass me to death, aren't you?"

"No way. I'm out to love you until death do us part, starting right now."

After five decades as an innkeeper, Adele Kincaid is up with the roosters, as her husband, Russ, says. She's so happy to be back on Gansett and thrilled that the boy she loves so much has found a wonderful woman to love him. Add to that the amazing job Owen and Laura did bringing the Sand & Surf back to life, and Adele is so proud. She recalls the awful scene she witnessed with her granddaughter, Katie, the day before. Thank goodness Shane was here to save her. If she wasn't mistaken, Adele had seen a spark between the two of them. She'll keep an eye on that situation. Maybe it's time for her and Russ to move back home to Gansett.

Katie runs into Shane and Holden, taking a walk on the beach. She is sticking around for a while. He surprises himself and her by asking her out to dinner. She declines his invitation and worries that she offended her brother's new brother-in-law.

At brunch, they end up sitting next to each other. Russ and Adele gift the Sand & Surf Hotel to Laura and Owen. Their other grandchildren will each receive a gift of the same value when they marry. The Lawry kids ask, what if they don't get married? They'll have to wait until their grandparents pass away, which they won't be doing for a very long time, so it'd be better if they fall in love and marry.

Charlie announces that he proposed to Sarah and she accepted. He promises her children that she will only know love and safety moving forward.

Adele shares the story of how she saw Shane save Katie from drowning the day before. Everyone is shocked and relieved they're okay. The moment Adele mentions the incident, Katie grabs Shane's hand and holds on for the rest of brunch.

Following brunch, Julia, Katie's twin sister, starts packing, and Katie breaks the news that she's not returning to Texas right away. She quit her job after the doctor she worked with attempted to attack her. Shane asked her out to dinner, but she said no. Julia badgers Katie to go on the date until she gets up, marches across the hall to Shane's room and bangs on his door. They make plans for later that night.

Shane meets his cousins, uncles and father to fish and ends up catching an eighty-pound tuna. Big Mac plans to grill the tuna for dinner, and everyone is invited. Shane made reservations for dinner with Katie, but she insists on joining his family to enjoy the fish he caught. He's nervous to expose her to his family, but it's fine with her. She already met them at the wedding. The entire McCarthy family and all their close friends are there for the fish dinner. After enjoying the delicious tuna, visiting with everyone and listening to Evan and Owen play, Katie and Shane head back to the hotel.

Shane talks to Katie about his ex-wife, Courtney, and her drug addiction. When they take a walk on the beach, Katie steps on a piece of broken glass. Shane takes her to the clinic, where Dr. David cleans her up and puts stitches in the cut. She's so disappointed because, aside from her injury, she was really enjoying her first date ever.

Shane takes Katie back to the hotel and settles her in her room. She asks him to stay with her. He keeps her safe during a thunderstorm, which scares her. Katie wakes up to a note on the pillow.

> *Morning! Hope your foot doesn't hurt too much. I have to work until about five today, but I'll come by after I get home and grab a shower. What do you think of Italian food? I had a great time last night. Shane*

Katie sighs with happiness as she rereads the note. He's so sweet and was incredibly kind and accommodating last night—not only when she injured her foot, but after she told him it was her first-ever date. He'd made her feel special, and she's eager to see him later.

Adele comes to take Katie shopping, but since she's injured, they settle for breakfast on the patio and plan to lounge around all day. Dr. David Lawrence stops by to speak with Katie.

"Sorry to barge in on your breakfast," he says.

"It's fine," Katie replies.

"After we met last night, I was thinking about how you mentioned you're a nurse practitioner at home. We're desperately in need of more help at the clinic, and I wondered if you'd have any interest in relocating."

Katie stares at him as her grandmother beams with pleasure.

"What a lovely offer," Adele says. "What do you think, Katie?"

"I, um, I don't know what to think."

"I'm sorry to drop it on you this way, but we've been overwhelmed for quite some time now, and our uptick in patient load has made it possible to consider hiring another full-time nurse practitioner. We already have Victoria Stevens, our nurse practitioner-midwife, but the two of us are utterly swamped. When you said you were a nurse practitioner in a family practice, my wheels began to spin."

Katie's wheels spun right along with his.

"What's your situation at home?" he asks.

"Funny you should ask. I recently quit my job in that family practice."

David places his hand over his heart. "Don't play with me."

Katie laughs at his boyish grin. "I really did quit right before I came here and was going to look for a job when I got back to Texas after some time here with my family."

"Would you consider relocating to our lovely island?" Katie reviews the momentous few days she's already had on Gansett and how much she's enjoyed spending time with her mother, grandparents, Owen, Laura, Holden—and Shane—not to mention the rest of the McCarthy family. What would it be like to be there all the time, surrounded by her family and new friends like Shane and his family?

"Katie?" Adele says. "What do you think?"

"I'd love to hear more about the job."

"Fair enough." David withdraws a business card from his wallet and hands it to her. "My cell number is on there. Feel free to give me a call when you're getting around better, and we'll set up a time for you to come in. Or just stop by, and I'll fit you in between patients."

"Thank you so much for thinking of me for the job."

"No problem. I hope you'll give it some thought and remember the word *desperate* as you do your thinking."

"Well, how about that?" Adele says when they're alone again.

"Rather unexpected."

"A very interesting offer, to say the least, and allow me to sweeten the pot by telling you that Pop and I are talking about moving back to the island in the spring."

"You are? Really?"

"Uh-huh. We've had enough of the Florida sun. We'll be looking for a little place on the island before we go home later this month."

They discuss her date with Shane the night before. Katie is concerned about getting involved because they're both carrying heavy baggage. He lost his wife to addiction and then divorce, which knocked him flat for a while.

Adele props her chin on her upturned fist. "You've waited a long time to take a chance with any man, so it's understandable that you have concerns. Let me tell you what I know to be true—everyone has crap. You don't get to be thirty years old without accumulating crap—some of it good, some of it not so good. If you're looking for someone with no crap, you'll be hard-pressed to find him. There are no guarantees in this life, and when we risk our hearts, there's always a chance of getting hurt. Speaking only for myself now, I'd much prefer taking a chance on being hurt over never knowing real, true love. I look at your grandpa after fifty-five years of marriage, and I still think, 'There he is. There's my guy.' I want you to have that, too, my sweet girl."

She gives Katie a lot to think about.

Shane is working in the kitchen at one of the new affordable housing units when Lisa Chandler and her boys, Kyle and Jackson, arrive to check the progress of the house that will soon be theirs. At five and six, the boys have a lot of energy, while Lisa looks exhausted from working at three restaurants to make ends meet. She also has a wicked cough that seems to suck the life out of her. When he asks about it, she says she's fine and will pick up some medicine.

Mac arrived as the boys came pounding down the stairs. The boys love Mac, and he always takes a few minutes to wrestle with them. Shane and Mac aren't sure what the deal is with the boys' father. Lisa has said only that he isn't in the picture.

Lisa comes down the stairs, coughing again. Mac will ask David to stop and check on her when he goes to the clinic with Maddie, who is pregnant. He jokes about having three kids. Mac asks Shane to stay for the winter and continue working with him, which Shane agrees to do.

Mac heads to the clinic to meet Maddie. This time, they'll be settled on the mainland long before the baby is due. He can't take any more traumatic births.

Victoria calls them into an exam room and teases them about getting pregnant again so soon after Hailey's birth.

"Suffice to say there was champagne involved," Maddie says with a laugh.

Before they start the exam, Mac tells Victoria about Lisa Chandler's cough and how she told Shane she can't afford to come to the clinic. Victoria promises to send David to check on her. Victoria performs the exam and ultrasound.

"Hang on just a second, Maddie," Victoria says before leaving the room.

Victoria returns with David, who performs the test again.

They can't find the baby's heartbeat.

In all his life, Mac has never heard a louder silence.

Mac and Maddie are devastated as they make plans to go to Providence for a D&C procedure.

Shane picks up Katie for their second date and finds Sarah in Katie's room. She invites Shane and Katie to dinner the next night, and Shane graciously accepts. "I love your mom and Charlie, too. They've become good friends since I've lived here. It's never a hardship to spend time with them."

He closes the door and steps closer to her. She's riveted by the intense way he looks at her. "And it's never a hardship to spend time with you either."

Shane thought about her all day, but specifically about kissing. "Shane…"

Her first kiss turns into everything else, too, and they end up staying in with pizza and a movie afterward.

Shane receives a message from Mac, who's going to the mainland for a few days. He'll fill Shane in when he returns. Janey fills Shane and Laura in about the miscarriage. Shane leaves to pick up their dinner and runs into Ned Saunders at the restaurant. Shane asks Ned about a rental since he's staying on the island for the winter to work with Mac.

David checks on Lisa Chandler and sees Seamus O'Grady at the mailbox next door. Seamus asks about Lisa and the boys as he glances toward the driveway next to his. "I know you can't talk about their private business, but if they need anything—anything at all—come to me. Caro and I get a kick out of those kids."

"I'll keep that in mind. You have a nice evening, Seamus."

David likes how island residents look after each other. He finds the Chandler boys running around in the yard. They take him inside, where Lisa is sleeping. The boys wake her up, and she's surprised to see David. Seamus knocks on the door to invite the boys over for dinner. They wash up and head out, which allows David to examine Lisa.

He's stunned to see tears rolling down her face.

"Everyone is so nice," she says softly.

"That's Gansett for you."

"I think I'm really sick." She looks down at the blanket that covers her lap. "As in really, really sick."

"Why haven't you come to see me before now?"

"I've been in denial. I kept thinking I'd shake it off the way I always do."

"Do you mind if I take a listen?" David doesn't like what he hears and convinces Lisa to rest while the boys spend the night at Seamus and Carolina's house. Lisa agrees to see David at the clinic in the morning.

David is deeply concerned about Lisa and is sorry she waited so long to get medical help. As a seasonal worker in several of the island's restaurants, she didn't qualify for insurance coverage. He arrives home feeling exhausted and out of sorts but is excited to see Daisy after a long day apart. She makes everything better just by being there. As he parks next to his landlord Jared's Porsche, Jared and his wife, Lizzie, come out of their house, dressed up for a fundraiser.

David suggests they host a fundraiser for people who can't afford basic medical care.

They ask if he knows someone who needs help.

"Yeah, I actually do. I've got a young mom with two young boys who might be seriously ill. The boys are five and six."

"What can we do?" Lizzie asks.

"Can I get back to you about that tomorrow when I know more about what we're dealing with?"

"Absolutely," Jared says. "Anything she needs, you let me know."

"I was having a horrendously shitty day until about five minutes ago. Thanks, you guys."

Lizzie hugs David. "Whenever you encounter something like this, you come to us, okay? We have everything we could ever want or need, and it's my pleasure to spend Jared's money on worthwhile causes and people in need."

Jared snorts with laughter. "She's quite good at it, too."

"I don't believe in doing anything if I can't do it well," Lizzie says.

"And that's why I love you so much."

"You two have a great evening," David says, amused by them, as always.

"We'll expect to hear from you tomorrow," Lizzie says.

Smiling, David goes up the stairs to the apartment he shares with Daisy.

For the first time in her life, Katie Lawry wakes up to a man in her bed.

Shane kisses her forehead and then her lips. "Morning."

"Morning."

"Best night of my life. Hands down."

"Really. Well… That's quite nice to hear."

It's okay if he doesn't feel the same way. He's been married after all, and by all accounts was crazy in love with his wife. Of course, he's had better nights than the one he'd shared with her.

"I know what you're thinking," he says, startling her.

"How do you know?"

"You're thinking that I was married, so naturally this was just another night for me, but it wasn't. It was really important—and special—for me, too. For many reasons, but primarily because I got to spend it with you."

"And that's the most perfect thing you could've said."

He smiles. "I thought you might like that." After another kiss, he says, "I really do mean it. I've been stuck in a bad place for a long time now, and it's so nice to feel good again. The time that we've spent together has made me feel very good, which is a huge improvement in a short time, so thanks for that."

"Happy to be of assistance."

After a shower, they go downstairs for breakfast and run into Laura as they're debating whether Shane should've carried her due to her injured foot.

"Are you two kids already bickering?" Laura asks from her post at the reception desk. "Shouldn't you still be in the rose-colored glasses stage?"

"Who's in the rose-colored glasses stage?" Abby asks as she comes out of the gift shop. "Oh," she says when she sees Shane and Katie. "I know who. Come down and tell us everything."

"While that's a lovely offer," Shane says sarcastically, "we'll pass."

"I'll get it out of him and fill you in later," Laura says to Abby.

"No, you won't," Shane says firmly. Though she was horrified by the idea of Laura "getting it out of him," Katie laughs at their banter. They remind her of the way she speaks to her siblings now that they're older and out from under the black cloud of their childhood.

"We're going to breakfast," Shane says. "Leave us alone."

"Do I have to?" Laura asks, chin propped on her upturned hand.

Katie is amused by them and appreciates Laura's invitation to an upcoming girls' night out.

"She's busy," Shane says before Katie can reply.

"I am?" Katie asks him.

"Very, very busy."

"Doing what?"

"Come with me, and I'll tell you."

Katie smiles at Laura. "Thanks for the invite, but it seems I have other plans." Then she decides that she doesn't like having him make decisions for her and tells Laura she'll be there.

Katie and Shane go into the restaurant to have breakfast. While he took a seat, she took an interest in the menu.

"Katie."

She glanced at him, hoping he couldn't somehow tell that her heart was racing and her hands were trembling ever so slightly. This, right here, was why she'd avoided men all her life.

"I'm sorry. I shouldn't have done that. I was doing what I do with Laura. I shouldn't have answered for you. If you want to go out with her and the others, that's exactly what you should do." He smiled. "I'll find a way to get by on my own for the evening."

His adorably heartfelt apology and innate understanding of what had upset her went a long way toward calming her rattled nerves. "Thank you for apologizing. That scenario…" She gestured toward the lobby. "Sort of a hot-button issue for me."

"I understand. It won't happen again."

She stared across the table at him.

"What?"

"I… I didn't expect that to be so easy."

"Why not? I was way out of line and realized it about two seconds after I said it. You don't think I'm going to fix that ASAP?"

Katie appreciates that he immediately understood the issue and fixed it. That makes him different from other men she's known.

Katie goes to the clinic to talk to David about the job. David is walking a patient out. The woman is young, with long dark hair and doesn't look well.

David escorts Katie into his office. "Another day, another bout of insanity. Tough case this morning. Thirty-one-year-old single mother of two. I suspect late-stage lung cancer."

"Oh, my God. That's awful. Was that her who just left?"

He nods and then grimaces. "She put off coming in because she couldn't afford it."

"I hate hearing that."

"You and me both. Anyway… Let's talk about you and your plans."

Katie agrees to take the job.

Back at the Hotel, Katie greets Shane when he comes in from work. He convinces her to go for a swim in the ocean, a place she's always loved but has been afraid of since the near-drowning. During their swim, they talk about how they're staying on the island for now. Katie notices the lights in Newport in the distance and says she's never been. Shane decides to take her the next day.

During a great day touring Newport, Shane realizes he loves Katie. As they're walking from the ferry back to the Surf, someone calls Shane's name.

He turns, realizes it's Courtney and drops Katie's hand. Courtney asks to talk to Shane. She tells him things he didn't know that have him reeling and rethinking everything he thought was true. The information weighs heavily on him.

Katie is hurt that he'd act embarrassed by her. Laura hears why Katie is upset and goes out to give Courtney a piece of her mind. Shane sends Laura away and talks to Courtney in the sitting room. Laura convinces Katie to go out for girls' night out. As they're leaving, Shane comes out of the room with Courtney and sends her away. Laura tells Courtney to leave, that she's not wanted there.

Shortly after Shane gets to his room, he realizes his mistake and races to find Katie. Unfortunately, he runs into Owen, who questions his motives towards Katie. Shane convinces Owen that he cares about Katie and wants to make things right with her. Owen tells him he knows where the girls are, and he'll take him—eventually.

Sydney waits for Luke to come home. With both Big Mac and Mac off island, Luke was stuck running things at the marina.

"Very happy to see you."

He lifts her into a hug. "You see me every day."

"And I'm always happy to see you but today is special."

"How so?"

"Put me down, and I'll show you."

He let her slide down the aroused front of him but kept a firm grip on her hand.

She towed him into the bathroom that adjoined their bedroom and stepped aside so he could see the objects she'd arranged on the countertop.

"What's all that?"

"Take a closer look."

He leaned in, his brows furrowed adorably the way they did when he was concentrating on something. And then, as she watched, his eyes widened with surprise and pleasure.

"Really?"

Sydney nodded, tears filling her eyes. "Ten tests. Ten positives."

"We're pregnant?"

"We're pregnant. It's not official until Victoria says it is, but ten tests—" She didn't get to finish the sentence, because he was kissing her. Sydney wasn't sure whether the dampness on her face was from her or him, but what did it matter?

Jenny was first to arrive for girls' night out, followed by Grace, Stephanie, Abby and Janey. Soon after, Laura and Katie came in. Laura was still upset that Courtney had dared to show up just as Shane was starting to be happy again. Soon, Maddie and Tiffany arrive, and they rally around Maddie, hoping to provide a much-needed distraction after the trauma of losing the baby.

Owen forces Shane to wait an hour, then drags him to dinner with the guys, most of whom are his cousins. When they see how upset Shane is, Evan, Adam and Grant take him to crash girls' night, much to the dismay of the other men, who had promised to give the ladies more time before their usual crash.

Once at Luke and Sydney's, Shane goes right to find Katie and asks her to talk to him. Katie joins Shane on the deck.

"I'm so sorry, Katie. I've been trying to get to you for hours now so I could say that to you. I was completely shocked to see her, and I reacted badly. It kills me that I hurt you and made you cry after you put such faith in me. I've loved every minute we've spent together. I told your brother earlier that you've been more right for me in five days than she was in five years. He said I ought to tell you that."

While Katie believes Shane wants to be with her, she asks him for time to think, which he reluctantly gives her. Shane goes home to the Surf, where he spends the night wondering what happened to his perfect day.

Katie cries herself to sleep and wakes to a thunderstorm. She hears a soft knock on the door, and then Shane is there holding her. "I thought you might be scared."

Thrilled to see him and overwhelmed by his kindness, she takes his hand and all but drags him into the room, closing the door behind her. They get into bed, and Shane reaches for her. Katie snuggles up to him as another loud boom of thunder makes her whimper.

"It's okay, honey. I'm right here." He holds her close as the storm rages, reassuring her with soft words and the gentle caress of his hand on her back.

Katie falls asleep in his arms, no more certain that she belongs there than she'd been earlier but comforted nonetheless by his tenderness.

Katie starts receiving letters from Shane the next day. He tells her he sent Courtney away and wants to be with her and only her. She catches her grandfather delivering the notes and learns her grandmother has more letters for her, but Adele insists on following Shane's delivery instructions. Katie waits another hour before her grandfather delivers the next note.

"How many more are there?" she asks her grandfather.

"I don't know. Don't shoot the messenger."

"Love you, Poppy."

"Love you, too, pumpkin. For what it's worth, he seems like a nice guy."

"He is."

"Don't let me keep you. Go see what he has to say. You know you're dying to."

"I am!" With a smile for her grandfather, Katie steps into her room, closes the door and tears open the envelope.

> *Dear sweet Katie, More food for thought… Since we're both sticking around on Gansett this winter, how about we get a place together? One with a fireplace. I love fires in the winter. Do you? Are you convinced yet that I'm serious about you? Do you believe me when I tell you you're the only one I want? Love, Shane*

Hoping to catch her grandfather making another delivery, she throws open the door and gasps when she finds Shane standing there. There's nothing left to think about as she jumps into his arms or when he lifts her into his kiss. Holding her tightly, he carries her inside and kicks the door closed behind him.

"What're you doing home?" she asks. "I thought I had to wait hours to see you."

Katie asks about his friend Lisa Chandler and learns she has terminal cancer.

"Apparently, David consulted with his colleagues in Boston, and they agree it's too far gone for treatment other than making her as comfortable as possible," Shane said.

"Oh, God."

"David's friend Jared and his wife, Lizzie, have donated nurses and equipment to keep Lisa at home. Seamus and Carolina have offered to help with the kids, and there's a fundraiser next week at the Beachcomber for the family."

"The Gansett Island community doesn't fool around."

Katie wants what he wants, but they need to slow things down and spend more time together. Katie isn't sure what it feels like to fall in love. Shane shares what it feels like for him.

"Last night, when I couldn't find you and Owen wouldn't tell me where you'd gone, I was out of my mind. I felt like I was going crazy or something, knowing you were nearby and that I'd hurt you badly enough to make you cry. When I heard that, I would've given everything I had to touch you, hold you and tell you how much I care about you and how badly I want to be with you. I had to wait hours—hours and hours—knowing you were upset because of me.

"And then when I walked into Luke's house and saw you there, everything that was wound up inside me settled. Even though nothing had been resolved between us, I felt calm because you were there. I could see you, touch you and talk to you. It was like everything I needed to survive was right there in one beautiful, sweet package. That's what it feels like to me."

He glances at her. "Why are you crying?"

"Because," she says, wiping the tears from her cheeks, "that was the most incredible thing anyone has ever said to me."

Seamus is getting coffee at the diner when he hears about Lisa's diagnosis. He rushes home to see how he can help. He sees David in the driveway.

"I came as soon as I heard what's going on," Seamus says. "How is she?"

"Overwhelmed," David says, seeming overwhelmed himself.

"There's nothing that can be done?"

David shakes his head.

"Where are the kids?"

"At home for now. Jared and Lizzie James have pulled off a minor miracle and brought a whole team of people out here to tend to her and the kids."

"What happens to them?" Seamus asks, relieved to hear that some immediate help has arrived. "After?"

"We haven't gotten that far. She's still absorbing the news."

Seamus nods in understanding. "You'll let me know if there's anything we can do to help?"

David assures him that he will.

Seamus tells Carolina about Lisa. He wants to step up for the boys.

Big Mac and Linda hold a party to introduce Mallory to the McCarthy family and their friends. Mac, who is still devastated over the loss of the baby, wants to stay home, but since Maddie is acting as if everything is normal, they go to the party. The gathering includes his brothers, their significant others, his Uncle Frank and Betsy, Laura, Owen, Holden, Shane, Katie, Uncle Kevin, Riley, Finn and Mallory, the guest of honor.

Joe, Janey and PJ arrive a few minutes later, Janey seeming hesitant as she's introduced to Mallory.

"It's nice to meet you." Mallory takes the hand that Janey offers. "I've heard so much about you."

"Nice to meet you, too. I'm sorry I wasn't here the last time."

"No worries," Mallory says. "You're here now."

"Just don't call me Brat, and we'll get along fine."

Mallory laughs. "You got it."

Katie and Shane attended bachelor and bachelorette parties for Grant and Stephanie. When Shane comes home, he's too drunk to bother Katie. He finds a note from Katie saying she loves him and that she knows he is preoccupied with something. She asks him to talk to someone about what's weighing on him.

Shane wakes early and is upset that Katie noticed his distress. He thought he was doing a better job of hiding it. Shane goes to see his Uncle Kevin, the psychiatrist, who convinces him to give himself a break after everything he's been through, but also encourages him to tell Katie what's on his mind.

Mac and Maddie are on the way to Grant and Stephanie's rehearsal dinner when Mac can't take Maddie's silence any longer. He pulls over, begs her to talk to him and they finally grieve for the baby they lost. They name him Connor.

The morning of the wedding, Ned shows Shane a house for rent. It's everything he's hoping for, and the best part is that it's within walking distance to the Surf, where his baby nephew lives.

Stephanie wakes up on her wedding day at Charlie's house and hears giggling coming from her father's bedroom. Knowing he's happy with his love, Sarah, and living a life free of the past warms Stephanie's heart. Her best friends come to help Stephanie get ready. With tears in his eyes, Charlie says his daughter is "breathtaking."

Grant and Stephanie are married on the deck of the Sand and Surf. At the end of the evening, Shane takes Katie to see the house he found, although he's worried he made such a big decision for both of them.

They sit in the corner of the empty living room. Always the lady, Katie curls her legs under her, tugging her skirt down to cover her knees.

"I want to tell you a few things that normally I'd prefer to keep to myself for several reasons. One, I hate talking about this stuff, and two, it really has no bearing on you, us, or how I feel about you. But it's important to me that I be honest with you, so I want to tell you, okay?"

"Okay…"

He hates the trepidation he sees on her face and hears in her one-word answer, but he knows he has to come clean with her. "Earlier this week, when you wrote me your adorable note, you said you'd noticed I had something on mind. You told me that if I couldn't talk to you about it, you wished I would talk to someone. You were right. I did have something weighing heavily on me, and I talked to my Uncle Kevin, who's a psychiatrist."

"What was weighing so heavily on you?"

"The things that Courtney said to me… I was messed up afterward. I didn't want to be, because I've come so far from that situation, and I have so much in my life now to be grateful for. I'd started this awesome new relationship with you, and I was happy again for the first time in a very long time. So much of that happiness was because of you."

"Did Kevin help?"

"He helped a lot. We talked it through, and he said a lot of things that made so much sense, but one thing in particular really resonated with me." He takes hold of Katie's hand and links their fingers, needing to touch her while he talks about his past for what he hopes will be the last time. "He said that with this new information about what really happened, it was no longer possible to make Courtney the villain in our marriage. I couldn't hate her anymore, and I had to find a way to deal with the things she told me without derailing my new life."

"And have you? Have you dealt with it?"

"Not entirely." He gave her the honesty she deserved. "But I will in time. The important thing for you to know is that I have absolutely no desire to go back to her. I loved her very much for a long time, but I don't love her anymore. I love you. You're the one I want to be with. I want to live here with you or somewhere else, if this place doesn't do it for you. I want to be close to our nephew and the new babies when they're born. I want to spend time with my family and friends and your family when they come to visit."

He leans his forehead against hers. "I want to be with your mom and Charlie, Laura and Owen and Holden, and I want to help out with my friend Lisa and her kids, who are going to need all the friends they can get. I want to be here with you. I want a life with you. I know we haven't known each other long, but it took me no time at all to know you're special, and the more time we spend together, the more proof I get that my initial gut feeling about you was spot-on."

"Shane…" She takes a deep breath and places her free hand over her heart. "You take my breath away."

"In a good way?"

"In the best way possible."

His relief at hearing that was overwhelming.

"I love you, too," she says. "I want all the same things you do and a couple of other things that it's too soon to tell you about."

"No, it's not too soon. Tell me. I want to know so I can help you get everything you want."

"I've mentioned this once before, but when I was younger," she says tentatively, "before I understood just how screwed-up my family really was, I pictured myself with a lot of kids. I'm thirty-two, so the reality of a big family is starting to slip away."

"Then we ought to get started on this project of yours sooner rather than later."

She stares at him, seeming astounded. "You're serious."

"Completely serious. I remember you telling me before about the horde of kids you want to have. My life has been on hold for a long, lonely time. I'm ready to get busy living again, and in case you haven't noticed, I love babies. Well, I love Holden, but I'm sure I'll be crazy about our kids, too. I want the same thing you do, and there's no time like the present to get busy living."

"Is this really happening?"

"It's really happening, and it's amazing, and it's only going to get better."

 An interview with Shane and Katie...

Your story is so sweet and full of beautiful moments, such as Shane's letters and Kate's reply. I love the way you two had to work out a lot of baggage from the past to find your happily ever after.

Katie: We definitely worked for it.

And when Courtney showed up in the middle of it...

Shane: I thought I was hallucinating when I saw her. And when she told me more about what really happened… She sent me into a tailspin right when I was finally beginning to move on.

Later, when she dies suddenly, you're again revisited with shock.

Shane: I'll never forget the state police coming to find me to tell me that news. I was so hoping she'd get a fabulous second act, and I'll always be sad that she didn't.

Katie: That was a very sad time for us.

And it happened close to when you lost your first baby to miscarriage.

Shane: Yes, that was a rough period, but we got through it together. And then our son, Ben, was born. He's eight now and fills our lives with such joy and laughter.

Does he have siblings?

Katie: Does he ever! We had four kids in four years, which I don't recommend.

Shane: What she said. Holy shit, literally… That's a lot of diapers and sleepless nights and nonstop madness.

Katie: I was getting old. We had to hurry.

Shane: Stop. You're ageless.

Katie: If you say so, but my eggs were curdling.

(They laugh.)

Four kids. That's so exciting! Tell us about the other three!

Katie: Our Claire is seven, Jameson is six and Emerson is five. It's complete madness and we wouldn't have it any other way.

Wow! You wanted a big family, and now you have it. How does it feel?

Katie: Even in the midst of absolute chaos, I'm so, so happy to have this family and to give them the magical childhood I didn't get to have, except when my father was deployed or we were here on Gansett with our precious grandparents. I do wonder how my mother ever handled seven of us, though.

Shane: Katie makes every day special for our kids and me. She's the magician who makes it all work.

Katie: You more than do your part, too, Dad. We're a great team and do far more laughing than crying these days.

Are you still working at the clinic?

Katie: I do twenty hours a week now that everyone is in school all day, but I took a few years off during the baby boom. It's nice to be back to work and to have that time just to be Katie, the nurse, rather than Katie the mom to four little ones.

Shane, are you still working with Mac?

Shane: I am, and we're busier than ever. It's still so much fun to work with him and my other cousins every day. Speaking of laughter… That crew is still a comedy team.

I can only imagine. Congratulations on your beautiful family and life together!

MARIE FORCE

Love After Dark

Book 13: Love After Dark
Published: August 18, 2015

> *Life has a way of changing your plans. Sometimes for the better…*
> Paul Martinez has been run ragged by the demands of managing the family's landscaping business and his mother's battle with dementia. It's been so long since he had sex that he can't remember the last time. The arrival of nurse Hope Russell brought some badly needed help to Paul and his brother Alex in managing their mother's illness, but Hope's presence has sparked a whole new problem for Paul—lusting after one of his employees, something his late father would never condone.
>
> Hope and her young son Ethan badly need this second chance on Gansett Island, and she's determined to make her new job work for both of them. Kissing her boss, however, was not part of the plan. The more time she spends with Paul, the more she admires the way he cares for his mother and the attention he pays to her son. But when Paul finds out about her shameful past, will he still want her and Ethan in his life?

Main Characters:
*Paul Martinez, co-owner of Martinez Lawn & Garden, member of Gansett Town Council.

*Hope Russell, nurse, mother of Ethan Russell.

*Indicates recurring throughout the series

Supporting Characters:
*Alex Martinez, engaged to Jenny Wilks in MEANT FOR LOVE.

*Jenny Wilks, engaged to Alex Martinez in MEANT FOR LOVE.

*Marion Martinez, co-founder of Martinez Lawn & Garden, mother of Alex and Paul Martinez.

*Erin Barton, new lighthouse keeper, twin of the late Toby Barton, who was engaged to Jenny Wilks Martinez.

*Chelsea, bartender at Beachcomber

***Chloe,** owner, Curl Up & Dye Salon.

***Ethan Russell,** son of Hope Russell.

***Katie Lawry,** nurse practitioner at Gansett Island Clinic and involved with Shane McCarthy in KISSES AFTER DARK.

***Lisa Chandler,** neighbor of Seamus and Carolina O'Grady, mother of Kyle and Jackson.

***Mallory Vaughn,** nurse practitioner.

***Seamus O'Grady,** married to Carolina O'Grady in GANSETT AFTER DARK.

***Carolina O'Grady,** grandmother of PJ Cantrell, married to Seamus O'Grady in GANSETT AFTER DARK.

***Kyle Chandler,** age 6, son of Lisa Chandler.

***Jackson Chander,** age 5, son of Lisa Chandler.

***Dan Torrington,** engaged to Kara Ballard in MEANT FOR LOVE.

***Dr. David Lawrence,** living with Daisy Babson in TIME FOR LOVE.

***Victoria Stevens,** involved with Shannon O'Grady in TIME FOR LOVE.

***Jared James,** married to Lizzie James in CHANCE FOR LOVE.

***Lizzie James,** married to Jared James in CHANCE FOR LOVE.

***Blaine Taylor,** married to Tiffany Taylor and stepfather of Ashleigh Sturgil in TIME FOR LOVE.

Carl: Hope Russell's ex-husband and Ethan's father.

***Mac McCarthy,** married to Maddie Chester in FOOL FOR LOVE, father of Thomas Chester McCarthy in MAID FOR LOVE, Hailey McCarthy in FALLING FOR LOVE and Connor McCarthy (deceased) in KISSES AFTER DARK.

***Maddie McCarthy,** mother of Thomas, married to Mac McCarthy in FOOL FOR LOVE, mother of Hailey McCarthy in FALLING FOR LOVE and Connor McCarthy (deceased) in KISSES AFTER DARK.

***Grant McCarthy,** married to Stephanie Logan in KISSES AFTER DARK.

***Stephanie Logan,** married to Grant McCarthy in KISSES AFTER DARK.

***Adam McCarthy,** engaged to Abby Callahan in GANSETT AFTER DARK.

***Abby Callahan,** engaged to Adam McCarthy in GANSETT AFTER DARK.

***Evan McCarthy,** engaged to Grace Ryan in WAITING FOR LOVE.

***Grace Ryan,** engaged to Evan McCarthy in WAITING FOR LOVE.

***Janey McCarthy Cantrell,** married to Joe Cantrell in READY FOR LOVE, mother of Peter Joseph "PJ" Cantrell in TIME FOR LOVE.

***Joe Cantrell,** married to Janey McCarthy Cantrell in READY FOR LOVE, father of Peter Joseph "PJ" Cantrell in TIME FOR LOVE.

***Laura McCarthy Lawry,** mother of Holden Newsome in SEASON FOR LOVE, married to Owen Lawry in GANSETT AFTER DARK.

***Owen Lawry,** stepfather of Holden Newsome in SEASON FOR LOVE, married to Laura McCarthy Lawry in GANSETT AFTER DARK.

***Shane McCarthy,** involved with Katie Lawry in KISSES AFTER DARK.

***Judge Frank McCarthy,** involved with Betsy Jacobson in GANSETT AFTER DARK.

***Betsy Jacobson,** involved with Frank McCarthy in GANSETT AFTER DARK.

***Dr. Kevin McCarthy,** psychiatrist, father of Riley and Finn.

***Riley McCarthy,** works for McCarthy Construction, son of Kevin and Deb.

***Finn McCarthy,** works for McCarthy Construction, son of Kevin and Deb.

***Ned Saunders,** married to Francine, grandfather of Ashleigh Sturgil, Thomas McCarthy and Hailey McCarthy in GANSETT AFTER DARK.

***Francine Saunders,** grandmother of Ashleigh Sturgil, Thomas McCarthy, Hailey McCarthy and Connor McCarthy (deceased), married to Ned Saunders in GANSETT AFTER DARK.

***Tobias "Slim" Fitzgerald Jackson, Jr.,** pilot.

***Sydney Donovan,** married to Luke Harris in SEASON FOR LOVE.

***Luke Harris,** married to Sydney Donovan in SEASON FOR LOVE.

***Big Mac McCarthy,** grandfather of Thomas Chester McCarthy in MAID FOR LOVE, Hailey McCarthy in FALLING FOR LOVE, Peter Joseph "PJ" Cantrell in TIME FOR LOVE and Connor McCarthy (deceased) in KISSES AFTER DARK.

***Linda McCarthy,** grandmother of Thomas Chester McCarthy in MAID FOR LOVE, Hailey McCarthy in FALLING FOR LOVE, Peter Joseph "PJ" Cantrell in TIME FOR LOVE and Connor McCarthy (deceased) in KISSES AFTER DARK.

***Kara Ballard,** engaged to Dan Torrington in MEANT FOR LOVE.

***Tiffany Taylor,** mother of Ashleigh Sturgil, married to Blaine Taylor in TIME FOR LOVE.

***Tom Barton,** father of Erin and Toby (deceased).

***Mary Beth Barton,** mother of Erin and Toby (deceased).

66 LOVE AFTER DARK Headlines!

- Paul decides it's time to start dating again!

- Lisa Chandler passes away!

- Hope and Paul kiss!

- Marion needs to see a specialist on the mainland!

- Jenny is worried about losing Alex before their wedding, as she did with Toby!

- Seamus and Carolina take in Kyle and Jackson Chandler!

- Lizzie and Jared look into starting a senior care facility on the island!

- Slim finds Erin injured on the side of the road and drives her home!

- The island community comes together for Lisa Chandler's funeral!

- Paul talks to Big Mac about dating an employee!

- Hope and Paul take Marion to Providence!

- Marion slaps Hope across the face!

- Paul and Hope spend time at Cape Cod!

- Alex surprises Jenny with a wedding at the lighthouse to ease her worries!

- Jenny is pregnant!

- Erin is sad that her late brother's fiancée got married, but she's happy for Jenny!

- Erin finds out that Slim's real name is Tobias, like her late brother!

- Kevin and Chelsea hook up!

- Alex and Jenny's long-planned wedding is beautiful!

- Paul and Hope get engaged! She and Ethan are staying on Gansett!

Paul Martinez loves September, when the tourists have left and the island belongs to the year-round residents again. Since his brother, Alex, is in love with his fiancée, Jenny, and they've hired Hope Russell to help with their mom, Paul feels that life is passing him by. He decides it's time to start dating again. If things were different, his first choice of women to date would be his mother's nurse, Hope.

However, Hope works for them, and his late father, George, had a rule against Paul and Alex dating women who work for them. Hope and her son, Ethan, are settling in well and adjusting to island life, and the last thing Paul wants to do is screw that up. Hope has provided some much-needed respite for Paul and Alex since she took over Marion's care. Jenny tries to set Paul up with her friend Erin, the new lighthouse keeper. While Erin is great, they both agree they'd be better as friends.

Paul comes home from work to find Ethan waiting for him. Ethan's curiosity, willingness to help and boundless energy remind Paul of himself and his brother at that age. While they take a walk to check the pumpkin patch, Ethan never stops talking. He tells Paul all about school and what he did that day. Paul tells Ethan how he once rushed to carve a pumpkin and ended up at the clinic with stitches in his hand. Ethan wants to know if Paul's dad was mad at him.

"He was after he knew I'd be okay. I got a hell of a talking-to about the dangers of knives and doing what I was told. Tough lesson learned the hard way."

"I don't have a dad anymore."

Paul tries not to show any reaction to that statement. He's wondered about the boy's father, but neither Ethan nor Hope has volunteered any information about him, and Paul hasn't wanted to ask. "Neither do I."

"Yeah, but yours died. Mine's in jail."

Paul is unsure of what to do with that information, especially after Ethan runs off after dropping it on him. Hope never mentioned anything, and it didn't come up in her background check. What should he do?

Hope is waiting for Paul when he gets back to the house. She's grateful for the time Paul spends with Ethan but worries he is being a bother. Paul enjoys the time with Ethan, and she shouldn't worry about it. Hope says Marion had a rough day, which upsets Paul. Then Marion comes to the door and mistakenly calls Paul by his father's name. Having to constantly remind Marion they're her sons and not her husband is heartbreaking for all of them.

After dinner, Paul is sitting outside enjoying the stars and a quiet moment to himself. Hope comes from her cabin behind the main house to talk to Paul, and gets a text from Katie Lawry that Lisa Chandler, an island resident, single mother in the final stages of lung cancer, won't make it through the night. Hope has been assisting Katie and Mallory Vaughn with caring for Lisa. Paul encourages Hope to go to Lisa and brings a sleeping Ethan to his house.

In the early morning hours, Paul awakens when Hope comes to collect Ethan. Lisa died at four o'clock in the morning, and Hope is upset. While he comforts her, they kiss and end up wrapped up in each other on the sofa where Paul was sleeping. Hope, embarrassed by her behavior, puts a stop to the kiss and races back to her cabin with Ethan. Worried he pushed Hope away by kissing her, Paul is awake the rest of the night.

When he sees Hope later, she avoids eye contact. Paul can't let their middle-of-the-night kiss or worries that he upset her fester all day, so he meets Hope after she puts Ethan on the school bus.

Paul holds up his hands. "I come in peace."

That draws a small smile from her. She folds her arms into the protective pose she seems to prefer and drops her gaze. "I'm so sorry, Paul. I don't know what came over me."

"You aren't going to quit, are you?"

Gasping, she looks up at him. "Do you *want* me to?"

"Hell, no, I don't want you to quit. We'd be lost without you."

"It was very unprofessional of me to kiss my boss like that."

"Your boss kinda liked it."

"Oh. Um…" She seems to force herself to look at him. "You did?"

Paul nods.

"Still, it was extremely unprofessional."

"No, it wasn't. You were upset, and it just happened. We're in an intense situation here with my mom's illness and the isolation of the island and everything that goes with it. I'd like to think this isn't your typical job."

"It's not. It's the best job I've ever had, and I'd hate to do anything to mess it up."

"Then let's not allow it to mess things up for either of us."

"Thank you for being so nice about it."

They work together to convince Marion to go to the clinic for her physical. Dr. David Lawrence has been caring for their mother for quite some time. During the physical, David notes a significant decline in her health and would like to have her seen by a specialist on the mainland. Hope agrees with his suggestion and offers to go with Paul if Ethan can stay with Jenny and Alex.

Alex is worried about Jenny. She's quiet and withdrawn, which isn't like her. He convinces her to talk to him and learns that she's afraid of something happening to Alex before their wedding. She was right here, a month before her wedding, when her Toby died in the 9/11 attacks. She's worried they won't make it to their wedding day. Alex reassures her and vows to spend as much time with her as he can before their wedding day.

The Gansett Island community rallies around Lisa's sons, Kyle and Jackson Chandler. Seamus and Carolina O'Grady took custody of the boys a few days before Lisa's death, but they've had their young neighbors for some time now. Shane and Mac McCarthy were in the process of building Lisa, Kyle and Jackson a new home when she got sick. Grace Ryan offers to help with the service for Lisa. Stephanie insists on hosting a reception following the service at her restaurant. It's been twenty years since Seamus left his home in Ireland, and just as long since he felt at home, but watching how the community surrounds the boys, he finally feels at home on Gansett.

Alex, Jenny and Paul entertain their friends David Lawrence, his girlfriend, Daisy Babson, Jared and Lizzie Jame and Erin Barton and Hope, who had the night off with Ethan having a sleepover at a friend's house and Marion out with her friends for the evening. Hope talks about how the island needs a senior care facility to keep those who need care close to their families. David knows of at least ten families on the island that would benefit from something like that. Hearing of a need, Lizzie tells Jared they need to open a facility. He promises to look into it. Paul tells them the old school building will be going up for sale, and Lizzie has a new idea to pursue.

Seamus comforts Kyle in the middle of the night when the child wakes up crying and missing his mom. He asks Seamus if his mom really is not coming back. Seamus confirms it, and the boy sobs himself to sleep. After he gets Kyle tucked back in, Seamus worries he's not the right man to be raising the boys. Caro soothes him and reassures him that all new parents feel that way. She tells him, "You'll teach them how to be men, and if they're even half the man you are, you will have done an amazing job."

Later that night, after getting their mom into bed, Alex and Jenny head to the new house they built behind the store. Paul convinces Hope to join him for a drink, and they end up kissing. Paul brings Hope inside with him and takes her to his room in case Alex and Jenny return. They talk about how a relationship could complicate things. Paul convinces Hope to stay and let him hold her for a while.

Lizzie James is up and showered early on Sunday morning. She asks Jared to take her to see the school. Now that the seed has been planted about a senior care facility, Lizzie can't let it go.

Lizzie calls and wakes Paul, who takes the call out in the living room so that he won't wake Hope. When he returns to his room, Hope is embarrassed to be in bed with her boss. As soon as she can, Hope runs out of Paul's room and returns to her cabin. Paul laughs at the irony. The first time he spends the night with a woman in longer than he can remember, and she runs away like her ass is on fire the next morning—great way to start the day.

As Hope escapes back to her cabin, she tells herself she cannot be with her boss. She and Ethan need the stability of this job. She can't screw it up. Determined to return to the easy friendship she had with Paul before the kissing happened, Hope returns to the Martinez house to get Marion ready for her day.

Once Marion is off for the day with her friends, Paul goes to the store to get some work done. Shortly after he gets there, Hope comes in seeking shelter from the rain. Paul kisses her, and she stops him, telling him they can't do this and runs out, leaving Paul confused. He makes a date with Chloe, who owns the salon in town, for that night.

As Hope gets home and starts to warm up, she thinks about the many reasons she needs to keep her distance from anything that can upset their lives. Her ex-husband was a nice, desirable man, like Paul, until he wasn't. She can't risk it. She's confident she's making the right decision regarding Paul until Ethan calls Paul his bestest friend ever, bringing tears to her eyes.

Mac McCarthy invites his siblings, cousins and uncles for a cookout that the rain forces inside. He chose that day for the gathering because his parents are off-island for the day and he wants to talk about their upcoming fortieth anniversary. The group decides on a surprise party. After the planning is done, the guys discuss Alex's upcoming bachelor party. The ladies tell them that while they are celebrating Alex, the ladies have hired strippers to keep them entertained at Jenny's bachelorette party. The men are outraged, which delights their wives and girlfriends. Mac is especially upset about his wife cavorting with strippers.

Unable to sleep, Paul goes outside to sit and get some air. He hears Hope crying and goes to her. She tries to send him away but ends up crying all over him. Paul tells her he knows Ethan's dad is in jail, which upsets her more. Hope talks about her ex-husband, Carl. They met in college, he was in sports medicine, and she was in nursing school. They got married right out of school and had Ethan. He worked at a college and coached girls' lacrosse at a local high school. She worked overnight at a memory care facility, so someone was always home with Ethan. Life was good, and then it wasn't. She found out Carl had been arrested when police showed up at her work. He was having sex with a fifteen-year-old girl he coached. In court, she learned there were four girls involved. He was convicted, and even though she knew nothing about what he'd been doing, she lost her job, her home and her ten-year-old car. Ethan's friends weren't allowed to play with him any longer.

Paul is upset on her behalf and Ethan's. He says it changes nothing as far as he's concerned. She takes excellent care of his mother, and they consider her and Ethan as part of the Martinez family. They kiss again, but Paul pulls away, insisting she think about what she wants and whether this is what she wants. They will spend two days together on the mainland while Marion is with the specialists. Hope wants Paul to tell Alex that they're thinking about being together.

Slim picks up suits for the boys on the mainland. Seamus talks to him about his concerns regarding parenting Kyle and Jackson. Slim says, "Today was a tough day. Tomorrow will be a tough day. The next couple of weeks are apt to be rough. But one day, not too far off from now, they'll begin to act like little boys again, and you and Carolina will be there to show them the way through it."

As Slim heads home, he encounters Erin Barton on the side of the road in the dark. She was riding her bike when she blew a tire and sprained her ankle. He drives her home to the lighthouse and stays to help her.

The funeral for Lisa is beautiful and sad. Kyle and Jackson followed their mom's casket into the church. By the time they reach the front, there isn't a dry eye in the church. The gathering following the mass is full of concerned friends. Big Mac McCarthy notices Paul's interest in Hope. Paul asks Big Mac what he thinks about him dating an employee, considering his father's rules against it.

"I had a similar rule with my boys," Big Mac says. "Last thing I needed was messy entanglements during the busiest months of the year. Not to mention, I was always a little afraid of getting sued by a disgruntled employee who failed to land one of the McCarthy boys. Sounds sort of silly, but you can never be too careful."

"Yeah, true."

"That said, your dad and I were dealing with boys and young men who hadn't figured themselves out yet. You're a full-grown man now, Paul, and everything is different. You know how to handle yourself in any situation, and I have faith you'll do the right thing no matter what. Your dad would certainly feel the same, especially in light of what you and Alex have done for your mom in recent years. He'd be very proud of both of you."

Overwhelmed by Big Mac's kind words, Paul has to gather himself before he can speak. "Thank you. That means so much coming from you."

The next morning, Paul and Hope struggle to get Marion into the truck and onto the ferry for their trip to Providence for her evaluation. Once they arrive at the facility, Paul takes a phone call as Hope is helping Marion out of the car. Paul returns to them just as Marion slaps Hope across the face. Paul is infuriated as a bright red welt appears on Hope's face. Paul wants to rage against his mother and the hideous illness that's turned her into someone he doesn't recognize. They leave Marion with the well-trained staff at the facility, and, after getting an ice pack for Hope, they go to a bed-and-breakfast inn on Cape Cod.

Lizzie James convinces Jared to reach out to his brother, Quinn, to be the medical director at the senior care facility. Lizzie's plans are on hold until they find a doctor. Jared convinces Quinn to think about the facility and come spend time on the island. It's not the yes Lizzie was hoping for, but at least Quinn is thinking about it.

Alex and Jenny apply for their wedding license. Toby died the day after they applied for their license, prompting Alex to plan a surprise for her. He's arranged for a wedding at the lighthouse where they met.

Frank McCarthy is there to officiate the ceremony. "Jenny and Alex," Frank says, "I'm honored to have been asked to preside over this incredible moment in your lives, and I love a good surprise. Well done, Alex."

"Thanks, Your Honor."

"This, right here," Frank says, gesturing to the two of them. "This is the epitome of love. What you've done for Jenny today, Alex, is something she'll remember for the rest of her life. And Jenny, you'll someday have the opportunity to return the favor for your husband by easing his worries and his sorrows. As long as the two of you can do that for each other, everything else you face will seem easy in comparison."

Jenny wipes tears from her eyes, while Alex does the same. The import of the moment hits him all of a sudden, leaving him humbled by the knowledge that from this day forward, Jenny will be his wife, his partner, his lover, the mother of his children, the center of his world.

What began right here in this yard with flying tomatoes and angry shouts has become the best thing ever to happen to him. Alex can't wait to spend the rest of his life with her.

Paul and Hope check into their room at the inn and decide to take a walk on the beach. During their walk, Hope shares more about what happened with her ex-husband and how her family responded to the scandal. They end up back in their room, wrapped up in each other, making love and falling asleep in each other's arms.

Alex calls Paul to tell him that he and Jenny were married earlier that day and to explain why. Paul is thrilled for his brother and Jenny, but apologetic about them caring for Ethan on their wedding night. Alex says Ethan goes to bed early, and Paul begs him not to do anything that will traumatize the boy.

Jenny still can't believe what Alex did for her. She has a surprise for him that she plans to share at bedtime. She's pregnant!

Erin is crying for her brother. Toby would be mad at her for shedding more tears after all this time, but Toby's love, Jenny, has married someone else, and it's too much for her to handle. She's happy for Jenny and loves that Alex cares so much for her that he arranged the surprise wedding to ease her worries. Slim arrives after asking why she was crying and shows how kind and compassionate he is.

"She was supposed to marry your brother and today was hard for you."

"Yeah," she says softly. "As happy as I am for her…"

"I get it. I'm sure she would, too."

"She'll never know I was anything other than thrilled for her and Alex. They're great together, and she's certainly earned the right to be happy."

"You're a good friend to feel that way. She's lucky to have you."

"We're lucky to have each other. We've been through the fire of hell together and come out on the other side, stunned and altered, but we survived." She wipes her face and laughs. "How do you get me to tell you these things? I don't even know you."

"Pilots and bartenders," he says, making her laugh again. "What do you want to know about me?"

"Did your mother name you Slim?"

"No, my grandfather did, actually."

"I don't mean to be insulting, but you aren't exactly super skinny or anything." He has the muscular build of a man who takes good care of himself.

"Is that a fat joke?"

"Hardly! And you know it."

"Yeah," he says, chuckling, "I know. I was a skinny kid who had the same name as my dad, so my gramps started calling me Slim, and it just sort of stuck long after I wasn't a skinny kid anymore."

"What's your real name?"

"Was your brother's real name Toby?"

Surprised by the question, she says, "No, it was Tobias, after our grandfather, but he hated that name and always went by Toby. Why?"

"My real name is Tobias Fitzgerald Jackson, Junior."

Stunned and overwhelmed, Erin believes her brother has sent her a new Toby to look after her, and the thought warms her heart. After that, she finally agrees to go to the dinner Slim has invited her to every time they've seen each other.

The guys are upset after hearing the women hired male strippers for Jenny's bachelorette party. Mac and Maddie argue about it in front of Dan Torrington, who then confronts his fiancée, Kara. Blaine, overhearing Adam and Joe discussing the strippers, brings it up with Tiffany. The women play up the drama and make the men promise not to ruin Jenny's surprise.

Paul and Hope meet with the doctor after Marion's evaluation. Most of the information is upsetting as Marion's condition has seriously deteriorated. Thank goodness Hope is there, because Paul can't listen as he tries to process everything the doctors are saying. The most pressing recommendation is a long-term care facility for Marion as soon as possible. When they share the news with Alex and Jenny back at home, Hope suggests they consider it and decide when they're ready. Alex and Paul decide to enjoy Alex's long-planned upcoming wedding and talk about it again afterward.

Without the job of caring for Marion, Hope and Ethan will have to leave the island and Paul. She doesn't want to go, she tells Paul, but it's what she has to do. They're devastated by the turn of events and decide to take a step back from each other, so it won't be even harder when she leaves.

Paul goes through the motions of working, eating, sleeping and getting up to do the same thing again. He keeps his promise to harvest the pumpkins with Ethan, but every moment he misses Hope, even though he sees her every day. A long, lonely winter stretches ahead of him. He'll tend to his wounds then. When they move Marion to the mainland, and Hope and Ethan leave, Paul will be alone in the house that now teems with activity. Alex and Jenny would soon move into their own home, and with Marion gone, there'll be no reason for David and Daisy to come by every day or the women from the church, who've been so generous about providing regular meals for them during Marion's illness. The house will be empty and lonely without the endless activity, a thought that only adds to his profound depression.

"You gotta snap out of it, man," he whispers to his reflection as he prepares for Alex's bachelor party. "Alex has waited a long time for this. It wouldn't be fair to bring him down." He gives himself a few minutes to summon the celebratory mood the night demands of him as the best man before he leaves the bathroom.

On the way to the bachelor party, Alex calls Paul out on his bad mood. "What gives with you the last couple of days, man? Other than the obvious, of course."

"Nothing gives. Business as usual."

"Try telling that to someone who doesn't see you every day and doesn't know you as well as I do. Something is wrong, and you may as well tell me what it is, so I don't have to beat it out of you."

"I'd like to see you try."

"We both know I could, so let's save ourselves the bother."

"Whatever."

"Come on, Paul. You know there's nothing you can't tell me."

"It's not the time. Tonight is about you. We'll talk after the wedding."

"We'll talk now."

Paul recognizes his brother's bullish tone and knows it's pointless to argue with him. Growing up with Alex, he would've at least tried. Today, he can't be bothered. "The thing with Hope isn't going to happen."

"Oh. Wow. I sort of thought it was already happening."

"It was."

"So what happened?"

"The meeting with the doctor happened."

"Umm, you want to fill in the blanks for me?"

"She realized if Mom leaves Gansett, her job here will be done, and she'll have to go elsewhere to find work. Her ex-husband wiped out their savings, so she has no cushion of any kind, apparently."

"So she called it off with you because of that?"

"She said she couldn't get further involved with me knowing she'd be leaving."

Alex scratches at the stubble he left on his jaw these days because Jenny likes it—and he'd told Paul that when Paul asked why he never shaved anymore. "That is a tough one. On the one hand, I can see where she's coming from. I don't know the details, but I assume the ex put her through the wringer."

"It was bad business."

"I figured it had to be if the guy's locked up."

Paul didn't feel it was his place to tell Alex her story, at least not without her permission.

"Have you considered asking her to stay with you?"

"Not really."

"Why not? I assume you want her to."

"Hell, yes, I want her to."

"Then tell her that."

"Am I just supposed to ask her to stay, knowing she has no way to make a living here?"

"I hate to point out the obvious, but she doesn't need to work if she's with you. She could focus on Ethan and make more babies with you and maybe get a job at this place Lizzie is determined to open on the island."

Paul's mouth waters at the thought of such an easy solution. "I don't think she'd go for that. She would say she's perfectly capable of taking care of herself, and no way is she putting all her eggs in some man's basket again. Not after what happened to her before. He totally screwed her over."

"And you'd never do that. Make the grand gesture."

"What grand gesture?"

"The *grandest* of grand gestures."

"Are you seriously suggesting I propose to her? We just started actually seeing each other a week ago."

"We were thrilled that you guys took some time away together while Mom was in the hospital."

"I'm glad you approve," Paul says sincerely. "But it's too soon for the kind of grand gestures you're suggesting." Although now he doesn't know how he'll think of anything but proposing and having Hope stay with him.

The party that Sydney and the girls throw for Jenny is fabulous and over the top. It seems as if every woman on Gansett is there, and everyone is thrilled that Jenny is finally getting her long-delayed happily ever after. Hope wonders what the others would think if they knew Alex and Jenny were already married. She loves being in on the secret that only Sydney and Erin know, too.

Hope loves being a part of this group of women. They've made her feel so welcome from the first time she met Jenny, who assured her there'd be no lack of fun things to do if she and her son moved to Gansett Island.

That had proven true, and this group was a big part of the reason why. Unlike the women she'd known back at home, these women don't thrive on gossip. They build each other up rather than tear each other down. They thrive on being happy and productive. They're also some of the funniest women Hope has ever met.

Take Tiffany, for example, who's relaying the fact that her husband, the police chief, wanted to do background checks on the male strippers the women hired for Jenny's party.

"Wait," Jenny says. "You guys got *strippers?*"

Hope isn't sure if Jenny is intrigued or appalled. Probably a little of both.

"No!" Tiffany screams with laughter that draws the others in, too. "We've been *telling* them that all week. They're out of their minds over it."

Much too early for the women's liking, Mac is first to burst through the door. "Get out of here, Mac." Maddie gets up to push her husband back toward the door. "This is a private party! No men allowed."

"Where are the strippers?" Evan asks as he enters, followed by the others in a big mass of angry testosterone.

The men search Sydney's house for the male strippers they were led to believe were attending the party, only to find they aren't there. "*Where the hell are the strippers?*" Mac roars.

"Did you hire strippers?" Maddie asks Sydney, the two of them looking like the picture of innocence.

"I didn't." To Erin, Sydney says, "Did you?"

"Nope. I wouldn't know where to find strippers."

"Don't look at me," Kara says as Dan glowers at her.

Blaine continues to glare at Tiffany while she cries with silent laughter.

"Gentlemen," Joe says, his gaze fixed on Janey, "I believe we've been had."

"We've been *what?*" Mac asks, his face red with barely suppressed rage.

"*Had*, Mac," Joe says. "It's a prank. An evil, *evil* prank."

"A prank," Mac says, advancing toward Maddie, who backs up until she encounters a wall. "*A goddamned prank?*"

"Hi, honey," Maddie says with a goofy smile. "Did you boys have fun at your party?"

"No, we did not have fun, because we were *preoccupied by the thought of our women cavorting with male strippers!*"

"What strippers?" Maddie asks, batting her eyelashes at him.

"As long as you're all here," Sydney says, "we ought to combine these two parties."

Paul drives Alex, Jenny and Hope home after the party. He drops Jenny and Alex at their new house. Paul waits until they're safely inside before he backs out of their driveway and turns toward home. When he kills the lights and shuts off the engine, the darkness engulfs them. "Be with me tonight. No commitments, no promises. Just us taking what we both want." Hope should say no. *More* won't make leaving any easier.

His hand finds hers in the darkness. "Please."

The desperation she hears in that single word has her saying, "Yes."

Kevin is at the Beachcomber bar, where Chelsea is bartending. She comes over to him, smiling warily. "Dr. McCarthy."

"Ms. Rose."

She raises a brow as she puts a napkin down on the bar and places an ice-cold light beer on it. "Glass?"

"Comes in one." The cold beer tastes good going down. "You gonna call my big brother on me tonight?"

"You gonna give me reason to?"

Kevin laughs at her saucy comeback. When she smiles at him, he realizes how pretty she is. They talk about the demise of his marriage. A low hum of desire takes him by surprise. It's been a long time since he's felt anything resembling desire. "You're easy to talk to, Ms. Rose."

"Thank you, Dr. McCarthy."

"I'm sorry for what you've been through, but I'm not sorry you're single."

"Separated."

"Permanently and legally?"

"Heading that way. Are you planning to go back to her?"

"No."

"What if she shows up here and says it was all a big mistake?"

Kevin thinks about that for a minute. "Even then." Permanent damage has been done, and there's no undoing that.

"Then that counts as single in my book."

"Does it, now?"

"Yep." She gives him that look again, the one that can't be mistaken for anything other than interest. "I slept with your niece's husband once."

"Joe or Owen?"

"Joe."

"Before he was her husband?"

"Yes! Years before."

"Okay."

"So that doesn't appall you?"

"Why should it? I assume you were both single and consenting."

"We were."

Kevin shrugs. "Sex happens."

"Does it?"

"That's been my experience."

"What do you think about it maybe happening tonight?"

For a moment, Kevin is rendered speechless. But then he recovers. "I'm fifty-two."

"Are you incapable?"

"No," he says with a laugh. "All the equipment works just fine, thank you, with no medication required. But I suspect I'm a hell of a lot older than you are."

"I'm thirty-six."

"That's sixteen years."

"A doctor who can also add." She fans her face dramatically. "You don't find that every day."

She's cute, sexy, funny and lovely. And young. Too young for him, but he'd gone hard as stone at the thought of taking her to bed. The confident way in which she propositioned him is a huge turn-on. He's forever counseling his female patients to take control of their own sexuality. To find a woman who clearly owns hers is incredibly hot.

"So what do you say, Doc? Would you like to come home with me tonight?"

He's never once, in thirty years together, been unfaithful to Deb. But his marriage is over, and she's moved on with someone else. There's no reason he can't do the same. Under the bar, he slides the wedding ring off his finger and stashes it in his back pocket. "Yes, I believe I would."

David makes some calls on behalf of the Martinez family to look into facilities for Marion. He finds a place that has an immediate opening due to the death of a patient. He encourages Paul and Alex to take it, as it may be a long wait before another spot opens. While Alex wants his mother at his wedding, out of concern for her comfort and well-being, they decide to take the spot at the facility and move her two days before the wedding. Leading up to the move, Hope helps pack Marion's things and label her clothing and personal items. When moving day comes, Alex and Paul decide to take Marion themselves, even though both Jenny and Hope offer to come with them. On the ferry ride back to Gansett, Alex comments that it was easier than he'd thought it would be. Paul says maybe it was easier because it was time.

That night, Paul hears Ethan giving Hope a hard time. They're moving after the wedding, and it sounds like Ethan doesn't want that any more than Paul does. He goes to intervene and helps Ethan understand that Marion's worsening health is the reason Hope no longer has a job. Ethan calms down, and after some time with Hope, Paul returns home, devastated that they're leaving.

Alex happens to be at the house when Paul returns. He convinces Paul to tell Hope he loves her and propose to her. He even suggests that Paul give Hope the ring their father gave their mother. It's what their mother would want.

Alex and Jenny have a beautiful wedding day. It's everything they hoped for. Alex meets Jenny's family and Toby's, which hits him hard, as he realizes once again that Toby's death had made room in Jenny's life for him. They honor Toby during the ceremony by lighting a candle for him.

Erin introduces her parents to Slim. After he charms her mom and dad, he leaves to get them a drink. Erin tells her parents that his real name is Tobias. Her parents recognize, as she did, that her brother sent him to her.

After the wedding, Paul arranges for Ethan to spend the night at Seamus and Carolina's with Kyle and Jackson. He convinces Hope to stay with him for the night. When they get home, he goes in ahead of her and lights a fire. "Remember when we talked about you and Ethan staying here, and I said I'd take care of you?"

She nods. "I remember."

"It occurred to me afterward that I'd left out a few important details."

"What details?"

His heart pounds double-time as he drops to his knees before her.

She gasps. "Paul…"

"The most important detail I forgot to mention is that I love you, Hope. I love you, and I love Ethan, and I want you both in my life to stay. When I said I wanted to take care of you, I meant it, but I also understand how important it is to you to be financially and professionally independent. And that's why I think you should go forward with your plans to get a job on the mainland, but maybe a part-time job one or two days a week? We'll rent an apartment over there for when you have to work, as long as you come home to Ethan and me when your shift ends. I want to make this our home—and you can do anything you want to the house to make it your own. I want to raise Ethan as if he were my own. I want to have more babies with you. I want everything with you, and I swear to you—on my life and the lives of everyone I love—I will never be untrue to you. Will you marry me, Hope?"

Tears slide down her cheeks, and for the life of him, he can't tell if they're happy tears or sad tears.

"Hope?"

"You… You love me?"

He laughs softly. "Did you hear anything else I said after that?"

"I heard all of it." She wipes away the tears that keep coming.

From his pocket, he produces the ring he's carried around all day like a talisman, hoping it would bring him luck.

"That's your mother's," she whispers.

"Alex gave it to me and told me to give it to you. He said our mom, the mom we knew and loved for so long, would want you to have it because she'd love you for me. She'd love us together."

Hope covers her mouth and shakes her head.

Is she saying no? He honestly doesn't know how he'll cope if she turns him down. Suspecting she loves him as much as he loves her, he slides the ring on her finger. "Well, look at that," he says reverently. "It fits like it was meant for you. My father gave my mother this ring on their twentieth anniversary. She loved it almost as much as she loved him. I want what they had, Hope. I want what Alex has with Jenny. And I want it with you. So, will you please marry me?"

"Yes," she whispers, so softly that he thinks for a second he's hearing things.

"You want to say that one more time so I can be sure I heard you right?"

"Yes, Paul," she says, smiling as tears continue to roll down her cheeks. "I'll marry you."

The next day, Paul and Hope drive to Seamus and Carolina's to tell Ethan their news. They pull into the driveway, where Ethan is playing soccer with Jackson, Kyle and their dog. When Ethan sees them, he lets out a happy cry and runs for his mother. She scoops him up and peppers his face with kisses. "Are you guys having fun?"

"So much fun."

She puts Ethan down and reaches for Kyle and Jackson, who ran to her, too.

Her sweetness to the boys hits Paul right in the chest.

"I don't hafta go home yet, do I?" Ethan asks.

"Not quite, but Paul and I wanted to talk to you."

"Is something wrong?"

"No, baby." Hope gathers him into her arms again. "It's really good news. At least we hope you'll think so."

While Kyle and Jackson look on, Paul squats so he can look Ethan in the eye. "How'd you like to stay here on Gansett?"

Ethan's big eyes widen with glee. "Really?" He looks up at his mom, who nods. "So we don't hafta move away?"

"Last night, I asked your mom to marry me, and she said yes. Now I'm hoping you'll say yes, too, so you guys will get to stay here with me."

Ethan hurls himself at Paul, who manages to keep his balance as the boy hugs him.

"Should I take that as a yes?" Paul asks, thrilled by Ethan's reaction.

"We really get to stay forever?" Ethan asks his mother.

"Yes, honey."

"And will you be my new dad?" he asks Paul.

The question hits him with the force of a gut punch. "If that's what you want," he says gruffly.

"It is." Ethan breaks free of Paul's embrace. "Hey, you guys," he says to Jackson and Kyle, "me and my mom are gettin' married!"

Paul exchanges glances with Hope, her smile as wide as his. He holds out his hand to help her up. As the boys run inside to tell Seamus and Carolina the news, Paul hugs her. "I guess it's official now."

 An interview with Paul and Hope...

I've always loved the Martinez family and the way Alex and Paul took such beautiful care of Marion for so long before Hope came to help. My heart broke writing the part of your story where Hope realizes she's going to be out of a job when Marion moves to the mainland.

Hope: It took everything I had not to bawl my head off during the meeting with that doctor. Ethan and I loved Gansett Island from the first minute we landed here, and the thought of leaving the island—and Paul, Alex, Jenny and all our other friends—was devastating.

Paul: For me, too. I felt like I'd finally found my future only to have it almost yanked away.

Alex played a pivotal role in helping you understand that you had to go for it or risk losing Hope.

Paul: Yes, he did, and he never lets me forget that. Any time I hassle him about anything, which is often, he reminds me that he got me a wife and I need to shut my face.

Hope: They're as ridiculous as ever.

Haha, I wouldn't expect anything different from them. How are Ethan, Scarlett and Charlotte?

Hope: We just celebrated Ethan's twenty-first birthday, if you can believe it.

Paul: With his first-ever beer—haha. As if.

Hope: That had better have been his first one.

Paul: I'm sure it was, honey.

Hope: Is he humoring me?

Um, I'd like to take the fifth on that. What's Ethan up to these days?

Hope: He didn't want to go to college, but we really wanted him to try it at least, even if it was brutal to move him off the island. The girls and I cried for days when he left!

Paul: I did, too, but in the truck.

Hope: I never knew that! Turns out he loves it. He's at the University of Rhode Island and runs home the second the school year ends to work with Paul and Alex. He can't wait to join the family business full-time.

Paul: And we can't wait to have him. He's double-majoring in business and landscape architecture, both of which will be amazing skills to have on our team.

Wow, that's amazing. Good for him. How about your girls?

Hope: Scarlett is ten and loves her dance classes at Miss Tiffany's studio, and she's a voracious reader. We're at the library every other day, or so it seems. Charlotte is seven and is into every sport there is. Paul had to take up running when she decided she wanted to try it.

Paul: It's been good for my waistline but humbling that I can barely keep up with her.

Hope: She's so good at everything she tries. We're not sure where she gets that.

Paul: Alex would say she gets it from him. He says all the good stuff in all the kids comes from him.

He's too funny!

Paul: (sarcastically) He's absolutely hilarious.

Are you working at all, Hope?

Hope: Now that Charlotte is in school, I'm full-time at the senior care facility. I'm Mallory's assistant director of nursing. I absolutely love it there. Second-best job I ever had.

Paul: I know what had better be first…

Hope: Haha, you know it.

We were so sad when Marion passed. I'm sure she and your dad are always with you as you run their business and live in the house they called home.

Paul: They are so much a part of our daily lives. Alex and I are always sharing memories of them. Hope and I talk about what they'd think of the changes we've made to the house. We hope they're proud of us.

There's no question that they are. No question at all.

MARIE FORCE

Celebration
After Dark

Book 14: Celebration After Dark
Published: December 1, 2015

> *One smile changed everything…*
>
> On the occasion of their 40th wedding anniversary, Big Mac and Linda McCarthy look back at how they came to be, while each of their children confronts a new challenge in their own lives. Come to Gansett Island to celebrate the holidays and the anniversary of the island's most loved couple!

🗼 Main Characters:

***Big Mac McCarthy,** grandfather of Thomas Chester McCarthy in MAID FOR LOVE, Hailey McCarthy in FALLING FOR LOVE, Peter Joseph "PJ" Cantrell in TIME FOR LOVE and Connor McCarthy (deceased) in KISSES AFTER DARK.

***Linda McCarthy,** grandmother of Thomas Chester McCarthy in MAID FOR LOVE, Hailey McCarthy in FALLING FOR LOVE, Peter Joseph "PJ" Cantrell in TIME FOR LOVE and Connor McCarthy (deceased) in KISSES AFTER DARK.

***Indicates recurring throughout the series**

🛟 Supporting Characters:

Frank McCarthy, Sr., father of Frank, Mac and Kevin.

Jane McCarthy, mother of Frank, Mac and Kevin.

***Judge Frank McCarthy,** grandfather of Holden Newsome in SEASON FOR LOVE, involved with Betsy Jacobson in GANSETT AFTER DARK.

Brett, Frank McCarthy's roommate.

Diana Vaughn, mother of Mallory, ex-girlfriend of Big Mac McCarthy.

Joann McCarthy: deceased wife of Frank McCarthy, mother of Laura and Shane.

Josie, friend of Joann and Linda.

Kathy, friend of Joann and Linda.

***Mac McCarthy, Jr.,** married to Maddie Chester in FOOL FOR LOVE, father of Thomas Chester McCarthy in MAID FOR LOVE, Hailey

McCarthy in FALLING FOR LOVE and Connor McCarthy (deceased) in KISSES AFTER DARK.

***Maddie McCarthy,** mother of Thomas, married to Mac McCarthy in FOOL FOR LOVE, mother of Hailey McCarthy in FALLING FOR LOVE and Connor McCarthy (deceased) in KISSES AFTER DARK.

***Thomas McCarthy,** son of Mac and Maddie McCarthy.

***Hailey McCarthy,** daughter of Mac and Maddie McCarthy, born in FALLING FOR LOVE.

***Adam McCarthy,** engaged to Abby Callahan in GANSETT AFTER DARK.

***Abby Callahan,** engaged to Adam McCarthy in GANSETT AFTER DARK.

***Evan McCarthy,** engaged to Grace Ryan in WAITING FOR LOVE.

***Grace Ryan,** engaged to Evan McCarthy in WAITING FOR LOVE.

***Mallory Vaughn,** nurse practitioner.

***Ned Saunders,** married to Francine, grandfather of Ashleigh Sturgil, Thomas McCarthy and Hailey McCarthy in GANSETT AFTER DARK.

***Grant McCarthy,** married to Stephanie Logan in KISSES AFTER DARK.

***Stephanie Logan,** married to Grant McCarthy in KISSES AFTER DARK.

***Laura McCarthy Lawry,** mother of Holden Newsome in SEASON FOR LOVE, married to Owen Lawry in GANSETT AFTER DARK.

***Owen Lawry,** stepfather of Holden Newsome in SEASON FOR LOVE, married to Laura McCarthy Lawry in GANSETT AFTER DARK.

***Shane McCarthy,** involved with Katie Lawry in KISSES AFTER DARK.

***Katie Lawry,** involved with Shane McCarthy in KISSES AFTER DARK.

***Janey McCarthy Cantrell,** married to Joe Cantrell in READY FOR LOVE, mother of Peter Joseph "PJ" Cantrell in TIME FOR LOVE.

***Joe Cantrell,** married to Janey McCarthy Cantrell in READY FOR LOVE, father of Peter Joseph "PJ" Cantrell in TIME FOR LOVE.

***Peter Joseph "P.J." Cantrell,** son of Joe and Janey Cantrell, born in TIME FOR LOVE.

***Dr. Kevin McCarthy,** father of Riley and Finn.

***Riley McCarthy,** son of Kevin and Deb.

***Finn McCarthy,** son of Kevin and Deb.

***Joan,** Linda's sister.

***Sydney Donovan,** married to Luke Harris in SEASON FOR LOVE.

***Luke Harris,** married to Sydney Donovan in SEASON FOR LOVE.

***Alex Martinez,** married to Jenny Wilks in LOVE AFTER DARK.

***Jenny Wilks,** married to Alex Martinez in LOVE AFTER DARK.

***Paul Martinez,** engaged to Hope Russell and stepfather of Ethan Russell in LOVE AFTER DARK.

***Hope Russell,** nurse, mother of Ethan Russell, engaged to Paul Martinez in LOVE AFTER DARK.

***Dan Torrington,** engaged to Kara Ballard in MEANT FOR LOVE.

***Kara Ballard,** engaged to Dan Torrington in MEANT FOR LOVE.

***Dr. David Lawrence,** living with Daisy Babson in TIME FOR LOVE.

***Daisy Babson,** living with Dr. David Lawrence in TIME FOR LOVE.

***Tiffany Taylor,** mother of Ashleigh Sturgil, married to Blaine Taylor in TIME FOR LOVE.

***Blaine Taylor,** married to Tiffany Taylor and stepfather of Ashleigh Sturgil in TIME FOR LOVE.

***Jared James,** married to Lizzie James in CHANCE FOR LOVE.

***Lizzie James,** married to Jared James in CHANCE FOR LOVE.

***Tobias "Slim" Fitzgerald Jackson, Jr.,** involved with Erin Barton in LOVE AFTER DARK.

***Mayor Chet Upton,** Mayor of Gansett Island.

***Verna Upton,** wife of Chet.

***Erin Barton,** new lighthouse keeper, involved with Slim Jackson in LOVE AFTER DARK.

66 Headlines in CELEBRATION AFTER DARK...

- Happy 40th anniversary, Big Mac and Linda!

- Big Mac fell in love with Linda at first sight!

- Flashback to Linda's first trip to Gansett Island!

- Maddie is pregnant!

- Abby has PCOS and wants to call off her engagement to Adam!

- Adam says they're getting married on New Year's Eve!

- Evan and Grace are going on tour!

- Grant and Stephanie are going to LA!

- Janey is pregnant!

- David and Daisy are engaged!

- Slim and Erin are spending time together for the holidays!

- Adam and Abby get married!

On the morning of his fortieth wedding anniversary, Big Mac McCarthy is reminiscing about the day he met his wife, Linda. He was due to sign the purchase and sale agreement for the marina the next day and had just gotten into yet another argument with his father about his marina "folly." Frank McCarthy, Senior, believed Mac was throwing away his inheritance from his grandmother on the broken-down marina in the middle of nowhere.

As he drives to his brother Frankie's apartment, Mac thinks about what his father said and how he's already given up a lot for the marina. He ended his relationship with Diana Vaughn because she wanted to travel and see the world, and he's putting down roots on a remote island off the southern coast of Rhode Island. Their life plans didn't match.

When he arrives at his brother's home, Frankie reassures Mac he's making the right decision with the marina. Frankie's girlfriend, Joann, is coming over and bringing friends. Frank and Joann have been together since high school. Mac thought they'd be married by now, but Frankie is finishing up law school first.

As a group of young women walks up the sidewalk, Mac notices a pretty blonde and asks Frank who she is. She's Joann's friend, Linda, from Providence College. Frank asks him not to scare her away, to which Mac responds, "Mark my words, she's going to live with me on my island." Mac asks her to take a walk with him, and she hesitantly agrees.

"Well, so, it's kind of like this…" he says. "Tomorrow, I'm signing papers that will make me the proud owner of a ramshackle marina on Gansett Island that I plan to turn into a gold mine. I was wondering if you might like to help me do that."

Stunned, she says, "Didn't I just meet you an hour ago?"

"Uh-huh."

"And you're asking me to come live with you on your island and help you turn your ramshackle marina into a gold mine. Is that right?"

"That's about it, yep."

"Are you always this forward when you meet someone new?"

"Nope. I've never asked a girl to come live with me anywhere, let alone on my island."

"I'm flattered to be the first, but you'll understand my reluctance, being as I'm in school and all that."

"What year?"

"Going into my junior year."

"I won't be able to wait two years to marry you. There's just no way that'll work for me."

"*Mac!* Are you out of your mind? Do you have some sort of condition that makes you delusional?"

"Do you believe in love at first sight?"

"No! That only happens in the movies."

"And on front porches in Providence."

"You… I…" She purses her lips, seeming to choose her words carefully. "Are you being serious right now?"

"Dead serious. You ever feel something right here?" He pushes his fist into his gut. "And you know? You just *know?*"

"That hasn't happened to me before."

"It's happened to me only one other time."

"Were you in love with her?"

He smiles at her catty tone. "As much as you can be in love with a dilapidated group of buildings, a sagging dock and a parking lot full of potholes. I took one look at that mess and felt like I'd come home. And I took one look at you, the most beautiful girl I've ever laid eyes on, and felt like I'd found the other half of me."

He asks Linda if she believes in fate, and when she says no, he tells her, "It might be time to start believing."

With the hindsight of four decades, Big Mac acknowledges he was damned lucky she didn't run from him, screaming for the police.

Mac McCarthy, Junior, wakes to his wife, Maddie, vomiting. Even though she pushes him away, he insists on holding her hair, cleaning her up and carrying her back to bed. She's pregnant again, following a miscarriage a few months back, and Maddie is scared. Mac reassures her, reminding her that the doctors told them there's no reason to worry about it happening again. They talk about names and agree to wait a while to tell anyone their news.

Adam McCarthy wakes up alone in bed in a hotel room in Providence, hearing his fiancée, Abby, sobbing in the bathroom. They've been trying to get pregnant for a while without success, so they traveled to the mainland to consult a specialist. Abby has been diagnosed with polycystic ovarian syndrome. While scary and upsetting to him, the news has devastated Abby. When he tries to comfort her, she says he doesn't have to follow through with their plans to marry. He wants children and should find someone who can give them to him. Adam wants her, and only her, and they're getting married on New Year's Eve.

Grace Ryan surprises her fiancé, Evan McCarthy, after his last night on tour. She's in his room when he returns to the hotel. For Evan, three weeks away from Grace was just too much. He was touring with Buddy Longstreet and everyone, including Buddy, was trying to convince him to keep touring to ride the success of his number-one song, "My Amazing Grace." But he just wants to be with Grace. He and Grace discuss how he'd always wonder what would've been if he didn't continue to tour. She decides to hire someone to run the pharmacy and go on tour with him.

Mac and Linda spend the morning remembering their first year on the island, recalling Mac introducing her to Ned, his first friend on the island, and their wedding. They were married six months after they met, even though both sets of parents were concerned about how young they were. Mac surprises Linda with a four-carat diamond ring, one carat for each decade they've been married. He also surprises her with her dream trip to Paris in the spring. They reminisce about all they have to be thankful for, especially their five children, their grandchildren and the gift of Mallory, the daughter Mac never knew he had until recently. They certainly have a lot to celebrate at the party the kids are throwing for them, which is supposed to be a surprise, but they can't get anything past 'Voodoo Mama,' their nickname for her.

Grant McCarthy isn't sure what took Adam and Abby off island right before the party, but Adam has left him to run around tending to last-minute party preparations. He struggles with the television he's carrying into the Sand & Surf. Even though they had a TV, Adam insisted that the video he put together for the occasion needed high definition and sent Grant on this errand. After the New Year, Grant is heading to LA to begin production on the screenplay he wrote about his wife Stephanie's struggle to free her stepfather, Charlie, from prison for a crime he didn't commit. Stephanie doesn't want to relive her story and wants to stay on the island while he travels out west. Grant convinces her to join him and promises to keep the details away from her while they're there.

Seamus O'Grady calls Joe Cantrell to inform him he's shutting down the ferries for the day due to bad weather. Worried that Adam, Abby, Evan and Grace won't get back to the island for the party, Joe sends their pilot friend, Slim Jackson, a text asking him to fly the foursome to the island. They have a bumpy flight from Westerly but thankfully make it home in time for the festivities.

It's one o'clock, and Joe's wife, Janey, is still asleep. He and their son, PJ, go upstairs to check on her. They find her curled up asleep in bed, but she startles awake when PJ makes a noise. She takes PJ to nurse him, apologizing for sleeping the day away. Joe concludes she's pregnant again. Scared after PJ's dramatic birth, he gently suggests she might be pregnant, which upsets her. He lists the familiar symptoms and reminds her she didn't know she was pregnant with PJ, either. They decide to confirm the pregnancy and immediately seek out a specialist to ensure a safe delivery after the trauma of PJ's birth.

Linda asks Mac to drive her to Luke Harris's house to give him her anniversary gift. Linda found a 1935 Chris-Craft 557. Luke has been restoring it for six months, ever since Linda located it rotting away in a boatyard in Wisconsin.

"You've got the pictures?" Luke asks.

"I sure do." Linda produces an album from her purse that documents the boat's journey from broken down to fully restored.

"Wow," Mac says as he flips through the photos. "This is incredible. What a great surprise."

"I figured we could do some cruising on this one," Linda says.

"We sure can." He hugs her tightly. "Thank you so much, Lin. And Luke, you did an amazing job, as always."

"It was fun. The best part was pulling one over on you."

Big Mac laughs. "Which is not easy to do."

"No, it isn't. Hope you guys are having a really great day. You surely deserve it after not only raising your own family but also helping out with a few special cases."

Big Mac releases Linda to put both hands on the shoulders of the man who showed up at the marina as a fatherless fourteen-year-old looking for a job and had become one of them in the ensuing years. "You're family to us, Luke, and we wouldn't have it any other way."

Luke swallows hard. "Thank you," he says softly. "You've both meant more to me than you'll ever know."

Big Mac hugs him, and then Linda does the same.

"We love you," she says.

"Same," Luke replies.

"Thanks again, you guys," Mac says, taking another long look at the boat. "I love it."

Smiling at Luke, Linda gives him a giddy thumbs-up, thrilled that their gift is such a hit with the man who's almost impossible to surprise.

Mac and Linda go home to get ready for their party. Ned and Francine come to pick them up. After fixing drinks, Linda and Francine talk about their favorite subject—their shared grandchildren.

Big Mac takes Ned aside. "I was thinking about you today."

"What about me?"

"Remember when you were practically the only person I knew on this island?"

"Sure do," Ned says with a chuckle. "Gave ya a ride over to North Harbor to check out the marina that first time."

Big Mac smiles at his old friend. "I was thinking, too, about how you sold me this house for dirt cheap."

"Ya had yer bride sleeping in the back room at the marina. Desperate times. Someone had ta do somethin'."

Big Mac lets out a big laugh. He puts his hand on Ned's shoulder. "Just want you to know—I never could've gotten through those first couple of years without Linda. But I couldn't have done it without you, either. Getting in your cab that day was one of the best things I ever did in my whole life."

Ned blinks furiously. "Aww, shit… yer all sappy today. Hell, yer sappy every day."

"Maybe so, but I wanted you to know, just the same."

"Means a lot ta me. Before Francine came back ta me, this was my home as much as yours. You and Linda and yer family… my family, too," he says gruffly. "Woulda been a lonely life without y'all ta keep things interesting fer me."

"This life of ours wouldn't have been the same without you, either. My third brother."

They arrive at Stephanie's Bistro for the "surprise" party with their children and grandchildren greeting them. Adam, Abby, Mallory, Janey, Joe, Evan, Grace, Mac, Maddie, Stephanie, Grant, Thomas, Hailey and P.J. made up the welcoming committee in the lobby.

Thomas steps forward to present a wrist corsage made of white roses to Linda and a white rose for Big Mac's lapel. "Are you surprised, Papa?" Thomas asks.

"So surprised, pal. How did you keep this a secret?"

The blond boy smiles widely. "I promised Daddy I wouldn't tell."

Big Mac hugs the little boy who'd made him a grandfather when Mac married his mother. "You did a good job keeping the secret."

As they enter the restaurant, they're pleasantly surprised by the large crowd of family and friends who've gathered to celebrate them. Big Mac's brothers, Frank and Kevin, hug him, as does his adorably pregnant niece Laura, his nephews Shane, Riley and Finn, Linda's sister, Joan, and her family, Alex and Jenny Martinez, Dan Torrington, Kara Ballard, Luke and Sydney Harris, Paul Martinez and his fiancée, Hope Russell, Shane's fiancée, Katie Lawry, and her brother, Laura's husband, Owen Lawry. Katie and Owen's mother, Sarah, and her fiancé, Charlie Grandchamp, are there, as are Carolina and Seamus O'Grady, Maddie's sister, Tiffany, and her husband, Blaine Taylor, David Lawrence and his girlfriend, Daisy Babson, and Jared and Lizzie James. Everyone who was anyone to them had come. Even Mayor Chet Upton and his wife, Verna, are there.

Mac makes a toast to his parents, which has everyone laughing at his irreverence. He introduces the video Adam put together with pictures spanning from the day they met, to their wedding, the purchase of the hotel, the births of their children, weddings, grandchildren, Mallory joining their family and concluding with a photo of Big Mac and Linda kissing at Alex and Jenny Martinez's wedding last fall. As the video ends, the room erupts into applause. Big Mac kisses Linda, lingering longer than he normally would in public, and then leans his forehead against hers, whispering, "What a story."

"What a story, indeed."

Evan, in charge of music for the night, begins with their wedding song, "You're the First, the Last, my Everything," by Barry White, for the happy couple.

Toward the end of the evening, Laura begins distributing keys to rooms upstairs for the family. Her gift to the aunt and uncle who saved her childhood after her mother passed away from cancer is having their whole family under the same roof for the evening. When they're down to just family, Laura sends everyone to change into something cozy and then to join Evan and Owen in the sitting room for music and snacks.

Leaving the party, Slim drives to the lighthouse. He can't wait to see Erin. They've spent the last few months talking on the phone and on FaceTime. He left after Alex and Jenny's wedding with just a kiss goodnight. He's wondered this whole time why he stopped with just one kiss. Slim tells Erin he's unsure of what she wants.

Erin asks, "How long can you stay?"

"I'm here until after the New Year and then back to Florida through the end of March. Were you planning to go home to Pennsylvania for Christmas?"

"Well, I was until I heard this pilot friend of mine might be coming to town for the holidays."

"And what did your mom have to say about your change in plans?"

"To quote her directly, 'If I had a choice between here or there with that sexy pilot, I'd pick the pilot.'"

They have twelve days to spend together to figure out their next move.

Back at the Sand and Surf, Linda is snuggled up to her husband as she reflects on one of the best days of her life. She's surrounded by her children and grandchildren, with Evan and Owen playing all their favorite music. After he asks why she's so quiet, Linda tells Mac, "Just taking it all in."

"It's a lot to take in."

"To think it began with you and me and led to this."

"It began with you and me forty years ago today."

She smiles at him and raises her glass to touch it to his. "You were right, you know."

He raises a rakish eyebrow. "About?"

"Everything. Us, the marina, the hotel, buying the house, raising the kids here. All of it. I don't know if I ever actually told you that. Everyone thought you were crazy for staking your claim here, but you knew exactly what you were doing."

"Hell, sweetheart," he says with a laugh, "I didn't know a damned thing other than I wanted you and I wanted Gansett. The rest was pure, dumb luck."

"It was a lot more than that, and you know it."

"None of it would've happened without you."

"Yes, it would have. You were on fire with ambition and determination."

"I was, but I wonder if I wouldn't have burned out here long before the marina took off if I hadn't had you to keep me company on all those cold winter nights."

They thank everyone for the glorious celebration. Adam announces he and Abby are getting married on New Year's Eve. Linda notices Abby is less than thrilled and wonders what's going on.

In light of the news they received from the specialist, Abby is still cautious about Adam tying himself to her. He loves her and only her. While making love that night, Abby remembers he's always loved her just as she is and realizes he'll love her through her health challenges. She shares her thoughts with him, and he tells her that as long as they have each other, everything will work out.

Over the holiday, the family learns of the two new babies on the way. They're happy that Stephanie decided to go to with Grant to LA. Evan and Grace will be married in nineteen days, and then they'll be traveling in support of his music with the encouragement of their family. Adam shares Abby's diagnosis with his parents and their worries about fertility. Now the only one left to worry about is Mallory. Big Mac is trying to convince her to move to the island.

Abby and Adam take over McCarthy's Gansett Island Inn for their New Year's Eve wedding. They follow Laura's lead and book rooms for all their guests at the inn so they can celebrate safely. Daisy, the head of housekeeping, helps them finalize details, as the regular event planner is off for the holidays. She's glowing with happiness following her engagement to Dr. David Lawrence. The McCarthy family has moved far past his breakup with Janey and is thrilled for both of them.

Adam's groomsmen are his brothers, Joe and Owen. His nephew, Thomas, serves as the ring bearer, and Uncle Frank presides over the ceremony. Abby asks Grace to be her maid of honor, with Maddie, Laura and Stephanie as her attendants. Abby had been skeptical that they could pull off a decent wedding with only eleven days to prepare, but as usual, Adam has shown her that anything is possible if you want it badly enough.

Finally, after many ups and downs, Adam gives Abby her happily ever after, and the best part is, she gets to spend the rest of her life with him.

 An interview with Big Mac and Linda...

I love this anniversary celebration and finding out how you two got together. Linda, I have to ask you… His opening salvo was pure insanity. How did you decide to give him a chance?

Linda: Well, he was absolutely gorgeous and on fire with ambition. I'm not sure which of those things was a bigger turn-on.

Mac: It was definitely my sexiness that did it for you.

Linda: (laughing) Well, it didn't hurt anything. Everyone in my life tried to talk me out of following him to Gansett Island. I'm glad I listened only to my own heart and not to what anyone else was saying.

Mac: I'm glad, too, because it would've been no fun around here without you.

Linda: During that celebration and the one we just had for our fiftieth anniversary, I thought a lot about how important it is to follow your own heart, even when the whole world is telling you you're making a mistake. The biggest mistake I could've made was not to take a big leap with you.

Mac: Aw, that's so sweet, and I feel the same way. Trust me, I know I was like a crazy lunatic that day at Frankie's party, but I took one look at you and your gorgeous smile and just knew… There she is.

Linda: You had enough faith for both of us.

Your family has grown since we last caught up with you. What's the grandchild count now?

Linda: Eighteen! Mac and Maddie have six, counting Connor, Grant and Steph have two, Evan and Grace have three, Adam and Abby have five and Joe and Janey have two. Of course, we consider all the other kids to be ours, too. It's a mob.

It must be something when they're all together.

Mac: Sure is, but we enjoy every second with them, and we love that they're all the best of friends with each other, like their parents are. When we're away, we can't wait to get home to see them. One of the great joys of our life is that all six of our kids and their families are close by and loving life on our island. We certainly never expected that when they were chomping at the bit to get the hell out of here as soon as they could.

Linda: There's no place like home.

Mac: Certainly no place like *our* home. That's for sure.

Are you guys still working?

Mac: Define "work." I still show up to the marina every day for the morning meeting, of course, but Mac and Luke are running the show there, and Daisy is the general manager of the hotel. Our granddaughter, Hailey, is interested in getting into the business after college and works at the hotel in the summer. Lin checks in from time to time, but we're sort of hands off these days.

Linda: You were hands-off at the marina from the second Mac came home to take over.

Mac: That's a bald-faced lie.

(They laugh.)

Linda: Sure, it is. We've been blessed to do a lot of traveling with our closest pals, and we're looking forward to the upcoming safari that Mac and Ned have meticulously planned.

We're so happy to hear you're continuing to enjoy good health and plenty of adventure.

Mac: I'm going to be *eighty* soon, if you can believe that, but I'm still going strong. Especially since I got my new knee. That's been a game-changer. Wish I'd done it sooner.

You at eighty is like most people at fifty.

Linda: That's a fact. He's tireless most of the time, and we're always up to something. We have a beautiful life, and we're tremendously thankful for all of it.

Thank you so much for reading Volume 1 of the Gansett Island Compendium! I hope you've enjoyed this trip down memory lane and catching up with all the characters from the first fourteen books who made Gansett Island so special.

Watch for Volume 2, Books 15-28, coming soon!

Also by Marie Force

Contemporary Romances Available from Marie Force

*The Gansett Island Series**
Book 1: Maid for Love *(Mac & Maddie)*
Book 2: Fool for Love *(Joe & Janey)*
Book 3: Ready for Love *(Luke & Sydney)*
Book 4: Falling for Love *(Grant & Stephanie)*
Book 5: Hoping for Love *(Evan & Grace)*
Book 6: Season for Love *(Owen & Laura)*
Book 7: Longing for Love *(Blaine & Tiffany)*
Book 8: Waiting for Love *(Adam & Abby)*
Book 9: Time for Love *(David & Daisy)*
Book 10: Meant for Love *(Jenny & Alex)*
Book 10.5: Chance for Love, *A Gansett Island Novella (Jared & Lizzie)*
Book 11: Gansett After Dark *(Owen & Laura)*
Book 12: Kisses After Dark *(Shane & Katie)*
Book 13: Love After Dark *(Paul & Hope)*
Book 14: Celebration After Dark *(Big Mac & Linda)*
Book 15: Desire After Dark *(Slim & Erin)*
Book 16: Light After Dark *(Mallory & Quinn)*
Book 17: Victoria & Shannon (Episode 1)
Book 18: Kevin & Chelsea (Episode 2)
A Gansett Island Christmas Novella *(Appears in Mine After Dark)*
Book 19: Mine After Dark *(Riley & Nikki)*
Book 20: Yours After Dark *(Finn & Chloe)*
Book 21: Trouble After Dark *(Deacon & Julia)*
Book 22: Rescue After Dark *(Mason & Jordan)*
Book 23: Blackout After Dark *(Full cast)*
Book 24: Temptation After Dark *(Gigi & Cooper)*
Book 25: Resilience After Dark *(Jace & Cindy)*
Book 26: Hurricane After Dark *(Full cast)*
Book 27: Renewal After Dark *(Duke & McKenzie)*
Book 28: Delivery After Dark *(Full cast)*

Downeast
Dan & Kara: A Downeast Prequel
Homecoming: A Downeast Novel

The Wild Widows Series—a Fatal Series Spin-Off
Book 1: Someone Like You *(Roni & Derek)*
Book 2: Someone to Hold *(Iris & Gage)*
Book 3: Someone to Love *(Winter & Adrian)*
Book 4: Someone to Watch Over Me *(Lexi & Tom)*
Book 5: Someone to Remember *(Full cast)*
Book 6: Someone to Save *(2026)*

The Quantum Series
Book 1: Virtuous *(Flynn & Natalie)*
Book 2: Valorous *(Flynn & Natalie)*
Book 3: Victorious *(Flynn & Natalie)*
Book 4: Rapturous *(Addie & Hayden)*
Book 5: Ravenous *(Jasper & Ellie)*
Book 6: Delirious *(Kristian & Aileen)*
Book 7: Outrageous *(Emmett & Leah)*
Book 8: Famous *(Marlowe & Sebastian)*
Book 9: Illustrious *(Max & Stella)*
Book 10: Momentous *(Olivia's story, coming 2026)*

Remington Family Law Series—A Quantum Series Spin-Off
Book 1: Acrimonious
Book 2: Contentious (September 2026)

The Green Mountain Series*
Book 1: All You Need Is Love *(Will & Cameron)*
Book 2: I Want to Hold Your Hand *(Nolan & Hannah)*
Book 3: I Saw Her Standing There *(Colton & Lucy)*
Book 4: And I Love Her *(Hunter & Megan)*
Novella: You'll Be Mine *(Will & Cam's Wedding)*
Book 5: It's Only Love *(Gavin & Ella)*
Book 6: Ain't She Sweet *(Tyler & Charlotte)*

The Butler, Vermont Series*
(Continuation of Green Mountain)
Book 1: Every Little Thing *(Grayson & Emma)*
Book 2: Can't Buy Me Love *(Mary & Patrick)*
Book 3: Here Comes the Sun *(Wade & Mia)*
Book 4: Till There Was You *(Lucas & Dani)*
Book 5: All My Loving *(Landon & Amanda)*
Book 6: Let It Be *(Lincoln & Molly)*

Book 7: Come Together *(Noah & Brianna)*
Book 8: Here, There & Everywhere *(Izzy & Cabot)*
Book 9: The Long and Winding Road *(Max & Lexi)*

The Miami Nights Series*
Book 1: How Much I Feel *(Carmen & Jason)*
Book 2: How Much I Care *(Maria & Austin)*
Book 3: How Much I Love *(Dee's story)*
Nochebuena, A Miami Nights Novella
Book 4: How Much I Want *(Nico & Sofia)*
Book 5: How Much I Need *(Milo & Gianna)*

The Treading Water Series*
Book 1: Treading Water *(Jack & Andy)*
Book 2: Marking Time *(Clare & Aidan)*
Book 3: Starting Over *(Brandon & Daphne)*
Book 4: Coming Home *(Reid & Kate)*
Book 5: Finding Forever *(Maggie & Brayden)*

Single Titles
In the Air Tonight
Five Years Gone
One Year Home
Sex Machine
Sex God
Georgia on My Mind
True North
The Fall
The Wreck
Love at First Flight
Everyone Loves a Hero
Line of Scrimmage

Romantic Suspense Novels Available from Marie Force

The Fatal Series*
One Night With You, *A Fatal Series Prequel Novella*
Book 1: Fatal Affair
Book 2: Fatal Justice
Book 3: Fatal Consequences
Book 3.5: Fatal Destiny, *the Wedding Novella*
Book 4: Fatal Flaw

Book 5: Fatal Deception
Book 6: Fatal Mistake
Book 7: Fatal Jeopardy
Book 8: Fatal Scandal
Book 9: Fatal Frenzy
Book 10: Fatal Identity
Book 11: Fatal Threat
Book 12: Fatal Chaos
Book 13: Fatal Invasion
Book 14: Fatal Reckoning
Book 15: Fatal Accusation
Book 16: Fatal Fraud

Sam and Nick's story continues…
Book 1: State of Affairs
Book 2: State of Grace
Book 3: State of the Union
Book 4: State of Shock
Book 5: State of Denial
Book 6: State of Bliss
Book 7: State of Suspense
Book 8: State of Alert
Book 9: State of Retribution
Book 10: State of Preservation
Book 11: State of Unrest (July 2026)

Historical Romance Available from Marie Force

*The Gilded Series**
Book 1: Duchess by Deception
Book 2: Deceived by Desire

***Completed Series**

About the Author

Marie Force is the *New York Times* best-selling author of more than 110 contemporary romance, romantic suspense and erotic romance novels. Her series include Remington Family Law, Fatal, First Family, Gansett Island, Butler Vermont, Quantum, Treading Water, Miami Nights and Wild Widows. She has also written 12 single titles.

Her books have sold more than 15 million copies worldwide, have been translated into more than a dozen languages and have appeared on the *New York Times* bestseller list more than 30 times. She is also a *USA Today* and #1 *Wall Street Journal* bestseller, as well as a Spiegel bestseller in Germany.

Her goals in life are simple—to spend as much time as possible with her adult children, to keep writing books for as long as she possibly can and to never be on a flight that makes the news.

Join Marie's mailing list on her website at *marieforce.com* for news about new books and upcoming appearances in your area. Follow her on Facebook, at *www.Facebook.com/MarieForceAuthor* and Instagram *@marieforceauthor.* Contact Marie at *marie@marieforce.com.*

9 781966 871484